MW01482523

HANNE
and her
BROTHER

ALSO BY BILL STENSON

Translating Women (short stories)

Svoboda (novel)

HANNE
and her
BROTHER

BILL STENSON

thistledown press

©Bill Stenson, 2016
All rights reserved

No part of this publication may be reproduced or transmitted in any form or by any
means, graphic, electronic or mechanical, including photocopying, recording, or any
information storage and retrieval system, without permission in writing from the
publisher or a licence from The Canadian Copyright Licensing Agency (Access Copyright). For an Access Copyright licence, visit www.accesscopyright.ca or call toll free
to 1-800-893-5777.

Thistledown Press Ltd.
410 2nd Avenue North
Saskatoon, Saskatchewan, S7K 2C3
www.thistledownpress.com

Library and Archives Canada Cataloguing in Publication

Stenson, Bill, 1949–, author
Hanne and her brother / Bill Stenson.

Issued in print and electronic formats.
ISBN 978-1-77187-114-3 (paperback).–ISBN 978-1-77187-115-0
(html). –ISBN 978-1-77187-116-7 (pdf)
I. Title.
PS8637.T47H35 2016   C813'.6   C2016-905254-0
C2016-905255-9

Cover and book design by Jackie Forrie
Printed and bound in Canada

This is a work of fiction. Names, characters, places and incidents are either a product
of the author's imagination or used fictitiously. Any resemblance to actual persons,
living or dead, events or locales is entirely coincidental.

Thistledown Press gratefully acknowledges the financial assistance of the Canada
Council for the Arts, the Saskatchewan Arts Board, and the Government of Canada
for its publishing program.

For Parker, Deacon, Leah, Macy, and Oliver

A person who deserves my loyalty receives it.
— Joyce Maynard,
Looking Back: A Chronicle of Growing Up in the Sixties

AN ACCOUNTING OF ONE'S LIFE amounts to a confession one way or another, and the place you live has a lot to say about how you live it. Where I grew up, life was regimented and routine. Weekdays most people worked at something for wages, and every day, weekday or not, was marbled with milking, feeding, watering, and keeping up with a slew of temporary repairs. Time was measured not in years, but in seasons. I know what I'm talking about because this is where I lived for most of my life and where the first part of this story takes place: at this end of the valley, Tansor, from 1953 to 1967.

Winters brought heavy rain, steady for days and days at a time, cloud cover so close to the earth it was difficult to breathe, snow predictable enough to claim its beauty and scorn the consequences, frost that kept a lightbulb burning in the pump house or something close to hell would freeze over. Summers were hot and dry — the earth cracked and fissured and begging for relief — and only the infrequent wind would push the searing air into the shade, and shimmer the surface of pools left in the painstaking trickle of spring-fed creeks that began at the foot of the two-humped mountain and snaked like a rumour through the dappled shade of forest floor. There were birds in spring and so many shades of green in the flora that the mind began to doubt the eye — yellow-lime shoots all the way to green so dark they were purple — while the bulls and roosters and rams and stallions, fenced or unfenced, strutted in the pull of the lengthening days. The slanting light of autumn was like a dwindling pile of delicious dessert, reduced by minutes daily, a pellucid light that dressed trees and bushes in competitive yellows and oranges, reds and browns that held, waning, until there was no light, and birds who knew how said their seasonal goodbyes and roofs were made ready, vegetables canned, hay stacked to the rafters, turkeys slaughtered — except the one given reprieve and fed extravagantly until Thanksgiving.

The people who lived here came from everywhere: Europe, across town — a callous persecution, a slight of fancy, a thin entrepreneurial dream, a second chance. They were here now and knew they were here to stay. Their mostly small, rectangular plots of land had a skim of fertile soil on top of yellow clay that demanded any agricultural aspiration had to be supplemented by work from town or a sawmill or setting choker in the woods. Reading consisted mostly of TV Guide and the weekly paper, and magazines and books that did exist were mainly used to swat the drunken slurry of flies that migrated from barns to houses as if trying to move up in the world. In Tansor, people didn't move in and they didn't move out: they clung to their existence like goldfish — thankful to be in bowls that held water.

Gardening for the beauty of gardening was an accident as a rule. One might find a geranium in a clay pot by the corner of the house and depending on the month it could be green and flowering or a paleontological exhibit of good intentions. Carrots, beets, and potatoes were common. Sometimes corn. Fruit trees, apple and plum mostly, were there but only because someone had planted them years before and if a tree bears fruit it may as well be picked. Many houses had a jungle of mother-in-law's tongue, the resilient, water-me-when-you-want plant of choice.

Most yards came with their own garbage dump where broken cars and pumps and tractor accessories were laid to rest, and offered spare parts for a few years, then rusted into the earth. It was possible to transport garbage to the dump several miles away but few bothered. Three or four years of exposure to the elements and a soup can would crumble like a thin cracker in your hand. Pigs would eat most of the refuse and goats would eat anything they could wag their beards over. The odd house had a uniform exterior but many were a patchwork quilt of temporary inspiration and material supply: tarpaper and cedar lath a common stopgap measure. Roofs were reshingled only when attempts to patch them became a losing battle and an attic full of drip-catching buckets became too numerous to empty. Fences were generally repaired, not replaced, and livestock took advantage of visitation rights. Mrs. Eaton, the local spinster, addressed as Mrs. though she had never been married, was wakened at least once a month to the sound of a neighbour's cowbell outside her bedroom window.

There were no babies here. Once-upon-a-time babies were now tough and sinewy and would soon be ready to make babies themselves with little contemplation. Armed with grade eight or nine education and having attained the magic age of fifteen, young men would threaten to join the navy and peel potatoes if necessary for a chance to see the world, but would instead take a job for close to the same wage their father earned setting choker in the woods or pulling lumber on the green chain. In another pocket valley further into the countryside they would settle like dust on a similar patch of scrub land to replicate what they knew. Young women would waitress or style hair and wait for their chance to build their own nest somewhere with someone and the sooner the better. There were rare exceptions, those who would grind their way through high school and move to Victoria or Vancouver to work for name-brand corporations and never be heard from again. They were relegated to past tense if their escape ever found its way into conversation and transported, along with the dead, to an uncertain world.

For those living in the shallow valley at the base of the twin-peaked mountain the future was brittle and tentative. Loggers made decent money when there was work, but summers often brought a four- to six-week stretch when the woods were so tinder-dry that logging was curtailed and unemployment insurance applied for. Come winter, a two or three week stretch, sometimes more, the ample snow made fallen logs indiscernible and the felling of trees impossible. When the logging was shut down for an extended period the mills ran out of logs to make lumber and the pulp mill ran out of chips to make paper and those who mended fenders had no work because . . . well . . . a fender can wait. Spring and fall were full-ahead months in the valley, months that any notion of surplus had to consider the paucity of the season to come.

Eight years earlier someone did leave. An old man who kept to himself up on North Road (his last name was a colour: Brown or Black or White, people couldn't remember) had been annually buying two or three Irish Lottery tickets for years and suddenly won some large amount in pounds that no one knew how to convert. He waited a week until his money arrived, then put his hat on his head and his coat over his shoulders (the spirit of his circumstance presiding over a not-quite-warm-enough day) and caught the bus into town and never returned. For a year or two local teenagers used the house as a place to drink, but it eventually caught fire and burned to the ground. The bracken ferns and fireweed and alder took over any notion that a house once stood there, and a life that had once existed turned back into the earth.

One

1

MY FATHER, ARTHUR LEMMONS, BOUGHT the house cheap and paid cash. I was only six at the time and that was ten years ago, but I remember the struggles we endured. Five layers of linoleum were removed from the floors and it took a dozen trips to the dump to empty the house of its predecessor's belongings: food, broken dishes, pinstriped suits, a two dollar bill thumb-tacked to the inside of the closet — the one spoil from the vanquished I got to keep for myself. The house was a small two bedroom with a diminutive living room and a cramped kitchen. My father fixed clocks and repaired jewellery because that was what he knew how to do. His bedroom was off the living room and for the most part the living room was where he worked. In one corner there was a small TV and an overstuffed chair where he watched the news before he went to bed, and where I would watch *American Bandstand* if he was out of the house. It was a black and white TV. Arthur Lemmons didn't leave the house often.

Mostly, when he went somewhere I went with him. He watched me like a hawk on the basis that he didn't care to witness corruption in a daughter he was responsible for raising and at the time I didn't question it. Once a month we drove our Volkswagen van to Youbou to visit friends he'd kept in touch with from Europe, and this was a big deal, a genuine highlight for me. Being obedient by nature, and in order to placate him, I took correspondence courses instead of attending school which allowed me time to spend a good part of each day watching and learning the art of being a watchmaker from my father. I knew enough about literature, mathematics, history, and geography to pass my courses every year, but my true erudition was full of bezels, mainsprings, hands, movements, bushings, bearings, time trains, pivots, and escape wheels. My father had a modest bank account at the local credit union and half of what was left over at the end of the month was deposited in a separate account for me. It was his wish that I would someday follow in his footsteps, but he didn't like to discuss such a prospect because it exposed an alternative. The rich were willing to pay to maintain their expensive clocks and people from all backgrounds eager to pay for the differences they thought jewellery made to their appearance and no one knew this better than my father.

There was an obligation to parent that my father was committed to. While he never blurted it out in a sentence, I knew there were times he wished I was his son and not his daughter. He complimented me sparingly, but told me I was as beautiful as my mother had been without the glitz his patrons adored — a natural beauty if there ever was one. Only once did he tell me this. It was the year I turned thirteen, and somehow it wasn't an easy thing for him to say.

Conversations between us were elliptical as a rule. The intricacies of a turn of the century clock or what he wanted for supper (as I grew older I always cooked) were common examples. There was little need to converse because for the most part we knew, or assumed we knew, what the other was thinking. We had come to Canada on a huge passenger ship and whether it was because I was seasick most of the time or too young to remember, I had no recollection of what the ocean looked like. My father didn't care if he ever saw the ocean again; he would drive to town for supplies and to make deliveries and every so often steer his way to Youbou but never to the edge of the Pacific Ocean which was less than fifteen miles away. And the library. That was one place he was willing to take me whenever I asked.

A watch that had taken in water and needed to be steamed dry and fine-tuned was what I was working on. I set the time on the watch to match the large Junghans clock my father was proud of, mounted on the living room wall. Then I stared aimlessly out the window.

"What shall I cook for supper?"

"I bought sausages," he said without looking up.

I knew the time, always, and knew there was plenty of it spread out into the future for me. The clock on the wall measured my life with its inexorable ticking and it had chimed every half hour since I could remember. Often there were four or five clocks ticking away, a metronomic symphony that was audible from every room in the house. Daily, I would saunter into the woods or sit in the abandoned hayloft of our small barn and revel in the absence of clock sounds. We kept a rooster and half a dozen chickens in a coop beside the barn and the rooster would belt out his song in the morning or whenever leaden cloud broke later in the day; otherwise there was nothing about time routinely marked outside the house. The train headed west every afternoon on tracks that paralleled the back of our property, but its schedule was not precise.

"I'll collect the eggs," I said.

I watched my father who had his head turned sideways over his workbench, listening to the intricate sounds of a movement as he always did before assembly. He could measure resistance with his ear and claimed he could predict within a few months the number of years a timepiece would last before needing attention. His work consumed him and I knew I could sit and watch him for another hour and he wouldn't notice my presence any more than he would my absence.

"Do you think this is all there is?" I asked. "Don't you ever want to just do something new?" He swivelled in his chair, slid his glasses down his nose so he could properly examine me from across the room. I realized by the look on his face that this wasn't a good time. It was never a good time.

"What do you mean, new?"

"I mean just do something for the fun of it. Without any planning. You plan to drive to Youbou at the end of the month. If you don't plan something, we don't do anything. Don't you ever want to go somewhere or do something else?"

My father looked out the window. He looked sad, almost ashamed.

"There's nowhere someone like me could go that would make life any better."

Both the question and the answer surfaced once a month like clockwork, and I might have felt guilty because of my persistence, but every time the issue came to the surface it was as if it were being observed for the very first time, or my father had a built-in amnesia when it came to the fondness of my heart. The older I got the more I realized he believed what he said — that there was no specific place or activity his mind could imagine that would make a difference to the sameness he wore like a uniform. For me, it was different. More than once I thought of myself (and my father) as living in a zoo. Not an ordinary zoo, but one with a single species. People would drop by once and a while and pay admission and that would keep us alive, but they rarely returned, and who could blame them? A zoo with only one species isn't appealing.

The only friend my father kept in touch with was Peter De Groot and he had a daughter, Sadie, who was five years older than me. Sadie wasn't at home in Youbou that often anymore because she was a stewardess for Air Canada, but for years I found her company a welcome distraction. She was always one stage ahead of me growing up and she introduced me to makeup when we would closet ourselves in her bedroom and away from my father, and she told me about her experiences with boys that were always filled with detail thanks to my inexorable questions. When she turned sixteen she got a part-time job and the two of us would walk to the general store where she would buy a package of Players cigarettes for herself and a chocolate bar for me. Being around Sadie was like having an older sister temporarily and I loved it. If I did have a younger brother, I thought, this is what it would be like. Going to Youbou was a salvation growing up but I wanted more. When I was twelve my father agreed I could stay and sleep over at Sadie's house for two nights in a row, but on the second day of my "holiday" my father drove up, saying he had changed his mind. He said he could smell tobacco on my breath and I refused to talk to him all the way home. As if Sadie was going to pollute my mind. His words, not mine.

My graduation was a line between me and my freedom he had drawn years back and he planned to stick with it, but I would be free to go soon and didn't know what to think of what I might do. I understood it was my father's wish that I stay home and help with the business, but the older I got the more determined I was to leave as soon as possible. I imagined packing a small suitcase, kissing him on the cheek and hitchhiking into town. That part felt good. But what would I do when I got there? I loved and obeyed my father reverently, but I had read *Jane Eyre* twice in one month and for me there was a lesson in that and it was a lesson I knew I had to learn for myself.

My father didn't have much of an existence and I should have felt sorrier for him than I did. He lived the life of a hermit for the most part, interacting with his clock repair customers and one friend he took only a mild interest in. And then there was me. An historical analogy would be the Dark Ages, and I was so consumed in the paltry rhythm of my own reclusion that I paid little heed to my father's pathetic survival and the hint of any kind of renaissance on the horizon. I remember one morning when he was up early and decided to fry eggs for breakfast. The only eggs we ever ate were fried eggs and they were always fried in the cast-iron pan he managed to bring with him from Belgium, a pan that was unique, he said, because of its deep design. He brought the frying pan over to the table and slid two eggs onto my plate, then did the same for his own plate, except one egg slid off the flipper and landed on the toe of his shoe. He put the frying pan down and took off his shoe and put in on the table beside his plate. "Look at that," he said, "still sunny side up." He then proceeded to eat the egg right where it sat on the toe of his shoe as if destiny had a hand in his morning breakfast. We laughed out loud at the incident and it wasn't until years later that I realized it was the only time I could recall him laughing like that. Unguarded. Without any inhibition whatsoever.

What was odd about my father's life during this time was he didn't appear to be suffering. He never raged or drank himself under the table or acted morose, although it could be argued his reflection was glum most of the time. It's when someone's behaviour changes drastically that we begin to ask questions, and my father's demeanour was a steady hum I'd grown accustomed to.

For my father it was all about rules, rules, rules. I don't know if they were rules he'd adopted from his native Belgium or if his set of child-raising conventions were his own creation, but his world was dominated by predetermined regulations and that was that. The problem was that with every passing day I felt a growing desire for something dramatic to interrupt part of my life and those rules, and I sensed my father began to notice it too.

2

WHEN THE MID-MORNING TRAIN PULLED into Duncan at the end of the summer there were only two people on the platform waiting for its arrival. Those planning to meet the train or catch the train were commonly late because the station was wedged between the Tzouhalem Hotel and the Commercial Hotel where it was convenient to take in a beer or two while waiting, and the radius between the station and the beer was the same whether one ventured east or west.

It was the end of an arduous two-day journey from Los Angeles for Robbie Tweedie, one made mostly by bus, then ferry, and finally train, where Hoxsey Borden, Robbie's blood-aunt, and her husband, Slick Borden, stood there waiting, uncertain of what they were looking for. No one disembarked. An elderly couple staggered out of the waiting room and finally boarded the train before Hoxsey confronted the conductor and found Robbie Tweedie fast asleep with his head on his knapsack, taking up an entire row of seats for himself, his feet poking into the aisle.

"Good job I checked," Hoxsey said, "or you might have ended up god knows where."

The two of them dragged the knapsack outside to where Slick waited with a toothpick flicking nervously in his mouth. "So, this must be Robert?"

"My name's Robbie."

The three of them drove a sightseeing tour up and down the three or four main streets of Duncan before heading out into the country. Slick owned a two-door Hillman and there was just enough room in the back for Robbie and his gear.

"You've grown like a string bean, young man. The last time I saw you was eight or ten years ago. You were four I think."

"Eleven years ago," Robbie said.

"What grade are you in now?"

"I didn't finish school last year. I guess I don't know."

Hoxsey knew to be careful what she said but was eager to get to know her nephew anyway. No point asking how he liked Los Angeles because according to her brother things hadn't worked out at all. Something about school and not getting along with his cousin Emily who was two years younger. Hoxsey felt some pressure to make a home for Robbie Tweedie because after his parents died in a plane crash in Montana five years earlier, Robbie had been shifted from aunt and uncle to aunt and uncle and Hoxsey and Slick were the end of the line. "It's your turn," her brother had insisted by phone *and* letter to emphasize his position was firm.

"I drink coffee," Robbie said when they pulled up to the house on the side of the hill.

"It doesn't sound like you got much sleep on the bus, you poor thing. Maybe you should have a bite to eat and a nap before supper. Maybe have some coffee when you wake up."

"I feel like coffee," Robbie said and walked into the house and found his bedroom at the back from the description his aunt had given. By the time Hoxsey had perked a small pot of coffee he had his clothes put into a dresser and a picture of Jane Mansfield in a bent frame sitting on top.

"Looks like you've been through this routine before," she said and immediately regretted saying it.

"I was wondering," he said, then drank from his coffee as if it were fuel needed to complete his sentence, "if I can call you Hoxsey? And Slick. Without the aunt and uncle before." Hoxsey looked across the room to where Slick was reading the funny papers. He refused to look up. "I'm not little any more as you can see. And no one ever calls me nephew Robbie. You know?"

When he finished his coffee he found an axe in the woodshed and practiced slamming it into the big cut of alder used as a chopping block. Slick watched from the window and said he would have to teach him to put some wood on the block before he expended so much effort. Everything is new, Hoxsey said. He has a lot to get used to.

Behind the house was a steep climb that eventually levelled off onto a plateau that became the cutting edge to a large gravel pit that was now mostly a crater. Robbie sat with his back against a young maple, the closest living thing before a steep drop into the cavernous pit. Over on the far side he saw a boy, younger than he was, slide down the gravelled slope on a piece of ratty cardboard, then climb up the edge from the shallow side and do it again. Robbie had never tobogganed down a snowy slope, even though he was born in Montana, and he had been looking forward to winter in Canada so he could do such a thing, and here, right before his eyes, was someone doing it without any snow in the middle of summer. He walked along the edge of the gravel crater, thinking maybe the boy would give him a turn, but the boy saw him standing up above, abandoned his cardboard and walked his way to somewhere through the sparse woods.

3

EVERY TREE UP AND DOWN the road for a five mile stretch and four or five acres on either side, Old Evans knew with the same familiarity his lolling tongue had with his seven remaining teeth. His family had owned the whole stretch at one time, but now there were thirty acres to his name: the five he lived on and twenty-five acres south of the railroad tracks. Fir trees, cedar trees, hemlock trees, maple trees, oak trees, arbutus trees, alder trees. The odd cascara and dogwood. He was there when seeds had fallen and sprouted then rooted their way into the earth, tree arms spread to welcome the haphazard sun. Some of the very big trees were older than he was, but at eighty-seven he'd scribbled on more calendars than most of the trees had rings.

The trees were the enemy when he was born the second son, and by the time he knew his way to the outhouse most of the land had been cleared for farming. That's what he'd sprung from — a family of farmers, hopeful as any and more successful than most, and growing up the way he did there seemed no good reason not to do all the wrong things early in life to get them out of the way.

When he looked back now at the archived newsreel that came at him more frequently with every passing year, it was what had gone awry that pleased him most. The chicken coop he'd burned to the ground when he was old enough to know that dry wood was eager tinder; running over his brother's leg with a tractor that left him with limp until the day he died; being suspended from school in grade six for pushing his teacher, clumsy fool, who fell and hit his head on a desk and had to miss work for three weeks. Things most men would be ashamed of, unless they were drunk, he clung to, sacredly, because they stood out from the rest of his life. He had an old man's memory, potent and full of responsibility, and he used it to ease the fruitless conjuring of a distant future.

The body belonging to Old Evans was no longer sound but his mind was sharp. His legs were like dead branches and forced him to use two canes and shuffle like a blind man navigating someone else's house, yet every moseyed step he cherished because most of the people he'd known growing up were six feet under the same earth he could still traverse. His house, a mile away from the one he grew up in, he'd helped build more than fifty years ago for a sister who'd stayed two years then travelled east to sift her way through three grey marriages. She was younger by birth but dead now. Gone too was his brother, two years older. He was the last of the Evans that for a short while dominated this part of the valley and now he was alone. The land for a time had been his brother's and for profit chopped up in the shape of ice cubes — small farms not big enough to survive, big enough to pretend. The eight or ten neighbours closest by paid him little attention and at his stage of life and being a social anemic, he didn't ask for any. A few would lay on the horn and wave if they saw him making his way from the house to his workshop, but with both hands anchored to canes he'd keep his head down, full of intent. Groceries, mail, newspapers were delivered. It had been twelve years since he'd set foot outside the margins of his own land.

Ask anyone living thereabouts: Who lives in the green bungalow? and the answer you'll get is Old Evans.

It was past supper and like he did most nights, after fixing something to eat and stacking the dirty dishes on the counter, he leaned slightly forward as if facing a headwind. He clutched his canes at the back door which opened onto a ragged field that ran into woods and a path leading past a ramshackle barn to his pumphouse and well. He wore pin-striped black and white coveralls with brass buttons and cream-coloured long johns underneath, the only clothes he would wear. Even a man who can no longer walk the earth in loose strides can enjoy the vision of a journey on land all his own that even a straight line would consume half an hour of a young man's time. It wasn't fall yet and the leaves were mostly green, but despite this he could smell death in the thin breeze. Morning was his favourite time of the day, but he respected evening — a time for auditing the affairs of the day. When it was a warm night, like it was now, he could stand for an hour or more watching the painting that was his back acreage, bordered by door frame, patient for the urge to empty his bowels, a ritual that allowed him to settle into bed with his magazines and his radio and not be bothered until morning. Had anyone been in the woods staring back at the house on one of these evenings, they would have observed another kind of painting, the old man with a fat and flatulent dog at his feet where he lay most of the time. The animal was old and smelly and nameless and both the dog knew and the old man knew that one of them would die first. The dog may have thought his name was Come-on. "Come on," the old man said, and the dog struggled to his stiffening legs and waddled toward the bedroom to sleep on the same rag-spun rug he slept on every night.

4

I SPENT MOST OF ONE YEAR enrolled at Tansor Elementary, and despite what happened it was a good thing I did. I was able to get by with my marginal English but my progress accelerated in the survival mode of a grade one classroom. I was getting encouraging report cards and my father was content until an incident at the school changed things forever. Two boys in the grade six class escorted two girls — Lana from my class was one and a girl I can't remember from the grade two class — into the woods behind the school at lunch time. It was early spring and a warm day and I remember our teacher, Miss Abbot, had a bouquet of pussy willows in a jar by the window and by not giving them any water, she explained, they would stay looking soft and fuzzy forever. The two boys had asked me to go with them too, but I was lunch monitor that day and had to stay behind to clean the boards and tidy the room. What might have happened was that the boys insisted the girls remove their underwear so they could have a good look. I don't think anything else took place, but no one really knows for sure. When they returned to school, Lana was obviously upset by what had happened and sat with her head in a nest of folded arms on top of her desk and eventually Miss Abbot took her to the health room to have a chat. The two boys were suspended for a week and in no time everyone in the valley was aware of what had transpired. That was enough for my father. He pulled me out of school the next day and my career in the Canadian school system was over a little more than six months after it had begun. My father's demeanor was passive in general, but the incident torpedoed the calm I was used to and to a degree I couldn't comprehend. I put up a fuss, of course, but my father was firm in his conviction that the incident was symptomatic of what can happen in a country school like Tansor.

I missed the friendships I'd made in school and was angry for months about what had happened. My father insisted he could help me with anything I had to learn, but there wasn't much attention paid to school books for at least a year because I was so busy helping him get established in the valley. While he wasn't eager to develop relationships with people who lived around us, he did show signs of wanting to fit in, and he bought a cow because everyone else had one. He was good at feeding it and making sure it had water and he even brushed our cow every night, but he needed our neighbour, Ernie Jagger, to teach him how to milk it. After two or three weeks of putting the cow through hell, he finally sold it to Ernie Jagger for less than he'd paid for it. We moved on to chickens, which Ernie threw into the cow transaction, and it became my job to feed them and clean their small coop and collect the eggs. It was his idea to plant a vegetable garden, which the two of us accomplished over several weeks. Whatever expertise was required to develop a verdant garden was missing from my father's repertoire and within two or three years our garden was home to potatoes only. The potato plants would brown in late summer then lie down on the earth and, because not all of them were dug up, the garden eventually replenished itself with volunteers, albeit pathetically, every year.

Later in the spring of the school incident, I began to miss my friends, Lana in particular, so much that it felt like an ache inside my bones. Lana and I got along famously and she loved to draw and laugh, that was mostly what I remembered, and when she drew she hummed and I could sit for hours and listen to her hum and watch her sketch a world under control. One day, a Saturday, when my father was immersed in his clock repair, I decided it would be a good idea to go and visit her house. I'd never visited anyone from my class before but Lana had described her house as sunflower yellow and told me she lived on Sathlam Road and had pointed west, so off I went in the direction I knew the sun would eventually set. It took me more than an hour to get there but the house was easy to find: sunflower yellow the perfect description. We spent most of the day in her bedroom and she told me all the things they were doing in school — that part made the whole day kind of sad. Her mother fed us a lunch of tomato soup and toasted cheese sandwiches and when Lana's dad returned home about four he offered to drive me home. I thought this was a great idea because I wasn't looking forward to the walk and it would be a chance for my father to meet someone who could be a friend. My father was home when we got there, but he'd been out driving up and down the roads of Tansor most of the afternoon looking for me and he yelled at me to get inside the house. I went inside, but stood by the door and heard him telling Lana's mom and dad that I was far too young to be spending a day at someone else's house and he would make damn sure it never happened again. After he ranted for a few minutes he stopped and everything was quiet. I stepped out onto the porch and I could see that Lana and her parents were bewildered. Then my father appeared to regain his senses and he thanked them for returning me home safely.

My father didn't hit me but I think he wanted to. Did I know how dangerous it was to walk on the Lake Road? he asked. He went on with a second chapter of raving and warned against wild dogs and mean people, that made my arrival at Lana's house on my own feel like it deserved an Olympic Gold medal in an event he didn't think anyone should enter. I was confined to house arrest for a week, which wasn't a unique punishment of any kind because that's where I spent most of my time anyway, and never, never was I to go anywhere in the future without his permission or there would be hell to pay. I didn't know much about hell because I was not yet seven and we didn't attend church, but the way he said it, I knew it was a place that resonated with dire consequences. After two days I was allowed to sit out on the back porch in the afternoon sun where I ate my three allotted Dad's Cookies and looked out on the weed-infested garden I wasn't allowed to rescue under the burden of house arrest.

I didn't comprehend what was happening at the time, but my father never did make any friends and I had lost all of mine. Eventually, he built up his clock repair business, which was the mainstay of his expertise. The relationships I developed were with people I met in books that I read, and except for a rare sojourn into town, my travel was confined to the pages of any texts I could get my hands on. I consumed three or four books a week, sometimes more. When you live a certain way for a long period of time you come to expect life will continue much the same way, which mine did. I had conversations running through my head constantly: I was Abraham Lincoln arguing for the abolition of slavery and delivering the Gettysburg Address; he was self-educated and that inspired me. I was Nellie McClung and I wanted to write like she did and someday get elected. Amelia Earhart was my favourite and I had read two books about her life. She was a lot like me because she often spent time playing by herself and she came to Canada after she was born, just like I did. It was in Canada she took an interest in planes and for her, planes were a way to escape.

In my imaginary world I would play with my brother. He was younger than I was and he needed my guidance. I didn't take to fishing, although I had caught trout out of the creek behind the railroad tracks, but my brother wanted to learn to fish so that's what I would do some days, stand at the side of the creek and explain to him how you had to be patient even though being patient was hard on me. The part he hated the most was skewering the worms onto the hook for bait, so of course I had to do that for him every single time. Once I told him he'd better learn to do the worm thing himself because if I up and left he would be on his own and how would he bait a hook then? As I expected, he didn't have an answer to that one and remained speechless.

When I mentioned to my father my deep-seated desire to learn to fly, he said it was too dangerous and too expensive. As if I didn't know that. I was certain that if I were a boy or it was my brother asking the question, it wouldn't have been so easily dismissed. I tried to share the world I lived in with my father, who half-heartedly listened to what I had to say but rarely responded. Like most people, the only thing he knew about President Lincoln was that he had been shot.

The clock repair and occasional jewellery creation my father was so adept at soon turned into a vigorous business. He advertised himself as a European Expert Clock Repairman and people from all around liked the sound of European. My father once told me that if you were from Europe people in Canada assumed you knew how to make cheese and chocolate and could repair a watch or a clock and he said it like a criticism. It was soon easy for him to forget the notion of farming altogether and the animal world was the better for it. At first he cooked and cleaned when necessary and did the laundry, but he taught me how to do every conceivable chore around the house and by the time I was ten I was doing almost everything that needed to be done. At first I just watched him repair the various clocks that made it into our house and eventually he took my observation as interest and began to teach me the craft. It took a few years for this to occur and I think he finally realized since he didn't have a son to pass his expertise on to, I was better than nothing. I was never as fast as he was but it got so I could do almost anything to the clocks and watches that needed attention. When clients came to drop off their precious commodities he insisted I be seated at the kitchen table, hunched over my correspondence courses. You do good work, he told me, but people don't like the idea of a girl your age fixing their broken clocks because if someone your age can do it, they figure they should have been able to do it themselves. It will be our little secret, he said, and our little secret it was.

5

IT WAS LATE FALL AND IVAN MAY was short of water. Even a deep well needs something to feed it or it may as well be just another hole in the ground, but in Mr. May's case it wouldn't have mattered because he didn't own a well. He was riding his bike up the Lake Road and neighbours, out stretching their legs in the horizontal light, watched to see whose driveway he would turn into. He asked most who lived close by for water once a week, give or take.

The bike that carried him looked like a bike made by someone who liked to make bikes and maybe this was a first try. It was black, a girl's bike with fat tires — a bike larger in frame than suited a man of small stature — with a wicker basket tied to the handlebars and a rat trap over the back fender, a board lashed to it with bailing twine. The board stuck out sideways and had two nails half-driven into each end and bent over to pin the handles of the two galvanized pails he planned to fill. One pail was medium-sized, the other small, so for balance he knew from experience to fill them both to the same level.

Karl Marx was deeply revered by Ivan May and it was his insistence on proselytizing ardent communist recipes for society and not the sharing of water that caused everyone in the valley to shun him like a virus. Every month he received mailings from the Winnipeg chapter of the Canadian Communist Party and he saved them up for his ebullient sharing during the eight or ten weeks each year when rain was tedious for the mind to summon and absent from the indigent landscape.

When Ivan May turned into the chicken farm, Ernie Jagger saw him coming and shooed his kids into the house the way he choreographed everything they did on the farm, with a wave of his hand, as if they were a team of border collies. The seat on his Massy Ferguson had taken to vibrating and he finished tightening it down with a wrench before he walked toward the fence beside the water tap where his visitor had settled his bicycle and waited, patient as the fence post he was leaning on.

"Help yourself," Ernie said, pointing at the tap. "I won't be needing any handouts, just so you know. I read what you gave me last time and it didn't agree with me."

"What part?"

"I don't remember. All of it, most likely. Have you read the Bible, Mr. May?"

"The Bible I have read. Have you read *Communist Manifesto*? All of it?"

"That I haven't done. I'm sure I've read enough of your bulletins to get the gist."

"So, if someone claimed to dismiss the teachings of the Bible without reading it first, you would accept that?"

The Jaggers had plenty of water, but the pressure out of the tap was weak. Ivan May started with the filling and knew it would take a while. Ernie Jagger decided not to engage his parched neighbour any further because he was a man who owned few accomplishments so far as he could tell, and easy to reject as dull, myopic, and shallow. But there were times, like now, when the old man said something to disturb his is preconceptions.

"What's wrong with your tractor?"

"Who said anything's wrong with it?"

"You don't use it much, I guess. It just sits there most of the time. Rusting."

"A tractor's handy no matter. You should know that better than anyone." Ernie Jagger had taken his tractor up Evans Road four years earlier, and chain-dragged a garden shed close enough to the shack Ivan May was living in so that he could say he lived in a house that was two shacks stuck together. That, and sharing his water, was about as close to communism as Ernie planned to go.

"It could be argued," Mr. May said, "that if four or five around here helped you own that tractor it would get more use and you would have someone to help fix it when it breaks down like that."

"Nothing wrong with that tractor. Your big bucket's almost spilling over. What about the small one?"

"I know. Once it's full I pour half into the small bucket and then I know for sure it's equally divided."

Ernie Jagger glanced back at the house. He could see the curtains flapping and knew his two kids, Gerry and Bonnie, were watching to see if a visit from Mr. May could occur without their dad receiving a pamphlet.

"Any cracked this week?"

"Pull up by the house. I'll see."

Mostly, the Jagger farm sold wholesale in town. Nearly everyone in and around had chickens, even if they didn't fancy themselves as farmers. Cracked eggs that couldn't be sold he routinely gave to those who could use them. Ivan May was the only neighbour who asked.

"Here. They're not cracked but you can have these two."

Ivan May slid the eggs into his shirt pockets, then pulled them out and tapped them on his handlebars. "They're cracked now. You don't need to feel bad giving them away."

Ernie Jagger waved his hand dismissively, walked into the house and closed the door: another iconoclastic standoff. Ivan May had an excellent article on Caring for the Elderly in his wicker basket, weighted down by a rock. He placed the article and then the rock on the top step of the Jagger house before focusing on the balancing act needed to deliver his water home.

6

ERNIE JAGGER WAS THIRTY YEARS OLD when he'd
taken up religion and at the time there had been plenty of
reasons to do so. He had brought his young English bride
to Canada in his mid-twenties and worked hard to establish
his egg business. It was what his father had done in Britain,
a business to be taken over by his older brother, leaving him
with a sum of money to move to Canada and do the same,
which he did. What got in the way was hard liquor and his
scurrilous behaviour toward his wife, and for a short time, his
kids; it was a period he was not proud of and one that needed
a solution. His wife returned to the old country, left like she'd
been pardoned from death row, and it wasn't long after that
he met up with Reverend Ridley and joined, with fervour,
the Pentecostal Church. Ernie Jagger was not naturally
evangelical, but would tell anyone willing to listen that the
church and Jesus Christ had saved his life.

He was still fond of his drink, but knew his limits. He
abstained on Sundays but otherwise took one shot a day of his
brown, throat-cleansing liquor made from his own still — a
condensed version of his undrinkable plum wine, trans-
formed into something heavenly. Religion had anchored him,
given him the vision and a newfound discipline he wished
he'd had years earlier. Every Sunday morning he would see
to it that Bonnie and Gerry, who were *his* kids now whether
they liked it or not, were spruced up enough to sit through the

service offered with great zeal by Reverend Ridley, an august figure who every week expounded on examples of people who could have been Ernie at one time, succinct reminders of the importance of keeping the faith.

When he looked back on who he once was, something he did habitually as it helped to reinforce his beliefs, several things were obvious. He had lived a life of pain in so many ways, yet there had never been any shame come to surface. Indignity was there, it had to be, but he had mastered the art of camouflage. He knew he had been thrashing the waters of a polluted river: one with strong currents of rejection from his family, a wife with particular ways he couldn't hope to replicate in this new country, being yoked with the responsibility of two children at such a young age, a penchant for mind-numbing liquor that brought temporary relief. His response to all of it had never been second-guessed.

The Jaggers owned four Bibles. Bonnie and Gerry had one each, kept in their bedrooms and read nightly with his supervision. One he kept on the coffee table in the living room and another was kept in the chicken coop. Certain images from his own life still tormented him, almost daily. Scenes where he beat his wife unmercifully, his kids hiding under the bed until the storm passed, a time he slaughtered five perfectly good laying hens before he passed out on the floor of the chicken coop, covered in blood and chicken shit. One that came back at him often was when he kicked the television in until smoke started pouring out the back because his wife, ironic as it seemed now, had tuned in to a Billy Graham crusade one Sunday morning. These demons, less frequent visitors as time passed, still haunted him without forewarning and when they did, as if struck by lightning, he fell to his knees in prayer and then accepted edification from a passage from one of his four Bibles. The prayer offered with every evening meal always ended with: God bless our chickens.

Neighbours didn't care for Ernie Jagger or his deleterious behaviour up until his transformation. He hadn't been aware of their discontent, but they liked him well enough now. And Ernie liked his kids, finally. He wasn't sure that had always been true. They were polite and helped out around the house, hated school but went without complaint and wrote to their mother once a year, at Christmas. Bonnie and Gerry had a few friends at school and a few friends from church, but little time for any of them because their father kept them busy on the farm. They did have a two week exodus each summer to the Pentecostal Bible Camp on the Cowichan River, however. Ernie took them there each year, even though it meant a lot more work for him at home, and he stayed for most of the first day to help out if he was needed. One of the things that united Ernie with his two children was that the three of them had been baptized and saved in the graceful summer flow of the Cowichan River.

The transformation that had taken over his life had real consequences. The friends he once knew were friends no longer, and it puzzled him that he had associated with any of them in the past. He now spent as much time with Reverend Ridley as with anyone. The two of them got together once a week to throw horseshoes behind the church, an activity that gave them something to do while they discussed life and religion and destiny. The reverend had watched Ernie closely for years and believed he was now a prime candidate to become a man of the cloth himself. One Sunday in the early spring, when Reverend Ridley was bedridden with a fever of a hundred and two, he asked Ernie to step into the breach and when Ernie complied he was energized by the experience. He delivered a convoluted sermon in which he had drawn a parallel between life and religion and the chicken and egg question. It was a discourse he couldn't repeat under any circumstances because it had started with only a few handwritten notes that he abandoned as soon as he got going. The congregation, possibly because they empathized with the pressure he deserved to be under, thanked him profusely for his illumination and a few hung around after church to discuss his platform. Gerry and Bonnie sat at the very back of the church that day, worried that their father was in over his head, but when the sermon was said and done with they were publicly as proud of their father as they had ever been.

Every horseshoe-pitching session the question of his spiritual future made it into dialogue, but Ernie always said no, it was not the time. He was satisfied with enjoying his sobriety and sense of purpose and he had two children to raise. The next few years were important years, and based on how their early childhood had gone, he had some loathsome times to make up for.

7

BEFORE NOON ON MONDAYS AND FRIDAYS was when
my father preferred to travel into town and then only when
necessary. I did what I could to delay such journeys later into
the day, or Saturdays if possible. He liked to avoid people and
traffic and noise, all of which he found confusing in a way
that made him hold his breath. Saturday afternoons there was
a livestock auction from one to three held not far from the
train tracks in town, and he would sometimes sit at the back
of the bleachers and take in the bidding, though he never once
considered bidding himself. All who attended the auction
were there to satisfy their own agenda and no one bothered
him or wondered why he came. He kept a notepad on his lap
and tried to predict what a milk calf would go for, a black
sheep, a plough horse. It was a practice he had participated
in often enough that he was generally only a dollar or two off
in his estimate of the going price. About half the bidders were
regulars and my father knew who in the valley had money
and who did not. I petitioned that I ought to go along with
him and take in the auction, but he told me an auction was no
place for a girl to spend her Saturdays. He was always willing
to describe what he saw there and after a few months I realized
I probably would have hated it anyway.

The library was two blocks from the auction yard and on
Saturdays he would pop his head into the library and wave
me to the car when he was done. Because he became so

immersed in the auction sale, I knew I would have two hours of unencumbered, avaricious library immersion.

Graham Puckett worked some afternoons and every Saturday stocking shelves and helping people find their way around the library. I didn't like his last name but I liked him. He was helpful to anyone who needed assistance but was especially attentive to my needs, or so it seemed, usually a research topic I'd made up five minutes before entering the library. Graham was in his last year of school and thought he would move on to UBC in the fall; he owned a dull green '51 Chev spruced up with baby moon hubcaps and a racoon tail attached to the antenna, had brown curly hair, dark blue eyes and sideburns past the bottom of each ear.

"Hanne looks different somehow," was how he greeted my entrance. I was wearing a tight white blouse I hadn't worn for a year but it still fit. In my small handbag I had stored a tube of hot-pink lipstick purchased from Rexall Drugs, the application of which had taken place in my reflection in the Hudson's Hardware feature window. Graham's comment made it all seem worthwhile, but the weight of what he said flustered me and I began to fidget with the pages of my binder.

"Elephantiasis. I want to know what causes it and where it comes from. And some pictures if possible."

Graham Puckett wrote it down two different ways on a piece of scrap paper and scrutinized the results. "I'm sure we can find something, though we may have to sift through some medical journals to find what you're looking for."

"What about Special Collections?" I asked.

Graham looked directly at me then and I averted my eyes. Three weeks ago, a Saturday, Graham had taken me into a separate room at the back where the special collections resources were kept. He helped me briefly with my research and the back of his hand had gently stroked my forearm, soft as a butterfly, before he left the room. I knew my words had been a mistake, too bold, too brazen. Elephantiasis felt like a topic one would find in Special Collections but apparently I was wrong.

"Well, let's start here," he said. "If nothing turns up we can see what might show in Special Collections."

"You got a haircut," I said.

"I know. It will look better in a day or two."

܀ ܀ ܀

"How was the auction?" I asked on our way out of town. I waited until he had to pay close attention to a knot of traffic before leaning toward the side mirror to make sure there was no evidence of lipstick for him to question.

"They had this bull enter the pen for bidding and they had a devil of a time getting him back out. It was something to see."

"I *like* getting out of the house. Maybe we could take a different route home?"

"Not today. I've got ice cream in the back and it needs to find a fridge."

It was the answer I expected, but I didn't care. I focused on what would happen eight days from now when Graham Puckett drove out to where I lived to take me for a long ride. I couldn't remember who had suggested a ride in his car but I knew I was the one to request a trip to Maple Bay, where there was a park and a yacht club and an ocean view of Salt Spring Island. I'd heard people talk about Maple Bay and once there was a black and white picture in the *Leader* of people swimming there. It was too late in the year for swimming but that was unimportant, and in any case it was just as well as

I didn't own a bathing suit and I didn't know how to swim. What I wanted most was the chance to sit beside Graham in his Chevy with only two feet of windswept air between us, and every time I rehearsed the journey I was wounded by joy. I couldn't imagine anyone I would rather have for company when I got to see the Pacific Ocean for the first time.

We were less than a mile out of town before my father pulled over to offer Lodie Stump a ride home.

"What happened to your truck?"

"Truck won't start for some reason. Started last week."

"You should have asked for help," my father said. He put the van in neutral and went around to help with the door which needed some muscle to open. The three grocery bags went in first, then he helped Lodie into the back seat.

"I didn't want to bother anyone," Lodie said. "I thought if I left it for a day or two it might decide to start. No such luck."

Lodie Stump asked me how my schoolwork was going and the rest of the ride home was given over to the sound of a Volkswagen muffler. We drove Lodie right to her door, one driveway over from our own, and he helped her in with the groceries.

"What took so long?" I asked. My father wasn't in such as hurry all of a sudden and the ice-cream was no longer an issue.

"I'm going to see if I can fix her truck. Just making the arrangements."

8

WHEN RED NEILSON LEFT THE HOUSE after eating in the morning, no one in his family saw him again until supper unless they went out back to the acre of jumbled carnage which was his auto wrecking business. He saw himself as an undertaker for dead cars, and dead cars were like dead people in the sense that most didn't want to deal with them, but for him there was a moderate living to be made with limited effort. The money he made from his hubcap collection alone, he figured, was enough to pay for his beer. Most of the time he was stripping cars and sorting parts, but on rainy days or days he felt less inclined to work, he would hold up in the tarpaper shack set almost exactly in the middle of the acre and disappear into his vast collection of *Playboy* magazines. He had several favourites he kept in the bottom drawer of his desk and the rest were stored in a cedar chest in the corner of the small room. The shack had a corrugated tin roof and a wood-burning stove and it was where customers, when there were any, tried first when they needed him. On an average day he would sell three or four vital parts, mostly to young bucks from town, occasionally from collectors in white suits. Once a month he would assemble enough parts to make a running vehicle and he would paint the tires black and sell it at the side of the Lake Road. His ambition had a short leash, but his wife worked part-time and the children had never gone hungry.

Kurt was two years older than his sister Daisy and seven years older than his brother Milo.

Compared to most, the Neilson household was a hub of activity. Cars were towed in and out, tires rolled down the driveway, and people parked out front then sniffed their way through the car parts — as if such activity may have been an art or a science that took years to perfect. People came and people went. Saturday nights a party broke out at the Neilsons with such regularity it was considered an option right alongside the Saturday night dance at the Moose Lodge. Liquor flowed like a spring creek and some nights there would be a hand of poker, a mystery game, or darts. If someone showed up who could bend a spoon just by thinking about it — so went the rest of the night. The three kids generally stuck around and sat on the porch in summer or the staircase in winter, afraid there would be something they'd be sorry to have missed out on.

Kurt was like a feral cat and he had a temper too. His nose had been broken three times before he became a teenager and most of his schoolmates were afraid of him. He never bothered his sister Daisy because his dad would make him pay if he did, but with Milo — well, that was a different story. When Milo was four he was roughhousing with Kurt in their upstairs bedroom on a rare day the kids had the house to themselves, and somehow Milo went flying out the window and fell into a radish patch that had gone to seed in mid-July. That may have been the only time Kurt had been scared in his life because looking out the window he could see Milo hadn't moved from where he landed. Kurt ran past Daisy who was lying on the bearskin rug watching Saturday wrestling and eating a batch of pink icing she'd made just for herself. "Shit. I think Milo's dead."

Screaming was all Daisy could muster when she came out and saw what had happened, so Kurt went inside and phoned Ernie Jagger, the chicken farmer who lived down the road. They drove Milo to the hospital, pinned between Daisy and Kurt on the bench seat of Ernie Jagger's Ranchero, and he started to show signs of life as they pulled into the emergency entrance.

Anyone who looked at Milo after that day would think he was a normal kid for his age, but when you talked to him it was plain something wasn't right. His broken arm healed in time but something inside his head never did, and while Milo went to school like the rest of the kids in the valley, mostly he coloured in shapes of his own creation that mildly resembled cars. Kurt was protective of Milo after that — his way of making amends maybe — and anyone who took advantage of the youngest Neilson got a close up look at his older brother. After the accident, Kurt was certain his dad would pummel him with his bony fists, but a whole week went by and nothing much happened except twice-daily visits to the hospital to visit Milo. It was an injustice too large in scope for retribution to soften.

It was easy for most to conclude that very little made it into the fatuous mind of Milo Neilson because he didn't react to much of the world that swarmed around him. What did make it in got locked in, especially things he took a shine to. Three years after the accident his Uncle Fred came for a week and told Milo that if he dug into the earth long enough eventually he would end up in China. Uncle Fred helped him get started and when he left to go back east, Milo was still digging. Every summer since then Milo charted out a patch of their yard and went to work and only gave up when the weather turned and the hole began to fill with water. His dad would eventually fill it back in and it would be forgotten until the next summer and Milo, insouciant as ever, would eventually find the shovel his dad had taken to hiding and get to work. It was with the same fixation that Milo had recently adopted with his brother, Kurt. They went to different schools, but when school was not an obligation, Milo wanted to trail behind his brother everywhere he went.

9

THERE WERE SO MANY WAYS to tell him about my upcoming ride in the country with Graham Puckett but none of them qualified as irrefutable and my mind went stir-crazy. I tried writing them down. Graham was hardworking and smart and planning to go to university. Graham was helping with my research and needed to show me something. Graham had been driving for a year and a half and had never had an accident. Graham was interested in clocks and wanted to visit first. Graham was a boy (who kept a comb in his back pocket and put it to good use) and I was a girl — that was clearly reason enough for me to go.

By Thursday I realized none of them would work and I would take my chances that Graham's appearance would somehow charm him. Graham was charming. Or maybe my father would be sleeping. He considered Sunday a day of rest even though he had stopped attending church since our arrival in the valley, and some Sundays he would lay down after lunch and sleep for two or three hours, in which case I would write him a note saying Graham had taken me to the library because there were books left over, due to overstocking, and I was free to help myself. He also might visit Lodie Stump to see how her truck was running, something he had done twice during the week since he'd replaced the battery. That would only work if he were inside Lodie's house, a building that had but a few windows.

In the morning I cooked his favourite breakfast: three eggs sunny side up with double-smoked bacon, three strawberries on the side and two pieces of burnt toast. I was nervous and cleaned first my workspace, then his.

"It's Sunday," he said.

"I'm not working on anything. Just cleaning up so we'll be ready to go tomorrow. I ironed your three white shirts if you need them."

The comic strips embedded in the local paper that came out on Wednesdays were absorbing his attention and if my words registered I couldn't tell. Eventually, he turned the radio on. He had little use for churches but liked to hear church music on Sunday and always managed to find some. I found the music depressing. I used the heat produced by the stove from cooking breakfast to heat water for a lukewarm bath then cleaned the bathroom even though that was usually done on Mondays.

I closed my bedroom door on the drone of organ music and flipped the pages of our only family album. There were four pictures of my mother; the one I liked best was the one taken a few weeks after we had returned from the hospital and my mother held me with such pride and beauty it always lifted my spirits. I was starting to look like my mother and I didn't mind it. The hairstyle was different but I had my mother's eyes and mouth. The picture was black and white but I imagined her wearing a light yellow dress and me a dress of pink or blue. There was another picture of my mother by herself, leaning against a tree. I found this picture fascinating because I wondered if she were pregnant for a second time when it was taken. There was only one picture of me and my mother and father together. I was very young in the picture and I had a dress with ruffles on the bottom and I stood smiling below my mother's waist. My father stood beside my mother and every time I viewed this picture I thought about the space in front of my father where a brother could have eventually stood.

If my mother were around she would be happy to see me head out to explore the ocean and the islands and sandy beaches. She would understand my desperate yearning.

"Is Lodie's truck running okay now?" I asked after lunch. The puzzle in the paper had taken over his focus and he was having trouble with it.

"It starts okay. It needs a muffler."

The small front porch, overgrown with ivy, was seldom used. I sat out on the first step and observed the golden light on trees that were beginning to turn with the season and drop their leaves, like memories, on the parched earth. Three Canada Geese followed a low flight path across the front acre, looking for companions for their impending journey south, and flew over Neilson's Auto Wreckers, ignoring the swearing and door slamming that comprised their Sunday routine neighbours had grown accustomed to.

From the doorway I could see my father sitting with his eyes closed and I wondered what he was thinking about. He wasn't one to share what was on his mind and something had to be on his mind because a mind can't stay empty for long. He could work away at clocks and watches indefatigably six days a week and then shut down on Sundays like he had an internal switch no one else had. Despite his deep reverie, he heard the sound of Graham Puckett's car crunching up the gravel driveway at the same time I did.

"Someone's here," he said.

"It's Graham. The boy who helps me at the library. He said he might drive out this way some day."

"It's Sunday," my father said. He got up and followed me out the back door.

The car pulled up close to the back steps and a cloud of dust from his arrival slowly drifted east over the car and Graham Puckett sitting in it with the window rolled down.

"Hi," I said with less enthusiasm than I wanted, sensing my father standing in the doorway.

"You look lost," my father said.

Graham got out of the car and walked up the steps to shake my father's hand. "Graham," he said. "You must be Hanne's father." He shook Graham's hand briefly but didn't say anything. I noticed Graham wince slightly. Since living in the valley, my father had adopted the local custom of offering a robust handshake or no handshake at all. "Hanne tells me you're the best at fixing clocks around here." Still, he said nothing. Graham looked at me, hoping for some clue about what to say next.

"Graham has offered to take me for a ride in his car this afternoon," I said.

"No."

"We won't be long. I'll go grab my scarf." I ran to the bedroom at the back of the house. If I grabbed my scarf and got in the car now maybe he wouldn't have time to mount an argument.

My father stepped into the woodshed at the back of the house and came out with the only weapon we had, a shotgun. He rested the butt of the rifle on his foot and held the stock in his right hand. The gun was empty. He had been given it by a client for work he had done but he'd never pulled the trigger and never bothered to purchase ammunition.

"Hanne isn't going anywhere with you," I heard him say. "I'd hate to punch holes in your car but I will if I have to."

Graham got behind the wheel and had the car started by the time I made my way back to the porch. "What are you doing? Where is he going?"

"Back where he came from. You're too young to be hanging around with boys from town. You might not know what he's after, but I do. Forget you ever met him."

Graham had the car turned around and he headed down the driveway without looking back. I stamped my feet on the back porch, as if that was going to do anything. I ran through the house to the front porch and watched the car turn onto the Lake Road. Graham ground his gears pulling out and I had the notion I would never see Graham Puckett again and it felt like the truth.

"Why did you do that? There's nothing wrong with Graham. You don't even know him."

He sat back down in the chair beside the radio as if what had occurred was an illusion. He didn't look at me but he didn't close his eyes either. He stared straight ahead, confounded by how such a serene day had been so promptly ruined.

"You can cook supper yourself if you're hungry. I'm going down to the creek. You're acting stupid, you know that? This is all stupid and more stupid. I'm not your wife, I'm your daughter. About time you figured that out."

I crossed the back acre in record time, over the fence and down a path the other side of the railroad tracks. This was my favourite pool in the creek, a bucolic place. I came to relax and it always made me feel good inside, watching the unwavering creek make its journey toward Somenos Lake. I fished here in the late spring and fall and swam in the middle of summer, but none of the attributes of my favourite hideaway brought relief from my current frustration and misery. I hated my father then with all the energy I could muster. The words

51

I'd spewed out in my rage offered a vengeful comfort and the fact that he didn't offer a rebuttal signalled their veracity. If my mother were alive I would have been able to travel with Graham to see the ocean, I just knew it. He was my father and he was supposed to stop me from doing stupid things, a job description he alluded to often. But driving to see and smell the ocean with a boy who didn't even smoke was as a good thing as any to do on a Sunday.

When the sun sat balanced on the horizon I retreated to the barn, wrapped myself with gunny sacks and cried myself to sleep in the hayloft. The last sound I remembered was the forlorn sound of an owl, all by himself as is the way with owls, in the trees nearby.

10

IF HE WROTE HIS FRIENDS back in California and told them he was living in Canada in a house without a TV they wouldn't believe him. Robbie Tweedie didn't have any friends in California to write letters to so it really didn't matter. His cousin Emily didn't know how good she had it with her canopy bed and her own TV with more than ten channels to watch anytime she wanted. She would invite him into her bedroom only when she wanted company and she had a fluid set of rules as to what Robbie could do and where he could sit. She could eat pizza in her room but he couldn't. She didn't want crumbs on the bed, not that he often got to sit on the bed even though it was the best place in the room to watch TV. Sometimes she invited him onto her bed — it depended on her mood. Emily hated sports of any kind so for the most part Robbie would glare at soap operas and listen to her moral interpretation of what was presented.

Now, without a TV, there was not much point hanging around the house. On Saturday mornings he was invited to go elsewhere, Hoxsey didn't care where, because she and Slick wanted some "private time" together. It didn't take long for him to figure out it meant they shared a morning bath and then screwed until lunchtime. Whatever Slick did for a living he was gone weekdays, but with the irregularity of a rain squall he would arrive home in the middle of the day and when that happened, if Robbie were home at the time, he knew that Saturday rules applied to his living in the house.

In September he found himself enrolled in a school he could walk to in ten minutes. Grade nine was their best guess as to where he belonged, though he was older than most in his class. He hated school, but at least it was somewhere to go. In California there had been a few cool teachers who could make you laugh once in awhile, but here all the teachers took everything so seriously he wondered how they could stand being who they were. The principal had short hair like a marine and would stand in the hallways between classes to make sure everyone walked on the right-hand side.

Robbie had a few things in common with Daisy Neilson. They both hated school for one. Daisy wasn't big on conventions of any kind and when the weather was warm she was sent home on two different occasions because her skirt was too short. "Fucking assholes," Daisy said. "What am I supposed to do? Sew an extra inch back on? Marine-face can't control his hard-ons, that's what it is." What Robbie liked about Daisy was she said what most of her peers were thinking and did what most would if they had the nerve. If her crotch were itchy she'd scratch it while talking to you and not think anything of it. Robbie was wary of her though. One day after school in the middle of September she and another girl went at it on Auchinachie Road and Daisy didn't take long to bloody her opponent without mercy. For a week after, Daisy walked home alone because everyone was afraid to go near her. Daisy could travel on the Lake Road or the back way using Auchinachie, the road Robbie lived on. "Hey, wait up why don't you?" she said one day and they stopped at his house for lemonade. Hoxsey always kept something cold in the fridge after that because she was happy to see Robbie with a friend.

"You're always so polite around Hoxsey," he said. It was a hot day in late September and they were sipping their lemonade in the shade of the woodshed.

"What do you mean? I'm friendly. I treat anyone fair and square if they don't screw me around. Your aunt's okay."

Robbie accepted the fact that he was not much of a fighter. Most of the kids at his school had a long established pecking order of mean and nasty and he had no desire to work his way up the list. Daisy's brother, Kurt, was at the top, along with the Olson brothers, and Robbie had been bounced around in the hallways because he was the new guy, a guy from California, and everyone wanted to know where he stood. Their P.E. teacher was big on Olympic wrestling and had them paired off earlier in the day on mats outside, and Robbie found himself matched up against a small wiry kid and then a boy wrapped in whale blubber and he lost both times. Daisy hadn't mentioned it on their way home so it appeared his strategy of non-aggression might work after all.

Daisy's two brothers were lithe and muscular, especially Kurt, but Daisy was short for her age and everything about her was rounded. She wasn't fat, just sturdy: round legs, round arms, a round and freckled face. She could beat any girl at school in an arm wrestle and half the boys too. She hefted the axe over her head and drove it deep into the chopping block. Robbie decided to do the same but struggled with getting the axe out of the alder.

She said, "I've got an uncle. Fearless Fred they call him. I've only met him once but he might come back out here some day. He went over Niagara Falls in a barrel when he was twenty-one. He wasn't the first but he did it."

"That sounds crazy. He could have killed himself."

"Fearless Fred told me when he was here: 'Daisy, you're going to die someday so you might as well die going after what you want.' Here, I'll show you something else he can do."

Daisy took the axe away from him and knelt down by the chopping block. She laid the back of her hand against the surface and extended her index finger, then lifted the axe over her shoulder and sunk the blade into the block an inch away from the end of her nail. "That's how Fearless Fred trims his fingernails. With an axe."

Nothing more was said. She handed the axe back to Robbie and they stood there, both stunned. Robbie put the axe down and found a second alder round and placed it on top of the first. Instinct told him what he had planned needed to be done in a hurry or he would change his mind. He unzipped his pants and pulled out his frail looking dink and laid it on the chopping block, just below waist high. He lifted the axe as smoothly as he could and after its descent it came so close to his penis, Daisy sucked her breath in panic. He didn't feel a thing and quickly tucked himself back in and left the axe in the chopping block.

"How are you two doing out there?" Hoxsey yelled from the porch.

"Good," Robbie finally said because Daisy didn't look like she wanted to say anything.

"I just made some oatmeal cookies. They're warm if you want some."

"I gotta go," Daisy said, then opened her mouth wide enough to take in a whole cookie at once. Before she left she turned back and gave him a punch on the shoulder.

11

IT WAS A STALEMATE. I SPENT the bulk of my time in my room working on my coursework, knowing the sooner I got through my last three courses the sooner I could escape, while my father hunched long, silent days over his workbench with the abundant orders that had arrived at our doorstep. He could use my help but didn't ask and I wasn't about to volunteer. We cooked our own meals, separately, when we were hungry. There was no trip to town the following Saturday, and the only time my father left the property during the week was to go to the corner store for groceries. I decided to write a letter.

It was embarrassing, what had happened on that fateful Sunday, and while I could understand if Graham didn't want to have anything to do with me in the future (who would want to cozy up to someone with an overprotective and neurotically insane father?) it felt like setting the record straight was the right thing to do. Despite grinding my teeth, my angry scrawl contained words carefully chosen, explaining my father's past and why he had overreacted. Clearly, he had overreacted. At the end of what amounted to a grand apology, I explained where the Tansor service station and store were located and that I would be there the following Thursday evening at seven, should he wish to see me again. I spent an hour writing the letter and posted it on Monday which would give Graham plenty of time to make up his mind. I had felt cleaner inside once the letter was written and made a batch of carrot muffins my father would enjoy and could partake in if he chose to.

My father was engaged in a charade that didn't take long to grasp. At first I found it odd that he stopped watching the late news before going to bed. He would sit in his overstuffed chair in front of a TV turned off and clean his fingernails while he re-read the weekly paper, then eventually nod off to sleep. I stubbornly continued my self-imposed exile in my bedroom, but observed my father's behaviour between pots of tea and late night snacks. Once he was convinced I had fallen asleep, he would leave through the front door, the door farthest from my bedroom, wander halfway down the driveway, and climb between the barbed wire fence and enter the house of Lodie Stump without knocking. It got so I could predict which nights he would make the stealthy sojourn because Lodie left her back porch light on the nights he was welcome. It was laughable, like something straight out of the *Nancy Drew* series.

As pathetic as the ruse was on the surface, I was still baffled. Had all this started simply because he'd replaced her battery? My father had rarely acknowledged our neighbour before then. And why would he, after all these years of perfecting the art of a hermit, take an interest in an abandoned woman living next door and do so surreptitiously? It was obvious he wanted me to know nothing about his visits and such secrecy felt misplaced — everything about how he'd lived his life for so many years had been nothing but plain and honest. Was it possible he thought his interest in Lodie Stump was a contradiction, based on his treatment of Graham Puckett eight days earlier?

It was obvious my father was a singular man and routine was the blueprint of his life. He was the only person I knew that I was related to and, as alone as I sometimes felt, I understood that were he not in my life it would be like living alone on Mars. Still, his ability to get by with so little stimulation, so little sense of the future, was puzzling whenever I took the time to consider the matter. Puzzling on a good day and infuriating the rest of the time. If he were a dull and stupid man I think I could have accepted everything about the way we lived, but he was clearly more intelligent than most, just stuck. For a few years my father listened to a syndicated radio broadcast with a woman psychologist as host and know-it-all. Sometimes it was reassuring to listen to other people's problems and maybe that was why I was so willing to pay close attention. On one show the psychologist told one of her callers: Time heals all wounds, eventually. This lady always spoke with such confidence and probably people believed everything she said on the radio, but I think she would have qualified her statement had she met my father.

I loved my father for all his frailties, but there were times I felt responsible for trying to hate him for failing to settle our whole family in Canada as he had promised. As a kid you don't know much about what goes on deep down between two people, and it may have been my mother who deserved to be the object of my disdain, but my father was the only one left for me to experiment on. A few times I settled myself in the hayloft and rehearsed a verbal armament I could unleash when the time was right, but the right time never surfaced. I would return to find him bent over a clock's puzzle pieces, humming to himself, not with pleasure but with mild resolution.

Often when I read a book I liked I read it again immediately, a bad habit probably but one I got used to. Late into the night I was re-reading Dickens' *Bleak House* and fell asleep without any sign of my father's return. I slept in and when I made it to the kitchen for breakfast (he had helped himself to two muffins, I noticed) he was seated at his work station, his back to my domestic musings, as if nothing unusual had taken place. I resisted asking him any of the numerous questions ricocheting inside my head. It was a role I was playing, I knew that, but I didn't know what else to do.

12

A SWIRL OF LATE SUMMER FLIES had a job to do. Some were circling the ceiling light in the kitchen counter-clockwise, others helping themselves to the half can of dog food set out in a bowl on the floor that had been untouched for two days and sported a skim of mould. There was no point replacing it with fresh food. When a dog refused to eat it wasn't a good sign.

Old Evans hated Thursdays but put up with them. His routine was to have breakfast then putter in his workshop, eat lunch, and putter his way to suppertime; Thursdays he left the morning free for the itinerant nurse to change his bandages, change his sheets and give him a bath. She monitored his medication and checked his vital signs, though Old Evans knew his vital signs better than anyone. The first week of every month she trimmed his toenails.

"Good morning, Dr. Evans. How has your week been?"

"Seven days long, same as last week."

Verna had been tending to the old man for close to three years and she looked forward to dropping in on him. He was stable, never complained and always had a story or two to share. He was ancient, as were many of her clients, and it was clear he knew more about the world than she did. She called him Dr. Evans out of courtesy, despite his efforts to get her to call him Art. He had practiced as a doctor in BC for sixteen years and had been the first in the province to use a microscope in his practice.

"You mentioned the left leg was a bit numb. Was it any better this week?"

"Better maybe. Starts tingling when I'm in bed."

Despite his modified mobility, exercise was important and Verna always threw a line or two his way to reinforce the fact. She knew he spent twelve hours in bed most nights but was on his feet the rest of the time doing something outside of sleeping, so her reminders weren't needed but had become routine. Without having to be prompted, he shuffled back to his bed, released his coveralls, unbuttoned his longjohns and lay down. He knew not to bother with shoes on Thursdays so it took her no time at all to remove his clothes and begin to unpeel his bandaged legs. She kept him informed about what was going on in the valley: roads being ripped up, roads being paved, rumors regarding the dismantling of the old water tower, a truck that had turned over north of the Silver Bridge. Through Verna's detailed reports he had a notion of what was going on in a world he no longer had access to and his treatment passed by quickly.

Once the bandages were removed she massaged liniment on his legs, especially the problem leg in and around his knee, and then left his legs to breathe for twenty minutes while she ran his bath. His bath took up another twenty minutes, or however long it was before Verna had his bed stripped and the sheets, along with the week's dirty laundry, in the wringer washer started in the spare room, his bedding replaced and a new set of clothes set out on his bed. It was easier to wrap his legs with fresh bandages while he was standing up so she dried him off and put the bandages on in the bathroom. Once he was dressed up to the waist she left him to finish and ran the clothes through the wringer and hung them to dry on one of two wooden racks that sat beside the washer.

By the time he was dressed and had made his way to the kitchen table, Verna had assessed the kitchen, which wasn't part of her job but she did anyway. He was capable of cooking his own meals but apparently incapable of washing the dishes.

"I don't see any vegetables in that fridge of yours."

"That's because I ate them up."

"You know we've talked about this before. Variety *is* the spice of life. You need to eat more than just mush every day."

He was the first to admit cooking had never been a bandwagon he'd climbed onto. His two wives, over the years, had looked after that department. He cooked porridge in a pot in the morning, left the rest on the back of the stove to be re-heated for supper. He ate his mush with brown sugar and a bit of milk if there was any and washed it down with hot water. That was all he ever drank, hot water. He would force himself to prepare something different for lunch and he had eaten a bowl of snow peas two days earlier but doubted Verna would believe him if he told her. Embracing hardy vegetables was a more desultory custom the older he got.

His dog seemed to understand Thursdays as well. He sat by the door and scrutinized their choreographed movements, knowing eventually life would return to normal. The dog watched, with mild interest, his mouldy dog food make its way into the garbage and a much smaller portion of fresh dog food take its place. Old Evans would then remind Verna she didn't need to bother cleaning up the kitchen and she would say she understood that and do it anyway. This was when he would tell her stories, not about what was going on now but what had happened in the past.

Verna's daughter was six months pregnant and the conversation turned in the direction of babies.

"I lost count after forty. I would say I delivered more than sixty babies. Mostly boys for some reason."

"All healthy?" Verna asked.

"All but one. It was the neighbour who called and asked me to come. The husband was fearful of what becoming a father would mean, had turned to drink and run off for two or three days. She was alone until a neighbour dropped in. There was a heartbeat when I arrived but the birth was difficult and the little girl that was to be never took a breath out of the womb. "

"That's a sad story," Verna said.

"What was even sadder was the mother didn't appear to be upset at all. Maybe she thought her husband would be relieved, it's hard to say."

"My daughter has a doctor lined up. She likes him but it's his second year in practice and he's so young. I can't help thinking she might be better off with someone who has more experience with all this."

Old Evans didn't respond. Verna looked over her shoulder to see if he had been listening, but he was in a trance, staring out the kitchen window and into the back acreage.

13

HIS FIRST FULL SENTENCE ALL WEEK was in the form of a question: *Do you want to take a trip to town for supplies?* It was Thursday, six o'clock in the evening, and the library closed at five every day except Friday and he knew that — a fact that disqualified his overture as anything close to a gesture of reconciliation. I told him no, I didn't care to. I didn't need anything and planned to spend some time meditating down by the creek. As soon as the words came out of my mouth I wished I hadn't said the word *meditating*, a concept I had read about but hadn't discussed with anyone, and I certainly didn't want to discuss it now. It was something I'd tried a few times, sitting in the lotus position, trying to focus on nothing, but even nothing seemed to be something and I hadn't made any headway in the practice. His decision to get out of the house couldn't have worked out better. If Graham accepted my invitation I would be up the road a quarter mile and now there would be no need to explain myself. It occurred to me, grimly, that he might pass Graham on the road into town, though I supposed it unlikely he would recognize his car.

"Are you taking anyone with you?" I asked. He looked at me like it was a question that didn't make any sense.

Once his Volkswagen was out of sight, I brushed my hair, traced my lips with my only tube of lipstick, and headed west on the Lake Road. Twice I had to stand halfway in the ditch when chipper trucks came barrelling down the road. I went into the store to ask the time and waited from five minutes to seven until fifteen minutes after, walking back and forth outside to appear intent on something. The fact that Graham didn't show up made sense in one way, but I felt let down all the same. The least he could have done was listen to my side of things.

I went back into the store and bought a Fudgesicle to console myself. The path that led to the railroad tracks and the creek was even further up the road, and this was where I went, so if my father made it back before I did my appearance by way of the back acre would make sense. The path to the tracks dipped steeply and was covered with loose gravel; I knew from experience it was safer to run down such a slope, planting each foot on the ground for as little time as possible, and because of my abeyance to one of the laws of the physical universe I didn't notice what I was to find out more than a year later, Graham pulling his car up to the pump for gas.

14

A FULL LIFE MEANT NOT ONLY looking out for yourself but looking out for others. Mr. May understood that most didn't see human existence the way he did, but he was determined to live by example. He knew who occupied every house for miles and miles and knew their ages, their passions and their squabbles. That others found him nosey and interfering didn't deter him one iota. When Mrs. Eaton broke her ankle walking the railroad tracks he offered to walk her dog until it healed and she accepted. When Milo was hospitalized for a week he monitored Red's auto parts business when the family visited the hospital. He was the only one to show up when Lodie Stump's husband came home drunk one afternoon and blasted their living room window with his .303. When he'd arrived Bert Stump was sitting on the sofa crying into his hands and Lodie had locked herself into the bathroom. Mr. May told him he needed to leave and get some help with whatever demons were haunting him and Bert walked out the front door and down the road and never returned, an action that resulted in Mr. May wondering, months later, if he'd done the right thing. He pulled the curtains over the gaping hole in the window and waited until late at night before Lodie was willing to extricate herself from the bathroom. She was not the kind of woman suited to living so far from town but he didn't feel it was his right to tell her so. She was innocent, like a fawn, but he didn't share that with her either.

Mr. May knew how to drive but hadn't driven for more than thirty years and went everywhere on his bicycle. Almost anything he needed he could get at Berkey's Corner, but once or twice a month he would ride to town hoping to share his incendiary thoughts with some of the town's influential citizens: the mayor, the owner of Hudson's Hardware, the Anglican minister: Reverend Street. He would pick up his monthly welfare cheque because he didn't trust the mail. Several social workers had tried over the years to find him suitable employment, but for the last decade he had been left to his own devices. He didn't have any reservations about collecting his stipend once a month because he thought of himself as a citizen providing services often needed and saw himself as supported by the state for that very purpose. Mr. May had made the front page of the *Leader* in 1959 because he was riding past the Royal Bank and saw a man run out with a mask over his face. The man was about to remove his mask and move on down the street but when he saw Mr. May on his bicycle he started to run, a shopping bag clutched to his chest. Mr. May peddled after him on his bicycle, keeping his distance of twenty or thirty feet, and followed him past Strawberry Hill where the railroad tracks head south out of town and suddenly the man keeled over from what was later determined to have been a heart attack. He rode his bicycle back to the closest garage and phoned for an ambulance. The man survived, was eventually brought to trial and imprisoned, and the money, amounting to several thousands of dollars, was recovered. Just that one day in his life had left him with a sense of entitlement. He was possibly the only one to pick up his monthly welfare cheque without the slightest trace of humility.

One project that had occupied him sedulously for nearly a year was trying to get the local library to stock a copy of

Communist Manifesto by Karl Marx. The head librarian told him there had been a copy many years ago but someone had stolen it. This incensed Mr. May. A stolen book was obviously a book in demand and besides, he had done some research and knew they could buy a paperback version of the book from Winnipeg for $2.49. The librarian said the Canadian Communist Party was not one of the agencies they were accustomed to buying books from and was he aware that shipping would be close to a dollar extra. Mr. May then offered to spend an afternoon stocking shelves to pay for the book but was told library policy entrusted library employees and carefully selected part-time students for such exact and demanding work. The head librarian's name was Cecil Biltmore and his heavy-handed English accent had suffered very little erosion in the twenty years since his immigration, but what jilted Mr. May the most was how the man seemed to enjoy the standoff. It wasn't every week he made it to town but a library visit was always included when he did. There was a suggestion box near the front desk and Mr. May always put in his request, and lately had taken to changing up his hand writing and signing fictitious names.

To be avoided at all costs was a return trip to home after school was out. He heard the town clock chime three in the afternoon and realized he wouldn't make it home until close to four and the reason for his late departure was because Graham Puckett, a young man he'd never before met, had the afternoon free of school for some reason and was in doing inventory under the scrutiny of Cecil Biltmore. The head librarian was overwhelmed with the task and more than willing to let Graham deal with the wizened old man and his petty complaints about biased book ordering. The young man was versed in the rudiments of communism and patiently listened to Ivan May elaborate on his existing framework of knowledge. Not unnoticed was his sympathetic understanding that all modes of thought ought to be represented in the public bastion of knowledge. The young man was so optimistic and mature it gave Mr. May a refurbished view of society's future.

Territorial dogs, and gravel slopped out of trucks and onto the road from the local gravel pit, were evils Mr. May was wary of and accustomed to coping with — it was the hoard of after-school boys who would wait until he had passed them going up the hill to the gravel pit before pelting him from behind with stones that filled him with trepidation. When the silly buggers were planted in their desks, their round, oily faces resting on upturned hands, engrossed in watching the flies hammer their flight of freedom against the yellowed window panes, his journey was flawless and filled with contemplation. It was fortunate that their aim was as misguided as their behaviour and it was infrequent that he would actually suffer the sting of their intent. It was his bicycle he depended upon that was his greatest concern and in the spring they had managed to bend one of his spokes and break another.

Contrary to his worst imaginings, there were no wily boys to be spotted on the way home. Only Daisy Neilson and the new boy who had moved in with the Bordens were at the side of the road and they were immersed in their own company and didn't pay any heed to his passing. He couldn't help thinking his positive meeting with the student worker at the library was in some way responsible and that maybe there was hope for the world after all.

15

THIS IS WHAT I REMEMBER. The move had been planned for months and it was all my parents talked about. They talked to me about moving to Canada, too, because I was almost six and had begun the disturbing habit of developing my own opinions, and they knew enough to lobby in advance. We arrived in Oostende three days before our scheduled departure because my father didn't want anything to go wrong, but what he wasn't counting on was my mother getting nervous and sick to her stomach. I had no idea until later that she was pregnant and I remember her health had not been good for some time. Now she was resisting the trip altogether, something I must have picked up on because I can remember the two of us having arguments with my father that we should return to our village of Lubbeek, just outside of Leuven. But it was much too late for that in my father's mind, for we had sold everything we owned, and he was convinced Canada would be a place where the opportunities were endless. I have no idea what my father did or said to convince my mother that the move was what we should be doing, but as soon as we arrived in Oostende, whatever powers he had exercised over her began to dissipate. "*Dom, dom, dom,*" my mother kept repeating, perhaps referring to our planned journey or maybe, by this point, she had my father in mind.

When it came time to board, my mother disappeared into the crowd. She was standing with us beside our luggage one minute and lost the next in a sea of travellers and well-wishers cluttering the landscape. My father panicked. He told me to stay put and went running, zigzagging around the dock like a madman, but had no luck finding my mother. He handed his tickets over and took me aboard and into a stateroom, then went back to look for her. It turned out he'd put me in the wrong stateroom and soon I was surrounded by an older couple and all their belongings. They tried to reassure me and said I could stay with them until my father returned. I, too, was nervous and sick to my stomach by this point, sure my father would never return and I would be off to Canada on my own. It was starting to get dark in the harbour when he returned with apologies to my temporary hosts and my mother as white as the sheet she finally fell asleep on.

The first day or so everyone, except my mother, was excited about crossing the ocean to North America. It was a huge ship we were on but the moody Atlantic showed little respect for the vessel and those taking refuge inside. My father was never physically ill but he didn't look his normal self; it may have been because of his concern for my mother. The first three days she spent on the edge of the small bed with a bucket at arm's length; she couldn't keep anything down and neither could I. A German doctor examined her twice and gave her something to settle her stomach but she showed no interest in eating anything.

I remember my father talking more than he normally did. He talked about where we were going and what a glorious time we were about to have in our new life in Canada, anything he could come up with to give my mother hope and strength to hang on. It appeared to have an impact because on the eighth day my mother finally ate something that stayed put. The same day I must have been running a fever because they had ice packs for my forehead and every hour they jammed a thermometer in my mouth, at least they did until I finally fell asleep. My father was exhausted from all that had gone on. I was the first to wake up in the morning to his rhythmic snoring and as a result I was the one to notice my mother was no longer lying in the same bed she'd inhabited since we had left our native land.

16

JORDAN RIVER WAS ALMOST AN HOUR and a half drive by car and since his dad refused to drive him, Kurt slung the leather strap of his creel over his shoulder, grabbed his fishing rod and starting walking confidently down the Lake Road with his thumb stuck out, hoping for a ride. He could still see his house when he turned and accepted a lift from a forest ranger.

"Plan to catch some big ones up at the lake?" the man asked.

"Not really. I'm river fishing."

There was no sense telling him the name of the river. The fewer people who knew about it the better. The man was a slow driver and a fast talker. He talked about his job, fire season, his wife and kids, and how he was in charge of staking out a suitable place for a telescope to sit on a mountain outside of Lake Cowichan. "No city lights out there to interfere is the reason why," he said.

Kurt accepted the ride almost to Lake Cowichan and started walking west. He walked into the town and out again, heading toward Honeymoon Bay. His sister Daisy had started to hang out with Robbie Tweedie, and when he heard Kurt was planning to go fishing he asked if he could go too. Kurt said not this time because it was tough enough to get a ride on your lonesome, let alone with another guy who admitted to never having fished in his life.

Two years ago on the same day, his Uncle Fred had taken Kurt fishing to Jordan River and between the two of them they'd caught more than fifty trout. Last year he had gone by himself, mostly to defy his fastidious father who thought a day standing and watching a river go by was a waste of time, and though he had only managed eleven cutthroats, he had enjoyed the independence of the trip and planned to make it annually. There weren't many cars heading out of Lake Cowichan and he walked almost two miles before a woman stopped to pick him up.

"Thanks," he said, and threw his gear into the back seat before opening the passenger door. "I was beginning to think I might have to walk all the way."

"All the way to where?"

"Well, I'm heading to Jordan River, so if I can just get as far as — "

"I know where it is. It'll be hard to get a ride into the logging camp this time of day. I'll drive you there. I don't mind."

Kurt looked at the woman closely. He was uncertain if she was serious or not and her insouciant manner caught him off guard. She was taller than his mother and younger and better looking too. She was close enough to him in age that it made him feel older. She had soft, black hair that danced on her shoulders as she talked, and wore a white, ruffled dress as though she had just come back from an all-night party. There was an empty Coke bottle on the bench seat between them, a seat that appeared to be set too far from the steering console and made her work hard at extending her white legs to work the clutch every time she shifted gears. He noticed she was doing so wearing fluffy slippers.

"You must have a name," she said.

"Kurt."

"Curt with a C or Kurt with a K?"

"It depends what kind of mood I'm in. I spell it both ways." The woman laughed. It was rare that he said anything clever enough to make anyone laugh.

"My name's Megan. Megan Todd."

Megan was willing to split the conversation fifty-fifty. She found out about his dad's wrecking business and his brother and sister. Megan explained that she helped her father with a ten-acre Christmas tree farm south of town and that their busy season was only a couple of months away. She said she was on her way to visit her high school friend, Yra, to play Scrabble.

"We play Scrabble for a couple of hours, but mostly she just likes to have me around. She married a man who doesn't offer much company in the daytime."

It felt like a short ride to the Jordan River logging camp turnoff, the place the river curled around and headed to Port Renfrew and the Pacific Ocean. It was a warm fall day, despite partial cloud cover, and they had kept the windows rolled up against the dust of the logging road. She stopped the car a hundred yards from the road leading into the camp and he didn't know why.

"There you go, Kurt. I hope you catch a slew of fish. If you'd be a gentleman and stay right where you are for one minute, I'm going to duck on this side of the car and pee in the dust."

Out of the corner of his eye, he could see her wrestling to get her panties off, then she disappeared from view and he heard the sound of her peeing. Kurt reached over with his left leg and depressed the clutch pedal. The car was on a slight incline and silently rolled forward at the side of the road. From his view from the rearview mirror he could see the startled look on her face. She gave herself a nervous looking shake, balled her panties in her fist, returned to the car and chucked them under her seat.

"There we go. That was a relief, let me tell you. I normally would have made it to Yra's by now. You're not quite the gentleman I made you out to be."

"I'm not gentle."

"You're not?"

"My daddy says I've got bad blood in me. You can't get rid of bad blood."

Kurt retrieved his fishing rod and reel from the back. Before he closed the door he looked at her one more time, trying to take her all in. "If you tell me where you live I could drop some fish off for you sometime."

"That's very sweet. It really is. My boyfriend catches salmon all the time and I only eat them to make him feel good. Thanks, though. You might turn out to be a gentleman after all."

He closed the door and scuffed his way down the road. Megan watched him for a long time before starting the car. She turned it around on the road and the car lurched a few times before she got going. Then she beeped a goodbye and sailed off in a funnel of dust.

He had a small jar of worms dug from his mother's compost pile, but his uncle had taught him it was the Dead-Eye-Dick lure that worked best in these waters. His uncle had never fished the Jordan River until the time he took Kurt, but had been wise and avuncular enough to inquire about methodology at Bucky's Sport Shop in advance. From the entrance to the small logging camp, it was only a quarter mile to where the river kept a close association with the road for seven miles. The valley had been scorched by a forest fire years before, and there were remnants of charcoal trees and stumps that were becoming harder to find because of the new growth that had taken place: cedar, hemlock, fir, and plenty of red huckleberry bushes now just past their fruitful prime. The river's dramatic demeanour was what stood out his first trip and he appreciated it again now, the way it twisted and turned and funnelled through narrow channels and brisk waterfalls, later to open out to a pool in a canyon of water twenty-five feet deep, fifty feet wide and a hundred yards long. This was where he and his uncle had spied the largest uncaught fish either had ever seen. It was a landlocked steelhead, almost three feet in length, cruising back and forth in the clear water, the master of his small den. For an hour they had dangled every lure Uncle Fred had in his tackle box in front of the beast and nothing would entice him. Uncle Fred said he was the size he was for good reason.

The canyon didn't hold such a fish last year nor this year. Kurt contented himself with skipping from pool to pool as he had been taught. He kept thinking of Megan. She had called him a gentleman. No one had called him a gentleman before and he knew she was wrong.

The fishing wasn't as lucrative as the year before. Maybe he wasn't trying hard enough or his heart wasn't in it somehow. He wished now he'd accepted Robbie's company.

It took longer than he would have liked to hitchhike back and it was starting to get dark when he arrived home. His parents and Daisy were watching something stupid on TV and Milo was in the backyard digging a hole to China. He cleaned the six fish he had and left three for his family. He wrapped three in a plastic bag and decided to give them to Robbie and the Bordens.

"I'm up here." Robbie was referring to himself and his position on top of the woodshed. Kurt climbed the ladder already in place and joined him.

"What you doing up here?"

"Waiting. Waiting for them to finish. Some Saturdays it starts in the morning and goes all day. This is one of those."

Once Kurt perched himself on the roof beside Robbie, he could see what he was looking in on. The curtains to the bedroom window's bottom section were drawn, but the fancy, curved section higher up was naked and so was the couple sprawled on the bed. From their vantage point they could only spy half of the bed and the Bordens were apparently all played out for the night. Hoxsey Borden slid from the side of the bed they were able to view, squeezed her shallow tits together with her hands as if weighing them and then disappeared.

"I brought you some fish," Kurt said, handing him the bag.

"Thanks. I bet they're good."

"I'll take you next time. If you still want to go."

"Sure," Robbie said. "I'd like that."

17

WHEN YOU'RE INSIDE A THING you don't really understand the thing you're in because it's impossible to be outside the thing and inside at the same time, and only by viewing it from the outside do you have a true sense of it. I was living in my own little fantasy world and it was rare and at times frustrating that my father did anything to interrupt it. I became two people: the sausage-frying and cleaning-the-chicken-coop Hanne and the Hanne that hours of seclusion had nudged into a world most could not imagine. An intense imagination can substitute for much of what we yearn for. Many people focus on something they want and either take the necessary steps to get it or, if that fails, sulk or resort to violence because it didn't work out, which makes sense because not everything does. The line between these two results disappeared for me when I learned I could have anything I wanted as long as I didn't expect it to be delivered the same way most people did. None of this did I understand at the time because I was too much in the thing to comprehend it.

I had imagined Graham Puckett would drive out to our house and take me to the ocean and we would laugh and tell stories and maybe later snuggle and kiss and it would be a turning point in my life. I would finish my coursework and I would move to Vancouver, with Graham of course, and he would be trained as a research consultant and I would become a writer and part-time jewellery maker because a well-articulated fantasy is always anchored by a thread of reality, and we had to have some way to pay the bills until Graham's stupendous salary was sufficient to support the two of us and our two children, one boy and one girl. My father would stay right where he was because that was what he wanted and he didn't like to talk much to anyone, and with no one around he wouldn't be tempted to be someone he wasn't. Reality is often difficult to change but imagination can be as easy as a whistle. Graham didn't show up at the Tansor store like I'd imagined and our worlds had stretched further and further apart like an elastic band that would either boost the yearning we had for each other, or possibly snap — sending us helter-skelter into worlds neither of us had yet imagined. Either way, there was both hope and desire and these two elements alone were enough to keep me going.

My father and I continued our week of ignoring one another, me mostly in my bedroom and the kitchen, him in his bedroom at night and otherwise in the kitchen and the living room. I didn't care that I couldn't access the TV for a whole week; I had my radio that I enjoyed listening to and I had lots of books to read. Actually, I was running short of books, but my penchant for re-reading the ones I liked best kept me going. The only song I really liked that year was "My Boyfriend's Back" so I kept the radio on low and cranked it up when my song arrived. We generally worked side by side on clocks all day in relative silence, but since the standoff he had taken to listening to the radio that was in the living room. Ever since Martin Luther King's "I Have a Dream" speech he seemed to want to keep tabs on the news.

One afternoon there was a rare knock on our front door. I was getting a drink of milk to go with my cookies and about to return to my den when a man in a suit and tie came calling and asked if we were interested in selling the house. He asked my father of course, not me, and so our visitor was flatly rejected without my input. I would have said, yes, let's sell, let's move somewhere different and do something useful with our lives, but instead the man, despite his promise of a more than fair price, was sent packing. My father saw me standing still in the middle of the kitchen and said, perhaps more to himself than to me: "That man's an idiot." I didn't want to stay silent but that's what I did. What I wanted to say was, "It takes one to know one," a line I got from an episode of *Laurel and Hardy*, but I popped a Dad's Cookie into my mouth, half dry and half dunked in milk, and closed by bedroom door.

18

ONE THING WAS CLEAR TO HIM: every woman came with a unique smell. Hoxsey smelled like perfume and bath salts, not just because she bathed once or twice a day; she smelled that way even when she was pulling the vacuum around the house or washing the windows. Robbie had observed Slick inhale the essence she exuded when he came home; it was like a rejuvenation to him that preceded the more intimate kissing and hugging they engaged in more often than seemed necessary. One of the few things he remembered from school in California was his science teacher explaining that in the animal world, mothers used their sense of smell to identify their offspring. Sheep, he remembered, was one example. The same teacher said human smell was taken for granted and that if we cut off our sense of smell we wouldn't be able to tell if we were eating an onion or an apple. Robbie had never tried it but he intended to someday.

Daisy smelled like damp earth on a warm day. That was the closest thing he could compare her to. Once, when Daisy was briefly standing in the same room as Hoxsey, he experienced their separate aromas radiating across the dining room table, competing for supremacy. It was a confusing and intoxicating experience that subsided only when he and Daisy returned to the woods and he had her distinctive smell all to himself.

It was hard not to like Daisy. Boys were drawn to her as readily as flies to rancid meat, and yet the relationship she was willing to establish with him was more like that of a friend. When a girl takes you into the woods and asks if you want to wrestle or look for an ant hill it doesn't feel like a first kiss is on the horizon. He *had* imagined kissing Daisy once or twice, usually when he was lying in bed and searching for sleep, but when he pressed his imagination and closed in with a slow, meandering style, she would bite him on the nose and laugh in his face. Daisy *could* act coy — he'd seen her practice — but it was not part of her repertoire when the two of them were together.

Unless Daisy had soccer practice, they always walked the same route home, hanging around his house one day and going to hers the next. Kurt liked Robbie and Robbie wasn't sure why. Kurt typically hung out with people he respected as having warrior status, but this didn't apply to Robbie. Kurt liked having a friend from California and was always asking questions about what it would mean to live there; it was easy to tell, though not spoken of directly, Kurt thought he could see himself living there someday — surfing, riding motor scooters, chasing chicks with deep tans, and staring at the stars most nights.

"The water's cold," Robbie said, to his question about surfing. "You *can* surf there all year round but most of the time people wear wetsuits."

This conflicted with what Kurt wanted to hear and he bit his lip. If he lived there, he was certain he would never wear a wetsuit. How cold can the ocean be in a state that is sunny most of the time?

Robbie liked Kurt well enough but he didn't trust him; however, at least when the three of them were together he got to be with Daisy. There was a short window of opportunity when the three of them had the Neilson house to themselves — not counting Milo who didn't mind what went on — before Beverly Neilson got home from working afternoons at Pearl's Beauty Salon and Red Neilson finished his day in the junkyard. The music they played — sometimes records on the hi-fi console, or when they were too busy to choose, top forty hits from CKLG radio out of Vancouver — was loud enough for Old Evans to hear from inside his workshop and loud enough that Kurt, Daisy, and Robbie communicated by yelling about whether they would make peanut butter and jelly or peanut butter and jam sandwiches an hour before suppertime. If Kurt wasn't around for some reason, Robbie and Daisy would escape to her bedroom where they could talk about anything: stupid teachers and what they imagined doing to them; death, as in whether it would be preferable to die from drowning or die in a fire; who they would marry right now if marriage was mandatory and they had their pick; Buddy Holly vs. Elvis Presley.

"Elvis Presley had a twin brother," Daisy said one day. "He died at birth. If he hadn't died maybe they would have been more like the Everly Brothers." Robbie tried to imagine two Presley brothers thrusting their hips side to side with perfect rhythm.

Kurt was astute enough to leave his dad's favourite magazines alone, but always kept, between his mattresses, one or two of the dozens his dad kept in a cedar chest. Because of this, Robbie almost preferred spending time in Kurt's room. The pictures of the women were a special kind of beauty. Robbie found them far more alluring than watching his aunt and uncle go at it from the roof of the woodshed.

"Still got the same top ten?" Kurt asked.

"Yeah, I guess," Robbie said.

At least once a week, Kurt wanted to go over the top-ten list of girls he would jump if he got the chance. Robbie dictated his favourites and Kurt kept a written record of both on file in his bedroom. Reluctantly, they both agreed they couldn't use any of the girls from magazines: these had to be real flesh and blood girls they knew. Never did Robbie mention Daisy's name in such conversations, but truthfully, she would have been near the top of the list if her brother weren't the one taking notes.

There was going to be a Halloween dance at the school in two Fridays' time. It wasn't mandatory to dress up but practically everyone was going to, including Daisy who was going as Wonder Woman. Kurt and Robbie wished it weren't a costumed affair, and with only two weeks to go they knew they'd better think up something soon.

Kurt said, "The Olson brothers are stocking their lockers with booze that Friday. So are a bunch of other guys. A Mickey is the way to go. I know a guy who can buy us some. Do you want him to get you some? Cost you five bucks."

"Sure."

"What do you want? I'm going to get rum."

"Rum sounds good," Robbie said. "But I want to know something. Every time you go over your top-ten list you always stop at number two. Why don't you have a number one?"

"I've got a number one, believe me. She's fucking gorgeous. She's not far from here but she doesn't go to our school. I'll show you some time. You won't believe it."

19

IT WAS AFTER TWO IN THE MORNING and the counter-point ticking of clocks about the house was the only discernible sound to indicate that the world hadn't completely ground to a halt. Arthur Lemmons was more alone now than he had ever been and he knew he felt the way he did because after years of not expecting much, after turning his back on social inter-action of any kind, he had taken a chance on getting to know Lodie Stump. It was hard to be disappointed when there were no expectations, but all that had changed.

Lodie had needed a new battery but that was not all she required. She was friendly in a shy kind of way and ever so thankful for his help and his company. She was as lonely as he was (something that had never occurred to him as possible) and slightly more determined to do something about it. Never was there any discussion about the covert nature of their relationship: it was as if they both understood it was something of a trial and error excursion that didn't need to lead anywhere in particular. Lodie was thirty-one and techni-cally married; Arthur was forty-six and raising a daughter through a critical time; the neighbours, they were certain, would twist their thoughts and slant their opinions at will and leave out any rational description of the two of them.

Lodie wasn't lazy exactly, but was slovenly in her ways: her house was always in the process of being cleaned up and set straight, but the process was ongoing and full of good intentions without a serious hint of completion. If Hanne were ever away for an extended period of time, something Arthur would never allow, he would cherish the opportunity for Lodie to visit his house to see what law and order looked like. But lifestyle was never discussed because there was no point. They were two elements in a vast universe and they just happened to dwell within walking distance of one another with only a flaccid barbed-wire fence standing between them.

Sitting alone in the definitive darkness of the country, Arthur traced the thread of time that had woven the last two weeks of his life. She needed help. He helped her. She offered him tea. He drank it. She said she stayed up late most nights and watched the twelve o'clock movie, and he agreed to join her. All of that seemed like a natural progression, but then everything, examined in hindsight, lost focus. The first night he sat on one side of the sofa and she took up the other side. As the nights progressed they sat closer and closer together and soon the movie was of no consequence. Arthur couldn't remember the names of any of the movies they watched, though he remembered the first one was a western with John Wayne. The Gillette razor commercial stood out, but that may have been because he'd heard it so often. Two nights before it had been a longer stay than usual and something in the balance between them changed. She kissed him longingly at the back door before he left and that seemed to confirm something. Tonight her back porch light did not come on, and while he considered going over there anyway, in case, for example, the bulb had burned out and she didn't know that, he thought better of it. Any demands he might have were not warranted.

Arthur turned on the lamp that hung forlornly above his chair and the shock of yellow light made it feel as though a thief had entered the house. Hanne had left their one family photo album on top of the TV and he started at the beginning and scrutinized every page. There were three colour photos at the end, but everything else that documented his life was in black and white. He had one picture of himself as a little boy, eight years old, wearing shorts and suspenders. There was a picture of his wife in a summer dress holding a large flat of strawberries and smiling like such days would go on forever. Arthur had viewed this same picture of his wife many times over the years and each time it was as if it were in the present. He looked at it now and imagined her right after the picture were taken, saying something about the strawberries or the beautiful day or life in general, optimistically, as was her way. The album was only half full. The life he expected would have seen this album and likely a second and third full of family pictures. When he uxoriously looked back upon the pictures of his wife, he wanted more than anything to accept reality: that what flashed in front of him were layers of an irretrievable past.

He glanced out the window toward Lodie's house. The porch light was not on and by now she would have taken her thoughts to bed for the night. He was tired but knew he was not ready to sleep, so he fetched a glass of water from the kitchen tap and settled down to finishing some of the paperwork sprawled out on his desk. It was the tedious accounting for things, so separate from exchanges of human endeavour, which tired him out completely.

20

I EMERGED FROM MY BEDROOM earlier than usual because my mind was made up: the cold war between us had gone on long enough. For the last two weeks I had waited until he'd finished with his own breakfast and got to work and then I would enter the kitchen and do the same. Today would be different. I would prepare bacon and eggs for breakfast, the eggs sunny side up just as he liked, and insist that our relationship be a civil one, hopefully in some way refined.

The porch light at Lodie's had not been on when I went to bed, though it was not quite dark when I did so. My goal, which I'd kept to myself, was to finish my coursework by Christmas and contemplate a new and adventurous life for myself — a life removed from my father. There was no point sharing my intentions: much better to finish this schooling business and consider my options when I had some. I could see him arched over his workbench, papers strewn everywhere, and because there had been no domestic stirrings I assumed he had worked late, had not gone to Lodie's house and then fallen asleep.

The sounds of my breakfast preparations didn't faze him, nor did the enticing smell of bacon and coffee. "Something smells mighty good," I said from the kitchen, but he didn't respond. I went into the living room and called him for breakfast but he failed to stir so I went up to him, nudged his shoulder, and his body slid off the chair and onto the floor, one arm of his reading glasses sticking out like an antennae.

I removed his glasses and turned him onto his back. I yelled into his ear. I grabbed his hand and his fingers were cool. My complete lack of experience with death was instantly replaced and came in the form of my father.

☙☙☙☙

It was impossible to account for the rest of the day. An ambulance took my father away and it left a hole in the house no matter which room I stood in. Apparently, the world was watching everything. Mrs. Eaton saw the ambulance arrive when she was walking her dog along the railroad tracks; Mr. May saw the ambulance leave when pedaling his bicycle; Beverly Neilson saw what was happening as she left for work; Ernie Jagger stood at the end of his driveway and deduced something had gone wrong; Verna arrived to attend to Old Evans and knew an ambulance had been summoned to the Lake Road and was relieved, in the compromised way a caregiver must, that it was not the old man she was about to see. We knew our neighbours but never interacted with any of them more than necessary; that was my father's choice, but that didn't prohibit everyone from knowing the circumstance that presented itself. Before the afternoon was complete, Mrs. Eaton brought over a dozen warm buns and a vacuum flask of homemade soup. Mr. May came up our driveway and knocked on the door and got no response because I was inside, walking in circles at that moment, and had no desire to talk to anyone. Ernie Jagger didn't know what to offer and did not make the trek to our door, but instead placed a card in the mailbox to say he was sorry and willing to help in any way he could. Beverly Neilson drove up our driveway and knocked on the door. I didn't respond, so she opened the door and entered anyway. I was curled up in a ball on top of my bed and she sat down and offered her sympathy and as much opportunity as I wanted to cry on her shoulder. I resisted but she got me up and made me some lemon tea and insisted I eat some of the soup delivered earlier. I didn't eat much, but it was something. The untouched breakfast I had prepared served as a blatant reminder of the day's event and Beverly cleaned up the kitchen as best she could.

Lodie Stump was the only neighbour I didn't hear from because as usual she was oblivious to most of what went on in the world. She used her phone to call the pharmacist in town, and because it was a party line and busy at the time, that was how she learned about the demise of my father. The man had been in her house for hours at a time for the last two weeks and now they were saying he was dead and she didn't believe it.

I was sixteen years old and had always felt older than my age — but on this day I felt like a child. For most of my life I'd been raised without my mother there to care for me, to confide in, to answer questions best answered by a mother. Now my father was gone too, and while I knew this to be true, it didn't seem at all real. Compassion had entered the house in small episodes off and on during the day, but the kindness that had been shown was swallowed in a murky dream overflowing with pathos. There was a difference between being lonesome and being alone, and the disparity between the two was unkind and made the last two weeks at our house unreasonable and full of regret. If only I had prepared his favourite breakfast earlier in the week, perhaps he would still be in the room with me, asking how my studies were going or what I thought of reconditioning a particular clock. He would often do that: ask me questions he knew the answers to so that my involvement was affirmed. He had offered me the only kind of life he was capable of providing, and with all its limitations and flaws, it was the only one I knew.

The phone rang and I answered it even though I had no desire to talk to anyone. It was a man on the other end, wanting to know if his clock was ready yet because his sister's family was coming to stay for a few days and the clock was a family heirloom and he would really like to have it running when they arrived. Will the clock be ready in time? he wanted to know. He had accidentally dropped it before handing it over. Were there any parts missing?

21

THERE WASN'T MUCH OLD EVANS couldn't do in his workshop. He had a furnace and could weld, he had a table saw, a lathe, a grinder and every hand and electrical tool listed in the Eaton's catalogue. A wood-burning stove sat in one corner and in the winter, though it took an hour of stoking, the room was warm enough for bread to rise. The place was chaotically messy and anyone who walked into his workshop found it hard to imagine a finished product making it out the door. Unless he could manoeuvre fallen objects with his two canes, what fell to the cement floor stayed there: sawdust, every shape and size of scrap wood, a tin of nails that obeyed gravity. If anything of importance needed retrieving he asked Verna when she came or the pimple-faced boy who delivered groceries.

Projects gave the old man purpose. Rarely did he build anything anyone asked for because nobody asked him to build anything, so instead he manufactured projects with intricate designs that took time and patience, two commodities he had plenty of. Lately he had been turning slabs of maple into bowls on his lathe. He was working on his third in a row and this one was nearly perfect. It was difficult to judge the potential of such a product because until you were inside the wood, the grain and hidden cavities — the legacies of living — were difficult to discern. Three coats of linseed oil over three days and it would be allowed to make its way to the house.

In front of one of his two workbenches sat a tall stool he'd made years ago, and it was here he would lean as much as sit and stare out the window at the five-acre field that surrounded the house. Once a year, late June, he allowed Ernie Jagger to mow his fields in exchange for shop supplies Ernie would buy in town and deliver to him as compensation. Ernie Jagger didn't own a baler, so he hired someone to turn the field into bales of hay, more than enough to feed his one horse and small herd of cattle and fill his chicken barn with nesting material. Old Evans suspected he sold some of what he reaped, but it didn't matter. He had no desire or ability to work the land and his shop was well supplied; in fact, so many resources had accumulated over the last few years that it was a challenge to give Ernie a list that made it feel like an equitable trade. He took the clipboard down from beside the window and wrote down "mahogany", which would be hard to find but give Ernie Jagger something worthy to complete their annual ritual. From his window he watched Milo and Kurt taking turns shooting arrows up into the sky and waiting for them to stab the earth in some sense of proximity to where they were standing. It was only a matter of time before disaster struck, he knew, but it was a game they played less often as they got older. Once the hay was scooped from the field he didn't care that neighbourhood kids used his fields as a playground and by virtue of his saying nothing it was common practice in the summer and early fall.

He wished he had put mahogany on the list last year. It would have given him inspiration for something new to tinker with now that he'd had his fill of turning wooden bowls. Marriage had come too early in his life, he realized in hindsight. Izzy, his first wife, was a redhead, flamboyant, easily distracted and sadly as unhappy with her relationship as he had been. She went for a drive with her sister one Sunday and never returned. He had spent eight years trying to track her down, earnestly at first, sporadically after the exercise appeared a fruitless endeavour thanks in part to a lack of cooperation from her family. He finally went back to school and studied hard to become a doctor. That was where he met his second wife, Morag, who was a stark contrast to Izzy both in temperament and wisdom. Morag expected the best out of him and he complied. The projects he conjured up in his daily routine were always, in a furtive way, built for Morag. His first wooden bowl led to a second bowl and eventually a third: one she would have approved of. A breadbox made completely of wood, one with a sliding door and a breadboard to match came to mind, only because Morag had seen one on their brief vacation in New England. It was a tricky project and the channel for the sliding door would be pivotal to the success of the piece. A mahogany inlay would make it an art object but he didn't possess any mahogany. Still, it was worthy of consideration.

There was a clatter on the metal roof that startled the drowsy dog lying under the table saw. The dog struggled to raise his head and finally sat up, his instincts as a guard dog not quite extinguished when confronted with such a distinctive and blatant racket. Old Evans looked out the window. Both Kurt and Milo studied his workshop from their position in the field and then ran off toward home, having learned an arrow will obey its trajectory until it runs out of energy or something stands in its way.

22

IT WAS FALL, THE TIME OF YEAR my father was occasionally prone to suggesting an alternate route home from town, a chance to peek at the many panoramic views to be found in the Cowichan Valley. One time he stopped the van beside a cemetery at the foot of Mt. Prevost and we got out and walked around the various plots, some elaborately marked, others with only a name, a few unmarked completely. The leaves were falling and the sun was shining and I remembered him saying this would be as good a place as any to be buried, so arrangements were made for his wish to come true. My father's only longstanding friend, Peter De Groot, came by several times over the days that seemed scattered in front of me and was a big help in arranging everything. Because my father was only known to his customers and a few neighbours, there was no formal service of any kind, only a few words spoken at the gravesite after my father had been laid to rest. It was only Peter De Groot and his twenty-one year old daughter, Sadie, and I who stood beside a minister from the Anglican Church who spoke slowly enough to draw the brief ceremony out into a five minute affair. There were three sets of flowers at the gravesite when we arrived. I don't think I'd given flowers much thought until that moment, but their presence signalled some recognition of my father's passing, which I appreciated. Peter and Sadie took me to the Dog House restaurant for an early supper, dropped me off at home, and were on their way.

When they left I didn't go into the house right away, I went to the hayloft instead. I'd climbed up the stairs to the hayloft hundreds of times over the years, sometimes to read or think, and more than once in a state of anger. This was the first time I'd come to one of my favourite places in the world feeling utterly sad and empty. Every other time I'd been there it was an escape of some kind that I wanted to last longer than it did because I knew that, when it was over, I would return to my routine life which was mundane yet comforting. Now, even though I was not looking forward to entering a house that had, more officially than ever, become a house one person lived in, I couldn't stay in the barn for more than a few minutes. What I didn't realize at the time was that I would never return to the secluded spot again.

The back door didn't lock. I pushed it opened and stood on the porch looking in. I could hear three or four clocks ticking but the house felt silent. I wanted to go somewhere, anywhere, but there was nowhere to go. The house looked like a museum, not a home. I pulled the door closed behind me and the fly strip that hung from the lightbulb in the kitchen, still loaded with August and September's ill-fated flies, pirouetted, drawing attention to the defeated who had succumbed and were now frozen in time. There were bills on the counter I would learn to deal with and a Bible left by someone, Ernie Jagger most likely, I would probably never read. There was a radio I didn't want to listen to, a TV I didn't care to watch, and dishes in the cupboard I couldn't imagine eating from. In my dolorous state the only place that didn't repel me absolutely was my bed which is where I lay down and fell instantly asleep.

23

FRIDAY, SCHOOL MAY AS WELL have been cancelled. Only a few students, those not planning to attend the dance, paid the least bit of attention to the roster of teachers, many of whom had given up on instruction and instead showed 16 mm films that had nothing to do with what they were teaching. It was going to be a long day for the teachers who had volunteered to supervise the dance. They hated the music young people listened to these days and found their wild groping of one another in the dark legions of the gymnasium pathetic and embarrassing — partly because the actions of fifteen and sixteen-year-olds were highly reminiscent of their own callow behaviour twenty years earlier. Some of the teachers planned to come equipped with earplugs.

The bulk of the students going to the dance had been successfully stealthy over the last two days and had equipped themselves for what promised to be a dance like none ever held at Mt. Prevost School. Lockers were stashed with beer and rum and gin and it was difficult for the students to contain their excitement. The usual procedure, when there was a dance, was to make the bulk of the school out of bounds for the evening, except for the hallway outside the gym that ran past the washrooms. Because of this, liquor had been surreptitiously placed close to the gym in lockers belonging to students, many of whom didn't bring any booze and had no intention of drinking. This consent had been obtained with a combination of bribes and threats and so far everything had gone as planned. The only exception that made the ringleaders nervous was Marsha Hamilton, daughter of one of the school board trustees and student council president. Marsha clearly knew what some of the students were planning but had accepted complicity. She was in charge of decorations for the dance and if it were cancelled all her creative Halloween inspiration would be for nothing.

Mr. Rodman gazed mindlessly out the window through thick bifocals while his students were supposed to be working on the science homework they could complete now instead of on the weekend.

"Mr. Rodman. Tell us about some of the dances you had in school," Kurt said. Mr. Rodman was notorious for telling stories and was easy to get off track. All eyes were on him, expecting a thirty minute treatise on life back when civilization had replaced the reign of the dinosaurs.

"There weren't many dances back in my day. I only went to two of them, I think. I was too shy. They were mostly tame affairs as I recall."

Several students found his description humorous. Mr. Rodman smiled but was uncertain about what was so funny.

❧❧❧

Daisy looked better as Daisy than as Wonder Woman, mainly because her dark wig didn't go with her freckles. Kurt spent Friday evening trying to decide between going as a gangster, a fisherman, a millionaire, or a railroad conductor, and settled on a hobo because no one in his family kept much in the haberdashery department that came close to fine cut or imaginative clothing. Robbie arrived at the Neilson's at 6:30 with dark pants, a white shirt opened to the first three buttons, his hair slicked back along the sides and gelled in a wavy statue at the top, a cigarette in his mouth. "James Dean," he had to explain. "You know. From *Rebel Without a Cause*." It was the first of many explanations he would be forced to make that night.

All of the teachers dressed up, which no one expected, the exception being the principal, Mr. Collins, who looked like a US Marine during the day and most thought it impossible for him to look any different once the sun went down. Marsha Hamilton used some of the student's council money to hand everyone a bag of black and orange jelly beans as they entered, even though Halloween was on Saturday. The administration had consented to having the emergency lighting on in the hallway that, like the gym, contained supplementary lights from strategically placed jack-o'-lanterns sitting on desks and on stepladders. It was a festive atmosphere, no doubt about it, and everyone, including the teachers on duty, was in a good mood. The dance officially began at 7:30 and students had been warned that no one would be allowed in after 8:00. At a covert student meeting on Wednesday they had drawn straws; Eddy Olson was the loser and had to use the payphone at Berkey's Corner at ten minutes before eight to call the school and explain that someone had smashed in the front window of Mr. Collins house and that fireworks were going off on his front lawn, then hurry back to the school in time to gain entry.

The dance started tentatively at first, mostly thanks to the first few songs, including "Puff the Magic Dragon" being orchestrated by Marsha Hamilton. Once Marine Collins headed to the parking lot and Buddy Holly music filled the gym the party began in earnest. No one thought about it until hours later, but Collins must have locked the door behind him because Buddy Olson never made it into the dance.

It turned out to be a blessing that costumes were the order of the evening because most of them had plenty of storage for the illicit booze that was consumed with greedy delight in the washrooms and dark recesses of the gymnasium. The five teachers on supervision duty couldn't be everywhere at once, and because of the gender neutral attire, they had no idea who was going into which washroom. There was alarm in the eyes of some of the teachers because everyone was ebullient and the pace of the evening kept gaining momentum, plus most were relying on Marine Collins to oversee discipline and now he had gone home. As the dance progressed, the booze boosted the temerity of both genders equally, and many who had no intention of joining in the drunk-fest, did so. Mr. Duvard, the French teacher, danced once with Marsha Hamilton because no one else seemed to want to. Making out with someone in the gym had to be modified or eventually one of the two teachers stationed inside would intervene and tap the libidinous partners on the shoulder like a referee parting boxers caught in a clinch. It didn't take long for the students to take their foreplay into the washroom cubicles and by 9:30 the aggressive fondling had left many costumes in such a state of disarray it was difficult to differentiate a French maid from an alien. The tone of the evening changed when Andy Murray vomited into a jack-o'-lantern in the corner of the gym, extinguishing a flame that had been burning brightly. Miss Dulcet, the Home Ec. teacher, took Andy into the sick room to lie down while she phoned his parents. When he flopped down on the small bed, a bottle of unopened beer rolled between the teacher's feet. Robbie overheard three teachers convening outside the sickroom and it had been the first indication all evening that they had a clue about the egregious behaviour surrounding them.

Robbie had danced with Daisy twice but had since lost track of her. He was wandering the hall leading into the school when he saw Marine Collins make his return, having clued in that the phone call was a lark. Robbie knew where Kurt was and skittered down the hall and into the girls' washroom.

"Hey, heads up. Collins is back."

Kurt was inside a cubicle with a girl and had just removed her pink panties which, in all the excitement, had fallen into the toilet. "Let's go. We got to get out of here." Kurt didn't hesitate to follow his own instructions. There was a wide but narrow window above the toilet. He pushed it open and stood on the toilet tank and squirmed himself to freedom. Robbie tried to leave as soon as he'd delivered the message and met Mr. Collins at the doorway. "Evening, sir," Robbie said, then turned left when Mr. Collins turned right, then right when Mr. Collins turned left: a quintessential Laurel and Hardy routine. Mr. Collins looked up at the sign that read GIRLS' WASHROOM and pushed Robbie against the wall before entering. The smell of beer was everywhere and several costume-clad patrons ran out the door when he entered. He opened one cubicle door and found Evelyn Franks with her head in the toilet, then opened the next and saw the bare legs of a female trying to make her escape. "Get back here, you. Did you hear me?" The escape artist either wouldn't listen or couldn't obey, he wasn't sure which, but grabbing on to her bare legs was the last option he considered. Someone outside was yelling for her to hurry up, so pull on her two white legs is what he did, and finally the half-clad female slid off the toilet tank and fell into his arms. The costume may have been a werewolf, but without the head or pants in place, Collins realized he was staring into the face of Marsha Hamilton, his student president.

～～～

"What about Daisy?" Robbie said.

"Don't worry about her," Kurt said. "She can look after herself."

A hundred or so students were left milling about the school after the aborted dance, but many who were walking home gathered at Berkey's Corner. When two police cars, lights flashing, sped toward the school, everyone started to head home. Robbie had a quarter of his rum left and Kurt had one bottle of beer, which he opened on a side road after he'd helped himself to a swig of Robbie's rum.

"Holy shit, I wonder what will happen now?" Robbie said.

Kurt tried to answer but was laughing too hard. The images of the evening kept coming one after another and the riot in his mind was more than he could take in.

Robbie said, "Thank God we got out of there. I wouldn't want to be one of the suckers left inside once Marine Collins took over. I've never seen his face so red, ever. Do you think anything will happen to us? Collins saw my face, plain as day."

"Jesus, man. You worry too much. What's wrong with coming out of the can? It depends if anyone squeals on us, that's all. Like Marsha Hamilton, for example."

"Marsha Hamilton got caught?"

"She sure as hell did. I had her close to naked in the john when Collins arrived. I gave her one rum and Coke, strong, mind you, and she was out of it. Her boobs are bigger than I thought. That's why she couldn't squeeze out the window. God, that was hilarious."

"Too bad it's all over," Robbie said. "It was just starting to heat up."

"The night's not over yet, my friend. The dance should still be going and the night is young. I don't plan on going home until my parents are asleep anyway. Follow me."

24

HAD ANYONE PAID ATTENTION TO the calendar on the kitchen wall, it had been ten days since my father had taken his last, uneasy breath. It could have been six months or thirty seconds; my mind was numb most of the time and I was working hard at the art of survival. The thought of cooking just for myself was unreasonable and I existed mostly on bread and peanut butter and a few vegetables from the summer's garden. My only remaining relative was gone for good, buried in a municipal cemetery out in the country under the watchful eye of a two-humped mountain. I had walked there once since he'd been officially laid to rest, to place flowers, daisies I'd picked from the side yard, because that's what people did. There was no stone to mark the location, but the mound of fresh soil heaped over where he rested was, for now, marker enough. I had entered his bedroom only once, looking for documents, but couldn't face dealing with his clothes and personal effects. I escaped for hours at a time to the woods, the creek, the railroad tracks: all nothing but excuses to be anywhere but in the house. Mourning the loss of my father had become a full-time job and in a few days the house was a mess: clothes and rags and dishes were strewn everywhere, something that would have never happened had he been sitting in the living room watching the evening news. For a few hours every day I felt angry and betrayed, but anger took a good deal of energy and it didn't take long for me to submit to an empty sadness.

Without any kind of formal plan I began putting things in order: washing clothes, washing dishes, removing clutter into drawers and cupboards. I fired up the wood stove for hot water and when I'd worked myself into a state of exhaustion, almost drunk from weariness, I slid into a warm bath and stayed there until the water had gone cold. I was chilled when I got out and put on my thick cotton housecoat to ward off the cool autumn air that had settled into the valley. I hadn't turned the TV on once since my father disappeared, but I yearned to have someone else's voice replace the nattering that frazzled my mind. I found a documentary on the mating habits of African elephants and I didn't bother to change the channel.

25

RED NEILSON KEPT HIS BEER and several months' worth of empties in the back of the garage. While Robbie waited out by the Lake Road, Kurt found three full bottles of beer. They were the only full bottles and his dad was sure to notice, but he took them anyway. Milo hadn't fallen asleep yet and leaned out an opened window and watched his brother leave.

"Never arrive empty-handed," Kurt said.

"I don't know about this," Robbie said.

"It's worth a try, man. She's way more gorgeous than anyone that goes to our school. She's like a prom queen."

Robbie had no idea who Arthur Lemmons was but he understood he had died. He didn't know Hanne Lemmons either. There was something out of tune, visiting the house of someone you didn't know so soon after a death in the family and he had mentioned this to Kurt. She'll be lonely, Kurt declared. We'll be a diversion. Wait till you see how beautiful she is.

A light was on at the front porch, but Kurt decided on the back and knocked firmly on the door. Robbie stood behind him.

"Trick or Treat," Kurt said, when Hanne opened the door and turned on the porch light. She looked out at them but didn't respond. "Just kidding. Halloween is tomorrow, but we were at the school dance and we dropped by for a visit. We brought you something."

"It's late," Hanne said, looking out at the darkness of the back acre and the irrefutable evidence.

"Later than it was," Kurt said. "We don't want to bother you or anything. We won't stay long. This is Robbie. He just moved here. He's a California dude."

Kurt held two beers out in front of him and walked precociously into the house. Robbie trailed behind and Hanne shut the door.

"You got a bottle opener? I know how to open them with my teeth but it hurts like hell."

Hanne got an opener out of the drawer and Kurt opened the three beers.

"I don't drink beer, really. My dad used to have one sometimes, but it's kind of bitter."

Robbie noticed Hanne lost in thought. He imagined her thinking of her father being there at that moment.

"Sorry about your dad," Robbie said. "Both my parents died when I was young so I know what you're going through. I'm sorry."

"Your dad was quiet," Kurt said. "But everyone liked him. Just take a taste of this beer. It's German style beer. I think you might like it."

Kurt led the way into the living room and sat down on one end of the small couch. Robbie sat in the over-stuffed chair. Hanne turned off the TV and, despite sitting on the couch as far from Kurt as possible, felt the heat of his proximity. There had been few visitors to the house over the years and she felt awkward, but despite this she did not pick up on the tone of her circumstance.

Robbie could see what Kurt meant about Hanne. She was beautiful and he tried not to stare. He looked around the room at all the clocks sitting on shelves and hung on walls and poking out of boxes, but his eyes kept returning to the girl on the couch who held her beer with both hands on her lap. If he turned his head too quickly she appeared momentarily as two girls sitting on the couch. He wished there *were* two girls on the couch. Identical twins would be perfect.

Hanne took her beer to her lips and forced a tiny sip.

"So, what do you think? Pretty good, eh?"

"It's not too bad," Hanne said. "I think I like Coke better."

"It's an acquired taste," Kurt said. "I love it now." Kurt had consumed half his beer and so had Robbie, though Robbie attacked his bottle in rapid, nervous sips.

"Your dad was a clock repairman," Robbie said.

"Yes. He was."

Hanne asked Robbie if he missed California. He told her the stuff she thought she would want to hear. About the gathering of people at malls and at the beach. About how most were blonde by nature or chemical. He told her how people went to great lengths to make themselves look like their favourite movie star or singer. When she asked questions or made comments on what he had said, Robbie could tell she was smarter than he was. It wasn't something he could measure in any definitive way, but it was obvious. Robbie would never say so to Kurt, but he thought he was way smarter than his friend, so that made Hanne clearly the most intelligent person in the room.

"I've watched American Bandstand a few times," Hanne said, "but I've never been to a dance, ever. Tell me about your Halloween dance."

Kurt put one arm in the air and used the other arm to stick his beer in his mouth and finish it off. He told his story about the dance and how it was planned subterfuge from the start. His eyes sparkled with fervour as he described their principal and the school and the hallways and the decorations. He told her everything as best as he could remember it, how couples got together in cubicles and had at each other and the music and desire and the frenzy of it all. He told her how everyone had some kind of costume on and about what they did when they came together in the cubicles or in the gymnasium. He looked into Hanne's eyes and moved closer to her on the couch. It all started with a kiss, Kurt told her, and put one hand on the side of her cheek and touched his lips to hers, like a feather at first and then he was kissing her firmly and awkwardly and Hanne found herself kissing him back. He said that if she had come to the dance as a maid or a housekeeper and looked like she did now, someone would take the sash of her dressing gown and pull on it and he tried to demonstrate, but Hanne balked and put one hand on her sash and tried to push him away. Kurt soon had her housecoat opened and Hanne squirmed and pleaded and tried to turn away. Kurt pulled her housecoat up over her shoulders and flipped her onto her back. He told Robbie not to be so stupid and to turn out the lights so Robbie turned off the lamp and went into the kitchen and turned out the overhead light while a muted darkness fell over the three of them. On his way back from the kitchen he looked out onto the front porch and staring in through the glass panel was Milo, not with any emotion registered on his face, just staring into the room at what was happening to Hanne in the thin light their eyes had grown accustomed to. Robbie could hear Hanne's muffled screams and he ran out the back door and around to the front of the house. Before he made his way down the driveway to home he told Milo, dressed in his pyjamas, to go home and Milo, sensing something was wrong, did as he was told, in his bare feet, diagonally across the field which was the most direct route home he could find.

26

EVERY KID GROWING UP IN THE COUNTRY felt cheated on Halloween because it was the one day of the year they wished they lived in town. The farmhouses were so far apart, trick-or-treating became a marathon with little to show at the finish line. For the last few years, when Halloween fell on a school night, a community event of sorts had been held at Tansor Elementary where there would be costume judging, with prizes given in so many categories that everyone who showed up was rewarded with a bag of candy that would replace two blocks worth of cavorting for most city kids. There was also a bonfire, with a wiener roast and marshmallow toasting, and fireworks about eight o'clock that were the same every year but never failed to marvel those in attendance. This year there was a new elementary principal, and while he thought the tradition had merit, he said it would have to wait until Halloween and school attendance were once again in synch. City kids knew to head out for their candy grab equipped with a pillowcase or flour sack; in the country most took a small paper bag or an ice cream bucket to store their Halloween rations; some just consumed their loot as they travelled. The odd family up and down the Lake Road would drive their children into town and park for an hour while their offspring perfected the art of hoarding, but most were not so lucky, and without a community event on the docket this year, the eagerness for the sun to go down was mollified at best.

What did make the rounds on Saturday was news of the fiasco that had started out as a school dance. Several families had been phoned already. Parents were informed certain individuals would be suspended from class on Monday and kept for questioning by the administration and by police. On Tuesday, parents would be given a morning or afternoon appointment to receive the results of the investigation and learn about the consequences for their child. The Neilsons were called, at first citing Daisy but not Kurt. A second phone call implicated them both and Red Neilson grounded them immediately. Robbie's aunt and uncle were given notice but Robbie was the only one home to receive the phone call. Kurt played innocent, though both his parents knew if his younger sister were involved he likely had been too, and they were informed it was their job to stay home and deal with any trick-or-treaters who came to the door. After the way Friday had played out, the dance was the least of Kurt's worries, and he was afraid to show his face in public in any case. He did tell Milo, on his way out, to be sure to bring enough candy back for him to eat, too, and Milo nodded that he would.

It had rained enough off and on during the day that the roads were lined with puddles, then as dusk began to fall it cleared up, leaving the valley with patches of fog in low-lying areas, making the farmlands appear as though the clouds had gotten it wrong all of a sudden and were hovering close to the earth instead of floating in the sky. Most houses sported a jack-o'-lantern on the front stoop or near a window, a glimmer of hope for the fairies, ghosts, goblins, and Robin Hoods soon to make their rounds.

Halloween was one day of the year Mr. May had not found a solution for. His house of glued-together shacks sat well back on his property and it was a dark walk from Evans Road to his doorstep. Most kids yelled *trick-or-treat* and were happy with whatever treat they received, but this sense of decorum did not apply to Mr. May. His dog, Lenin, wasn't much of a watchdog at the best of times but on Halloween the firecrackers made him cross-eyed, whiny, and desperate to hide under the bed. One year his dog, Lenin, ran away for three days, and since then Mr. May kept him in the house the whole night. Not many kids made the journey to his door. They assumed, because he didn't have much money, there would be little reward for their efforts, and some parents parading younger children wouldn't allow the visit in any case. Mr. May was a communist, after all. Despite the relative lack of customers, every year there was always some kind of problem. He now hid his bicycle in the trees, and he didn't bother with a jack-o'-lantern because it would only get smashed. The previous Halloween he opened his door and some older kids threw a lit Roman candle into his house, and he immediately shut the door because he didn't want his dog to escape. The incendiary device sent sparks of blue and red in every direction that he and Lenin couldn't avoid. Mr. May had asked around and consensus was his house was the only one to receive such treatment. This year he hoped he'd found the solution that would suit everybody.

On the post at the end of his driveway he nailed an old Japanese orange crate and placed a dozen chocolate bars inside, six Crispy Crunch and six O'Henry, with a note that said: SHARE WITH THE WORLD. 1 EACH. THANK YOU. Each chocolate bar was wrapped with a short slogan to give them something to think about, sayings like: *Abolition of exploitation; Everything for everyone — nothing for ourselves; No peace without freedom,* or *Each according to his abilities, to each according to his need*, attached with an elastic band. When it got dark he fed his dog and sat at the kitchen table with one lantern burning, hopefully enough to suggest he was home and his windows didn't need to be soaped.

Many country homes offered homemade treats, things like popcorn balls, chocolate chip cookies, and fudge. Mrs. Eaton always looked forward to Halloween because she dressed up as a witch and had cobwebs draped around her porch and without fail opened the door and gave trick-or-treaters a scare. She asked them to perform a trick of some sort or sing a line from their favourite song. Her way of thinking was they felt better if they earned their treat, and everyone who could walk there made a point of stopping by her house. The apples on her tree ripened by late September and she set aside fifteen of the best, roundest, worm-free apples and coated them with two layers of delicious red toffee and stuck a white stick down the middle; the apples were kept in the fridge and wrapped in wax paper and fastened with an elastic band so they wouldn't get caught up with competing candies. Some kids, those travelling without their parents, usually ate half their candy before they got home so they had a stronger case for laying claim to any remaining candy, but no one touched Mrs. Eaton's candy apple until they were safely home again.

The Pentecostal Church never said much about Halloween, but parishioners, including Ernie Jagger, got the impression that it was not a condoned event on the calendar. Despite this, Bonnie and Gerry were two who always made the rounds. Bonnie was destined to attend Mt. Prevost School next year but with the rumours circulating on Saturday, Ernie Jagger was weighing his options. Overall, Halloween didn't impact the world of Ernie Jagger, but that had not always been the case. When his kids were younger and right after his wife had left him, for two successive Halloweens the two large fence posts that guarded his driveway had been toppled by cars driven by recalcitrant youth from somewhere up the Lake Road. The first year he considered it a one-off and replaced the fence posts. When it happened a second time he waited a month and replaced the fence posts with diametrically larger versions and cemented them in place in such a manner he was convinced they would reside there long after his passing. Nothing happened on the third Halloween until well after midnight, and then from his bedroom he heard the crash. He got up and watched from the window to see an old beater that had taken the brunt of the collision and was hissing steam out the radiator. That spelled the end to a short Tansor Halloween tradition.

Old Evans was in bed by 7:30 most nights, reading for an hour or two before he fell asleep. Halloween was an exception. He received so few visitors it was a night he looked forward to. He didn't go all out, but he left the porch light on and his back door slightly ajar, then sat at the kitchen table and worked on a crossword waiting for the eight or ten children who might eventually make an appearance. It was difficult for him to get up and down so he invited them in and told them to help themselves to any two of the chocolate bars he had on a plate. However many were left at 8:30 he ate himself before he retired.

Hoxsey and Slick Borden detested Halloween. They didn't have any kids of their own and only played along to avoid having their windows soaped or firecrackers set off in the woodshed. They were surprised Robbie didn't want to dress up and go out for the evening. In the country, most were forgiving of young teenagers making the rounds, in a sense, perhaps, so that they could make up for the paltry haul they'd suffered through in their early childhood. Robbie held fast to the idea that he didn't want to, he was too old for that sort of thing and stayed in his room most of the day, brooding about what had happened the night before, events his aunt and uncle knew nothing about. He had tried reviewing what had taken place from as many angles as he could and the results were always the same: he had been involved in something that was terribly wrong. To take his mind off things, he offered to cater to the trick-or-treaters who came to the door, so his aunt and uncle agreed and snuggled on the sofa. At nine o'clock he put his coat on and announced he was going for a walk and he took two black liquorice sticks along as comfort food.

There were no lights on where Lodie Stump lived and the curtains were drawn. Her routine for several years had been to make caramel fudge bars for Halloween. She hadn't felt up to it this year, in fact she was tired, worn out, and depressed. The idea of confronting youthful hedonism pounding at her door, so full of expectation, was more than she could cope with. Arthur Lemmons was the opposite of youthful, but he had been extremely exuberant in her company. Part of her realized she didn't deserve him, a much larger part felt she had not deserved to lose such a gentleman. Her entire house was cloaked in darkness, save for one tiny candle at the edge of the bathtub filled with warm water and a myriad of bubbles and Lodie Stump in the middle of it all, prepared to feel unrepentantly sorry for herself.

At eight-thirty a few bursts of fireworks set off from individual homes could be seen and heard, but overall, it had been an uneventful Halloween eve. Milo came back with a smile on his face because he knew his brother would be thrilled he had done what he was told. He had about a dozen treats in his bag to share with Kurt, and they were clearly marked because almost all of them came from Mr. May's orange crate.

27

THE SKIES HAD CLEARED and the moisture skimming the roads had turned to ice. The quarter moon and bleary stars gave the brown and beaten grass fields a luminescent glow where Robbie was the only one out walking, and felt the eyes of the world were on him, though it was unlikely anyone in the neighbourhood took in his solitary figure. He went down a side lane and walked the railroad tracks to the back of the Lemmons' property. He had no idea how his visit would transpire and the anonymity of his route gave him the fortitude to continue.

He knew why he had fled the scene the night before: it was clear in his mind he was not about to be a partner in crime because he had known instantly that was what it was — a crime. Flirting with his cousin in California had been harmless, really. Hanne Lemmons was alone and vulnerable and they both understood that when they entered her house. She had no one to protect her. When he'd turned out the lights and heard her cries for help they were offered in his direction because he was the only other person there, and was equally culpable because he had done nothing to help her. Kurt had made it sound like she was lonely and eager for their company, but what Kurt had envisioned had turned into a nightmare. He now understood that Hanne must have been nervous and wary, sitting in a room with the two of them, holding a beer she had no interest in drinking. She had tried to make conversation to diffuse the situation when she asked about how the dance had gone. It had been months after his parents were killed, years after really, before he was able to properly see the world again, and in a manner like never before, Robbie comprehended the difference between how susceptible he had been as a boy without parents and what Hanne had to deal with, being a girl.

It wasn't his intention to seek exoneration; it was far too late for that. He had been a coward, he saw that now, and there was no defence to offer her. He didn't know what words he would use to ask for forgiveness, but he wanted her to know he was filled with regret and willing to help in any way imaginable. This visit would be a betrayal of his friend Kurt: that much was certain. He would testify on her behalf and accept the exposure of his own weakness — that would be part of it. His aunt and uncle, like two sets of aunts and uncles before them, would arrange for him to go somewhere, a foster home perhaps, and he would have to deal with whatever that would mean. He made his way across the frosty back acre toward the house and in the process imagined the hate and ridicule that would eventually come his way from friends and family and neighbours and likely from Hanne herself. He could feel them lined up on either side of him, a gauntlet he threaded bravely, their shoes and boots and slippers gouging the half-frozen earth, still soft because of the rain, the hatred ringing in his ears but his eyes focused on the house sitting in the middle of the middle acre where destiny had brought him, and through the loathsome stench of it all he heard the voice of his mother, singing a soft lullaby, certain of intention.

He stopped to consume his last string of liquorice and then climbed through the barbed-wire fence and into the barnyard. The chickens could hear an interloper and shuffled in fear and displeasure. The hatred had fallen behind, had not climbed through the fence to follow him, and he proceeded with equanimity and resolve. His mind was clear now and he felt more whole than ever before.

His eyes had adjusted to a darkness compromised by the soft light of a freckled night sky. Shadows were cast upon the ground from the chicken coop and giant fir trees and it was in one of the shadows he stopped his progress. He sensed he was not alone and soon he saw Kurt walking confidently up the driveway from the Lake Road toward the back of the house, saw him rummage through his pockets as if he'd lost something, then climb the stairs to the back door and let himself in.

He hated Kurt. However it had worked out the night before he had no idea, but he hated him now for laying claim to something that didn't belong to him. Or maybe it did. Maybe that was how these things worked. Kurt had known what he was after right from the start and Robbie only trailed behind, inquisitive and clueless. Kurt had what he wanted and what Robbie realized, too late, he had wanted too. Kurt hadn't bothered to knock and now he had the prize all to himself.

28

UNLESS SOMEONE SQUEALED ON HIM, Kurt wasn't about to take his impending hearing at the school as a serious threat. His palliation resided on the foundation that no one had caught him drinking and Marine Collins hadn't seen him squeeze out the bathroom window. Marsha Hamilton might have said something but he doubted she would — her state of undress was embarrassing enough without naming someone who helped her get there. He was one of the accused, he figured, because he hated school and most of the feckless teachers hated him.

He could tell his dad was ready to blow up over the incident. There were four empty beer bottles beside his favourite chair upon which he sat emptying another bottle. Beverly Neilson decided the small silverware set she owned needed cleaning, but Kurt could tell it was something to do while she mulled over a variety of reprisals her two headstrong children ought reasonably to face. The evening might easily have passed with intermittent grumbling had Beverly not insisted on a family meeting. Red Neilson scowled at the TV, his jaw slack and leaning into his collarbone and he refused to move but was drunk enough to go along with a goddamn family meeting if it was held in the living room and he didn't have to move from his throne.

Beverly had grown up being subjected to family meetings every Sunday and, like most parents, transferred the blueprint of success onto the next generation, though their occurrence was random. No one looked forward to a family meeting except Beverly. At first, Kurt refused to attend until his dad yelled that he had better get his ass downstairs and the tone of his voice suggested he would come up and tug on him if necessary.

"Just who in the hell do you think you are?" Red Neilson screamed, his face suddenly as red as his hair. "You think you can just come and go, make up your own rules around here? You've been skipping school. Don't think we don't know that. If you don't get your ass back there on Monday and smarten up you're out of there. Mr. Collins doesn't want you back."

"I'm done with school. I've got better things to do."

"Great. Don't go back, see if the world cares. If you're not going to school then get yourself down to BC Forest Products or MacMillan-Bloedel. They'd better have a job setting choker ready for you because you sure as hell aren't hanging around here all day with your head between your legs. A hundred bucks a month is what it will cost you to live here. Starting the first of the month."

Kurt jabbed his hands into his pockets from where he sat on the sofa. He usually kept his rabbit's foot with him at all times but he must have left it upstairs. The events of the past week had changed him in a manner he couldn't get his head around. He felt older, too old to bother with the institution he had been attending fitfully but was legally of age to leave. When he looked at his dad sitting half-stewed in his chair, he thought he was more like his dad that anyone cared to admit.

"Kurt will calm down and go back to school," Beverly said in her best imitation of a voice of reason. "You need an education these days, son. You don't want to work in the woods all your life."

Red Neilson said, "Don't waste your breath. There's poison in his veins. I don't know where it came from but he was born with it. He never gives a goddamn about anyone but himself."

Milo didn't like all the yelling. He put his forehead down on the coffee table and started to cry and his older brother looked troubled by it.

"It's okay, Milo," Beverly said. "Everything will work itself out. It always does. Kurt, you need to take some time to think things through. Daisy will go back and she will finish this year and three more and she'll be a secretary or something useful someday. You can do the same. You're smart enough, we know that. Don't think your dad and I don't wish we had more education." Red Neilson was about to defend himself, Beverly could tell, so she raised her hand and continued. "You can have just about anything you want in this world, Kurt, but you need to do certain things first. Daisy will be successful one day, I know that, and we want the same for you."

Kurt knew from experience it was best to say nothing. If he raised an objection of any kind his father would get wound up all over again. That's the way family meetings worked: his dad had a fit and his mother ameliorated and put into words the ultimate decree. It wasn't clear what he wanted, except more time in his life with someone like Hanne Lemmons. He would find a job, no problem. Then he would have money and people like Hanne would be there when he wanted them.

Daisy said nothing at all. She was going to go back to school and hoped Kurt would change his mind. Her dad put his empty beer bottle down beside the others and Daisy knew, without being asked, to fetch him another. Beverly went to clean the polish off the silverware and Daisy decided to help, so Kurt went upstairs to his room and Milo tagged along. He lay down on his bed and laced his hands behind his head and Milo lay down beside him and did the same.

"Don't worry, little man. I'll figure out what to do."

"Tootsie Pop," Milo said.

"Tootsie Pop. You like Tootsie Pops? I'd go get you one if things weren't such a mess. I've got to do something and soon. I'll be out tomorrow and I'll get you one for sure. Promise. Sound like a deal?"

"Tootsie Pop," Milo said.

It was late before Milo fell asleep, fully dressed, on top of the bed. His mother would usually come and check up on him, but tonight was an exception. Kurt could hear his sister and his mother working away in the kitchen and managing to laugh about something. When Daisy was around her mother they got along and he envied that. They finally went to bed and twenty minutes later Kurt went downstairs and put on his coat and shoes. His father had fallen asleep in the chair. He looked almost peaceful when asleep and anyone looking at him now would never have guessed his anxious state a few hours earlier. His dad had it in for him and he wasn't sure why he had developed into such an anathema. Maybe what had happened to Milo years earlier was the reason and if so there was nothing he could do to win his favour back. Maybe if he got out on his own the whole family would be better off.

The cool air was refreshing after feuding with his parents and it was a relief just to be out of the house. He was going back to see Hanne. His plan was to tell her that he had gotten carried away with himself the night before and approach her more like a friend. They were neighbours, after all, and would be seeing each other eventually. He knew if she didn't want him as a friend he would have to accept that and let things build up over time. He understood this was the way it should be and he hoped things would be fine with her. He was hungry for her beauty and while it hadn't worked out the way he planned, surely she had enjoyed it once it was all over. It had all come as a surprise to her and this time he would be gentler.

When he got to the back porch he checked both his pants pockets and his coat pockets but his rabbit's foot was not to be found. Milo must have taken it, the little bugger. Tomorrow he would make a point of getting Milo one for himself.

29

IN THE TWENTY-FOUR HOURS that had passed since it happened, my mind was constantly swollen with thoughts and I hadn't slept more than twenty minutes at a time. I had a raging headache and nothing in the house to take for it because one of my father's beliefs was that pain was a message from nature and meant to be felt, not numbed. I would go from being outraged to feeling pathetic and back again, and my assessment of things was obsessive and inconvenient. I wished more than anything my father were around to protect me.

From where I lay on my bed in a half-sleep I could hear the chickens complaining about something. Raccoons made an appearance in the spring and fall and I considered whether I had remembered to close the coop up for the night and stumbled to the back door, thinking I should probably check. I looked out and saw a figure making his way toward the house and terror strangled me and sucked up my breathing. There was nowhere in the small house to hide. I grabbed the cast iron frying pan from the stove and went first to the living room and then my father's bedroom, a place I hadn't ventured for more than a week. There was little in the room, just a bed and two small dressers. I hid behind the door and heard the back door opening.

"Hanne?"

There was the sound of the absence of sound for a long time. I considered the audacity of my predator standing just inside the door, planning his next move. A car needing a muffler ripped through the night on the Lake Road and silence closed in again.

"Hanne? Are you here? I need to talk to you."

I should have brought my father's gun into the house, I realized, but it was too late now. Even though it had no ammunition it might have done the trick. A kitchen chair skidded across the linoleum. Both bedrooms were dark because the curtains were closed, but the frail starshine was strong enough to cast slanted shadows in the living room. "Hanne?" The voice was without aggression but I knew all too well about such deception and there was no way I was going to let it happen again. The creaking of the wooden floorboards painted his footsteps in my mind. He was standing at the entrance of my father's bedroom, looking in at nothing he could see. I heard his breathing, smelled the heat of him. "Hanne?" His hand held the doorknob, less than a foot from where I was standing. He took a sudden step forward into the room and with all my strength I slammed the frying pan against his head. I raised my arms, prepared to do it again, but there was no movement from the body slumped at the foot of the bed.

When the overhead light flooded the room, I gasped. He looked helpless, almost friendly, lying prone on the floor with one arm jutting out behind his head, but I wasn't about to take any chances. I found a rope from the back porch and wrapped it around his legs over and over again and tied a tight knot to complete the task. When he woke up he would answer my questions or I would let him have it again. I felt my heart pounding and worked to control my breathing. I got the rifle from the porch and leaned it against the door jamb. If he had something to say for himself, he could say it staring into the barrel of a gun.

I waited, but Kurt didn't move. How long it took an unconscious person to wake up I had no idea. I kicked him once or twice but he didn't respond. I looked at him closely and saw that his head was resting in a small pool of dark blood on the linoleum floor. "Shit. You bastard. Wake up. Kurt, wake up." I threw a cup of cold water on his face. Another half hour went by and that was when I started to cry.

When the Junghans clock reported midnight I admitted to myself what I had known for two hours. Kurt was dead. He was dead and I had killed him. In twenty-four hours a boy had entered my house and raped me and had come to my house again and I had killed him. Twenty-four of the smallest hours.

When my father bought the house it was explained to us that there were two wells: a wet well and a dry well. The previous owner had dug out a second well not much deeper than the first and there was enough water most years. The dry well was dry now but might become a wet well again someday, so we were told. The dry well sat close to the garage and the boards covering it were failing and needed replacing — a job my father hadn't gotten to. I used a crowbar to pry the middle board away from the casing. I used an old towel and wrapped the head to absorb the blood and prevent myself from having to look at his face. Grabbing the rope from his bound legs, I dragged his body across the gravel driveway. I put the legs in first and he hung there, wedged between the sideboards, like a magician caught in the middle of an act. When I turned his arms parallel to the opening, he slithered through and I heard a splash. The dry well was not completely dry after all.

∽∽∽∽

My childhood was lost. That was the thought that entered my head with nauseating clarity. I knew I'd had one — you don't get to be sixteen years old through some biological leap — you grow up needy and dependent and wanting more of everything, but now all I had known was wiped out. The bathroom held the only mirror in the house and when I stared into it the person who stared back was unfamiliar. Someone I didn't recognize. Someone I didn't want to know.

I was so startled and gripped with fear I couldn't cry. Not for any of the events that had transpired in the last ten days and not for Kurt Neilson, a boy I hardly knew. I had panicked. It was easy to see the string of errors that I'd elbowed my way through, but now it was too late. I should have called the police and told them what had happened: how I had been raped one night and stalked the next and was trying to protect myself and one swing of the cast iron frying pan had killed someone who had come wanting more. You could kill in self-defence. One person trying to harm another had to expect the same thing could happen to them. Soldiers killed other soldiers, not just for freedom or honour, but so they themselves could survive. People killed other people out of fear, anger, hate, and all three were part of me when I was standing behind the door with the frying pan in both hands. I was terrified that night because I imagined the nightmare happening all over again. And I was plenty angry because I knew it was Kurt standing there, avaricious, breathing, calling my name. How dare he think he could come back and make use of me a second time. And hate. Yes, there was no shortage of that. I hated the image of Kurt and how he'd handled me on the couch as if I were nothing but an object.

Dumping the body in the dry well had been the last, most irretrievable mistake. My father was a man who rarely made mistakes but when he did he admitted them, and he had taught me to do the same. There were so many clocks in the house telling the same story: time moves forward and forward again, measured in seconds, minutes, it didn't matter, it passed through your life and you could never go back. Were it possible to go back five hours I would have left Kurt right where I'd felled him and called the police and told my story. If I could go back as far as Friday night I wouldn't have allowed into the house two drunken boys with an offering of beer. Why had I done that? Was it loneliness? Was I flattered? For the smallest of moments I had willingly kissed the boy I eventually killed. It didn't matter now because they did enter the house, and after they left, my life was changed forever. If I could go back two weeks I would have insisted my father and I come to terms with our disagreement. How could such a trivial thing in life seem so important at the time? If only one of us had been able to make the connection, none of this would have happened.

My circumstance could not be retrieved, clearly, and I was doomed. Self-protection was no longer a legitimate claim now that the body was at the bottom of the well. If only I hadn't moved the body, there might have been a story to hold on to. Now there was only a monstrous nightmare. An ugly crime.

It was six in the morning. In another hour it would be seven. At some point Kurt's absence from the earth would be noticed. I lit a fire in the woodstove and used rags to sop up the congealed blood that had pooled in the bedroom and then burned the rags immediately. I used a wet cloth and bleach to wipe up the smudges of blood left on the linoleum from when I'd dragged the body out to the well. There would be evidence that close inspection would reveal on the gravel driveway, and possibly on the boards guarding the well. These I would deal with once there was more light. It was starting to get light out now. For the last six hours I was convinced the sun was something I would never see again.

Now I had to act normal. This gave me pause for more thinking because I wasn't sure what normal was. Had I ever been normal? Was my life, even up until the last two weeks, one most people would consider ordinary? I was almost out of food, so once I had rid the property of any signs of death, I would walk to the corner store and buy groceries. That was surely what a hungry person would do. People would look out their windows and say to themselves: *There goes Hanne Lemmons with her arms full of groceries. It won't be easy for her, now that her father's gone.* And the chickens would need tending to. They would want to be fed and I could clean out the chicken coop — something I hadn't done for weeks. And I could sell some of the eggs at the end of the driveway. FRESH EGGS. $1.00 A DOZEN. People would understand that. Someone on their own trying to survive.

But first the blood. It was almost light now. I would use the hose on the gravel driveway. The blood would wash away, sink into the earth. It was cloudy out. The sky was heavy with clouds and it might rain hard and I wouldn't have to bother — wouldn't have to return to the well where I knew somewhere down below there was a body either floating or sinking, but certainly a body not rolling over in bed and smelling breakfast or imagining in any way what a Sunday could bring.

෴

I walked to the store on Monday because by then I was completely out of food. The wind was out of the west, strong enough to wrinkle the puddles at the side of the road. The clerk was the only person I'd spoken to for two days, but I had been doing plenty of talking to myself. I walked into the store, confident I could appear like nothing new had happened in my life that was particularly of note, but that changed when I saw a poster with a picture of Kurt thumb-tacked to the wall.

"Shame about young Kurt Neilson going missing," the clerk said, staring at me while she spoke. The lady lived two doors down from the store and I had known her name at one point but couldn't conjure it up now. She liked working part-time at the store, it seemed, because she liked to talk to people, and most days it was a steady parade of customers.

"It is," I said.

"I don't think he's missing at all," the lady said. "I think I know what happened." She glared at me and I didn't say anything long enough that the monologue continued with its own momentum. "It doesn't make sense to say he went missing. If he were a little kid, maybe, but he's about your age I'd say. Someone that age doesn't go missing like they got lost. No, I don't think for a minute that's what's gone on here. I think he's a runaway. He's always been rebellious. If I don't keep an eye on him he steals like a gypsy. Beverly Neilson says he was in good spirits but what does that mean? We never really know what goes on in families. I think he had a tiff of some kind and the Neilsons don't want to let anyone in on it. The whole family is wild if you ask me. The Neilsons I mean. I think it would be hard for anyone to live in that house."

The clerk had said her peace and now turned her attention to the canned goods, two loaves of bread and quart of milk that were on the counter. There was a display of Tootsie Pop suckers near the till and I put two down beside the groceries. It had been years since I'd had a Tootsie Pop as a treat.

"The thing is the truth will be known eventually. That's always the way. He'll hitchhike somewhere and get scared and come home with his tail between his legs. Or be found dead at the side of the road. No way it will be a mystery forever."

It was a bit more than a mile walk and I had bought the Tootsie Pop suckers so I could eat one, nonchalantly, on the way home, but both were buried at the bottom of the bag and forgotten now. What kept haunting me was the body at the foot of the well. How long would it float? Because it was such a small cavity in the earth, maybe it would be lodged between the walls and be near the surface indefinitely. The previous owner of the house had told my father it might become a wet well someday down the road — that's the way it was with underground streams — they were healthy for a few years, then dry up, and sometimes come back to life. I had woken up in the middle of the previous night and in my dream it had started to rain hard, for days it rained, and when I looked out into the backyard the water had pushed the boards away from the casing and Kurt was floating on the surface with a sneer on his face.

As if to reinforce the unknown power of nature, the skies above sent a downpour through the valley and onto my walking and it was only by clutching the two paper bags together close to my chest that I was able to make it home with all I had bought.

∾∾∾

I didn't see him standing by the garage for a long time and was startled to find Milo watching me with a sanguine grin on his face. Depending on how long he'd been there, he might have

132

observed me make innumerable trips to the garden where I filled the wheelbarrow with dirt I then dumped into the well through the hole created by the absence of the middle plank. I had been employed for a good part of the morning and early afternoon doing the same thing and my arms were hot and sore from the effort.

"China?" he said.

"What?"

"China," he repeated, pointing to where I had been digging.

I ignored him and returned to the garden with the wheelbarrow and Milo was right behind me. He grabbed the shovel and started filling it up and followed me back to the well. After a second such journey, I had had enough and sat down on a stump beside the garage and pulled a Tootsie Pop out of my pocket.

"Tootsie Pop," Milo said and stepped closer.

"You like these do you? You helped me with the dirt so I guess you can have this one. I've got another one in the house." Milo threw the wrapper on the ground and stuck the candy into his mouth and I went into the house to fetch another. When I got back to my stump, Milo had his Tootsie Pop in his mouth like he was smoking a fine cigar and was busy filling the wheelbarrow. Once it was full he couldn't move it so I helped him push the wheelbarrow over to the well. I showed him how to fill it only halfway and sat back on the stump. Each trip to the well, coming and going, he watched me with a silly grin like he knew something I didn't. I waited until he had completed several more trips and I worried that it was getting close to his suppertime and they might come looking for him. I gave him my last Tootsie Pop and told him it was time to head home to eat and that was what Milo did.

Filling the well no longer produced a splashing sound and I knew I was making progress. The bit of help Milo had offered fortified my spirits and I completed three more loads before fetching a flashlight from the back porch. The line of black earth contrasted with the yellow clay walls of the old well and as best as I could judge there was still another fifteen feet or so to go. The body wouldn't likely be able to float to the surface now, but I wasn't about to take any chances. However long it took, I was determined to fill the well in completely so no one would ever know there had been a well beside the garage. I would know, of course. I would know forever, but no one else would.

30

THE GAME OF HORSESHOES WAS STARTING to rub off on him. At first he had thought there was nothing to the game and anyone who could work a farm could surely throw a horseshoe, but there was a technique to holding the implement, to flipping it in the air so it had a chance to corral the metal stake. Reverend Ridley had taught him a lot and now had competition for their weekly ritual. The game of horseshoes was not all Ernie Jagger was getting out of their meetings.

Education was a commodity Reverend Ridley believed one could never get enough of, and once or twice a year he went somewhere to prove his theory. *It's one thing to have a strong faith, another to know how to impart it,* he repeated weekly. Ernie Jagger had taken his place in the pulpit a second time, only on this occasion it was less like he was attending an emergency service; he had planned his sermon a week in advance and when he was finished he knew in his heart he had what it took to be as good as Reverend Ridley, if not better. He was still firm on his commitment to working his farm until both Bonnie and Gerry were finished with school, but in the meantime he had ordered some correspondence materials from Langley which he read with as much passion and consistency as he did the Bible.

Part of what he was learning fought against his nature and he knew adjustments would be needed. Securing outlets for his eggs had not been his favourite thing to do, he realized looking back on it now, but he had done it because it was something that had to be accomplished. He had just read an article on "closet faith" — the notion that practicing a strong and ardent belief in God in isolation was not going to have much effect on the world — one had to find the means to express to others, the splendor of God. When Arthur Lemmons passed into another world (Ernie Jagger had not known the man at all well and was unsure to which world he had departed) he left a postcard offering his condolences to his daughter, Hanne. That was it. That was shameful.

While it was technically still autumn, there were now only a few trees that held their colourful leaves; most had fallen to the earth in a wash of violent storms where they layered around roots in a waxy sheen, not to be raked and burned, but left to the slow process of decomposition and the promise of renewed growth. Naked and forlorn, that's how the trees looked as Ernie Jagger made his way up the long driveway to the Lemmons' property. The trees appeared to be prepared to suffer for now, but there was a faith he could see all around him, an all pervasive knowing that this period of inner contemplation would offer rejuvenation in a very short time.

He stopped halfway up the ragged cement steps that lead to the back door because he heard something, the sound of digging, in the backyard. He walked around the garage and found Hanne filling the wheelbarrow with dirt.

"Someone is hard at work," he said.

"I guess I am," Hanne said, and swiped the hair away from her eyes with the back of her gloved hand, leaving a trail of dirt across her forehead. "I'm filling up the dry well. It's of no use and falling apart. My father meant to get to it."

Ernie looked back at the well he had walked by without taking any notice, then out at the garden area where she had been skimming the earth. There were patches visible where the fertile soil had been lifted to expose the yellow clay which was the common underbelly of the land. It was an inconsequential task in the grand scheme of things, but he considered that it gave the young woman something to do in her time of grief. What he saw before him was a perfect opportunity to offer Christian charity and he was glad for it. It was easier for him to express himself in actions than words.

"I can lend a hand, if you like. It seems a shame to dump the best soil that the providence of God has provided into the well when the well once held clay."

Hanne was sceptical as soon as she heard the word God, but what her neighbour explained to her made sense and the blisters on her hands were broken open, offering evidence of her toil and delivering pain. By the time Ernie Jagger had gone home and returned with his small front end loader, Hanne had the remaining four boards covering the well pried off and leaning against the garage. She then remembered what had been her intention when the day began and fetched the cast iron frying pan from the house and threw it into the well without it making a sound.

Ernie used his machine to scrape the useful soil into mounds, then gouged the clay out of the earth and began the process of filling the well. Each load of clay was five times the size of a wheelbarrow full of dirt and in less than an hour he had the cavity filled. He then took a load of good soil and mounded the location of the well with black earth. Before he shut his tractor off, he scraped the black soil that remained in the garden around as evenly as possible, so that a garden would be feasible, albeit in shallow earth.

"I built it up just a tad. No matter how you fill a hole like that there's bound to be some settling."

He looked at Hanne, hoping she would understand his logic. She looked back at him and didn't say anything, but appeared to understand that some settling was likely to occur.

"Thank you," Hanne said, staring at her feet as she spoke. "You saved me a lot of work."

"Hey, it's the least I can do. Anything else needs doing, just ask."

"I don't want to bother with the chickens anymore. It gave my father something to do but I despise them. I know you have a lot of chickens already, but would you be willing to take a few more home with you?"

Ernie looked over at the chicken coop. He could see three chickens inside the run and three outside. All of them looked well past their prime.

"I'll get Bonnie and Gerry to come by after school. They'll pick them up and you won't have to worry about them anymore."

Ernie Jagger climbed back onto his tractor and started the engine. Hanne took a step forward.

"What can I do to say thank you?" she asked.

Ernie stared down the driveway where he would soon travel. It was a straight line to the Lake Road, then a jog to the left and straight again to his house. Looked at this way, it occurred to him that the two farms were almost connected.

"You could come to church with us on Sunday. Service starts at 10:00. I take the kids every week and they get a lot out of it. I'll pick you up about 9:30 and have you back home by noon. Sound okay?"

Ernie had shouted his plan over the sound of the tractor, but Hanne didn't have it in her to raise her voice. She felt tired all of a sudden, as if all the work that had just been accomplished had been done by hand.

"He's watching us," Ernie said with conviction, pointing up at the heavens. "He sees everything we do down here." Hanne nodded her head mindlessly and watched Ernie Jagger bounce his tractor down the gravel driveway.

31

WHEN MY FATHER DIED there were five clocks sitting on the workbench looking forlorn and neglected. Two of them were subsequently picked up, the owners saying they would look elsewhere. Three were left for me to work on and one that had been taken away was returned two days later, which led me to understand why my father always had multiple projects on the go. I began working on the simplest first, a Doric Seth Thomas that was in for balancing and cleaning. There was a record of the same clock years earlier and when the owner came to pick it up I charged him ten dollars more than the last time and he didn't question it. I was working on a Tivoli next, a more complicated repair because the gong was badly twisted, almost, as often happened, like someone had messed around with it. I had to keep my mind occupied and fixing clocks was the kind of busy I needed to be.

The view out the window from where my father normally was positioned, took in the front acre and the road and Lodie's house and the egg farm. It had turned cold the night before, and while snow in November was not out of the question it was rare to have it come this early. My best guess was a healthy inch had fallen and grudgingly begun to melt. Anything to do with snow my father hated and he only shovelled it if he had to take the car to town, but I loved the way it adorned the landscape, like icing on a cake. The house didn't have eaves-troughs and the slightly warmer temperatures sporadically sent drops of water to the ground like giant tears, and it felt like the house was as sad as I was to see the snow melt. I turned back to the clock in progress and when I looked up again I saw a car tracing its way through the snow on the driveway. It wasn't just any car, it was the RCMP.

Despite the cooler weather I hadn't bothered to light the stove or start up the small oil burner in the basement and as a result the inside of the house was cool, but I was warm all of a sudden; I felt clammy, as though I had a fever and my whole body needed to sweat. I stood up but didn't move until I heard the knocking at the door.

"I'm Constable Jespersen. How is your day going?"

"I'm okay."

"Is your mother or father in?"

"No, there's nobody here but me."

"Do you know when they might be back?"

"They won't be back. They're both dead."

"I'm sorry. I . . . That means you're living here by yourself?"

"Yes, I am."

Constable Jespersen took his hat off and held it in both hands in front of him. He had begun a journey toward baldness and the hair he had was slicked over to one side. He looked more like a man of authority with his hat on and he stood there unsure of how to proceed.

"We're scouting the neighbourhood asking a few questions. If you don't mind I'll ask you the same questions."

I opened the door wider and the officer stepped inside. I didn't offer him a seat because he said there were only a few questions. He put his hat on the back of the overstuffed chair and took a notebook and pen out of his vest pocket, prepared to write down anything that was said.

"Do you know what questions I'm about to ask?" he said.

I felt faint. There was a hierarchy of questions I could imagine would be possible to ask about Kurt Neilson, and if he asked some of them I felt like I would collapse into confession. I sat down on the arm of the chair for support.

"Are you okay?" he asked.

"Yes, I'm fine. I've just been working long hours." I pointed over to the dismantled clock as indisputable evidence.

"Do you know Kurt Neilson who lives down the road?"

"I don't know him, no. I read a poster at the store that said he was missing. I don't go to school so I don't know many boys his age."

"Would you know him to see him?"

"I'd have to study the poster. We've never met."

"I see. What's your name and how old are you?"

"Sixteen and a half. Hanne Lemmons. Hanne with an 'e' at the end."

"And you don't go to school anymore?"

"I take correspondence. I'm almost graduated. I fix clocks if you know anyone with a broken one."

The constable scanned the workplace scattered with dismembered clocks and his face reflected a distrust of my erudition. How much of what I said was of interest was unclear, but he was writing things down. When he finished he stared at his notebook like he couldn't believe what he'd written.

"Okay, Hanne. That's all for now. Thanks for your time. If you catch sight of Kurt you'll let us know immediately, I'm sure. His mom and dad are frantic about it and there's a $1000 reward for any information that will track him down. If you're out driving tonight do be careful. It hasn't melted in places and it could freeze again."

"Thanks," I said.

I sat back at the work bench and watched the car retreat down the driveway and back up the driveway belonging to Lodie Stump. He spent about the same amount of time at her house, maybe a little less. When he finally drove off into town, I lay down on my bed because I felt exhausted. I lay on my side with my eyes open because I knew if I fell asleep I wouldn't be able to control the thoughts in my head.

☙☙☙

I got back to working on the clocks that were waiting patiently and now kept an eye out the window, thinking the constable could return at any time. He had seemed uncomfortable with the answers I had given, possibly because he didn't expect to find me living by myself, but there may have been something else that didn't feel right. Had he looked around the yard he would have seen a skim of snow covering everything, including the old well. Now the snow had melted and the evidence of the scarred earth was obvious. I was almost out of food again but resisted the urge to go to the store because I didn't feel like being out in public.

I knew I should eat better. My energy level was low and made it difficult for me to work for more than a few hours at a time, when I knew over the years my father routinely sat tinkering with his clocks for a full day and sometimes into the evening. Eating out of cans with toast as a side dish became common practice; it was too much bother to prepare a meal just for myself. Or it may have been my troubled episodes of sleep: I had a series of visions that woke me two or three times each night, one where Kurt's head miraculously rose from the pit of the well and sprouted out of the earth, another where I imagined waking up from sleep, completely naked, with Kurt standing at the side of the bed, a drunken grin on his face.

And now there was a new scenario where Constable Jespersen was knocking on the front door, but when I opened the door he wasn't there, then the knocking started at the back door and when I opened it the knocking resumed at the front door. I went to bed late every night because sleep was tiresome and when I woke up I felt sick to my stomach.

It had been my father's practice to deliver most of the clocks once they were repaired; many required delicate handling or all of his work was futile. I made it clear that from now on the refurbished clocks would be picked up by the owners with careful delivery being their responsibility. Two more clocks had been completed and picked up and, for now, there were two left to deal with. One required a new part that had been ordered, and the last project I had no experience with and needed time to figure out. I kept the TV on most of the time so it felt like someone else was in the room with me, but for the most part I had no idea what program was on, it was just background noise. I paid attention to the evening news in case the name Kurt Neilson was mentioned, but it never was. At seven in the evening I turned the TV off and heard something rubbing the front door. In the glass pane at the top was Milo's face, fitted with a half-smile.

I opened the door and saw Milo standing on a chair on the front porch, awkwardly, like a man on stilts. How long he had been there, staring at me, I had no idea.

"Milo, what are you doing here? You scared me half to death." Milo looked admonished but didn't speak. He didn't get down from the chair either. "What is it you want?"

"Tootsie Pop."

"Tootsie Pop? You came here at this time of night looking for candy? Milo, I don't have any more Tootsie Pops. You can't just stare into someone's house at night. You'd better get yourself home before your mom finds out."

Milo stepped down from the chair. He looked at me as if there was something he didn't understand. He reached out and brushed my sweater with the back of his hand, then walked in a daze off the front porch and down the driveway.

Once Milo made it to the Lake Road I checked that the front door was locked, wedged a chair against the back door and turned on both porch lights. That felt too conspicuous so I turned off the porch lights and every inside light and sat watching TV in the dark. I turned the volume down and listened. Despite not hearing anything I checked the front porch but there was no one there. From my bedroom window I could see a light on at Old Evans' house. I put on my coat and went outside and soon found myself standing at the barbed wire fence that separated the two properties. There was no gate and the fence wires were drawn tight. My coat got caught on the top wire making it impossible to free myself without wriggling out of my coat and into the cold air. I considered going back home but thought I would just get caught all over again. The back door to Old Evans house was never locked. I knocked and heard him yell, "Come in." The light leaking from his bedroom led me to where he was lying in bed with a magazine on his chest. His dog was half asleep on the far side of the bed and when Old Evans turned the radio off the dog uttered a feeble growl.

"Do you mind if I visit for a while?" I asked.

"Not at all. I'm always glad for the company. I was sorry to hear about your father. He was gentle and hardworking. I'm sure you miss him terribly."

I hadn't given much thought about what I would talk to the old man about. The cold weather. The books he was reading, maybe. I wasn't prepared for the statement he offered: non-judgemental and understanding. Immediately I started crying, sobbing uncontrollably from the wooden chair that sat beside his bed. Old Evans didn't say anything until it appeared I was over the worst of it, then he passed me a box of Kleenex.

"I'm sorry," I said. "I didn't think I'd ever do that."

"Never apologize for crying. Tears wash away our misery if we're lucky. That's what my mother always said."

I sat by the bed and talked about some of the things I needed to talk about. He never asked me any pointed questions, he just listened and nodded from time to time. After a while I looked down at my watch, a watch that once belonged to my mother, one I'd started to wear after my father died. It was almost eleven o'clock and I had been pouring my heart out and the old man was likely way past his bedtime. The thought of going back home to the empty house made me feel cold to the bone.

"Would you mind if I slept on your couch in the living room? Just for tonight."

"Help yourself. You'd better grab a blanket from the closet over there. It might be cool in that room without the heater going."

I thanked him and took a Hudson's Bay blanket to the couch. The blanket smelled musty, like it hadn't been out in the air for years, and both couches wore slipcovers. I removed one and folded it up, grabbed a pillow and curled up in the dark. It was so quiet I could hear from the other room the laboured breathing of the dog or the old man, I wasn't sure which.

32

WHEN THE RAINS BEGAN there was no shortage of water, a circumstance that would continue until mid-summer. It was the time of year when Mr. May curtailed his weekly neighbourhood visits for his drinking water and typically neither he nor his bicycle were seen with any regularity. This was not a typical year. The rain had been plentiful enough that discarded pennies at the side of the road turned green, but he was out on his bike almost every day (barring snow) and he was on a mission. Beverly Neilson appreciated his help and furnished him with a laminated picture of Kurt that he used to query everyone he met. Red Neilson told anyone who would listen that he thought Mr. May was doing a hell of a lot more than the police were. There had been a picture and a small article on Kurt's disappearance in the *Leader,* but he knew it was the kind of thing people saw, became agitated over for a day or two, and then forgot.

The Neilsons were desperate for any news relating to Kurt. Beverly, in particular, felt responsible, though when asked she refused to pinpoint why exactly, but in her mind it had to do with the last family meeting. Mr. May was keen to alleviate the muddle they were in, but he was also cognizant of the $1000 reward being offered. This equalled many months of social assistance and would allow him to buy a new propane hot plate and get new tires for his bicycle. When his imagination stretched to ridiculously extravagant bounds, he saw himself with a battery-powered light for his bicycle to replace the generator-fed light he now owned, one that made it difficult to climb the hills out of town on the way back home in the dark. He didn't care for those spells during the day when his mind wandered this way. His main focus was humanity and equal distribution of wealth and opportunity. Still, the thousand dollars had been collected by local businesses that, he was certain, had far more resources than he ever would, so the distribution of wealth was technically still a reality.

Mr. May was exhaustive in his search. Not only did he accost everyone he met in town with Kurt's disappearance, he wandered off into the bushes, the gravel pit, down by the creek. He rode his bicycle part way up Mt. Prevost until it got too steep, then walked to the summit on a day when the sun teased its way through the clouds. He knew he couldn't cover every square inch of the valley, but after two weeks of intensive searching he concluded that if Kurt were lying dead somewhere it wasn't in any of the most obvious places a young man might wander.

He tried some of the neighbours again and he was glad he did. Mrs. Eaton gave him a clue worth investigating. She told him: "He was a young man. Think about that for a minute. What is the one thing a young man is desperate for?" Mr. May listened to her line of reasoning, but it had been so long since he had been a young man, nothing came immediately to mind. "Girls!" Mrs. Eaton continued. "Girls is what they're after. They slobber over them. If I were the police I'd be questioning every girl close to his age. See if any of them have gone missing. See if any of them are pregnant. Every man wants money but only a few will risk robbing a bank, but every man wants a female and they rarely get thrown in jail for catching one. Girls is what they should be focusing on."

Mrs. Eaton lived two farms over from the only young girl he knew of, besides Daisy. He had talked to Daisy twice and while at first she was mad at her brother for running off, now she was as worried as anyone. He would talk to Daisy again, though. She was close to her brother and might know something. He had forgotten about the Lemmons girl, living all by herself now. Just before he peddled to her doorstep a rain squall opened up and he stood on the porch like a drowned rat, knocking at her door.

Hanne opened the door. "Hi," she said. She had only been home a few hours and was finishing up an order for someone in Ladysmith. The heat still wasn't on because she'd slept at Old Evans the night before and it didn't seem worth it to heat up the house half way through the day. She stood there unconcerned over her dishevelled appearance: she had sweatpants on, a fisherman's knit sweater and leather slippers. Over top she wore a housecoat to preserve her body heat, the only source of heat in the house. If her attire looked odd it wasn't caught by Ivan May.

"Do you mind if I come in for a few minutes? This rain won't last long."

Mr. May had come to the house often over the years, always to attain water and distribute propaganda. Never had her father invited the old man in, but the look of him, frail and wet, resonated as pathetic rather than threatening so she opened the door wide and he took off his rubber boots to reveal woolen socks that were missing a lot of wool.

"Thanks," he said. "It didn't look like rain when I started out. The weather has been something lately."

Hanne looked away from Mr. May and out the front window. The Lake Road was filled with children. Younger kids parading their way from Tansor Elementary and older kids heading west from Mt. Prevost School. Both sides of the road they filed, mostly walking by themselves, like lines of migrating lemmings.

"What's going on?" Hanne said. "Why are all the kids out of school?"

"They probably let them out of school so they could think about what's happened. Haven't you heard? President Kennedy was shot."

"Kennedy was shot?"

"I don't know all the details but he's dead so they say. He's not the first American president they've turned on."

Hanne was rattled by what she'd just heard. She stood transfixed, watching the children head home. Mr. May watched too, but his attention to the event was short-lived.

"You're still here I see and carrying on with the clock business too. You know how to fix those things?"

"I've worked on most of them. Some I have to figure out."

"You must be smart then. I have a hard enough time keeping my bicycle running. You've seen this boy around, I'm guessing." He pulled the increasingly tattered picture of Kurt from his shirt pocket and held it up like a trophy.

"I've seen it. I know he's missing."

"Well, there's a theory going around that he may have hooked up with a girl. Run off with one maybe, but you're still here so he hasn't run off with you. Do you think he might do that?"

"It depends. I don't know him, but he might have if he could find someone to run with."

"That makes sense. Would you run off with a boy do you think?"

"Depends. I suppose if the right boy asked me I might. Never met the right boy."

He studied the picture, contemplating the idea of whether or not Kurt could have been the right boy for someone. Hanne didn't fancy him — that much was obvious. But maybe some girl might think differently.

"There's another theory, too. One that says maybe he got someone pregnant. A girl. And that he ran away because he didn't want to face up to being responsible. That might be, don't you think?"

"I suppose a person can run away from anything when it comes down to it. You'd have to find a pregnant girl and ask her yourself. I can't believe President Kennedy is dead."

The rain hadn't stopped but had let up. Mr. May carried his boots to the back porch.

"You been doing some digging out here, looks like. Something's different."

"I just filled in the dry well. We haven't used it in years." Hanne's pronouncement stopped Mr. May right where he was on the back porch. He turned and looked at her as if he might see the spoken words sluggishly trailing out of her mouth. "What?" she said. "What's the matter?"

"I collect all my water off the roof. I don't own a well. At least if I had a dry well there'd be hope. It seems like a crime to fill in a well of any kind."

33

THERE HADN'T BEEN THIS MUCH excitement in the air since Ernie Jagger had started up the egg farm. All week he felt invigorated and inspired because everything was leaning toward a greater cause now: his evangelical aspirations had risen above entrepreneurial necessity. For the first time he understood where Reverend Ridley found the heat in his sermons.

Bonnie and Jerry were excited because their dad was excited. Ernie was always encouraging them to invite their friends to church, and what better way to accomplish such a thing than by putting forward a good example.

"How are we all going to fit in the Ranchero?" Jerry asked.

"Don't worry, we'll find a way. Let Hanne sit by the window. She'll feel less squished that way. I wish now I'd vacuumed the car."

Bonnie liked hanging around girls older than she was, even if it had to involve church. She wondered what Hanne might wear, how she would do her hair. Her brother was polishing his shoes and his dad's shoes — a weekly mandate — and the smell of shoe polish became the smell of Sunday morning. "You sit beside Dad," she told him. "I want to sit right beside her." The Pentecostal Church frowned on makeup, so Bonnie settled for a layer of lip gloss no one would notice.

What Hanne would be wearing and how she would prepare herself may or may not have been settled when the three of them pointed the car down the Lemmons' driveway. Hanne was climbing through the barbed wire fence, returning from Old Evans' house, and she didn't look at all dressed for a church service. Hanne started running toward them when she saw their car. It was Sunday morning by all accounts and her promise to accompany them had been forgotten.

34

WHEN I SAW THE JAGGERS creeping up my driveway I was immediately ashamed and then mad at myself for promising to attend church in the first place. "I'm running late," I yelled. "I'll be just a minute. Sorry."

I didn't own many dresses. I grabbed the longest, plainest one I could find, a beige, floral outfit, put a blue three-quarter button down coat over my shoulders, and grabbed my clutch purse. I ran a brush through my hair until I convinced myself I looked presentable, then brushed my teeth to camouflage the bowl of porridge Old Evans had given me.

"Sorry I'm late. I remembered but then I forgot it was Sunday."

Ernie looked at me, as if trying to comprehend such a notion. His whole week built toward Sunday, but the look on his face suggested he didn't believe everyone didn't feel the way he did. Gerry shuffled close to his dad and Bonnie opened the door for me. Before I got in I put a dozen eggs they had brought over for me into the back porch.

"I have an idea what the sermon will be about this week," Ernie said.

"Tell us," Gerry said.

"I can't tell you. It's a secret."

"You do this every week. You say you know but then you won't share. If you're not going to tell us then why mention it?"

Ernie laughed out loud but no one else did. It was plain he got a kick out of doing the same thing every Sunday.

"Thanks for picking me up," I said.

The church was in an older neighbourhood close to town. It was a long, beige, stucco building that looked like a house except for the wooden cross above the door. The parking lot was small and full by the time we got there and parked on the street out front. The Werke family turned the sidewalk corner in a long line, heading for the church, all thirteen of them dressed in black and white. They lived further out the Lake Road than Ernie did but offering them a ride would never work, and since they had no vehicle of their own they left home early every Sunday morning, rain or shine, and walked in a row, from tallest to smallest, into town. They were, by a significant margin, the largest family in the congregation, and it was common knowledge they claimed legendary status in the valley because each time they added to their flock they were celebrated and given elaborate gifts, too elaborate some thought, because there seemed to be no end to their progeny.

"Let's head inside," Ernie said. Getting a seat close to the front, he claimed, would be impossible once the Werke family entered the church. Reverend Ridley was at the front door and Ernie made a point of introducing me and explaining that I was his neighbour.

The church smelled like no place I had ever been before and I was unable to discern the source. It could have been the hymn books, the people, or the polished wooden pews. The frail light of a cloudy day managed to gleam through the four stained-glass windows and it was the light from the windows I focused on to take my mind away from the aromatic puzzle the church presented. Bonnie sat beside me and pointed out certain things about the church: a selection of the people who trailed in, the small organ donated by the Belamy family, the picture of Jesus on the far wall that had been restored when a church in Delta had succumbed to fire — the kinds of things she wondered about her first few Sundays.

The organist, not a Belamy herself but one who had married into the Belamy family, played "Abide With Me" and "Blessed Be The Name" to ameliorate the spiritual accessibility of the congregation that wore a week of grunge that needed shedding. The congregation was familiar with the maroon, pebbled hymn books and they blended impressively with the sonorous organ. Once the two hymns were completed, Reverend Ridley took over and embarked upon a sermon that warned of the evils of deception.

"Eliphaz reproveth Job: Thine own mouth condemneth thee, thine own lips testify against thee. How much more abominable and filthy is man which drinketh iniquity like water."

Reverend Ridley looked out at his flock between verses and then leaned over his sermon to unveil more nuggets of wisdom. Perhaps because I was new, his steely eyes always found mine before he briefly scanned the rest of the room, and each time I felt a pang of admonishment.

"The wicked man travaileth with pain all his days and the number of years is hidden to the oppressor. He dwelleth in desolate cities and in houses which no man inhabiteth, which are ready to become heaps. For what is the hope of the hypocrite when God taketh away his soul."

The reverend took it upon himself to translate the meaning of the words he had chosen from the Book of Job, to show those in attendance that the rigid doctrine did indeed have application in their lives. I felt weak and suddenly claustrophobic. I was trapped in the small pew between Gerry and

Ernie Jagger on my left and Bonnie and an elderly lady on my right. The lady, when she wasn't shouting out "Hallelujah" or "Praise the Lord," was fanning her thick perfume toward me and a wave of nausea began to build. I forced myself to be calm but soon it was evident something had to be done. I barged my way past Bonnie and the older woman, who looked shocked at my blasphemy as our knees touched, and I ran my dark blue oxfords past the last six rows of pews and out the front door. At the bottom of the steps I deposited the porridge Old Evans had so kindly shared onto the gravel and then pushed the muddy stones around with my shoe to hide the evidence.

"Are you going to be okay?"

I turned to find Bonnie standing on the bottom step, looking white and sickly herself all of a sudden.

"I'll be fine. I think it was the perfume or something. I feel better now."

"Do you want to go back in?"

"I don't think I should. Just in case."

"It's almost over anyway. A couple more hymns maybe. Let's just sit in the car and wait."

I had a two dollar bill folded in my purse for the collection plate but didn't mention it. My first church experience was far different from what I had anticipated, and instead of feeling cleansed I felt dirty and reprimanded. Whatever it was that had just been delivered, it didn't feel like something one should pay for.

"I didn't like going to church my first time," Bonnie said, as if sensing that I had already come to some conclusion about the experience. "Reverend Ridley knows a lot of stuff. He can say the name of God in forty-eight languages and he once told my dad that the word reverend only appears once in the whole Bible. He can really pour out a powerful sermon some days.

One time, in the middle of the service, a man fell out of his pew into the aisle and started quivering on the floor, almost like he was having a fit. Some people were concerned about the man but Reverend Ridley waved them away and came down from the pulpit and continued his sermon while standing over him. He memorizes his sermon every week and only looks down at his papers to appear like he is seeking God's help. That's what my dad says. Anyway, he finished his sermon and talked the man to his feet and that was that. The man thanked Reverend Ridley when it was all over. It was wild."

I leaned my cheek against the cool of the car window. Learning about Reverend Ridley, the religious virtuoso, I wasn't in the mood for. I imagined with horror the image of myself putting on a performance like that. It made my early escape to be sick almost palatable.

Physically, I was over the worst by the time Ernie and Jerry got to the car. Their usual routine was a visit to the Dairy Queen for a Dilly Bar or ice-cream sandwich before heading home, but this was abandoned because I was clearly not feeling well. Gerry pouted most of the way home because it was the small sliver of Sunday he looked forward to.

"Thanks again for driving me. Sorry I got sick. I'm going to have to give going to church some thought, but for now I don't think I'll go again." As soon as I had spoken, Ernie checked his wristwatch like what I had said wasn't supposed to happen when it did. I opened my purse and lay the folded two dollar bill on the front seat beside Bonnie. "I meant that for the collection. You can hand it in for me next week."

By the time I got to the porch, Ernie had the car turned around and was driving away. Had I remembered the eggs sooner I would have given them back, too.

35

THE DAYS OF THE WEEK repeated themselves and were filled with the concentration needed to work on the clocks at hand. Two more had arrived and it seemed there was no end to them. While I worked I listened to game shows on TV and drank coffee until I ran out of coffee and then tea, in quantities that forced me to take frequent breaks from my work to relieve my bladder. When it was light out and I kept myself busy, I could cope, but once darkness closed in at five o'clock the world began to close in on me as well. I ate something — mandated by my instinct for survival. I loathed buying groceries and survived on what I had around the house until my continued existence became problematic. One night I ate a piece of toast and a whole bottle of pickles. By six-thirty I couldn't stand it any longer and put on my coat and headed over to Old Evans' house. It was an easier journey now that I'd taken wire cutters to the top strand, and in the daytime I could see a beaten path between the two houses had already started to form.

The old man looked forward to my visits. This I would have been able to determine without his mentioning it but mention it he did. He was a fascinating character with an historical past he shared lucidly and I discovered more about him every day. Old Evans was always clement in our discussions and wanted to know more about me too, and at first I felt tempted to make things up that weren't part of my sheltered life because what I had accomplished didn't add up to much, but I began to relish the telling of the life I had experienced with my father and the old man learned things about me I didn't realize I knew. Tapping the reservoir of memories from long-ago allowed me to forget the present and my recent past temporarily. The more comfortable we became in each other's company the more intimate the details we shared, and in a matter of days he knew more about Hanne Lemmons than anyone else alive.

"Sundays, me and my brother would take off after church. We would take off before church if we thought we could get away with it. If we hung around, our dad always had extra work to be done, it was such a big farm, so we were never home on Sundays. In the summer it was the most fun. We would go to the Cowichan River and we had this rope swing tied to a tree over the Bean Pool and we took turns being Tarzan. Mom would pack us a lunch and we were free for the rest of the day. That was my favourite part of growing up."

When Old Evans started in on one of his tales, particularly when they involved his youth, he stared out across the bedroom and could clearly see something else besides the grey, faded wallpaper.

"What did you and your dad get up to for fun?" he asked.

This was a question I had investigated myself many times over the last few years. I didn't have an answer then and didn't know what to offer up now.

"My father wasn't one to look for pleasure. I realize that now, looking back. He didn't yearn to have a good time or if he did he disguised his feelings well. When we first got a TV, I was about ten and we watched a few shows together. *The Wonderful World of Disney* was one. When I got older and didn't want to watch kids' shows, we didn't watch much TV. He would watch the news but that was about it. For a few years we watched *The Ed Sullivan Show* but I think he did so just to keep me company. He would stare at the screen but I don't remember him laughing out loud once."

"So just the two of you came here. What happened to your mother?"

"I was pretty young when my mother died. I remember a few things about her but not many. No one knows what happened exactly. We were on a big boat coming here, I know that. My mother had been ill and one night she disappeared. My father said it was only two days before we were to reach Halifax and she was gone. They searched the boat once they realized she wasn't with us, but by then we were hundreds of miles across the Atlantic. My father wasn't much of a talker at the best of times, but growing up that was one topic he avoided. I tried, but it was something that was history and he wanted to leave it in the past."

The bedroom housed an old dog and an old man for ten or twelve hours a day and it smelled like it. The night table on the side where he slept held a dusty lamp and an odd collection of books and magazines and newspapers and, opposite the bed, was one dresser that had once supported a mirror but the mirror was missing. At the side there was one window that looked out on my house but the curtains were always drawn shut. Late each night a giant spider made its way across the bedroom linoleum toward the hallway, unbeknownst to the old man or the dog, as if it were well behaved and obeying curfew.

"The thing is, it wasn't just about my mother. It was my brother too. My mom was pregnant at the time and so it wasn't just her. My dad told me once it would have been a boy. I don't think they knew for sure. I should have had a mother and a brother all these years. Now I have no one."

The living room where I often slept on the couch was the largest room in the house. The first few nights the room felt eerie and inhabited by spirits because everything in the room was covered in cloth or dust, as if a once-upon-a-time life had been curtailed, but it was beginning to feel like home. The walls were painted with a hint of green and a foot from the ceiling a band of wallpaper, six inches wide, circled the room with a repetition of apples and pears. There were 144 pears and 143 apples in total. From what I could tell, even the dog avoided the room.

Everyone called him Old Evans except me. I addressed him as Mr. Evans, reasoning the tag *old* was clearly not needed and carried a tone of insult. Our chat had gone on longer than usual, mainly because I had answered many of his questions with long-winded answers. He tried to stifle a yawn and I figured if I were going to broach the subject I had better get on with it before I lost my nerve.

"I was wondering . . . " I said and then stopped. Old Evans turned his head sideways, suddenly appearing alert. "Well, you've been kind enough to allow me to sleep here a lot lately. I find it hard to live in that house by myself now. And this house . . . well it isn't a large house, really, but it's . . . "

"Of course you can stay here."

"You don't mind?"

"Why would I mind?"

Moving into the old man's house had been theoretical, a straw to be drawn that might have been long or short. My imagination hadn't considered all that it might take to accomplish such a thing. There was a spare bedroom where he had the wringer washer hooked up to plumbing, but really, the only place I could conceive of sleeping was on one of the two sofas in the living room. And then there were my personal

162

belongings. Old Evans removed his glasses and started his usual late night lens cleaning ritual. The lenses were so thick that when he removed them and held them in the air, the room on the other side appeared refracted as though seen through a prism.

"Thank you. I'll be able to help out. Do things around here."

Old Evans didn't answer. He turned off the lamp and readied himself for a peaceful sleep.

✿✿✿

After breakfast, porridge and hot water for Old Evans, porridge and milk for myself, he shuffled to his shop for the morning and I began packing my wares from my house to his. I was too late, on one of my return trips, to stop the filling of my oil tank. I had yet to turn the furnace downstairs on once because I hadn't been sleeping there, and now a full oil tank would have to be paid for unnecessarily. It took time to sort through what it was I wanted to bring, and eight trips later everything except the business surrounding the clocks had been transported. The conclusion I came to was that I would have to return to work on them in my house — there were simply too many tools and too many clocks with nowhere to go.

There was a loaf of bakery bread in the fridge and by the time he had returned to the house there were egg salad sandwiches on two plates and a pot of tea ready.

"You made lunch." I could tell by the tone of his words that he hadn't expected I would prepare lunch. He stared at the table like he didn't trust what he saw or what was before him was somehow an intrusion into his normal routine.

"I did. I hope you like it."

163

"I don't eat much that's fancy, but this looks good. I haven't bothered to make egg sandwiches for years." The old man sat down without washing his hands and took a bite of his sandwich. His eating habits were abstemious by anyone's standards and I was nervous watching him dig in. "Would you mind passing the salt? Too much is bad for you but salt can make anything taste good. It's good already, I didn't mean it tasted bad. Just a habit."

He read as he ate. I imagined this is what he did every day — sat by himself and ate lunch and read until it was time to get back to work. I loved the selection of magazines that arrived at the house: *Life, Popular Mechanics, National Geographic,* so I joined him in his silent gastronomy. He also subscribed to the *Vancouver Sun* which arrived a day after its publication but still felt like news when you got hold of it for the first time.

"What are you building out in the workshop?"

"Fiddling, mostly. I'm kind of between projects right now. It's a lull but it won't last. It never does. Something always needs doing."

"Do you want me to get some groceries? I don't mind."

"No need. I've started a list on the counter over there. You just add what you want that's not already on there and phone it in to Berkey's. Tomorrow is delivery day so the timing is right. Just tell them it's for Arthur Evans and consider it done."

"Arthur?"

"That's what my mother decided. My dad favoured Robert, but Arthur is was. You should call me that. I'm an old man already and there's no sense making it worse by adding Mr. What? You don't like the name Arthur?"

"No, it's fine. It's just that . . . Arthur was my father's name."

36

BEVERLY TOOK A DIFFERENT ROUTE home each day in her '56 Studebaker, a reclamation project her husband had configured years back, and by now her insistence on alternate courses from work to home were nothing more than a feeble attempt to sustain her optimism. Kurt had been gone almost four weeks and despite her putting up posters, arranging for an article in the *Leader* and harassing the RCMP into doing something productive on the case, Kurt had not returned. He had not written. He had not phoned. He had simply disappeared from the face of the earth.

Molly, her boss and co-worker at Pearl's Beauty Salon, after hours of consoling her during their slack times, went on to explain that there was always an inordinate amount of guilt that gripped the parents of a missing child. Where Molly had heard or read such an idea she had no clue, but it certainly applied in her case. The last time she saw her son was at their last family meeting. In the ensuing weeks there had been numerous times when she was tempted to call another such meeting, but she was afraid of them now. Could it be she had forced her own son to flee? It didn't seem logical. Kurt had gotten himself into jams in the past and no matter how directly he was implicated, nothing seemed to bother him. Life had been a roller-coaster of emotions for the whole family. Beverly had been angry at Kurt for the first two or three days, thinking he had taken up living at a friend's house, waiting with glee for them to suffer his absence. But no, every possible friend and acquaintance and relative had been contacted and Kurt was obviously not living close by. Kurt's favourite meal was pork chops, and while there were two or three meals worth in the freezer, she refused to prepare them until Kurt was safe and at home again.

Daisy's response was to hibernate. She attended school and went through the motions but was clearly not herself. The coach begged her to join the basketball team where everyone knew she would be a star, but she refused. Instead, she went to school and walked home, by herself most days, then helped her mother with dinner and did her homework half-heartedly. All that she had resented in her brother she now missed and she was left with an emptiness that had no cure.

What had happened was inevitable — that was the stance taken by Red Neilson — a position that drove his wife to distraction. Kurt had been getting too big for his britches, was his standard line of thinking, and eventually he would have gone off on his own. Red believed his son would show up some day driving a car big enough to take up a lane of the Lake Road with a blonde wife in the front seat and three kids fighting in the back. His son Kurt was a wild stallion and only the raw energy of life was potent enough to tame him.

Milo went mostly unchanged. He still smiled when his mind was lost in thought, though Beverly was certain he smiled less since his brother had vanished. The two of them had shared a room upstairs since Milo was two and after the first three days of Kurt's absence, Milo had taken to sleeping in his brother's bed. This sent his mother into convulsions the first Saturday without Kurt. Beverly, who routinely found it difficult to differentiate between happiness and confusion, had gone up to see why Milo hadn't bothered to come down for breakfast and the first thing she saw when she opened the door was a body wrapped in blankets on Kurt's bed. For three or four seconds her shredded life had all been neatly sewn back together. Three or four seconds that made the weeks that followed all the more difficult to reconcile.

"Where are you going at this time of night?" Red Neilson asked his wife. She had her coat on, a scarf wrapped around her neck and a hat in her hand she hadn't committed to.

"Somewhere you wouldn't think to go. I'm going to pay a visit to the young Lemmons girl, Hanne. I haven't seen her since just after her father past. She must be lonely in that house all by herself."

Red guffawed loudly as if to suggest it was a stupid idea right from conception. Daisy, sitting on the couch and doing her math homework while her father watched a detective show, glanced at her mother queerly then buried her head in her books. The truth was, Beverly wanted to be around someone else besides her remaining family planted like stubborn weeds in front of the TV.

She would be at her neighbour's door in less than five minutes, but it was chilly enough out that Beverly wished she *had* decided on the hat. Tansor was often dark and quiet at night this time of year: an absence of moon or stars or street-lights. No one ventured away from home unless they had to, and crunching down the gravel driveway on the Lemmons' property she felt like an interloper, someone sleepwalking unbeknownst to others. It wasn't until she was almost at the front of the house that she realized there were no lights on anywhere. She had come all this way — it felt foolish not to knock — so that is what she did, lightly, in case Hanne was sleeping. Beverly knocked again and again, then opened the door and called after the owner but got no response. She closed the door, sat down on the cement steps and tried unsuccessfully to stifle the wave of emotion that took over. She wanted to help and she wanted help, and now another night would pass without accomplishing either one.

37

TWO DAYS AFTER I MOVED IN, Verna arrived for her weekly check on Old Evans and things changed. There were two sofas in the living room and one (not the one I had been sleeping on) was functioning as a pullout bed. I arranged the furniture so that the pullout was tucked away from the entrance and this became my bed. There was no TV in the room but there was an ancient radio that still worked and I turned it off and on with a plug I could reach from the side of the bed. Some nights I listened to music or talk shows that came from distant cities and pulled the plug when I was ready to sleep. The extra couch I positioned in the room in the unlikely event I had visitors, and the coffee table, crafted from oak by Old Evans years ago, sat in front of it as if to suggest people were welcome. The furniture, the floor and the windows had all been scrubbed to erase years of dust particles obeying gravity and the two lamps were fitted with bulbs that brought a receptive sallow glow to the room once the sun went down.

A sense of order had been established in the rest of the house as well, especially the kitchen. The week's dishes were washed and put away, the fridge and oven were sparklingly clean, and the kitchen table, normally given over to months of old newspapers and magazines layered haphazardly, now held only newspapers from the last two editions and the magazines sat neatly stacked with members of their own species. To someone like Verna, these physical alterations were meek compared to the political atmosphere present in the house. When Verna arrived, I was at the door to greet her and I informed her that I was now living with the old man. Verna's response was reactive, though not intentionally dismissive, and she asked to see Dr. Evans immediately.

I could hear a wide range of intonations being exchanged in the bedroom behind closed doors and finally Verna emerged, startled somewhat, but resigned.

"So, you're Hanne, apparently. The neighbour next door."

"I am. And you're Verna, the nurse he can't say enough good things about. He talks about you all the time. He says you have helped him out in so many ways for years and years."

"Well, I do my best. It looks to me like there will be less to do with you living here. Sorry to hear about your father. Dr. Evans told me. I suppose this arrangement could work out for both of you. Temporarily. I don't imagine you see yourself staying here long."

"I don't know, really. This feels better than living in that old house by myself. I enjoy his company."

"Well, that's good then. He has a lot of stories to tell, that much I can vouch for."

Verna rubbed her hands together, as if this were a routine warming up exercise to prepare her for the task at hand. She turned without further explanation to help Old Evans, and I took the keys and unlocked the shed where he spent a good part of every day. I picked up what must certainly be scraps of wood, dusted his tools and the platforms that held them, organized the screws and nails he had in jars that screwed into lids nailed to the bottom of cupboards, then swept the floor until grey cement was once again visible. A miscellaneous assortment of wood in a variety of sizes and shapes leaned against all four walls and I was tempted to reorganize these as well, but resisted and only straightened and dusted them where they stood. Before I left I started a fire with some of the rescued wood scraps so that the workshop would be warm for his afternoon shift. I had been returning home most days to work on my clock inventory and Old Evans was eager to build me a workstation, based on the description I had given him, so I could carry on with my business from his living room.

"He's getting dressed," Verna said, standing at the entrance to the kitchen with her leather satchel in hand. "I usually take a stab at the dishes and empty the washer, but I'm guessing that won't be needed now that you're here."

I had heard all about Verna pestering him about the lack of variety in his diet, so while they were finishing up his treatment in the bedroom, I'd organized lettuce, tomato and cheese sandwiches and prepared a pot of tea, though I knew he would insist on hot water.

"I'll look after those things. No problem. I have some lunch prepared for the two of you. He looks forward to catching up on things when you come each week. I'm going to head next door to get some work done."

Verna looked too stunned to say anything and didn't.

⌘⌘⌘

Old Evans sat down at the kitchen table where Verna sat waiting for him. He understood Verna had to see the lunch preparations as somehow extraordinary, but he sat down to eat, tucking a napkin in at the neckline of his overalls — a ritual he'd taken up since Hanne arrived — and started in without comment.

Finally, he said, "My bet is she has tea ready on the stove."

Verna helped herself and brought him a mug of hot water.

"She's done a lot around here," Verna said.

"She certainly has."

"She doesn't seem dull like so many young girls today."

"I'd call her sharp as a honed axe," he said.

Verna finished off her sandwich. It tasted better than expected. The salt perhaps.

"It does seem odd though, wouldn't you say, for a young girl her age to be living here?"

"She's lonely and a bit confused right now," Old Evans said. "Think back on your own life, Verna. You don't have to be old to be lonely."

"That's true enough," Verna said. "It's just so sudden and everything. You don't know her all that well and for that matter she doesn't know you, either. I'm just thinking of your safety, that's all. She's a pretty girl, I'll give her that. She doesn't come across as dishonest, so I suppose she can be trusted. That must be what you've decided, then, that she can be trusted."

Old Evans didn't take the opportunity to respond to Verna's concerns. The sandwiches had been cut in two and he helped himself to another half. If there was anyone around who made a better sandwich he had yet to run into them.

38

BY THE FOLLOWING THURSDAY, the rudimentary structure of my work station had been constructed in the workshop, and I had a hand in building it because some of the pieces were more than Old Evans could handle. It would take another week, possibly more, before it was ready to move into the living room where I could finally set up my workspace. In the morning I was up early and helped him with breakfast, but soon after I went back to bed and was not there to greet Verna when she arrived.

From inside the cocoon I had fashioned with my bedcovers, I heard Verna make an enthusiastic entrance.

"You won't believe what I saw on the way out here. Just past the gravel pit as I was coming around the corner there was this deer, a buck with at least three points on his head, standing in the middle of the road. Good job I saw him in time. So I slowed down but he just stood there staring at me. Soon there were two cars behind me but the deer wouldn't move. He looked me right in the eye as if to say *I got here first, you drive around*, which is what I might have done but another car coming in from the lake pulled up and stopped and stared at the deer staring at me. He had no interest whatsoever in getting out of the way. We beeped, the car behind me was impatient and beeped first, but all the horns in New York city weren't about to budge this beast. The guy in the other lane was getting a kick out of this, I could tell by the look on his face, and he backed his car up a few feet and turned into our lane, right up to the deer and nudged him in the behind with his bumper. The deer moved a couple of feet so the guy did it again. It took three tries before he pushed him off to the side of the road and when he was done the deer was still standing there staring at the cars like some kind of injustice had taken place. I've never seen anything like it in my life. They're usually so frightened. With a cow I could see it, but not a deer. Do you think he was retarded?"

Old Evans didn't say anything right away. Obviously, he had never heard of such a thing either. "He must have been sick. Wild animals go on instinct as a rule. They're too smart to be stubborn."

"Well, if I'm a little bit late, that's why. My neighbour in town is a hunter. I should call him up and tell him there's a deep freezer's worth of venison parked at the side of the Lake Road."

He had shuffled halfway to the bedroom before Verna started the story and finished the journey by the time she was done, then the bedroom door was closed behind them. "Where's your new roommate?" Verna asked.

"I do believe she's lying down for a nap. I don't think she's feeling all that perky today."

I heard Verna comment on the bandages she was removing from his legs and then she started filling the bathtub with water that was warm but not hot, a specific request. When she got back to the hallway she poked her head into the living room.

"Hanne, you okay?"

I made no response, so Verna sat down on the side of the pullout bed and touched my forehead with the back of her hand and as soon as she did I began an extended bout of muffled crying. "What's the matter? Are you hurting somewhere? Tell me and I'll see if we can get to the bottom of it."

I pulled my head out from under the pillow and looked at the wall, not at Verna. "I think I'm pregnant."

"Oh my," Verna said. Being a nurse she was clearly busy reorganizing the thoughts that popped immediately to mind. "Well, we'll have to arrange to have you examined to make sure. You've missed your cycle, I take it?"

"Yes. Plus I've been sick almost every morning. I leave the radio on hoping he won't notice. That's what happens, isn't it? You get morning sickness?"

"Well, many do, that's for sure. My daughter is six months along now and she didn't get sick once. Everyone's different. My daughter, Emily, has a doctor she swears by. He's young, you know, but she trusts him. I'll see what I can do to set up an appointment."

Verna got Old Evans settled in his bath and made a pot of herbal tea and after some coaxing had me come to the kitchen table to drink it. Verna was prepared to enjoy my crisis. Last week she had fewer responsibilities to deal with at the Evans' household, but now she had more.

"Best not to mention any of this for now," Verna said. "I have a run out this way tomorrow and I'll see if I can't get an appointment for the early afternoon and I'll come pick you up. I may have to leave early if that stupid deer is still standing in the middle of the road."

I tried to stifle a giggle and it didn't sound much different from the whimpering I'd offered up earlier. But now I felt comforted, at least, and realized Verna was everything the old man had suggested. I was positive I didn't need a doctor to tell me I was pregnant, but it made sense to be sure.

175

While the usual Thursday treatment finished up, I prepared sausages and beets and toast for lunch. Arthur Evans didn't crave many vegetables, beets being the exception, and protein was not something he consumed on a regular basis, but sausages he didn't seem to mind. He preferred his toast burnt like my father used to and I had the toaster set to accomplish such a task, so that when the three of us sat down for lunch I was surprised when Verna ate one sausage, one beet and one piece of burnt toast. She didn't appear to find it at all odd, but she might have been acting out of politeness.

Verna wanted to revisit the deer episode, only now the tale was told with even greater enthusiasm and possibly more than a little hyperbole. The deer, for example, was a four-point buck this time around. Only after everything with a modicum of relevance to their lives had been discussed, did Verna mention she would be dropping by tomorrow afternoon to take me into town for a doctor's appointment. It has been several years since I had seen a doctor, she explained, and that was something that just shouldn't happen these days.

Old Evans loved having a project that held some urgency and purpose, and it was obvious he couldn't wait to get back out to his workshop. I decided I had better finish off a clock that was supposed to have been completed earlier in the week, even though it was the last thing I felt like attempting at that moment, and headed back to the dreary house that had been my home for so long. I felt lonely, once Verna drove off. What Verna offered me was something motherly I may have been blessed to receive many years ago, but it felt like I was experiencing it for the very first time.

39

ROBBIE NEVER HAD A LOT in common with Kurt Neilson, but his friend's sudden absence unequivocally changed the dynamic of his new life in Tansor. For the first two weeks after his disappearance, everyone at school thought it was a matter of time before Kurt returned with unpasteurized tales of adventure everyone could admire. But Kurt didn't return at all and what Robbie hadn't realized was that all along Kurt had let it be known that Robbie was officially off limits in the pecking order that existed among the boys at this end of the valley. Soon, the Olson brothers declared him an adversary, beginning with threatening glares and comments, bumping into him when he was retrieving his books from his locker. The incidents escalated in severity and each time there was a shroud of silence, a waiting for a response Robbie was loath to give. By the middle of November the Olson brothers sporadically ignored their bus ride home, nearly five miles, in order to pester Robbie on his walk home, away from school authorities. They would saunter behind him, kicking rocks at his heels, throwing insults his way that were moronic and almost made him laugh were it not for the threat that hung like rain in the belly of a black cloud. Robbie refused to engage with the enemy and he could tell he was frustrating Buddy and Sam Olson, much like the way a cat playing with a dead mouse begins to lose interest. But Robbie wasn't a mouse and he wasn't dead. Eventually they walked beside him on Auchinachie Road and nudged him and his books into a late afternoon thaw of sword fern and blackberry. The next day they left him alone and he considered this might be the end of it, but he wasn't about to be let off that easily, and two days later the brothers trailed him home and sidled up beside him at the same juncture in the road as two days previous.

What happened next was something Robbie was unable to explain for a long time after it happened. He felt overwhelmed, suddenly, by the many irritating events accumulated over the last sixteen years: the loss of his parents, his itinerant time with three sets of aunts and uncles, the episode that night in the living room of Hanne Lemmons, these and hundreds of other irritations that had festered for years, coalesced into a ball of energy he could no longer contain. One minute he had his satchel of books in his hands and the next his hands were around the throat of Buddy Olson, the elder brother, and pushed him into the woods, his hands held fast around his throat until they both crashed into the snarl of brush, fallen saplings, and rocks. Robbie rode his man into the jagged terrain and landed with all his weight on top of Buddy Olson who lay there with fear in his eyes, gasping to breathe. Robbie could never replicate what came out of his mouth when he started kicking Buddy Olson in the head, but the words that came were all rage and hatred and it wasn't long before Sam Olson tackled him from behind. Sam was younger and lighter than his older brother but Robbie knew he carried a knife on him, one that opened with the press of a button, something he bragged about and demonstrated often at school. Sam had him pinned face down and his head was jammed against a log and he couldn't move. When Sam released him, Robbie knew it was to fetch the knife out of his pocket and it was the opportunity he took to dislodge himself from his prone position and

178

buck Sam off. Robbie got to his feet and saw Sam standing in front of his brother, who was now on his knees and puking into a bed of salal. Sam didn't appear to know what to do: tend to his brother or deal with Robbie, who picked up a large rock and screamed, "Drop the fucking knife, asshole. Drop it!" Sam looked back at his older brother for directions but got nothing in return. Robbie heaved the rock that caught Sam high in the chest and sent him on top of his brother like the last two pins standing in a bowling alley. The knife fell to the ground and when Sam went to grab it Robbie stomped on his hand and heard something crack. He picked up the knife and pressed the button. The knife snapped open just as it had when Sam had demonstrated the mechanism behind the backstop. Buddy was having difficulty breathing and Sam, curled up in the foetal position, started to whimper.

With one Olson brother incapacitated and the other writhing in pain and radiating fear, Robbie's sudden rage dissipated. He closed the knife and slid it into his pocket.

"If you two want to brag about this at school, go ahead. I have my side of the story and a knife to prove it. I just don't care anymore, understand? Try to fuck with me again and I'll kill you both. I have no reason not to."

He retrieved his school work, still tucked inside his satchel at the side of the road as if none of this had happened, and glared down at the Olson brothers. Sam knelt beside his older brother, the two of them gathering their altered circumstances together. Robbie was thirsty all of a sudden. Thirsty and ready to go home.

∾∾∾∾

The relationship Robbie was hoping would develop with Daisy deteriorated after her brother disappeared. She wasn't as brash as she used to be and not as open to hanging around him. She was in her mother's camp: waiting for the day Kurt would saunter home with his tail between his legs. When she heard about what had happened with the Olson brothers, she gave him a brief hug and then punched him on the shoulder. "Kurt always said they were useless scum," she said.

Two weeks after his run-in with the Olsons, it was as if a new order had been established. No one bothered him. If anything, he went completely ignored by the boys at school who somehow got the message that Robbie Tweedie was not to be messed with. While this was a relief, nothing useful had been accomplished from Robbie's point of view. So much of his life had been lived on the outside of his family and peers, and moving to the valley had done nothing but reinforce his situation. It was not difficult to find something to do outside and be out of his aunt and uncle's company when the late summer and fall weather hung in the air, but now it was cold and the rains had begun, and sometimes even snow for a nauseating day or two. Saturdays he stayed out of the house all day, wandering around town and spending time at the local pool hall and it was there he met a guy called Jake who was days away from joining the navy. Jake painted a vivid picture of travelling the world and getting an education on the way and nothing had come Robbie's way since moving to the valley that sounded as good. Technically, one had to be seventeen, but a sixteen-year-old could enlist in Halifax and continue with his education and join the navy. They paid a paltry $45.00 a month, half of what a seventeen-year-old got, but it was money he wasn't getting now and nowhere in the navy were there uncles he was related to. Hoxsey felt he was acting a bit hasty, but Slick did everything he could to accelerate his application and took time off work to take him to Victoria for an interview. Robbie's mother had been a Canadian and that was not difficult to document. Robbie had no idea what he would do in the Canadian Navy, but the ambiguity didn't bother him. He had been raised in a bed of uncertainty, only this time it would be a bed of his own choosing.

40

LITTLE WAS SAID ON THE DRIVE back home. Verna offered a comforting phrase or two, I could hear her saying things, but I was unable to take anything in. There had been a short stop at the drugstore and the evidence was sitting on the seat between us: some sort of daily dosage of vitamins and minerals to support a weakened immune system. Verna had handled everything and now she pulled the car to the bottom of Old Evans' driveway and left it to idle.

"What am I going to tell him?" I finally said.

"The truth. That's your only option. Remember, the old man has been through it all in his time. If there's anyone who will understand your circumstance, it's him."

I started to cry then. I hated myself for doing so but it couldn't be helped. Verna waited a few minutes, then pulled a small package of Kleenex from the glove box and handed it over.

"Every day we wake up to a new reality. Most days it's much the same, but yours has changed, it's that simple. At least a million other women in the world are where you are now, Hanne. You're not alone. What will make your life worth living is where you go from here. It can all turn out splendidly, but that's going to be up to you."

Only when I had composed myself did the car make its way to the house. Smoke slithered out the workshop chimney, so Verna told me to make myself useful putting on a pot of tea and went out to chat with Arthur Evans.

"What took so long? What did he say?"

"What took so long was he needed me to help him turn over that thing he's building for you. He waited all afternoon until someone came to help him out. If the man has nothing else, he has patience."

"But what did he say when you told him?"

"Not much. 'Poor Hanne' was how he addressed the situation, but what he was meaning is poor Hanne compared to what you already have to deal with, not poor Hanne like the world is coming to an end. He'll help you, if I know him, but he won't feel sorry for you."

Verna let me take that in.

"The food served around here the last few weeks has been a vast improvement over what used to go on at this house. That's because of you. Now things are different again and diet is more important than ever. I'm going to make a list of groceries to order and unless they're bound to make one you of sick to your stomach I suggest trying them. If he says anything about my list just wait until he's in the shed and order them anyway. Some of nature's good foods he hasn't tried for so long he can't remember if he likes them or not."

Someone fussing over me, like Verna was prone to, was hard to decipher at times. The details I comprehended, but the emotion behind them floated in the air, looking for a home. Verna had been a nurse for so long and used to people doing exactly what she told them that it made it easier to accept.

The three of us had tea and cookies together and my being pregnant didn't come up until the end. Verna offered the closing chapter and reminded us both that exercise was important, diet was important, and doing at least one thing a day that brings pleasure was important. She said she would be back in six days and while she thought she had covered everything, were there any questions. There were none.

When she left and drove way, Old Evans looked up at me and said, "She makes everything sound so easy, doesn't she?"

∽∽∽

A few days later the workbench, designed to my specifications, was complete and varnished and left to dry. Arthur Evans said it best he leave it to air out for a day or two because a pregnant woman had better things to do than breathing toxic fumes. I was looking forward to moving everything into my new house because the thought of being alone in the place I had grown up in was depressing. But I did go there and persevere with the clocks at hand because, so far, Old Evans had paid for everything and I was determined to bring in some money to account for my share of the expenses.

For two days I took the pills prescribed, in the morning and just before supper, and then I stopped. In the afternoon when I had the house to myself, I lingered in the bathtub and reflected upon my reflection in the mirror. I didn't look pregnant. I looked like I always had and something in me said that was how I wanted things to stay. The doctor had guessed at my due date, but if this were to be timed exactly as nature intended I knew precisely when I would become a mother. This was only the beginning and maybe it wasn't too late.

Verna would know but, Verna, I could tell, would be ready with a pat answer ready to dispose of. She was a nurse, after all. Arthur Evans had been a doctor for more than a decade and, while it had been a long time ago, I suspected he would know about such things. His mood lately had been lighter and more purposeful since he found out I was pregnant, giving the impression that helping me out was a good thing and helping me and my child-to-be was imperial. Time was against me and another forty-eight hours of it passed before I found the will to ask.

"I'm only sixteen, you know."

Old Evans was reading in bed, earlier in the evening than usual. He had described the book he was reading as a novel about a man climbing a mountain.

"You never mentioned exactly how old you were. Sixteen is about what I figured."

"Sixteen is still pretty young," I offered. My age was the perfect way to open the discussion, I realized, and wished I'd done so two days earlier. "Sixteen," I continued, "is young to become a mother. I know it happens, even younger for some, but sixteen is young because you don't know much. About mothering."

He set his bookmark in place precisely, with just a hint poking above the bound pages. He removed his glasses and put them on the side table like he always did when I sat by his bed, as if seeing and listening were not viable simultaneously. Out of the corner of my eye I saw the daddy longlegs spider dart out from the closet, stop, then skitter back to where it came from.

"Back in Shakespeare's time," he said, "it was common for girls to marry and become mothers at twelve or thirteen. But then I don't imagine any of them knew the first thing about how to fix a clock. I think you'll be just fine."

"I'm not very pregnant yet. I was wondering about what it would take to not be pregnant at all. That's what I've been thinking lately. I want things to be back like they were and I was wondering if you, because you've been a doctor, would help me."

"Would you bring me a glass of water and some baking soda? There's a lot of rumbling going on down here."

I returned with a glass half full of water and popped an Alka-Seltzer tablet in before handing it over.

"What's that?"

"It's Alka-Seltzer. Verna told me to buy it. She says baking soda is bad for your blood pressure. You're supposed to drink it now while it's fizzy."

He did as he was told and grimaced after, complaining that it didn't taste any better than baking soda. Then he fingered the brass buttons on his coveralls, a sign that he was thinking.

"The why always comes before the how. The how I can help you with. What is needed is an emmenagogue — a concoction that stimulates menstruation. A midwife taught me the formula years back but nothing is guaranteed. It tricks the body and deprives the uterus of progesterone. It involves an overdose of ascorbic acid or vitamin C and drinking parsley tea every hour for two days. It wouldn't be a fun time. The how is not the problem."

I wanted him to continue, to commit to helping me so I could rest my mind, but he clearly wasn't about to do that.

"So you want to know the why? Is that what you need to hear?"

"I need to hear the why and so do you. I'm not after an answer tonight. This might be the most important decision you'll ever make and you've got some thinking to do. Tomorrow night maybe, or the next night. Then we can discuss it."

He gave a long, drawn-out belch, which the dog heard and responded to with a whimper, and then he picked up his novel. I was desperate for his approbation but wouldn't be receiving it tonight. I had done nothing but fret about my decision for the last two days and now he wanted me to do it all over again.

The next day when the groceries were delivered, Arthur Evans had the delivery boy help me cart my work station into the house. The furniture was arranged so I could sit and work and look out onto a small field that ran down to the Lake Road. The old man was gleaming with pride and I was too consumed to thank him the way I wanted to. I leaned my head against his shoulder and mumbled "thank you," then put on a heavy coat, gumboots, and a toque and went for a walk in the rain. It wasn't easy access to the railway tracks and the creek from the Evans' property, so I walked down the Lake Road to Holliday Lane, the long way, and found refuge down by the creek. I walked down the aging ties to where the tracks passed over a hundred-yard-long trestle. When I was very young my father had taken me that far in the springtime, and he had to hold my hand to convince me to cross. My fear stemmed from the stuttered vision of the creek far below and also because I was afraid a train might come charging toward Lake Cowichan when we were partway over. My father had a hard time persuading me he knew when the train was due and we turned around halfway across. I was older now and knew the train schedule and, while I was still not fond of heights, crossing the trestle was easy.

My father liked to use certain phrases he had picked up since moving to Canada and one of them was: *We'll cross that bridge when we come to it.* It was the perfect phrase for him because in his life there was little movement and the bridge never appeared. I was now at a point in my life when there was more than one bridge to cross and I knew a choice would have to be made. The child that was growing inside me could be a girl, but when I thought of delivering a baby it was a miniature-sized Kurt Neilson that came screaming into the world with revenge on his mind that I imagined. The child could look like

Kurt, I knew, with reddish-brown hair and freckles and like any child he would expect a father to surface sooner or later. A young boy would grow up to be an older boy and if he began to look just like his father people would begin to ask questions. In one of my more memorable dreams, Constable Jespersen paid a return visit in which I had seen his car coming up the driveway. It was raining hard and I bundled the child up and covered his head with a hat and put him in the carriage to go out for a walk. The policeman intercepted me and commented on how odd it was to take a baby for a stroll in such horrid weather. Horrid weather? I questioned, and the officer said yes, a child could catch a death of cold in horrid weather and then he leaned over and pulled the hat from the boy's head and said: Aha, just as I suspected. This child is the spitting image of that Kurt Neilson fella that went missing. What have you got to say for yourself now, Hanne Lemmons?

I didn't say anything because I woke up in a panic, but the vision and dozens of variations hounded me thereafter. The creek the bridge was built over was a bubbling slurry of coffee-stained water that was accustomed to change. First it had been clouds, then rain and now it was a vigorous creek, confident in the last two hours of its transformative journey toward Somenos Lake. My fingers tickled the surface and the water was warmer than it appeared. A lot of things were different from what they were presumed to be. The child growing inside me, the child that was likely larger than it was when I left the house two hours ago, might at this very moment be turning into a girl. The girl could have black hair and look more like my mother and have a steady heartbeat, as regular as a Junghans clock, a child that would squeal when tickled, take the world in with blue eyes instead of brown. Anything, imagined or not, was possible.

41

ALL THE NEIGHBOURS HAD BEEN watching the Lemmons' house and the house belonging to Old Evans for weeks, more specifically, the journey Hanne made between the two on a daily basis. It was hard to make sense of it all because few people ever visited the old man. Then Hanne stopped making the trek and her house was left in darkness at all times, except for one porch light. The obvious fact that Hanne was now living at the Evans' house triggered a variety of responses. Mrs. Eaton was glad Hanne had found a place to go but was somewhat miffed that the girl hadn't come calling two properties west, instead of one property east. She had made overtures of food to Hanne when her father passed and having never had children of her own, she would have enjoyed the company. Ernie Jagger thought it less likely now that Hanne would once again attend his church, not that he was about to give up, but he did consider that there might be two more acres he could mow, for a small fee, each summer. Mr. May concluded that come summer the well on the Lemmons' property would have plenty of water if no one was living there, and maybe he could get permission to get his water there whenever he wanted. Red Neilson wouldn't have had an inkling about the relocation had his wife not informed him. He wasn't clued into much of late, falling asleep in a stew of beer in front of the TV, where he sometimes remained wedged into his chair in the foetal position until morning. But Beverly noticed. She believed she noticed everything.

Do good things. Beverly believed if one did good things in life good things would be returned. She tried hard to do just that, though she knew that despite her best intentions she had not always been successful. She had seen the forlorn character of Hanne trudging her way down the road past her house the day before, soaked before the journey began, and waved to the girl who was oblivious to anyone else in the world. She would have rapped on the window and called her in for a visit, but she had nothing baked at the time. Preparations were now in place; she had risen early in the morning and baked a delicious chocolate cake which she cut exactly in half because with Kurt not around, half a cake was plenty for her family. Secured under her arm in a Tupperware half-cake plastic container, she made her way proudly, between showers, over to the Evans' bungalow and knocked on the door.

Hanne was working at her new workplace and might have seen her approach had she not been frustrated trying to reclaim a suspension spring she had ordered and had stupidly bent out of shape during installation. She heard the knock at the door. No one knocked on Old Evans' door — the few who came knew to just walk in.

"So you're living *here* now. I went to visit you a couple of weeks back but there was no one home. I brought you a cake . . . well, half a cake. I thought you and the old man might like dessert from time to time."

Hanne thanked her and took hold of the cake. When Beverly stood in the doorway, she invited her in and took the coat that was handed to her and watched Beverly remove her shoes. "You don't need to bother with your shoes," she suggested, but it was too late. Beverly stood there eagerly in stocking feet and both of them took in the kitchen floor that Hanne had considered cleaning but hadn't gotten to.

"Would you like some of the cake? With tea?"

"No thank you, dear. I have the other half at home and to be honest I'm not much for sweets. I won't be staying long. I just wanted to drop by and see how you were making out. You've had a lot of changes in your life lately."

The small kitchen table hadn't been cleaned from breakfast, so Hanne invited Beverly into the living room that was also her bedroom and workplace.

"So, you've carried on your father's legacy in clock repair, I see. Now that must be difficult work."

"It's not so bad. I've worked on a lot of different clocks. You get the hang of it."

"Well, it's a mystery to me. But then, life is a mystery, isn't it?"

Hanne nodded in agreement. She sensed the polite thing to do was to inquire about Kurt, ask had there been any news, but she had no interest in going there. Hanne had done everything in her power to obliterate the image of Kurt Neilson from her mind, but looking at Beverly now, it was obvious Kurt took after his father and not his mother. She picked up one of the clocks she was working on and described its German heritage and what was wrong with it. It was a speech Beverly listened to without much interest.

"You have adapted well," Beverly said. "You look much better than the last time I saw you. It's great that Old Evans is company at a time like this. I've said to Red over the years: go on over and pay the man a visit, but my husband says the old fella is too smart to visit. Men are funny sometimes, aren't they? They say they want company and they don't go find it.

Sometimes I think Red's best friend is a bottle of beer but a beer makes for a short conversation."

Hanne listened and nodded and commented briefly to appear polite. She had been raised in a house where conversation was an abstraction at best. Beverly, on the other hand, was a part-time hair dresser and words out of her mouth flowed like water out of a leaky tap. Her customers enjoyed her banter — the trick, she knew, was trying to remember which stories had been imparted to whom. That's why she liked to keep up with current events which were only current temporarily and soon replaced with others.

"Ernie Jagger, the egg farmer? You likely know him. Word is he's being swallowed by the Pentecostal Church hook line and sinker. He's thinking of becoming a minister himself. Imagine that, an egg farmer one day and a man of the cloth the next. So, you yourself. You're keeping well? I imagine you're a big help to the old man."

"We help each other. It's working out okay."

Beverly hadn't run out of things to say, but she had committed to a short visit, and Hanne's eyes kept returning to the clock sitting patiently on the bench, so eventually Beverly got up to take her leave, but not before noticing Hanne's hair.

"I work at Pearl's Beauty Salon, as I'm sure you know. I do the odd job on the side, for neighbours mostly. You have such lovely, thick hair, I can see that. If you ever need your hair trimmed or want a perm, anything like that, just give me a call. Save you going into town and paying town prices."

Hanne saw her to the door and returned her coat. It had started raining again and she would need it.

"I'll just pop into the workshop and say my hello to Old Evans. Don't want him to think I'm sneaking cake into the house just for you." Beverly laughed and Hanne watched her laugh.

Beverly walked from the house to the workshop. She took in the view of her house that Old Evans would have, a view from a distance that made her house look vulnerable in some way. She found him leaning against his stool and drawing something detailed on a sheet of paper when she knocked on the inside of the workshop door. He was surprised to see her, as her last visit was nearly five years back.

"I just dropped off some cake for you and the young lady. Everyone deserves a treat now and then."

"Thank you," he said. "Any word on your oldest boy?"

"No, I'm afraid not. We keep hoping. And praying. I'm not religious much at all but I do pray he's safe somewhere. That's what the police think — he's run off and doing what young people do. Not a day goes by I don't look out the window and expect to see him lumbering up the road. What are you busy designing over there? It looks complicated."

"Likely more complicated than it needs to be. I'm thinking of building a crib. Never attempted one before but there's a first time for everything. I might make a crib. I might not make a crib. It's been one of those kind of days."

Beverly said her goodbyes and patted Old Evans on the shoulder as if to confirm he was still alive and standing in front of her. He was a very old man and doing well for his age. She couldn't imagine her husband living that long, and if he did survive to that age, the last thing she expected he would build was a crib.

42

I WAS TOLD TO TAKE twenty-four hours to consider things, and I took almost forty-eight hours only to find myself still scrambling with convictions. He knew how to help me out of my situation and said he would once I was sure. I wasn't.

Nothing that could be decided felt right and I had resigned myself to choosing between two avenues, knowing there was a good chance I would resent whatever decision I made forever. When Beverly Neilson had sat on the couch and talked to me, there was a connection between the two of us I hadn't asked for. The woman was silly and consumed and caring all at the same time, and while she didn't know it she might soon become a grandmother. This she would never know, of course. No one would ever know it as a pure fact. If I decided to get rid of the baby once and for all, nobody, except Old Evans and Verna, would be the wiser and I could get on with my life, whatever that meant.

The old man was cagey and prescient at the same time. I had ordered a jumbo-sized bottle of vitamin C and also a bunch of parsley, since no one at the grocery store had heard of parsley tea. We both knew everything I needed was sitting on the windowsill above the sink and all I had to do was tell him it was time to get on with it.

"I like my workbench a lot," I said while we were eating supper.

"Good. I'm happy it worked out."

"I don't really like this liver, do you?" Both of us had eaten some of it. Both plates had treats for the dog left on them.

"I can eat it but it would be easier if I could plug my nose. No offense, mind you."

"Verna says liver once a week is something I should cook up. She says it's a good source of iron."

"It probably is," Old Evans said.

"Maybe I'll cook liver twice a year instead of once a week. What do you think?"

"You won't get an argument from me. The insides of a pig are a pig's business."

"I think these are from cows."

"Pigs. Cows. I'd give them both the benefit of the doubt."

"Thank goodness we have chocolate cake from Beverly."

"I don't eat cake as a rule," he said. "But after that liver I think I'll join you. It's been more than a year since I've eaten any, so make it a good-sized piece if you don't mind."

I made a pot of tea for myself and a cup of hot water for Arthur Evans. We sat at the kitchen table eating our cake and trying to think about the cake we were eating. It was, as Beverly suggested, thick and smooth, but we both knew the dessert was a temporary diversion.

"Would you like a second piece?" I asked.

"No, I'd better see how this one settles first. You going to eat another?"

"No I'm not and I'm not going to abort my pregnancy either."

"You're sure about that?"

"As sure as I can be about something like this. I've thought about it, like you suggested. There isn't a right decision to be made."

"Nothing we decide is ever a hundred percent good or bad. A good number of my bad decisions had a streak of goodness running through them I realize now, but at the time I couldn't see it that way. It's easy to pin our hopes on part of something only to see that something disappear."

"So you think I've made the right choice?"

"I can't be the judge of that. People on the sidelines will judge you, be sure of it, but you've given it serious thought, so my guess is things will work out all right. Which brings me to a question I have to ask. If one were to build you a crib for down the road, what colour crib would you want?"

"You'd build me a crib?"

"Well I wouldn't be worried about the colour if I wasn't going to make the damn thing. What do you say?"

I said, "That's an important decision. I'll need a couple of days to consider it."

⁓⁓⁓⁓

Verna came the next day and was satisfied when liver was mentioned. The house was like grand central station with two customers picking up clocks and one delivering a box full of clock pieces. I had renewed the ad my father had always run in the *Leader*, only I changed it to say discount for seniors. Most of my customers were elderly anyway, and if I upped my prices ten percent and gave them ten percent off, they were thrilled.

Old Evans agreed I could bring my coveted Junghans clock over and pin it to the living room wall. The first few nights he woke every half hour when it signalled the time, but now it was background noise and he was able to sleep. I felt at home working away with the rhythmic ticking, a sound that mimicked my own heartbeat and, I supposed, a second heartbeat as well. He also agreed I could bring the TV over. It was heavy, so he paid the grocery boy an extra large tip and I helped him. My father had arranged two antennas, a large one that protruded twenty-five feet into the air from the top of the roof, and a smaller one that sat on a pole on the ground. I wasn't about to mess with the large antenna, but I got the small one set up on the south side of the house and channel 12 and channel 4 were watchable. The first night Arthur Evans came and sat on the couch beside me and watched *Mr. Ed*. He said it was interesting and went back to bed to read.

Once the decision to accept being pregnant had been made I began to view the world differently. I put more energy into keeping up the house for the old man. The floors were washed, the bathtub cleaned, the kitchen drawers emptied and scoured. First thing every morning I went out to the workshop and got the stove going so it would be comfortable when he set to work. I had a lot to learn and just when I was reluctantly considering a trip to the library (I hadn't been back for months, wary of running into Graham Puckett). Verna brought a small library of books about the lives of expectant mothers.

"My daughter found these useful when she realized she was pregnant. She's read most of them twice, so help yourself. Don't fret too much about the chapter on swollen ankles. Cut back on your salt and you'll be fine."

"Guess what? He's going to make me a crib. I never thought that far ahead, but of course a baby needs somewhere to sleep."

"I know. He told me. He's excited about it. My daughter slept in the same crib I did and my grandchild will do the same. His will be special, you can count on that. Maybe you'll pass it on to generations in your family."

The thought of a child was alarming on its own, without contemplating a family down the road and future generations. Being inside my head was a troublesome place and one thing I was thankful for was that Verna had no notion of the abortion debate that had been raging inside me for the last seven days.

Verna stayed for lunch that included a good-sized piece of chocolate cake, mostly so there would be less for Arthur Evans to eat. Old people tend to crave sweets, she told me, but someone his age shouldn't make it a habit.

There hadn't been one thing I had asked of Old Evans that had been refused. This I found puzzling. My father was very good to me and had provided me with most everything I needed, but there were requests I'd made of him that were flatly denied and left no room for argument. Together, we had been to the movie theatre a handful of times, mostly Saturday matinees in the winter. He forbade me the right to stay in town on a Saturday night and go to a movie on my own. There was a time when I asked if I could join Girl Guides (the thought of it repulsed me now) but my father said there was no point in wearing a uniform and learning to obey other people's rules. Except for the one family we saw occasionally in Youbou, my interaction with others was restricted to clerks in stores or customers that infrequently came to our house. Anything that gave off the aroma of freedom and independence was a foul smell to my father, and because the confines of my upbringing had been narrow it was all the more staggering when Old Evans made a proposal to me that night after supper.

"Did your dad ever teach you to drive a car?"

"No. I asked but he said it was complicated. It doesn't look all that complicated."

"You're going to have to learn how sometime. Now would be good. Soon, you'll have more than enough to keep you busy. Is your dad's old car an automatic?"

"It has a stick shift. That's the part he said was complicated."

The plan that came spilling out of his mouth had obviously been rehearsed. The next day he shuffled painstakingly down the driveway and across the road to the auto wreckers and found Red Neilson on his way out to the back. He explained that I was looking for a car, an automatic, and had a 1958 Volkswagen Van for trade. If he had something suitable to swap we would consider it, otherwise we would head into town. The next day, Red Neilson pulled a 1952 Plymouth up to the door and said he could see making the trade if a hundred bucks were thrown in since he could only use the Volkswagen for parts. We took it for a drive up to the Tansor store with Red Neilson behind the wheel, and when we returned, Old Evans said it was a deal so long as four new tires were put on the car. The ones on there now, he said, were slick as a baby's bum. Red Neilson agreed, though everyone understood any tires he put on wouldn't be new, just better, and the transaction was complete by mid-afternoon.

"An automatic is easy," Old Evans told me. "Just press on the gas when you want to go and press on the brake when you want to stop. Stay on your own side of the road and that's about it."

Getting in a vehicle was a slow process for the old man. He had to open the door, back himself in, swing his legs around, and secure his canes. Getting out he needed someone to pull him to his feet, but he was committed to teaching me and sat looking out the windshield while I fiddled with everything in front of me.

"Forget about the radio for now. Just start it up. Hear that? Now put her in drive and touch the gas pedal and make sure you hit the brake before you get to the end of the driveway."

I did as instructed. The car sat there wondering what was next.

"Do I back it up now?"

"Let's worry about moving forward for the time being. I see we're low on gas, which doesn't surprise me with Red Neilson being the seller. Turn right and we'll head down to Berkey's corner and fill her up."

"Are you sure I should do this?"

"Of course I'm sure. A car won't run without gas."

I was nervous and thrilled at the prospect of driving on an actual road. I stared out the windshield the whole time, trying to judge my position between the dotted line and where the road met the gravel. Old Evans never said a word on the way there, but I could see his grasp on his cane jog from side to side as I made my adjustments to the lane that was mine.

We got eight dollars and forty cents worth of gas, which filled the tank. He insisted I turn right, toward town, and since I hadn't hit anything so far, I obeyed. We drove down the hill into the old part of town known as Chinatown and he had me pull up beside the government building that looked like it could topple over in a strong wind.

"I think this is where you got to go. There should be an office in there called motor vehicles. Tell them you need the book to study so you can pass your test. Don't dally around. They close in ten minutes."

I was back in no time and felt flustered. "What are we going to do now?"

"We'll head back home, I suspect."

"They said I'm not allowed to drive, even if you're with me, until I pass my learner's permit. That's the guy I talked to in the second floor window. He's staring at us."

"That's his job to tell you that. Just wait a few minutes. They close soon and knowing government workers like I do, he'll be putting on his coat any minute now."

We waited, and as Old Evans predicted, the man disappeared from the window.

"Okay, now there's nothing much to driving backwards. It's the same as going forward only it's the wrong way. Stick it in reverse and go slow. Turn the wheel that way, sharp. That's it. Now stop. Okay, back into drive, find the right lane and stay there until we get home."

I hugged the right side of the road all the way which made him nervous, I could tell, but he didn't say anything. Progress was slow and a man in a truck behind us started beeping at me to get a move on. Without warning, I turned right, down a side street.

"Where you going?"

"Around the block. By the time I get back on the Lake Road that idiot will be gone."

We got home without incident, except that I misjudged the distance between the bumper and the garbage can at the back of the house and knocked it over.

"Wow. I did it. Thank you so much. I'm learning to drive. I never thought I'd learn to drive on my own."

"You did all right for your first time. You need a good deal of practice but we'll get there. The hard part is learning to park and the hand signals they make you do. Just don't hit anything and study that book. Next week we'll schedule a time and you can write the test. Once you get the hang of it you can pick up the groceries yourself whenever you need them. Baby needs to get a checkup you can go on your own some day. I might even get you to drive me to visit some friends. I just have to think if any of them are still around."

43

WHAT CHRISTMAS MEANT EVERY YEAR in Tansor was anybody's guess and most took a stab at it. This one came on the heels of a year with no labour disruptions in the forest industry and only a week and a half lost due to fire season. All of this carved a path for those willing to embrace optimism, a guarded journey at best, and then came the middle of December when heavy snow carpeted the valley and the surrounding mountains, effectively shutting down much of the valley's industry and the confidence of those who fed off nature's harvest. It could last a week or two, maybe until just after Christmas, but it could also last until early February as it had two years earlier.

Families were caught between the weatherman's tentative predictions and the allure of the Eaton's catalogue. Had the heavy snow not come as early as it had, Gerry Jagger might have been able to negotiate an electric train set that had been on his Christmas wish list for three years running, Daisy Neilson might have realized the manicure kit and guide book she had taken a liking to and Milo would have received a substantial gift of some kind that would have depended on timing: he pointed out something new he wanted for Christmas on a daily basis. But now the two-week snows that could turn into eight-week snows had changed expectations and it began to feel like every other Christmas in memory.

The connection between the accumulating snow pack and the vaporizing of Christmas dreams was pretty obvious to children of all ages, but its reality was tempered when the snow offered such luxurious activity. By now every house had one or two snowmen that were always built facing the house and with their backs to the Lake Road. Thermometers were studied rigorously and afternoons when the mercury climbed above 32 degrees Fahrenheit, the hopes of school being cancelled were given a severe blow. One day of school had been missed already, but it was because the boiler at the school had broken down.

Christmas trees were plucked out of the woods by the middle of December, and every year several were extricated from the twenty-five acres Old Evans owned south of the railroad tracks. Mrs. Eaton was busy setting up her crèche, something she had done for as many years as she could remember and there had been some years when she was the only one to view it. Ernie Jagger let Bonnie and Gerry look after the Christmas tree, and he ran a string of red Christmas lights along the inside of his chicken coop. He had done this for three years running and for some unknown reason his egg production increased because of it, right in the middle of winter. Christmas was a time for standing back from the bustle of life, a time of contemplation, however short a time it received, and as a result none of the remaining Neilsons were looking forward to the season that was suddenly upon them. Beverly Neilson helped Daisy set up the tree under the scrutiny of Red Neilson in his easy chair, a tree that filled the corner of the living room as usual, but this year the tree was not adorned with a blue star at the top. That was the one job Kurt had always completed and, without any discussion, they all understood this would be the ritual from this day forward until Kurt returned home to change it.

Hanne and her father had always put up a small tree weeded from the shoulders of the railway tracks. Most years Arthur Lemmons had taken his daughter down to Eatons department store early in December and asked her what she thought of this dress or that blouse, then went back the following Saturday and purchased several that had caught her eye. Christmas had always been a sad time of year for both of them because it was when their circle of family was most obviously incomplete.

Christmas for Old Evans was a change in the music played on the radio and not much else. Hanne listened to his version of what Christmas would mean and retrieved the decorations from her house to make things festive. The only logical place for a tree was the living room where she slept so she set it up near the entrance so he could see it as he shuffled to and from his bedroom. The crib he was working on was obviously going to be her Christmas present this year and she monitored its progress every morning when she lit the stove.

Mr. May had liberated himself from anything honouring Christmas since he was a young man. He viewed the fuss made by others as foolish, needlessly commercial, devoid of spiritual connection and a complete waste of time. The only thing that came close to ritual this time of year was a package of dog bones he could get for free from the butcher because everyone else had turned their attention to turkeys. He made soup with them first and Lenin got to gnaw on what was left over.

44

DESPITE THE FACT THAT MOST of my clothes didn't fit, there were large tracts of time when I felt great. My days were so full I had no time to dwell on my sinister past. I didn't have a lot of money but after I had passed my learner's test, Verna was willing to accompany me on trips around town and I bought Old Evans a new level for Christmas because the one he owned was broken. My driving stints had petered out with the heavy snow, but I was confident I could pass a driving test once I got the chance. The smallest turkey I could find was ten pounds, and when I was finished with Christmas dinner the old man said it was the best turkey he'd ever eaten. I didn't believe for a minute mine was the best out of eighty-seven turkeys but I didn't say anything.

The crib was the most meaningful Christmas present I'd ever received. It was sitting in the workshop, airing out. Because I couldn't decide what colour to paint it, he'd decided not to paint it at all, but stain and varnish it with three coats. Each side had seven spindles, turned on the lathe, so the baby could see out, and he placed a decal of a stork delivering a baby on one end. Not once had he inquired about the baby's father, so perhaps a stork was fitting.

I had finished up as many clocks as I could before Christmas arrived, partly because my customers demanded it and partly so I would have some extra money for Christmas. I was busy with other matters once the calendar had been turned over to

January because Old Evans had convinced me it was best to finish off my correspondence courses before the baby arrived. I knew he was right and it felt good to have someone tell me what to do.

The weather mellowed halfway through the first two months of the year and I was eager to have my driver's license behind me. Verna had been helpful, but was busy with the pending birth of her first grandchild, so Arthur Evans accompanied me to the appointment on a Wednesday afternoon. He insisted on sitting in the back seat while the test took place, despite the examiner's repeated announcements that this was not possible, and it may have been his presence that earned me a pass because it took me three times to parallel park successfully and I nearly hit a dog that darted across Canada Avenue.

"I can't believe he passed me," I said, my temporary license firmly in both hands.

"I wouldn't worry. You don't need to park that way in a town this size. Just keep an eye out for dogs. Dogs don't know any better than to be dogs."

I was used to living in seclusion and in my present state in life I was comforted by the fact that I could continue with my customary mode of existence living with Old Evans. He was independent by nature and busy in his shop most of the time, but with the advent of the car he was the one to embrace the opportunity to get out from time to time. He had a pair of electric hair clippers at home and Verna would run the machine around his ears three or four times a year, customarily at her suggestion. It had been years since he'd gone to a real barbershop, and on a whim late in February that was his desire one Saturday afternoon. I sat and read magazines while he got his haircut, a shave, and the small hairs that sprouted from his ears trimmed back. I asked him if there was anywhere else he wanted to go, but he said no, that was enough adventure for one day. We stopped at a second-hand bookstore to satisfy my penchant for reading and allow me to avoid the library and Graham Puckett. It was a perfect outing for both of us until we stopped off at Berkey's Corner for a can of snuff the delivery boy had forgotten.

I went up to the counter to place my order and the lady had to go to the back to find it. When I turned my head to the left I noticed Robbie Tweedie sitting at the counter sucking away at a strawberry milkshake. We wordlessly exchanged stares until Robbie offered to say hi. I said hi back. I could see by the look on his face that he was bewildered. I hadn't seen him, not even walking down the road, for four months, and I knew he was taking in my present condition.

"I'm joining the navy," he said. "I'm going away in two weeks today."

It was impossible to tell if he was pleased with his announcement and proud to be going or if he was offering the proclamation as news I might want to hear. "Okay," I said.

The clerk came back with the snuff. It was the right name brand but the can was the wrong colour. I wasn't about to have her disappear to the back again so I opened my purse to pay, and when I did the bell over the door chimed and Mr. May walked in with his gunny sack of coins. He tipped his hat to all present and went to the dog food section.

"I don't imagine this snuff is for someone in your condition," the clerk said. "They're starting to say things about pregnant women smoking, so I don't imagine chewing this god-awful stuff would be any better. You don't appear to be too far along."

"Four months."

Four months. In my present company it sounded like a death sentence. Mr. May turned away from the cans of dog food to observe me. I gathered my purse and thanked the lady and when I turned toward the door it had been opened already. It had been opened by Lodie Stump.

I had seen Lodie driving into town often in a truck that now ran as smoothly as her expensive time piece, thanks to my father, but I'd never run into her in person. I couldn't believe what I was seeing.

"Well, will you look at that?" the clerk said. "I've worked here for three years and I don't believe I've ever had two pregnant women in the store at the same time."

I slid by Lodie and got to the car. I wanted to drive up the Lake Road and I wasn't in the mood for interruptions. I told Arthur Evans I would cook dinner but it would be later. I needed some time to myself.

The old man had mentioned a can of snuff earlier in the week and I omitted it when I phoned the order in. It was because of my own doing that we had stopped at Berkey's Corner and now my world was a different colour. I wasn't the only pregnant woman in the valley, Lodie Stump was too, and by the look of things she was as far along as I was and that pointed directly at my father. The woman lived close enough to yell at across the acreage and she was carrying around inside her what would become my half-brother or half-sister. It had to be, and because Robbie Tweedie lived the other side of the gravel pit I had hoped I would never again see his face, but we did meet, and by the look on that face he knew I was pregnant and would assume he knew how it came about. Would he have anything to gain by telling the world? Surely having been there that fateful night he would have more to lose by letting anyone know how he came to my house with a friend who had his way with me and that he had done nothing to prevent it from happening. He was leaving in two weeks to join the navy. Maybe he had mentioned it for a reason.

45

TWO FLAT TIRES IN ONE week had never happened to him before. Mr. May patched one, then replaced the back tire that was nearly worn down to the inner tube. He needed his bicycle more than ever now and regretted the delay caused by its upkeep.

The snow had stopped falling but refused to go away. The roads were mostly bare and traversable; he pushed his bicycle through the winter's accumulation of a foot and a half of snow that surrounded the house ever since Lodie Stump had taken to parking close to the Lake Road and hadn't employed a shovel. She was a woman who hadn't received a visitor for months, based on the pristine covering of snow, and she answered the knock on her front door to find Mr. May shivering in a black overcoat.

"Do you mind if I come in for a minute? It's freezing."

Lodie didn't answer but opened the door and let him in. She watched him remove a pair of threadbare gloves that offered protection for his knuckles but not much more.

"I didn't realize you were about to have a baby," he said.

"Well you know now. What about it?"

Mr. May stuffed his forlorn gloves into his coat pockets. "Well, it got me to thinking. Your being pregnant did, of the Neilson boy."

"And what the hell would a missing boy have to do with me being pregnant?"

"There's a theory out there. About why he went missing."

"Look, I don't know what kind of theories you're peddling this time of year but they're not welcome around here. You communists can come up with some zany arguments but this one tops them all."

"It has nothing to do with communist doctrine, its just — "

"It's just nuts is what it is. Don't move. Stay right where you are."

Lodie Stump went into the bedroom closet and came back with a black and white scarf. "Here, take this with you. It used to belong to someone and I don't want it around. And give your theories some thought before you spew them around the neighbourhood. Try to think like a normal person."

He passed the driveway that led to the Lemmons' property and the snow in the driveway that hadn't been disturbed since the first storm. It seemed a shame to leave a good house like that empty, a better house than the one he lived in. He could see smoke trailing out of Old Evans' workshop and the car was parked beside the house so he knew he would have Hanne to interrogate all to himself. He felt rebuffed by the reception Lodie Stump had given him and was determined to dance a jig around his next conversation, at least for a minute or two.

Hanne didn't see him make his way up the driveway and didn't hear him knocking on the door; the old man was busy mornings, and afternoons she had taken to listening to the radio while she worked. After spending most of her life in silence, sprinkled with the ticking of innumerable clocks, her preference was to blast the radio as loudly as she could without disturbing Old Evans in his workshop. She was immersed in her clock repair and belting out her accompaniment to "I Want To Hold Your Hand" when she turned and jumped at the sight of Mr. May standing by the living room door holding his new scarf in his hands.

"Sorry. I knocked as hard as I could but the radio was on."

"What is it you want?"

"Just a neighbourly visit. I was wondering how you were making out living here with old Doc Evans."

Hanne turned the radio off. She was ready for some tea and made her way past her bewildered visitor. She supposed if she made tea she should offer him some. The tea-drinking interval would at least offer parameters for the length of his visit.

"This must be a good place to live. You've got some company and Old Evans has a deep well."

Hanne turned her attention from the teapot to her visitor. Being social, especially in the company of a wizened old man like Mr. May, was something she had to work at. "No problems with water so far as I can tell. The company's not bad either. He's an interesting character with a thousand stories to tell."

Hanne didn't ask if he wanted tea. She poured him a cup. There was sugar and milk on the table if he wanted it. Mr. May always smelled musty when she'd been around him in the summertime, but after a winter of being cooped up in his cabin it was a pungent sour odour he gave off.

"I guess you don't know if it's a boy or a girl?" he asked.

"No clue."

"I knew a lady once who could suspend a wedding ring on a thread over a pregnant belly and tell you boy or girl. She swore she was right a hundred percent of the time. That was a long time ago, mind you. And a different place. She's probably dead now."

The diminutive figure across the table from Hanne was a conundrum. He'd lived alone for as long as she had been in the valley and people either hated him or were suspicious of his nature.

"I guess you have your dog for company?"

"Lenin doesn't do much anymore. He's getting old like me."

Hanne desperately wanted to ask how old he was but knew some people found the question a violation. He had to be close to sixty, maybe more. He was one of the smallest full-grown men she'd ever known and he looked like he needed to be fed.

"Is life okay for you?" she asked. "Do you look back and think your life could have been better?"

"Life can always be better. My problem is I was born at the wrong time and the wrong place. I know how life could be good but it's hard to do by myself."

"You mean we all should be communists? Is that what you mean?"

"When you spend most of your life just thinking about yourself like most people these days, it doesn't lead anywhere. You either get what you want and step on someone doing it or you don't get what you want and feel miserable. That doesn't sound good to me. And besides, a lot of rich people lead guilty lives."

"My dad didn't like you much."

"Most people don't."

"He said taking over another country was always temporary. Like what Russia has done to parts of Europe."

213

Mr. May helped himself to a second cup of tea and unbuttoned his coat. His house only got this hot in the middle of summer.

"Well, your father has a point. The Russians were only trying to show people the way. They're not the only ones to take over another country. People have to decide for themselves in the end. So, they haven't found a trace of the Neilson boy. That's what I heard."

"Apparently not. "

"He's running away from something. Something he couldn't handle staying here. Does that sound like the truth to you?"

"I have no idea. I suppose it's possible."

"People have ideas. Some say he might have run away from owning up to being a father."

"You the one saying it or someone else?"

"I'm just saying it's an idea swimming around out there. The Neilson boy goes missing and two females in the valley are four months pregnant four months later. You can see why people might wonder about that."

"I could never figure out, growing up, why my dad didn't think much of you. I've got a ton of work to do and don't care to discuss what these *people* of yours might be thinking. I've got my own life to live and I suggest you get on with yours."

"Somebody knows what happened to that boy and I'll find the truth in time. I don't plan on giving up until I do. You make a good pot of tea, I'll say that much."

46

ARTHUR EVANS KNEW SOMETHING was bothering me, and while he seldom made unsolicited overtures into my personal saga, he did ask one night over supper how I was making out.

"Fine," I said. "Just a little tired I guess. There's more of me to pack around these days."

He looked at me over his reading glasses as if to suggest that was not the whole truth, and of course, it wasn't. Two weeks after running into Robbie Tweedie at Berkey's Corner, I made an excuse to drive into town by myself. I told him I had some shopping to do and I needed to be alone because I was considering what to get him for his birthday. The old man was turning eighty-eight in less than two weeks and I had to get him something. I parked in the Commercial Hotel parking lot where I could keep an eye on the train platform. The train on its way to Victoria passed through about 3:15 and if he wasn't boarding the train, there was a bus heading the same direction at 4:30. Just before three o'clock the Borden's grey Hillman pulled up to the station and Robbie got out with a small suitcase in hand. It wasn't the kind of departure I expected to witness; Hoxie gave him a hug and Slick shook his hand before the two of them quickly piled into the car and drove away. As soon as it was obvious Robbie was leaving town I should have been satisfied and departed myself, but I stood across the railway tracks, transfixed, and eventually Robbie came out of the station, ticket in hand, and stared at me staring back at him. The train sounded its horn, crossing James Street by the water tower, and was soon wedged between us. I waved haltingly to Robbie and he waved back. I was in the car and on the road before the train headed south.

I drove down Canada Avenue, past a couple of drunks feigning interest in starting a fight on the sidewalk in front of the Tzouhalem Hotel. The few people still in town late on Saturday walked around them without serious interest. I parked across the street from Eatons and it took me a minute to realize why I was there. Robbie Tweedie had left town and he hadn't said anything to anyone as far as I could tell, and who knew how long he would be gone. Unless he came back to visit his aunt and uncle he may have left for good. There was a mannequin in the showcase window of Eatons, the finely cut figure of a male who looked like he might hold down a job as a file clerk but was dressed in work pants and a startlingly blue-checkered work shirt that caught my eye. Arthur Evans had light blue eyes that still sparkled when he laughed and in the cold weather he only had two other shirts he wore alternately: it was the perfect gift. I had the clerk put the shirt in a box and then, perhaps buoyed by the knowledge that Robbie Tweedie was no longer around, I started to envision a birthday the old man would never forget. If I suggested a party he would rule out the possibility immediately, so I decided I would plan one without his knowing. It had likely been years since anyone had baked him a birthday cake.

I was still preoccupied with the fact that Mr. May was running around the neighbourhood almost certainly sharing his theory with everyone he met. He had nothing to go on that I was aware of but his prodding sent my mind into a tizzy. The only sound sleep I was getting was late at night and into the early morning, often after Arthur Evans was up and eating his porridge. A partial dream that kept reoccurring saw me standing trial for the murder of Kurt Neilson and the only part I could ever remember was my taking the stand and giving testimony. My guilt felt like a foregone conclusion because I had apparently admitted to the deed. There were times when I wanted my mind clear so badly I thought about what it would mean to drive down to the police station and tell them everything, but the consequences I envisioned were not likely to be in my favour despite the story I had to tell. I had no idea what they would do to someone convicted of a horrible crime if they were female and expecting a child in a few months. I had a little someone inside me to consider and that was what I did.

My father always said if too many good things happen in a row you had better be prepared for the roof the cave in. I was soon to learn that when life becomes as predictable as the sequence of telephone poles at the side of the road, then something was bound to come along to stir things up. My mundane life was built around helping the old man, looking out for my health, fixing clocks, and waiting. Waiting for the birth that I knew would change my life but I didn't know how. I finished up my last two correspondence courses and Arthur Evans was as happy as I'd seen him. He insisted we go out to dinner to celebrate and he wouldn't take no for an answer. We went to Cecil's Café and he ordered meatloaf and I had a hamburger with remarkable caramelized onions. I considered the evening a success because we didn't run into anyone we knew.

The one thing I had planned to break the monotony was his party and it turned out to be a complete flop. Mrs. Eaton may have been too shy but she never came. Ernie Jagger may have felt rebuffed because I abandoned his church but neither he nor his kids attended. Mr. May likely didn't show up because of the way I had invited him to leave on his last visit, and Lodie Stump I didn't invite, but she wouldn't have considered it anyway, so that left one guest, Beverly Neilson, who brought him a card and a lace handkerchief, a complete surprise the way it was cleverly wrapped in an elongated rectangular box. Verna was busy that evening but she did drop by in the afternoon with a box of oranges. He loved the shirt I bought him and he put in on immediately. Because he didn't know I had invited so many who didn't show, he was overwhelmed with the attention given to attaining the grand age of eighty-eight and the size of the cake presented. It wasn't until after Beverly went home that he told me he had one ritual every time his birthday caught up with him. In a cupboard above the sink he had some brandy and he asked me to pour him some. I didn't want any, though he offered, and I poured his glass half full. There was so little left he said I might as well fill it up. He drank half the glass and asked me to put the rest on the table beside his bed because he figured if he drank it all at once he wouldn't be able to make it there. No one in his family acknowledged Arthur Evans' birthday, though his daughter did send a card that arrived two days late. Once he got himself settled, I cleaned up the kitchen, and though it didn't last long, I could hear him in the bedroom singing songs I'd never heard on the radio.

The next morning I slept in and when I got up he was still in bed. He said he didn't feel like working in the shop and thought he would read instead. I checked on him a couple of times and he slept until mid-afternoon, got up to use the washroom and then went back to bed. His dog with no name was used to his routine and expected to be outside by mid-morning so I dragged him by the collar and let him outside for an hour. When Arthur finally woke up again I brought him supper to eat in bed but he barely touched it.

I kept an eye on him but didn't phone Verna because her next scheduled visit was the following day. She arrived and I met her at the door to give her an update and it was like she left the land of the living; her demeanor and focus changed and she spent the next hour with him in his room. When she came out she said he was exhausted, but that all his vital signs were steady. I told her about his birthday ritual of a dose of brandy and she practically had a fit. She asked where his liquor cabinet was and I pointed to the cupboard above the sink and told her he had finished off the last of his supply.

"His constitution is a delicate balance, Hanne. I've seen this movie before, believe me. Their birthday rolls around and they revert back to being twenty-one. If he ever orders more brandy you let me know right away. I'll threaten this adolescent behaviour out of him if I have to."

Verna changed his bandages but left his bath to a later date. He was simply too weak to handle any more. She left but phoned every day for the next week to hear me report that he had been up for a few hours to eat, that he slept most of the day and night but was in remarkably good spirits. One day he did shuffle out to his workshop but was back in the kitchen table two hours later. That was the first time I'd seen such a defeated look on his face that seemed to say he knew he had taken one step closer to the grave.

∾∾∾

For the next several months I was in a survival mode that consumed my energy and felt tedious, but I was getting closer to the big day and it was as if I couldn't remember as far back as the birthday party. Most days Arthur Evans made it out of bed, but when he wanted to sleep in I made sure his dog was up and out of the house. One morning I went to grab him by the collar and as soon as I did I could tell the dog was dead. I looked up from the dog to the bed and the old man obviously knew and had been crying.

"Poor old dog," I said. I didn't know what else to say about a stinky animal I had no liking for but was obviously the old man's longtime companion. "I'll take him out back and bury him if that's what you want me to do." Arthur Evans was unable to speak but he nodded his head. It took me a long time to drag him out to the side of the workshop that was without windows. For some reason Milo was not in school that day but was standing in front of his house bouncing a tennis ball onto the road and catching it again, and he saw me out there with a shovel in my hands, struggling over my girth to dig a hole, and came over to where I was working. He didn't say anything but took the shovel from me and dug a decent-sized grave for the dog. He helped me slide him into the hole and he arranged his ears neatly at the side of his head and spread his legs at a slight angle so that it looked like he was taking a nap and not dead at all. He placed his tennis ball beside the dog's muzzle and then patted him gently on the head for a long time before he stood up and began to fill the hole back in.

"Tootsie Pop?" he said when the job was completed.

I didn't have anything like a Tootsie Pop in the house. I ruffled my hand over the short hair on his head and he seemed to understand there would be no treat coming his way.

❧❧❧

Nothing much changed for two months. Arthur Evans was not his active self until a temporary reprieve in June, when he spent most of two days in the shop and was enthused about his plans to build a rocking horse. I had never even seen a real rocking horse, only pictures, but he thought every kid should have one. This burst of energy was followed by days mostly bedridden and Verna started coming Mondays and Thursdays to monitor things. I spent time at his bedside in the evenings before he fell asleep; he was a man who could pull stories up from his past and there seemed to be no end to them.

"What's the worst thing you've ever done?" I asked him one night. It occurred to me that most of his stories, while filled with drama and often conflict, always came out with a satisfactory solution, more or less. Once the words fell out of my mouth I regretted asking. The question was too pointed toward personal indictment for anyone to ask without ill intent. I watched his reaction and was certain he was going to say he was too tired to talk anymore and needed to rest. There were thoughts chasing other thoughts inside his head and he was deciding which ones he might consider letting out.

"I did one thing in my life that I regret and can't take back. It was a mistake and a big one. I was on night surveillance duty during the war. It was the First World War and we were in France and there hadn't been much action for several days. Canadian troops had successfully broken through the Hindenburg Line and the altercations were sporadic and spread out after that. The war was coming to an end, though we didn't know that as a sure fact, it was just something that became common judgement. Our battalion was worn down, tired and on edge and I had been feeling sick for a few days. Others were not well either so when it was my turn for duty I carried on when what I should have done was confessed the state of my health and risked the ridicule it might have earned me. Anyway, sometime after midnight, I can't judge what time it might have been, I broke out in a fierce sweat and started hallucinating. By the time I realized I needed help it was too late because I was too weak to even speak let alone retrace my steps. My focus was on trying to stay awake in case the enemy mustered an attack but I passed out and only a day later, lying on a makeshift bed beside several wounded soldiers, did I find out what happened. The enemy had engineered an offensive just before dawn and three men in our platoon were killed as a result. It had been my job to alert the troops of any hint of aggression and I wasn't there when they needed me. Three men died because of my mistake."

"How did *you* manage to survive?" I asked.

"I have no idea, really. I guess I was unconscious and face down and not found until the next afternoon. Everyone thought I was dead so maybe the enemy did too. I wasn't wounded of course, so it was obvious to everyone that it was my negligence that caused the tragedy. I was taken out of active duty once I got my strength back but the war was over before anything came of it. I remember to this day the faces of the three men who died. I don't even remember their names but I remember their faces. They never had a chance to grow old like me."

Verna suggested I attend a series of birthing classes but I only went once to a church hall where the class was full of beaming young couples filled with high expectations, and me. There was one other woman by herself but she kept staring at her hands, respectfully, like they were the only part of her that hadn't undergone a huge transformation, and she didn't want to talk to anyone unless she had to. It was too much, and after one session I thought I would stick to the library of books

Verna had loaned me. I was shuffling around the kitchen on a Wednesday, preparing to make the morning porridge, when my water broke. Arthur Evans said to phone Verna right away but I decided to make my own way in the car.

I thought I'd drive up and they'd put me in a room and within an hour the baby would pop out and it would be done with, but it took more than an hour for them to check me in and another hour before a doctor appeared and examined me. I insisted they phone Verna Miller, the transient nurse, because Arthur Evans was home alone and hadn't had breakfast. They found me a bed in a room with three other women and gave me some magazines to read and said the baby was obviously not ready yet and I should try to relax. I wished, then, that I had phoned Verna. Not that I expected her to drop all her patients and sit at my bedside holding my hand, but I would have welcomed her reassuring voice. The nurses I had contact with were all business and I was clearly nothing more than another birthing machine in the assembly line. I read every magazine they owned and spent the afternoon staring out at the blue sky I wanted so much to stand under. About six-thirty my contractions made steady progress and at eight-thirty I gave birth to a baby boy. It felt like all the turmoil and misery I had experienced in my entire life was consolidated in the final hour before he was born. The pain was excruciating and it felt like there was a knife down there carving his exit. When it was finally over, one of the nurses commented it had been one of the easiest first babies she'd ever seen delivered.

"Have you decided what you're going to call him?" the head nurse asked me. When I told her the truth, that I hadn't given it much thought, she looked at me with such disappointment I felt like a visitor from another planet and I had to look away or I knew I would start to cry. Had it been a girl I would have called her Eva after my mother, but a boy was a consequence I hadn't expected.

When the nurse brought the baby back for feeding I was emotionally overcome in a way I hadn't contemplated. He was a greedy little bugger and so reliant on me that I felt like a completely different person, as if Hanne Lemmons was someone who had existed but no longer did. He kept his eyes closed almost the whole time, so intent was he on getting his fill. He opened one eye briefly like he was winking at me to confirm an embryonic relationship I could never turn my back on.

The next morning Verna was my first visitor. My little boy was swaddled in the bed beside me at my request and she was a geyser of emotion, congratulating me in such a way that made the birth feel like it had been a lifelong dream. A teddy bear outfitted with a blue top and blue shorts she propped up on the pillow beside me. I had a hunch it was going to be a boy, she told me, though she admitted she did check at admissions before she bought it. Only after her monologue dissipated and I asked after Arthur Evans did her demeanor change.

The day before she had gone to visit him and he was so weak he could hardly speak. She called an ambulance immediately, overcoming his objections in doing so, and he was admitted and in stable condition on the second floor of the hospital.

"He's still awfully weak, but the first thing he wanted to know was how you made out," she said. "I knew you had a little boy so I told him and he looked very peaceful when I gave him the news."

"What are the doctors saying?" I asked.

"Well, like doctors tend to be, they're pretty tight-lipped. His heartbeat is irregular, apparently, but they have him on medication to try to even things out. I think at this point all we can do is hope for the best."

The nurses told me I would likely be confined to the hospital for a week and I objected immediately. I wanted to go home as soon as possible, but I wanted Arthur Evans to be there like he had always been. They said it was best to get back into the swing of things at a snail's pace: get up slowly three or four times a day to use the washroom, read magazines and try to relax. Visiting hours were between 6:00 and 8:00 in the evening but I had no visitors and didn't expect any. After feeding my little guy and eating the most bizarre gruel that made Arthur Evans' porridge look like a palatial meal, I took the elevator down to the second floor and asked where he was staying. I was told Arthur Evans was not well enough to accept visitors just yet, so I explained I was his daughter, admitted in maternity, and I just wanted to look in on him, not disturb him in any way. As soon as I made my plea I realized I should have said granddaughter; the nurse didn't look at all convinced and said she didn't feel comfortable with the notion but told me his room number and instructed me to keep the visit short and not wake him up.

There was an opening in the curtain drawn around his bed and he was hooked up to an intravenous bag half-filled with a clear liquid that menacingly looked like his only hope for salvation. His arms were at his sides and his whiskered face was slightly elevated. I gently stroked the mottled skin on the back of his hand but he didn't seem to notice. I waited there for more than half an hour and I whispered in his ear, telling him about my baby boy and how he was such a good eater. I wished I'd brought something to leave on the side table to let him know I had been there, but I had nothing. I got up from my chair and started to leave. I looked back one more time and his eyes were opened, though his face didn't turn to take me in.

"Arthur, it's me, Hanne."

When I spoke to him, he blinked his eyes and I could swear the muscles on one side of his face twitched. I kept talking to him and what I had to say I had pondered for two days and I didn't know if there would ever be another opportunity to speak to him. I reminded him about how he had told me of the one thing in his life he had regretted doing and I told him that I, too, had something like that. I told him briefly about what happened to Kurt Neilson and how he had come to my house and I had killed him by hitting him over the head and how I had panicked and buried him at the bottom of our dry well. When I told him how sorry I was and how I had an ugly secret kept from a family waiting for their boy to return home, I started sobbing at his bedside and sunk my blubbering face into the pillow. I eventually gained control of myself and started to apologize for my outburst when I saw his lips open and quiver like they were rehearsing something. I feathered the back of my hand along his cheek and it was clear he wanted to say something. I leaned as close as I could and watched him try again and again until I finally heard the two words he wanted so desperately to impart. "I know," he said, then closed his eyes and breathed a small sigh that suggested for tonight that was all he was willing or able to say.

47

EARLY IN THE MORNING the nurse waited until I had finished my breastfeeding ritual and then broke the news that in the middle of the night Arthur Evans had passed away. Despite the mounting evidence of the last two months it was something I had managed to believe would never happen.

"Are you going to be all right?" she asked.

"Yes," I said. "I'll be fine."

I believed it because of course I had no choice. In the space of two days a new being had been brought into the world and another one had disappeared. I had been making a habit of holding my little boy at my bosom and walking up and down the hall to prove that I was strong and fit and ready to go home, but now I didn't care to impress anyone. The thought of going back to the green bungalow alone filled my whole being with emptiness.

Verna arrived in the middle of the afternoon and she was clearly upset by the news. She told me he had been ready to go and was only hanging on until my baby was born. Her words were meant to comfort me, but the more I thought about it the more I realized they were probably true.

There was a small waiting room down the hall and after supper I walked by and looked in and there was Lodie Stump, her back to me, fussing over a newborn baby in a bassinette. Part of me wanted to keep on walking but I decided it was time to face my fears so I walked up behind her and waited until she turned around.

"Oh," she said and her baby picked up on her alarm and started to fuss all over again. "I thought there was a chance you might be here about the same time."

Her baby, also a boy, was a curiosity for good reason and I was pleased to see that he took after Lodie more than my father. "Have you named him?" I asked.

"I named him right away. His name is Samuel. It was my grandfather's name and I've always liked it. What's the matter? Is something wrong?"

"I guess not," I said. "I guess it won't matter. I was going to name this fella Samuel as well. I don't have a good reason, the name just appeals to me."

The truth was I had a reason, just not a very good one. An orderly, who worked the night shift and left for home before most woke up, was a kind man who stopped by to see how I was doing every morning before his shift was over. His name was Samuel. The nurses kept asking me about a name, and I thought if a name has any power over who we become, maybe there was a chance my Samuel would grow up to be a kind and considerate person as well.

Lodie looked at me quizzically. "I guess if we had two Arthurs on the Lake Road it won't matter if we have two Samuels. People will call him Sam, I know, but I read somewhere that first and last names sound better when they have the same number of syllables. Sam Stump. I like the sound of it."

I didn't want to offend Lodie or her theory, but I wanted my boy to be Samuel, not Sam. Samuel Lemmons. Together, they sounded musical enough.

"Old Evans died last night," I said.

"Oh, my god. I had no idea he was sick. That must be quite a shock for you, living with him and all."

"He was so good to me I can't imagine him being gone. I can't imagine living without him."

My Samuel was in a deep sleep so I excused myself to return him to the baby factory. Lodie said she was going home tomorrow, and while she had given birth two days earlier than I had, I decided I would get Verna to talk to my doctor. I was sick of hanging around all the patients and nurses floating through the hallways like apparitions. I was ready to get on with the rest of my life.

∽∽∽

Verna didn't show up the next day so I bundled Samuel up in a cuddle seat, packed my two bags, and told the nurses I was going home. They had no idea what to do with my demand and just watched me walk out, glaring at me like I was ungrateful, which was far from the truth. I was plenty grateful: mostly to get out of there.

At the same time I was afraid to go back home. It wasn't my home, for one thing, and the only person who made it my home was gone. Samuel didn't fuss much but he was wailing when we left the hospital as if he were protesting my decision. As soon as we got in the car and started moving, he calmed right down like he had given me credit for thinking things through. When we arrived, the first thing that stood out was a series of notes taped to the back door.

When will my clock be ready?

Is this the place that fixes clocks? I have two in desperate need of repair.

Why don't you answer your phone?

I had no idea what I was going to do or where I would be living in the future, but I was certain that my foray into the world of clock repair was over for good. I had my own little human time machine to manage now and catering to the demands of people like this wasn't going to work.

The first thing I did was take Samuel into the room where Arthur Evans spent most of his life. It was sad walking into his bedroom because the bed hadn't been made and the twisted sheets lying there were in the shape of his absence. I told him about the old man and how he was so good to me. I gave him lots of details, like his eating habits, the newspapers and magazines he read. Then I took him into the living room where the handmade crib was ready and waiting for him. He listened to everything I told him, really concentrated on what I had to say. My father was never much for talking, but I think I remember my mother as a talker, at least that's how I preferred to remember her. I had likely talked more in the eight months I'd lived with the old man than I had before in my whole time with my father. Anyway, I liked talking to Samuel and he was going to learn a lot about the world from me long before he went to school.

I was nervous because of him. When you are in the hospital with a baby you know that if something goes wrong there will always be someone close by who knows more than you do about how to make it right. Now I was on my own and my goal was to keep him alive until my doctor's visit, scheduled for the following Tuesday. Feed him, change his diaper, talk to him, rock him back and forth. These were the things I knew how to do and I hoped they would be enough.

The second day home, the visit I had been dreading took place. Beverly brought Daisy and Milo over to see my baby and to offer their condolences that Old Evans had died. Milo was excited for me to open a present, a snuggly that looked like it would be a few months before it would fit, and a cow that mooed when you squeezed it. Everyone who saw Samuel for the first time said pretty much the same thing and I was worried Beverly would be the exception.

"Isn't he just the cutest thing you've ever seen? It's such a privilege to bring a child into the world. Just think, Daisy, someday this might be you."

Beverly went on and on like she had a script memorized. If she noticed any features that resembled her son she didn't mention them. They arrived just as I was about to breastfeed him and that was what I did. Beverly and Daisy accepted the process for what it was. Milo stared in fascination and stopped playing with the cow. Everything was proceeding as well as could be expected until Beverly asked: "Is the father going to support you in any way? I know how it is. Some will, some won't."

"I don't want any help," I said, like I too had a script prepared. "It's just me and Samuel against the world and we're determined to win."

∽∽∽

Verna came to visit later in the week and brought her daughter, Maggie, and her grandson, Corey, along for a visit and to drop off a huge supply of baby accoutrements. There were so many clothes and shoes and bibs and even a stroller that would easily get me through the first year. I offered to pay her for what she'd brought but Verna said it was what happened when you had a large extended family and a new baby made an appearance: everyone gave you the same thing at the same time and Corey had more than all of this back home. I realized then that Verna was one of the kindest people I had ever met but a terrible liar. Somewhere down the road I would make it up to her.

The service for Arthur Evans was to be the following day. So consumed was I with my own life that I hadn't thought about the inevitability of this event. I had promised to attend, of course. The service was being held at Sands Funeral Chapel and he was to be buried in the same graveyard as my father. Two Arthurs, as close together as they had always been.

The next few weeks were a blur. Mrs. Eaton came for a visit and left me with a photo album because, she said, I would want to paste snapshots of my family history there for the future. I thanked her but never mentioned I didn't own a camera. I had one picture Verna had taken of me and Samuel and her daughter and granddaughter sitting on the couch. It was a start and I understood the importance of the gesture she had made. Mr. May came by as well. He didn't stay long and barely looked in on Samuel, but he left two jars of baby food, one apple, one prune. One visit I expected didn't materialize, and that was from Ernie Jagger and his two kids. I thought for sure a new baby would have sent alarm bells ringing in his ears that a soul had arrived that ought to be saved. I found out that the three of them had moved to Langley where Ernie was studying to be a minister and that his egg farm had been dismantled and was for sale.

I continued to live in the house belonging to Old Evans and knew that my future there was tentative. Only one family member, his daughter, made it to the funeral and she left immediately without talking to anyone. Someone said he had one sister still alive but that she lived far away and was likely too old to make the trip, but from what I recalled all of his brothers and sisters had passed on to another world. There were only a handful of people at the memorial service because Old Evans had outlived most of the people he knew in the valley, and while it was true he was an independent, self-contained individual, it was sad to contemplate his family out there somewhere and aware of his passing but without the inspiration to honour him. My father's situation was similar, but he had purposefully left his homeland and all that he'd known there and was never eager to embrace close relationships in his adopted land, but it made me realize there were at least two ways to be alone: move to a place where you knew no one or outlive all the people you knew. I was determined not to end up alone, at least not for the same reason my father had. I'd never had many friends growing up, and any blood relatives I had any claim to were far away, out of touch and certainly not around to shower my newborn with superlatives. I knew Samuel needed other people in his life and I was resolute in my quest to find him some.

I told Samuel it was time to share. He had more stuffed animals than any kid had a right to, so I jammed a baby kangaroo and some homemade chocolate chip cookies beside him in the stroller and off we went up the Lake Road. When very young babies face one another they tend to go into a trance, as if trying to determine if what they're seeing is a genuine miniature version of a human being. It was much the same for Lodie and me. She was likely ten years older than I was but circumstances neither one of us could have predicted had manufactured common ground. Breastfeeding hadn't worked out and her baby Sam was on the bottle already.

"My mother came to visit for two days," Lodie said. "She came all the way from Saskatoon to tell me how to raise a child. It was hilarious. I told her she should write a book on the subject so other mothers could benefit from her knowledge, and can you believe it, she thought I was serious!"

Lodie was a talker more than I realized. She hated changing diapers, she said, but she loved to sing Sam to sleep which meant she was singing most of the time because he was a baby who catnapped. Lodie meant well, I was sure of it, but when I heard her employing her singing voice as a soothing agent I thought I knew why Sam had trouble sleeping. I'd overheard a few conversations over the years about babies being rated as easy to raise or not so easy. By the time our visit came to an end I understood that my Samuel was not such a handful after all.

"I heard the Jaggers have moved away," I said. "I thought for sure he would have actively recruited Samuel as soon as I got home."

Lodie said, "He stopped by here for a visit and it was strange. I got the feeling he was suggesting that Sam and I could move to Langley to live with them if we wanted. Can you imagine? The man must be forty-five if he's a day."

Lodie Stump was friendly and I enjoyed being in her company, as odd as it was. I was still undecided if she was one of those people who spoke without thinking, or if she was stupid. My dad was forty-six when he died and she had allowed him to do a lot more than install a battery.

When the weather is exceptionally hot, people slow down and so does the time that surrounds them. I finished up my last two clocks and was committed to not accepting any more clock repair business and before I knew it the Labour Day Weekend had arrived. From the day I officially earned my driver's licence I knew I had in front of me the opportunity to go down to the ocean, but while I was packing Samuel and a picnic lunch for the journey, I did so with a heavy heart. I had planned on making my first trip to Maple Bay with Arthur Evans, a trip he would have enjoyed. In my mind I was going to pack a lawn chair so he could sit in the shade and watch Samuel crawl in the sand, but Samuel wasn't quite ready to crawl, and like many things I found myself imagining, it was a hopeless vision. But I did take Samuel to the beach where the water was still somewhat warm and some kids were swimming their last swim before school resumed. I took off my shoes and socks and waded through the salt water with Samuel in a backpack and while the whole beach was filled with screams of exhilaration and joy, no one was happier than I was that afternoon. My father had turned his back on the ocean after our fated journey to Canada and I accepted that. For me, the views, the smells of seaweed and fish, the motorboats and canoes, the canopy of maple and arbutus trees all felt irresistible and I had no desire to return to the Lake Road. I wished the old man had been there to share it with me.

We arrived back home at six o'clock to a world that had changed completely. I recognized the daughter whose name was Beryl and her husband who went by the name of Richard. They had gone through the house and laid Arthur Evans' clothes out on his bed. Two boxes sat on the kitchen counter filled with what they believed the old man had owned that had some value, or maybe they were trinkets to remember him by, it was hard to say. On top of the second box sat my father's Junghans clock.

"We don't have a lot of time this trip," Richard explained. "We leave tonight to catch the ferry back and there's a lot of cleaning up to do. Not that it's your responsibility, of course. We'll take care of everything."

Between the two of them I was told that they planned on selling the house immediately. I was welcome to stay until the house sold but an empty house showed better and did I have a place I could go? I listened to their litany of expectations and then took Samuel into the living room to change him and Beryl followed me.

"We hope this doesn't upset you too much, dear. But you must have realized you couldn't stay here without paying rent if my father wasn't living here. I'm sure you were good company for him but everything comes to an end eventually."

I told them I understood. I said I could find a place to go by the end of the month and I would get out of their way to do whatever they had in mind. I also told them the Junghans clock belonged to me and I took it out of the box and hung it back on the wall.

"When you do leave," Richard said, "just lock up and leave the key under the mat. The real estate people will make extra copies."

"There is no key," I said. "Arthur Evans always left the door unlocked, so anyone who wanted to was welcome to come in."

48

WHEN A BABY SMILES AT YOU, those few seconds leave nothing in your mind but the inspiration and pleasure of the smile. Samuel would thrash his arms and feet in the air and offer up gurgling sounds and this was how we communicated. I told him there was nothing to worry about, meaning *he* had nothing to worry about: the worry was all mine. The last thing I wanted was to move back to the home I grew up in, but realistically it was my best option. I understood that some of what we plan works out and some of the paths we travel appear before us with seemingly no contemplation. Lodie and I spent more and more time together, at her house and the one I was living in, and when she saw the upheaval of real estate agents and auctioneers I was surrounded by, she suggested I move into her house. We get along fine, she said, and the boys will have someone else to stare at.

By the time the leaves were ostentatiously waving their fall plumage, Lodie and I had a routine that might best be described as idle consumption. With Lodie as my navigator and guide (she had lived in the valley most of her life and introduced me to places I hadn't imagined) we scoured the valley and beyond, the two boys variably screaming or sleeping in the back seat. There were so many roads in the valley you tend to pass by, but we would drive to the end of them and when we did it always felt like something had been settled. When the weather was foul we played Scrabble (always Lodie's choice of a fun thing to do), or she would watch TV and I would read. She never appeared to be extraordinarily happy or sad about anything we did or talked about. Lodie was not one to think too far into the future and for the time being I was willing to do the same.

"That looks like an elephant. See the trunk sticking out?"

Lodie and I were sprawled out on a blanket with the two boys squirming between us. We were examining the cumulous clouds that moseyed by overhead.

"I can't see an elephant," Lodie said. "It looks more like a fat sheep if you ask me."

"Well, it does now. You've got to look right away. They change in seconds sometimes. My brother and I used to play this all the time."

"You have a brother?"

"No. Not a real one. I used to pretend I did when I was little. Sometimes we'd spend a whole afternoon naming clouds. Look just above the tree line. Don't try and tell me you don't see a star up there."

"It could be a star, I guess, but it's missing a point if it's a star."

Lodie set about searching for something to name and I kind of lost interest. I missed Old Evans more than I would have imagined. Nobody wanted to buy his green bungalow for a few months, but finally Red Neilson agreed to buy it and immediately rented the house out to a man who owned a big truck. Red Neilson claimed he planned to open a tire store on the property, since it was directly across the street from his auto wreckers, and he did start the project by bulldozing the front field enough for construction to begin, but that was where the project stalled so that driving by all you could see was a house dwarfed by a huge dump truck, and a scarred field that had been operated on and was waiting to heal.

∽∾∽

Lodie was not much of a reader at the best of times but she began thumbing through the library of baby books I'd brought with me. One of them mentioned that breastfeeding is the most advantageous for a newborn, at least for the first year. She couldn't let it go, and of course by now she had pretty much dried up. She would play with her breasts from time to time and manage to squeeze a drop of yellow milk to the surface, an event at the intersection of proud and the miraculous in her mind, but her breastfeeding window of opportunity was clearly over.

"Maybe you've got enough milk for two," she said. "You could try it anyway."

I told her it was a preposterous notion and that Sam wasn't going to end up retarded just because he was bottle-fed, but she kept harping on it so I gave it a try. Sam took to the practice immediately and soon I felt like a commercial milking station with no downtime. Lodie bought a bottle of cream for my cereal, thinking it was the natural supplement to my servitude to the infant world. The immediate effect of Sam's breast-feeding was he stopped his colicky episodes completely and often slept for three or four hours at a time. "Sam taking on your milk is as close to natural as you can get," she told me, and I was unsure whether she meant the process in general or if she meant because I was the daughter of his father. I didn't ask for clarification.

Lodie loved an adventure of any kind and we had just returned from digging clams at Bamberton Beach and the house was filled with the smell of the sea. I was euphoric, partly because of the event-filled lifestyle the two of us were leading and also because for the first time in a long time I felt like the events of my recent past were far enough behind me that they no longer demanded ongoing self-incrimination.

"Do you ever think life can be too good to be true?" I said. Lodie looked at me like I must have just bumped my head.

"No. Why would you think that?"

"I don't know. Things seem to be moving so easily right now. I know I'll have to find a job eventually, but for now, things just feel right."

"If they feel right I don't see why they can't keep being that way. A sunny day can be followed by another sunny day."

"But eventually it rains," I said.

"Of course it rains eventually. And when it does it feels as good as the sun because if it didn't rain we'd all be dead."

The one thing Lodie had mastered was pragmatism. Most people were devastated when President Kennedy was shot, but Lodie said he'd already consumed more caviar in his short life than she ever would, and anyway, he was probably shot for a reason.

She kept an eye out for movies filled with dangerous possibilities and that evening, after we had put both Sam and Samuel down for a period of sleep that might last for two or three hours or fifteen minutes, it was never clear which, she was curled up in her favourite place on the couch with a quilt around her legs, keenly anticipating *Psycho*, a movie starring Anthony Perkins she had seen before and promised would be good. Then we heard the back door open.

"Hello. It's me. I'm back."

We both got up and stood in the doorway to the kitchen, and there was Bert Stump over-dressed in a thick winter coat with a duffle bag full of clothes.

"What are you doing here?" Lodie Stump asked. It struck me as a brash question but pertinent at the same time.

"I'm back because this is where I belong. I don't drink anymore. I haven't had a drink for more than six months, Lodie. I'm a completely new man."

I was unsure how Lodie received the statement, but she helped him drag his bag into the bedroom the two of us had been sharing. Her place only had two bedrooms and the two boys took up all the space in the other one. The movie had started and Lodie was missing the beginning. She hated missing the beginning. They talked back and forth until the movie was almost over and eventually the headboard began reverberating against the wall with such force both boys woke up.

"Would you mind checking on things?" Lodie said, her head the only part of her that stuck out of the bedroom.

I didn't say yes or no to such a stupid question. What did she think I was going to do?

The next two days were awkward for everyone. Bert Stump claimed he had a good paying job on pulp mill construction up north and he was on a two week vacation. Whether this was true or not was hard to determine, but he acted like he was on vacation, lying around the house with Lodie waiting on him hand and foot. How much she told him about the two newborns living with her I wasn't sure, but Bert didn't take much interest in them in any case. Anytime he tried to pick Sam up, the baby screamed until he was released.

They were legally married, of course, and some of the rights and privileges that come with being married, based on Bert's prolonged absence, were ones they were intent on making up for. Unless it was raining, I took Sam and Samuel out for a long walk in the afternoon, manoeuvring the two strollers side by side as best I could, and when I returned they were either barricaded in the bedroom or sipping a beer on the couch, their faces sly and flushed. I was determined to sleep on the couch and wait out the two weeks to see if Bert intended on returning to his reputedly high-paying job, but I didn't have to wait that long.

"Bert has booked a motel for one night for the two of us," Lodie said. "Up in Bowser of all places. He wants to know if you'll look after Sam for one night and a day. I want to know too. It would mean a lot to both of us."

This request spilled into the room just before lunchtime and I was in the middle of feeding Sam. I was living in her house and using her electricity so I felt I owed her something. From where I was sitting I could see she already had a suitcase packed and sitting on her bed.

"Okay," I said. "But give me a phone number in case something goes wrong."

Bert said he didn't know the phone number but that they would give me a call me in three or four hours. As soon as they got there. A few minutes later I was the only adult in the house. I watched from the window when they drove off and I knew then that they wouldn't phone in three or four hours. They didn't phone later that night or the next day either.

Neither Sam nor Samuel had any notion of Christmas being less than a month away and yet for some strange reason I felt compelled to do something that would at least fake Christmas spirit. Six weeks had gone by and it was pure survival, trying to cater to two infants competing with one another. When Lodie had been around we were able to spell one another off or run

242

childless errands from time to time, but now I did everything with them both in tow. Lodie didn't as much as write a letter of explanation, though every day I stolidly approached the mailbox with this anticipation in mind. She never clarified if she were making payments on the house, and whatever utility payments were due she must have made arrangements for, because the phone kept working and the lights always turned on. My only choice for getting a tree, outside of paying for one, was to cut down a small, pathetic fir tree that was twenty feet from Lodie's back door. I used the same tired decorations I had inherited and tied a large pinwheel lollipop on the top instead of the angel my father had used. I had given up, long ago, on heavenly angels.

Sam preferred getting around in a stroller and Samuel liked it when he was carted around in a backpack slung over my shoulders and both were content when we were in and around people. The three of us did our Christmas shopping at Eatons. I bought them each matching denim pants and a toy truck that was bloody expensive and one they would have to learn to share. It would be years before either one of them would consider what I might want for Christmas, so I bought and wrapped a bottle of cheap perfume to have something under the tree when the big day arrived.

Verna dropped by about two weeks after Lodie had taken off and I didn't mention Lodie had gone AWOL. I thought she would return soon, that's how naïve I was. Lodie's truck was still parked at the side of the house so maybe no one noticed she was gone. Mrs. Eaton stopped by in the middle of December, during our second snowfall, to drop off a tin of Christmas cookies and I could tell she sensed something was awry and that it was only a matter of time before the valley residents would be asking for answers to questions that were none of their business. The last thing I wanted was an army of curiosity seekers nibbling away at my serenity. As it turned out, Mrs. Eaton was the least of my worries.

49

HIS BASIC TRAINING WAS FINISHED, a modified high school education complete, his hair a simple crewcut, and he had an anchor tattoo on his right arm, but it was more the way Robbie Tweedie carried himself that differentiated him from the thin character that had left the valley a year earlier. He was home for one week before being assigned to the *HMCS Mackenzie* and he was about to begin his navy career as a communications technician. While it wasn't true, he felt like he had learned more in the last year than he had during the scattered years of his life, and he was home to stay with his aunt and uncle for one day short of a week. He intended to clear his conscience at the same time. This last point was a decision he had made shortly after his basic training; his commitment to do so was what had propelled his life into a realm of confidence like nothing his previous experience had earned him.

Hoxie and Slick were abnormally welcoming. They could put up with almost anything for a mere six days, and Robbie assured them he would be busy catching up with old friends. His first full day back he walked into town and into the RCMP detachment on Duncan Street and told Constable Jesperson his recollection of the last two times he saw Kurt Neilson alive. The only thing that might have stopped him from doing so was if he found out Kurt had returned home, but he was told there had been no sign of Kurt for well over a year, and so he explained how they went to visit Hanne Lemmons to be friendly and to share their beer and that when things had gotten out of hand he had panicked and fled and didn't stick around, and that while he didn't know what happened for sure between Kurt and Hanne that night, he had a pretty good idea. Robbie had given serious thought to leaving out the part about how he came back the next night and saw Kurt walk uninvited into Hanne's house, but he knew such an omission was as good as a lie and he was determined once and for all to clear his mind about information he had that might be useful. Constable Jesperson waited until a fellow officer returned to the detachment and had Robbie repeat the story again, only this time notes were taken and his story read back to him.

"No one knows where all of this might go," Constable Jesperson said. "Maybe nowhere. But if a court case ensues you may be called upon to explain the testimony you've given. You understand that part."

"Yes sir. I do."

"And did you ever visit the Lemmons' house after that night you describe?"

"No. I never went back."

"So you haven't talked to her since then?"

"I did see her at the store before I joined the navy. I told her I was leaving. That's about all that was said."

Robbie got the impression they would have kept him for more questioning, but any questions they could conjure up had been asked and answered. Telling his tale after so many months felt good but not as good as he expected. He could tell by the officers' reactions that he had muddied the waters rather than cleared them. He went to the Fountain Lunch and ordered a milkshake and sat by himself at the corner booth. His confession was only partly accomplished, he realized, because if the worst case scenario unfolded and there was a court case of any kind, he would likely be summoned and his aunt and uncle would learn about everything that had gone on. He had to tell them and he didn't want to, but after they had eaten supper that was what he did. Slick didn't say much when he heard the news and Hoxie was noticeably disappointed.

The next morning he slept in and when he got out of bed he found himself alone in the house. Hoxie rarely went anywhere by herself and he knew that Slick had to work. He walked up the Lemmons' driveway and found the door had a new latch on it and was locked. From the back porch he noticed the '52 Plymouth Hanne had been driving a year ago, sitting in Lodie Stump's driveway. He slipped through the wire fence and knocked on the door.

Robbie could hear the sound of a baby crying lavishly and Hanne impatiently demanding she had had enough. He knocked again, louder, and when the door opened he found Hanne Lemmons standing in front of him holding two babies in her arms. It was not difficult to assess that she was not expecting or wanting to see him.

"You had two babies?" he said.

"It's a long story, but no, I only had one. This one belongs to Lodie. She's away."

"Look. I don't want to bother you but I need to say something."

Robbie, despite his pronouncement, didn't say anything else. Hanne opened the door; he stepped inside and sat down at the small kitchen table.

"About that Halloween — "

"I don't want to talk about that night. I work every day trying to forget it so I don't need you coming here to remind me."

"I'm sorry. I don't want to talk about that night either. I just want to say that I'm sorry I ran away. I had no idea — "

"Okay, you've said you're sorry. You can go now."

"There's one more thing I need to say. It's the reason I came back here. I told the police about going to your house that night and about me taking off. I thought you should know that."

Hanne didn't respond, other than to stare across the room in thought. Both babies stopped fussing and stared at Robbie as if trying to figure out why he had come. He excused himself and walked out the door. There was still no one home at his aunt and uncle's place so he left a note saying he had been called back to Victoria early. He didn't want to be around anyone who had known him in a past, and in the bowels of a Canadian destroyer he would soon get his wish.

"Is there a problem with your car?"

"No, my car's fine."

"Then please head down the ramp and park on the right hand side. Miss? Is something wrong?"

"I don't want to get on."

"You paid for your ticket."

"I know I did. I know what I paid for."

"We can't . . . "

It wasn't that they couldn't, it just would have taken too long. The man wearing an orange vest told me to drive onto the ferry, turn the car around, and wait until the rest of the cars had been loaded. I did what I was told and kept my head slumped forward. I looked up once and saw the man in the vest talking to another ferry worker who wore a blue coat. It was obvious they were talking about me.

I was in Crofton, busy not taking the ferry to Salt Spring Island. When I was about to drive back to dry land the man in the orange vest stopped me one more time. He looked in at Sam and Samuel sleeping in separate cuddle seats in the back of the car. "Those look like two twin boys you got there."

"They're close to twins," I said.

"Stop at the booth on your way out," he said. "Captain says you can get your money back."

If there hadn't been a ferry lineup I believe I would have gone to Salt Spring Island as planned, but sitting there for forty minutes gave me a chance to watch the seagulls drop shells on the rocks while I debated the merits of my visceral thinking. I had panicked and reacted and I was determined not to do it again. Robbie Tweedie's visit had driven me down a tunnel of despair, an evil place filled with the unknown and based on the worst possible outcome of the information he apparently shared with the authorities. I imagined them linking me to Kurt's disappearance, finding the body buried twenty feet deep, sending me to prison and separating me from Sam and Samuel for twenty years so that when I got out they wouldn't know me from Eve. The thought of spending twenty years in prison was repulsive but a stronger urge to fulfill my role as a mother was what dominated and I wasn't about to give away the privilege without a fight.

I also knew that my disappearance from the valley would implicate me so soon after being questioned and that my only hope in fleeing was to go undiscovered. I knew nothing about Salt Spring Island. If things turned on me I might have to run from it all, and I would if I had to, but this was not the time.

50

BEVERLY NEILSON ARRIVED HOME on Tuesday at four thirty and found a police car parked in front of the house. Whoever was inside had the window down watching Milo demonstrate his faltering ability to juggle two tennis balls at once. It had to be related to Kurt's disappearance, and because Kurt was not around, she was afraid to get out of her car because it could only be bad news.

"Mrs. Neilson, Constable Jesperson here. You might remember me from — "

"Yes, I remember."

"There are a few things we need to discuss, if you and Mr. Neilson have a minute."

"You've found him?"

"No, I'm afraid not yet. But we do have a few things to discuss."

Beverly sent Milo into the wrecking yard to fetch his dad and when they were assembled at the kitchen table, Daisy was asked to go to her bedroom and Milo was allowed to watch TV in the living room. Constable Jesperson summarized what had been reported two days earlier by Robbie Tweedie. His speech was delivered in the form of a run-on sentence because he didn't want any interruptions, which he knew from a previous visit, he would likely get from Red Neilson. He wanted their reaction to the mounting evidence, but not until they had heard him out.

Beverly slumped in her chair and stared across the room. Red Neilson went to the fridge to look for beer. There were none so he sat back down.

"I know on top of all that has happened this is not what you were hoping to hear," the officer said. "But it's information we now have to deal with."

"It's just what the kid told you," Red Neilson said. "It could be a bullshit story as far as that goes. Why would he say something like that about Kurt?"

"That's a good question. I can tell you it wasn't easy for him to come back here and say what he had to say. He feels bad that he went there that night and even worse because he ran away. He knows if he had stayed there it might not have happened."

Beverly hid her face in her hands. She wanted to say something. She just wasn't ready yet.

"So, the sleazy girl. The one with the baby. Lemmons or whatever her name is. Is this her story too?"

"She will be questioned. And you need to know that if she confirms the story she could lay charges."

"What bloody charges does she have a right to lay?"

"Rape, would be my guess."

Beverly began to sob. There was no longer a disguise for her emotional state. Red Neilson got up to check the fridge again. There still weren't any beer to be found.

"It could be anybody's kid," Red said. "God only knows how many boys she had hanging around. This could all be a setup."

"If it comes to that you might want to confer with your lawyer. It would be possible to determine who the father is if they had to."

Beverly found a box of Kleenex and asked a vague question and Constable Jesperson explained it all over again before he left. The dizzying array of facts that had been presented began to settle in her mind. As awful as the news was, it wasn't the worst news possible.

"I didn't think it had anything to do with the school," she said.

"What didn't have anything to do with the school?" her husband asked.

"His leaving, of course. He was in trouble at school and then we had a big fight that night and he was gone. It had nothing to do with the trouble he'd gotten himself into and it wasn't the way you practically kicked him out of the house that sent him packing. Don't you get it? He got the girl in trouble and then he ran away. That's what's happened. And it means he's out there somewhere. Probably feeling terrible about it all but he's out there."

"You need a beer worse than I do. You're not thinking straight. Even if the boy's story is true, which I doubt, there's no way she would know she was pregnant in two days. And if it *was* Kurt he wouldn't have a clue she was pregnant either."

"I know," Beverly said. "But he would have known he raped her."

Red Neilson slammed his fist on the table and reaffirmed his belief that it was bullshit, then left for the Commercial Hotel to pick up some beer. Beverly didn't doubt he would return with some beer but knew he would stop and drink four or five at the hotel first.

51

SAMUEL AND SAM WERE BOTH happy to be home. They sat in cuddle seats on the kitchen counter watching me fry eggs, making gurgling sounds and high pitched squeals of delight. Whatever sound Samuel would produce, Sam would repeat it as if he were an echo. If I was lucky I'd get a chance to eat before I was called once again to be the great provider.

I did eat and was intent on cleaning up the few dishes when I looked out the kitchen window and noticed a police car parked outside my house, and an officer walking around looking in the windows. He walked to the side of the garage and stood staring out at the property as if I might mystically appear out of the woods, and he stood on the site of the dry well for a long time. It was obvious he didn't know I wasn't living there anymore. I could have done nothing and he would have gone away, but he would have come back and found me eventually. I knew why he was back and I knew what he had on his mind. Robbie Tweedie's return to the valley had altered the landscape as far as I was concerned and I was determined to deal with things right now because waiting for another now would have driven me crazy. When he started back down the driveway, I stood out on Lodie's diminutive back porch and flagged him down.

Of course by the time he drove up, both boys began to make a fuss. It was the same officer, Constable Jesperson, the one I'd been having nightmares over. He wiped his feet on the mat and I told him he could leave his boots on. He left his hat on too which was a relief. With his hat on it was easier to take him seriously.

"There have been some changes in your life," he said, taking in my new living quarters and the two boys.

I told him it was true. Life had dealt some changes for sure and I sat and listened, and even though I knew precisely what he was going to say, hearing the words spoken made the event of that fateful night sound like a documentary, a reporting on a life that wasn't my own. Hearing it spoken objectively like that was more palatable than the thoughts that were constantly pin-balling inside my head.

"That's the essence of what Robbie Tweedie has reported. Would you care to comment on any of it?"

"I'd rather not comment, actually."

"Well, is it true, what he has told us? Is it true that Kurt Neilson came to your house and took advantage of you?"

"You'll have to excuse me," I said. Sam ate more than Samuel did most days and he wanted my attention immediately. I opened my blouse as discreetly as I could and let him get to work. The constable fumbled in his pocket looking for his notebook.

Samuel was often triggered when Sam began to feed, but for some reason he sat in his cuddle seat and stared across the room as if trying to figure out if he knew this man. It may have been the hat. No one who had dropped in so far had kept their hat on, as close as I could recall.

Constable Jesperson was as eager to feed on my words as Sam and Samuel, who replaced him a few minutes later, were for their dinner. I told him that yes, it was true, and then came a battery of questions about the relationship the two of us didn't have and whether Robbie Tweedie was implicated in any way. He wanted me to confirm the day it happened and the time. Mostly, he wanted to know why I hadn't reported the violation, especially since, according to his records, he had visited my house asking questions about Kurt Neilson within a few days of the incident occurring.

"I was scared and confused," I told him. "My father had died in the house the week before and when they arrived I didn't know what to do. They had beer with them and they said they wouldn't stay long, they just wanted to visit."

"And these two boys," he said, "would have Kurt Neilson for a father?"

"Samuel does. Sam here belongs to Lodie Stump but she's gone off with her husband and I'm looking after things for now. She should be back any day."

"I see," the officer said, not at all sounding like he did see, then he wrote down a few notes in his book. He flipped through his notebook and read some things he'd written down earlier.

"Your confirmation of the evidence provided by Robbie Tweedie changes things significantly. Robbie was, I assume, not a witness to all that went on and he ran off in the middle of it all. Kurt Neilson hasn't shown up yet, but based on what we now know he likely will. You've had no contact with him since that night?"

"No. Absolutely not."

"That means Kurt Neilson took off without knowing you were pregnant. "

Had he stated the obvious for a reason? Or was he thinking out loud? Sam spit up a good portion of what he'd eaten, so I cleaned him up, held him against my shoulder and patted him on the back.

Constable Jesperson hesitated and then divulged his line of thinking. "People generally run away only when there's a strong reason to do so. Can you think of something that might have scared him off?"

"Yes, I can. If I'd done to someone what he did to me and I thought there was a chance people would find out about it, I would run away too."

"You don't have to answer this now if you don't want to, but have you considered laying charges of rape against Kurt Neilson?"

"I can answer that now, no problem. I'm not interested in laying charges. He's gone and I don't care if he ever comes back. All I want is to put this behind me and get on with my life. Is that something *you* can understand?"

"Yes, of course. You sound very convincing in your position. If he ever does resurface at some point you should know you can change your mind. You can take him to court down the road."

"I will never meet up with Kurt Neilson in a courtroom. That's something that will never happen."

The police car drove down the short driveway slowly, and Constable Jesperson sat with the car idling for a long time before pulling onto the Lake Road. There was a thin layer of relief floating on top of a deep-seated misery and I was conflicted and knew I would have to live the rest of my life as the person who had, almost simultaneously, ended one life and started another. I couldn't imagine anyone wanting to be who I was in my situation, and at the same time I felt indignant about the story I was holding onto. There was nothing I had done that anyone, if they knew all the facts, would say had caused the attack that night; it was the way I had acted out of fear that complicated things. Robbie, I realized, had done the same thing. Neither of us could turn the clock back nor could we earn expiation, but there was a big difference between the two of us now: Robbie could carry on with his life with a relative absence of guilt, and that was one privilege I would never be able to call my own.

52

SOME NIGHTS RED NEILSON DRANK himself to sleep in his favourite chair, but on the nights he made his way to bed, he and Beverly engaged in an argumentative debate until he fell asleep, leaving Beverly alone in the middle of the night to sift through their repartee in search of something to hold onto. If something either interesting or contentious was in the air, Daisy knew to leave her bedroom door open which allowed her to eavesdrop effortlessly. After tuning in for two nights in a row, she knew the essential details of Kurt's debacle and, like her mother, spent many darkened hours assessing the information.

On Friday school was out two hours early because of meetings at the school and, though she knew she should head home to mind Milo who would be bused home early, she walked right past her house and stood on the back porch of the place belonging to Lodie Stump. She could hear Hanne inside, singing a song about a mockingbird. Her mother would have brought something when paying a visit, but Daisy had nothing to offer except herself and it might be the last thing Hanne would want to receive. The song sounded cheerful and sad at the same time, and she waited until it ended before she knocked.

"Hi," Daisy said, and then, despite the mild January day, jammed her hands into her coat pockets. "I heard about my brother. I'm sorry."

Hanne didn't say anything but opened the door for her to enter. Hanne walked into the living room and Daisy followed her and looked at not one but two babies lying on their backs on a shared blanket and cooing at a mobile of gaudy-coloured stars.

"I had no idea about all that happened until a couple of days ago. It must have been awful for you all this time. He didn't come home after the dance was cancelled and he was gone for a long time and my parents don't have a clue sometimes. I would have come to see you earlier if I'd known."

"Do you want a cookie?" Hanne said. "I made some."

"A cookie would be great."

"And some tea? Or coffee if you like, but it's instant."

"I love instant coffee."

Daisy was asked to mind the two babies while the coffee was made. Sam participated in a self-regulated workout, his arms and legs churning the air, while Samuel lay inert, watching. The house felt comfy and familiar, in part because a variety of things were piled on chairs and in corners: the way Daisy tended to keep her bedroom.

"Where's Lodie?"

"She's gone off. Her disappearing husband reappeared."

"She took off and left you with her own kid? What are you going to do?"

"Look after him, I guess. He's good company for Samuel."

"Kurt will come back one of these days," Daisy said.

"You think so?"

Daisy took a wad of stale gum out of her mouth and hesitated before perching it on the edge of her saucer.

"Mom thinks so. She thinks Kurt just has to grow up a little and learn to face his issues. Mom's big on the facing issues thing. Once that happens, he'll be back. These cookies are delicious by the way."

Sam needed changing and Hanne took him into the bedroom. As soon as Sam was out of the room, Samuel started to cry so Daisy picked him up to soothe him.

"You've got a lot of responsibility," Daisy said. "Most times there are two parents to look after one baby but you're all by yourself with two. That must be tough."

"It is what it is. If there's an argument in this house I always win out. For now, anyway. I guess some day these two will give me a run for my money."

"How do you survive?"

"I get by. My dad had some money saved so that helps. I will have to get a job someday, but for now I'm content to look after my two little guys."

"You mean Lodie's not coming back?"

"It's been almost four months now, so I kind of doubt it. My dad always said not many people move away from Tansor, but when they do it's rare they come back."

53

WHEN MY DAD WAS ALIVE and we discussed someone in the news whose enigmatic behaviour was out of line in one way or another, he would always ask me to think about what that person might be seeing at that very moment. He believed people based their actions on how they saw the world, and while I didn't always agree with his analysis, it did lead to some thoughtful discussions. I tried to imagine what Lodie was up to, where she was and why she had done what she'd done. She seemed to care about Sam when she first brought him home, but looking back on it, it was as if he were a plant that needed watering, whereas I felt tied to Samuel forever, long after the umbilical cord was severed. Could it be she felt her connection with my father had been a huge mistake? An episode of misplaced passion? If she didn't cherish her baby the same way I did, why hadn't she arranged to give him up for adoption? After more than four months I came to understand that was exactly what she had done. Rather than give her baby up to a strange couple, she had deliberately handed him over to me.

I didn't want to move back to the house that was my own but I knew where I was living was Lodie's house and eventually, if she didn't want it back, she would want to sell it. I imagined the only reason I was able to stay where I was, revolved around her not wanting to return to face up with being responsible for Sam. If that were the case, maybe I could stay here forever.

Daisy fell into the habit of coming to visit me every Friday after school was over, and I always had something baked when she arrived. She was good company and said she wanted to learn as much as she could about babies, and that may have been the reason, but I thought it was her fascination with Samuel who was, after all, her brother's progeny. She was good with Sam but she paid special attention to Samuel and brought a camera over on her third visit and asked if I'd take a picture of the two of them sitting on the couch. She didn't say so, but I thought in her mind the pictures would be markers captured for her brother at some point in the future. Every time she came she stayed two or three hours and I liked hearing her stories about school. It got me to wondering if I would have thought about education and boys and teachers the way she did had I attended school. There were only two and a half years between us but in some ways she seemed much younger.

The fourth Friday I heard a knock at the door and I was busy changing Sam so I yelled for her to come in. I heard the door open and close and when I got out to the kitchen it was Beverly standing at the door, by herself.

"Hanne, I hope you don't mind my coming. I've been too embarrassed to come earlier, after what happened. Kurt is a good boy in so many ways but what he did was shameful. I guess I needed to tell you that."

I pointed to a kitchen chair and she sat down. I had been dreading a visit with Beverly, even though she had tried her best to be kind to me since my father passed away and was supportive and encouraging when Samuel was born. But things were different now that she knew. I couldn't look at her objectively any longer and more than once I wished instead of Red Neilson expanding his business, the family would move away somewhere and let me live my own life.

The boys were both napping and I could hear one of them stirring. I went to the bedroom and brought them both to the kitchen and Beverly started to cry.

"What happened, happened," I told her. "I really don't want to think about it anymore."

Beverly gained control of herself and I made a pot of tea. She asked if she could hold Samuel and I saw no reason not to let her. She stared at him fixedly and I could see her tears threatening to flood once again.

"He's just like his father," she said.

I thought she meant Samuel, of course, but she went on to describe how Red Neilson had been wild as a young man and had ended up spending two months in jail for his violent temper. As Kurt got older it was as if he were growing into his father's life, she said. So many things had gone wrong for him and now this.

I listened to what Beverly had to say but did so dispassionately. Their screwed up family dynamics hadn't served me well in the past and her history lesson wasn't about to change anything.

"Daisy has been dropping by on Fridays," I said. "I was expecting *her*."

"She's coming by later, if that's okay. I told her I wanted to talk to you first. She likes coming here and you're all she talks about when she gets back home. And I brought a little something the two of you could warm up for supper. I certainly don't expect you to feed her. She has offered to look after the two boys tonight so you can head into town. See a movie maybe. It was her idea."

I told her it was a kind gesture and I would think about it. She said her husband was questioning his intention to open a tire store on the Evans' property because a new tire store had just opened closer to town, and they were selling Japanese tires for next to nothing. It didn't take much effort to visit with Beverly. All you had to do was sit and listen.

"If you need any help at all," she said, "you know where we are and you just need to ask. I do have one favour to ask of you."

"Which is?"

"If even the smallest communication from Kurt comes your way, you will let us know immediately?"

"I don't expect that to happen," I said. "But if it does, I promise you'll be the first to know."

As soon as Beverly opened the door to leave, Daisy walked in to take her place. We had supper together and after the boys were fed and played with and put down for whatever portion of the night they were willing to sleep, I did drive into town by myself. I needed a few things from the drugstore and shopping without two babies in tow was a freedom I had forgotten. Daisy said there was a movie on downtown with Steve McQueen and I had to go see it because Steve McQueen was in it and he wasn't in very many films. I walked into the movie theatre and the show had just begun. The usher guided me with her flashlight down the carpet until an aisle seat appeared. The movie was called *The Great Escape* and it didn't take long to buy into the drama. I guess anyone who is captured wants desperately to get away. In time my eyes adjusted to the dim light and I could see a boy and a girl snuggling together in the middle section of the theatre, three rows ahead of me. When the screen grew bright I could see it was Graham Puckett and someone he had grown close to. When the movie was almost over and before the lights came on, I made a great escape of my own.

54

IT WAS RARE THAT MR. MAY found a source of money outside of his welfare cheque and when he did it was usually picking up pop bottles on the side of the road that the kids in the neighbourhood couldn't bother to return. Two or three times a year he would work at Neilson's Auto Wreckers, usually because Red Neilson was incapacitated and needed to keep his eyes closed. On Friday night, Red was half cut and alone in the house when Mr. May peddled his way home and because Red was lonely he invited him to join him in his drinking fest. Mr. May initially drank two beers and had to walk his bike up Evans Road to home because after Red Neilson passed out, he sat by himself and drank a third. The next morning Red Neilson couldn't see anything he recognized when he opened his eyes, and Milo was sent to fetch the withered figure of a man to watch over the grounds because some car collectors from Vancouver were scheduled to rummage through his Studebaker parts. Mr. May agreed to come but did so reluctantly. He wasn't feeling all that perky himself, and based on the information Red Neilson had imparted the night before, he had better things to do.

By 11:30 the collectors were gone and Mr. May had amassed forty-six dollars selling car parts, and received five dollars for his efforts, which translated into half a month's dog food for Lenin. Soon after, he peddled his way to Lodie Stump's house because he now had good reason to scrutinize Hanne

Lemmons. So far as he knew the reward for finding Kurt was still a possibility and the only person he knew that had a link with him was the girl he had raped. He couldn't understand rape. The strong sexual urge that was the source of its evil he could vaguely recollect from his own youth, though even with the passing of time he thought it must have been only a moderate exigency he owned at the time. The desire and passion of the impulse he was familiar with, due to a frenzy of activity in his late twenties when working on the railroad. It was with Bernice, who was similarly employed, and she was willing to let him into the arena that harnessed raw sexual energy, but it was always on her terms, terms with varying rates of execution. He couldn't imagine pressing his carnal pleasure on Bernice or any other female he had met — the act, based on his experience, surely had to require a certain level of submissive cooperation.

Hanne wasn't paying attention and almost ran him over when he turned his bicycle up her driveway. She rolled down the window.

"I need to talk to you," he said.

"Not now, Mr. May. I'm on my way to do errands. Lots of them. I'll talk but not today."

Before Mr. May could protest the window was rolled back up and she was gone. If that wasn't proof she had something to hide, nothing was.

55

THERE WERE A FEW THINGS I needed to pick up, baby aspirin being one of them. I didn't know if my boys were old enough for baby aspirin and thought I would drop by to visit Verna before returning home. Verna wasn't a doctor but she'd seen a lot of babies and she would certainly have an opinion on aspirin. Sam had always fed ravenously from my breasts from the very first opportunity provided him, and while Samuel was not as greedy, he had been a steady eater and it was alarming that for almost a week he had been eating less and less every day. He would suckle, but more out of comfort than anything, and his green eyes were clouded with a look of uncertainty that unnerved me. His forehead felt hot to touch but I didn't have a thermometer. Verna would.

Verna was almost in tears herself when I arrived with Sam and Samuel in tow. She was trying to learn to knit, now that she had a grandchild, and she had been at it for weeks and hadn't yet completed the back of her first sweater. When I apprised her of why I had come unannounced in the middle of a Saturday afternoon, she threw her knitting needles and semblance of a sweater onto the floor and focused her energy on something she was clearly suited for.

"Has he lost weight?" she asked.

"I don't know. He weighed eighteen pounds two weeks ago when we saw Dr. Shamberger."

Verna then told me to stand on the set of scales she owned and then hand Samuel to her. She got down on her knees before and after as if she had lost an earring on the floor. "Well, he hasn't gained any weight. This isn't accurate, of course, but he might have even lost a pound. How long did you say his appetite has been off?"

"Eight or nine days. Maybe ten."

She took his temperature and made a humming sound. "What?" I asked.

"His temperature is a bit high but he's clearly out of sorts. Sam has been fine through all of this?"

"The beat of his own drum," I said.

He needed changing and a sore-looking diaper rash had developed so Verna gave me a mild antiseptic unguent to ease his discomfort. She said absolutely no to the aspirin and told me to make an appointment with Dr. Shamberger on Monday. "If his appetite falters any more you need to take him to emergency. Call me if this happens and I'll go with you. Babies are normally very resilient and he will likely be over this by then. Let's hope so."

Before I picked up the babies to leave, Verna hugged me with a desperation that made Monday feel like a long ways away. "My own daughter didn't digest well for three months after she was weaned. We had to feed her soymilk as a substitute. Mothers. The things we have to go through."

They were both asleep on the way back home which was not unusual. Whenever we were on the road they dozed off and it was just as well because from their cuddle seats they couldn't see where we were going anyway. I nosed into our driveway and then backed out onto the Lake Road. I would go visit Mr. May myself and let him get his latest melodrama off his chest rather than wonder when he might next poke his head into my kitchen.

I had never been inside his house and I doubted that anyone else had, and I knew I wouldn't gain entry that day as he was sitting on a stump beside an old plane that sat just north of his two shacks. The plane had crashed years ago but nobody seemed to know the story. It was mysteriously missing one wing and the fuselage was half buried in forest now and it was where his dog Lenin preferred to sleep on hot days.

"You wanted to talk to me about something?"

"Yes, I do. I found out what happened with the Neilson boy."

"I guess everybody knows now. What about it?"

Lenin rolled over to have his belly scratched and Mr. May complied with his wish. It occurred to me that he was the only true friend the old man had.

"I don't want to insult you. Especially after all you've been through, but you must know what happened to him."

"I don't get it," I said. "Why is Kurt Neilson so important to you?"

He thought about my question as if it were one that was difficult to answer. He even stopped rubbing the dog's belly. Then he told me about the reward and how much it would mean to him if he were the one to track Kurt Neilson down. When he was finished he looked relieved that he'd said what he had.

"Has anything horrible ever happened to you?" I asked.

"I've had a few bad things happen along the way."

"And do you think about these things every day?"

"I try not to."

"Well that's me. Don't you see? It was a horrible night and it's over now and I don't want to think about it ever again. And every time you start poking around and asking questions it all comes back to me. Kurt Neilson left and he will never be coming back to talk to me about it, that much I can assure you. I think you should just forget about it. You're wasting your time."

I could see he was weighing my words, but wasn't convinced. The reward was something he couldn't let go of.

"Look, I have a proposition for you. If I ever hear from him again I promise I'll get a hold of you right away. If there is a reward you might as well be the one to get it. But in return you've got to stop poking around my business and leave me and the thoughts about that night alone. Forever. Does that sound fair?"

"Might be fair."

"It's going to get hot and dry soon. And so long as you never bother me with the topic again, you can go to the outside hose at my place and help yourself to water any time you want, all summer long."

It was hard for him to let it go, that much I could read by his facial expression, but the offer of unfettered water without having to pester the neighbours all summer and early fall was what cinched it. He shook on it and said it was a fair deal. If it were honoured, it would be a fair deal for both of us.

56

DR. SHAMBERGER WAS UNAVAILABLE Monday and Tuesday and because Samuel had only eaten twice on Sunday and once Monday morning (and spewed most of what he'd eaten back up immediately) I drove to emergency in the morning. It didn't take long for a doctor to examine him and listen to the story of his picky eating habits. I was informed they would have to keep him for several days for observation and to run some tests to see if they could get to the bottom of it, and when they took him out of my arms it was the most painful thing I had ever experienced. He was so helpless and reliant upon me, and now I was abandoning him to the care of the medical profession, so full of mystery and knowing. After almost seven months of his life he was back where it all began.

The doctor and the admitting nurse told me I should go home. I couldn't do it. Despite their best efforts to dissuade me, I sat in the reception area and talked to Sam and told him everything was going to be okay. I asked every hour if there was any news to report and I was told no, of course not, the observation of an infant would require several days if not more. I phoned Verna and told her what had happened. Not long after, she arrived and talked to the doctor administering to Samuel and invited me to dinner. She told me exactly what the doctor had said, and coming from Verna it made sense. I declined her offer for dinner and took Sam home. I fed him and changed him and gave him a bath. Then I sang to him until he fell asleep. Verna phoned to ask if I was okay and I lied and said I was. Sam didn't sleep for long: he knew something was amiss and it upset him. It would be one of those nights where sleep would be scarce for him but it would have little effect on me. I knew I couldn't sleep anyway.

∾∾∾

The weather had been uncharacteristically clement for most of January, and February was just the opposite. Snow it did but it was almost too cold to snow and the accumulations were noticeable only by virtue of accrual. Despite the change in the weather, I took Sam out in the stroller every day for at least an hour. The outdoors had to be good for him and it certainly felt good to me.

It's easy to forget that hospitals are not only theatre for tragedy. Babies are brought into this world in hospitals, broken arms are set to heal, and diagnoses save lives every day, but with the sight of Samuel, my tiny baby oblivious to the insanity that surrounded him, lying there with tubes and breathing apparatus the necessary thin threads tethering him to life itself, it was easy to feel only the pathos of the place. It depended upon which nurse was on duty whether or not I could bring Sam into the room with me, and it also determined when I bawled my eyes out. I didn't want Sam to pick up on the fact that I was a complete nervous wreck, but despite my best efforts, he knew. I went every day, twice a day, and every evening Verna would mind Sam in the waiting room so it was guaranteed I could spend time with Samuel. The first time the test results were explained, Verna was with me. The report went on and on about substantially reduced white blood cell count and the rarity of such a condition in a child that young. Most of it went over my head but when Verna's face went white and she didn't ask for any clarification or ask about future treatments for my little boy, I knew what was to come. The next day Verna suggested that Beverly Neilson ought to be informed and I told her that was probably true, but I wasn't the one to inform her. The next few days were scattered and both Beverly and Daisy from time to time could be found staring through the window at the babies in intensive care. I didn't want to talk to either of them and they seemed to understand my position. Every afternoon, Verna's daughter took care of Sam and I came to rely on Verna's no-nonsense demeanour when it came to sorting out all that I was facing. Nine days later the short journey of Samuel Thomas Lemmons came to an end. I was there when it happened and I had told him over and over that I loved him. He couldn't say anything and his eyes had been closed for the last two days, but I knew, right up until the end, he was sending his love my way.

57

I WAS COMING TO UNDERSTAND that at the funeral service, what was said and what was left unspoken formed a spirit cloud around the departed and the story that was told was not up for revision. What one does with one's life until they have no life left to live is the only veritable source of material. When my father died there were so few people who came to honour his passing it felt like a lonely and sad ceremony, even though I knew my father wouldn't have been disappointed. He had lived his life and done some things and these were recalled, almost as if the act of living was like getting away with something. There was nothing celebratory when my Samuel was laid to rest. What could the average person say other than he was cute (he was) or he was brave (he was that too)? During the two hundred and fifty-nine days he was alive I came to understand who he was, what he wanted, and though I may have dealt myself a hand of deception, I believe I knew the kind of man he would have become. He was easily startled, but once he understood what was going on around him, he was loath to give up the things he loved, like his nightly bath. If I were near him and he wasn't distracted by Sam, his eyes were always on me, as if there was a deep discerning he needed to carry out. When he was first born I was the same way with him, stunned by the miracle of his birth and coming to grips with the journey we were about to share, and now our collaboration was over. In a rational way I understood this to be true, but a much larger part of me would never completely understand what had transpired.

If a person traverses this earth long enough and does enough favourable things, he may, once it is all over, be referred to as a great man. Samuel Thomas Lemmons was a great baby. The story he told was a short one but its impact was great. There were many more mourners at his service than had shown up for my father and I understood that most were there to support me and I accepted this. The affection present in the room took on many forms: a glance or the avoidance of a glance, the liberal flowing of tears or the stoic evasion of emotion, a hug or a feathery pat on the back. The experience impacted us all equally and, I believe, for the better. My little Samuel, the briefest of raging comets in the middle of the night, would not soon be forgotten in Tansor.

The year of 1965 offered a good spring for some in the valley, but for me, although I had always found a spiritual lift when a new year unfolded, it was downright depressing. Everything that was growing taller, fatter, or greener only reminded me of what was not growing taller or fatter or any colour ever invented. Sam kept me sane through these months that were filled with lengthening days — days I began to sense were nibbling away at my future. Sam could crawl anywhere, and while he wasn't walking on his own, when I held his hands in mine and acted as his guide, he would walk around the house laughing out loud, knowing he was getting close to a new kind of freedom. Verna said plenty of babies learn to walk by their first birthday and I just knew Sam would accomplish the feat well ahead of schedule.

"Good morning, Sam my man. How did you sleep last night? You woke up once and went right back to sleep. I'll bet you were tired after all the fresh air we got. Am I right? I'm right, aren't I?"

I got in the habit of talking to Sam as if at any moment he would turn around and answer me back. Often, I imagined what he would say to me if he could. "I slept well, thanks. The reason I woke up is because my diaper was wet. I hate when that happens. I think I could sleep the whole night through if I could wake up dry. I won't be sorry when this whole diaper thing is over and done with. Diapers make me look fat and all my pants feel tight."

It felt good just to talk to him. I'd experienced too many days cushioned by silent conjecture when growing up with my father. If Sam would remember me as anything he would think of me as good company. That's how I saw it, anyway.

It had been my intention to turn my back on the clock repair business for good, but despite the fact that my ad was no longer running in the paper and I was no longer living with Old Evans, people managed to search me out and practically insist I fix their broken timepieces. I no longer had the work bench that was built specifically for that purpose, but I still had the tools, and it wasn't long before I was doing one or two a week which was like a part-time job: a good thing because Sam was outgrowing his clothes so quickly it was hard to keep up. Thankfully, Verna's daughter continued to pass some of her little boy's hand-me-downs my way. Before I knew it the time came to turn over July on the calendar and the warm weather slowed everything down. Sam loved to play outside whenever possible and he hated wearing shoes. He was starting to say a few words and one of them was "mama" which became my favourite word in the whole wide world.

Not a day went by that I didn't miss my Samuel. People I met at the store or the gas station were friendlier after the funeral, or so it seemed. It wasn't so much that they were taking pity on me or feeling sorry for me, but I was a survivor living in Tansor, had been through some hard knocks, and somehow this gave me credibility as a worthy member of the community. I had given serious consideration to moving back into my house, something I wouldn't have thought possible, but it felt like it would be an important step in accepting myself living here. That was something that felt more and more like it was inevitable: living in Tansor until I won the lottery or was buried six feet under. It felt that way until one Friday when a letter arrived from Lodie Stump.

She had been gone for so long it was hard to imagine her ever living here even though this was rightfully her own house. She left sometime in September and it wouldn't be long before September would be back again. For the first few months I expected her to arrive with a tale of woe, but by the time Christmas came and went I expected I might not see her again. Her husband, Bert, had no interest in living here with a kid that wasn't his, that much was obvious, but I assumed the house was in both their names and eventually they would want to sell it. This was what I both feared and expected to happen, until the letter arrived.

Hanne

You can't teach an old dog new tricks. Bert has turned out to be an old dog. I didn't want to shock you with my arrival because things may have changed for you, but I have a few loose ends to tidy up and I will be back in a few days. I need to start my life over again.

Your friend

Lodie

She was returning after all and it wasn't just the house she wanted back. In her old life she had been looking after Sam and she wanted to start over again. That was the logical conclusion I jumped to, and yet it was foggy because she hadn't mentioned her own son in her letter or even wondered how he was doing. Starting her life over again may have meant before she had Sam. While this was possible, I knew I couldn't take a chance. There was no date on her letter and who knows how long it would take to get here. I sang to Sam until he fell asleep and then I busied myself through the night. I left a letter of my own on the kitchen table. It was short and sweet. *The house is all yours. Hanne.*

Two

1

FOUR TANKS OF GAS, two quarts of oil, and a bottle of gunky liquid put in my radiator was enough to get me to Calgary. I had no interest in Calgary and tried to drive around it but that didn't work out at all. Sam, who was usually so road-worthy, had put up with things until we'd made it to Kamloops and the run-down motel we found on the outskirts the day before, but once we started on the road again the next day, he was outright irritable all the way to Cowtown. I was prickly myself but I had no one to complain to. It was a relief to be on the road and on the way to somewhere.

Winnipeg was my goal. I'd never run into anyone from Winnipeg and situated as it was in the middle of the country, I was certain obscurity would be waiting for me there. The road and maybe the tension of everything had a wearing effect, and both Sam and I were up at 8:30 the next morning in our second modest motel east of Calgary, in the middle of nowhere. I fed Sam and ate a banana; we both fell asleep until 11:30 and didn't hit the road again until mid-afternoon. In my mind I wanted to get to Winnipeg as quickly as possible and figure out a way to get us both settled, and on the way I found Alberta had a lot of country music radio stations which I found soothing at times and depressing at others. It was getting dark by the time we passed into Saskatchewan but I had no desire to stop; we'd gotten off to a slow start as it was and the fewer days incarcerated in my '52 Plymouth the better.

It was dark when I stopped again for oil and gas and that was when I made a big mistake.

It seemed clear enough from the map on the wall of my last gas station: stay on Highway 1 and drive until I run into Winnipeg. When I got gas I must have taken the wrong turn because I passed through a town called Maple Creek, but without a map I had no idea I was veering south. The road was good enough but not busy at all and an hour or so later it wasn't busy with my car either; the car had no oomph and I could see steam pouring out of the hood. Sam had dozed off but woke up to murmur his concern at the hissing steam that obeyed the breeze and floated over the windshield before offering its token humidity to the parched prairie landscape.

I lifted the hood of the car and a burning smell was my reward. I left the hood up so the sibilant beast might cool off and took Sam for one of his practice walks down the country highway. We both needed the exercise.

I was in the middle of nowhere and it had been at least twenty minutes of driving since I had seen any semblance of civilization. There were fences that cordoned the road off from the wave of rolling hills but no sign of a farmhouse on the horizon. I sang Sam the mockingbird song which he found reassuring and the stop did us both some good, at least for the first half hour. Then panic set in. I had no food with me and nothing to drink. Sam had me at least, and he indicated it was time to help himself to what was available.

While he was attached to my left breast like a ravenous leech, I heard a car coming over the rise, so I opened the car door and stood there holding little Sam in one arm and my free hand fluttering in the air indicating a polite suggestion to stop. And stop someone did after giving it some consideration. A truck slowed but drove for a long way down the slight incline before backing up to where I stood, hip against the front fender.

"Looks like you're having trouble with your car?" a young man said. I believed that was what he said but my conclusion was based on the context I found myself in more than a clear reception of his voice. From inside the truck an eight-track tape of a male country singer reported on the day Jesus would return and it was loud enough to scare wildlife nearby deep into the prairie night. Sam was almost finished his main course and about to dally around dessert which was mostly a waste of time, but he stopped feeding altogether and turned his head around to find out what this sudden flurry of action was all about. The man seemed to notice I had a baby then and went back and turned the truck off.

"It's overheated, I think. It just stopped running."

The man listened carefully to what I had to say, twirling a hay straw around in his mouth like it was a trick. He went up and hovered his hand over the tired engine.

"How long you been parked like this?"

"About half an hour. Forty-five minutes maybe."

"Well, you're right about the overheating but cooling things off may not be enough. Where are the two of you headed?"

"Winnipeg."

"*Winnipeg?*"

The way he said it I imagined Winnipeg must have moved. Either that or it was a damned unpopular choice around here. I didn't say anything back because it was a simple fact and not worth restating. I *was* heading to Winnipeg.

"Well, Winnipeg in this car right now is a pipe dream. Here's what I can offer you. I can drive you the wrong way for fifteen minutes because I got to deliver supplies, then I'll be turning around and going back home where we can find you a place to stay because you're going to be more than a day tending to this Plymouth here. Total running time will be less than an hour. Does it interest you or not? My name's Leonard."

I thanked Leonard and put two large suitcases, the ones I'd used to get in and out of motels, into the back of his pickup truck. Leonard put the supplies he was delivering into the back too because otherwise there wouldn't have been anywhere for us to sit. We drove for a short spell in the direction I had just traversed and he pulled the truck into a small farmhouse not far off the main road. There was a porch light on but the rest of the house was in darkness. Leonard said he'd be back in a jiffy and took the box of supplies to the house, opened the door and turned on all the lights. I could hear him talking to someone inside but I couldn't make out what exactly they were saying. Before he returned to the truck, the only light remaining on was the porch light.

"Okay," he said. "Let's get you where you're going."

"Who was in there?" I asked. I had no right to ask but I couldn't help it.

"That's my grandmother. She's eighty and on her own and blind to boot. She won't come live with us. She can't see the land anymore but she says it speaks to her."

Leonard liked to drive fast, that much was evident. When we came to a corner I put one hand on the dash to protect Sam and he noticed and slowed down. We didn't talk much on the way to where we were going. He asked me why Winnipeg and I told him it was just a place I'd never been. This gave him plenty to think about all the way to the town we drove down into, a small town with sparkling lights like a secret spaceship situated in the middle of the prairie. We drove along what appeared to be the main street but was still the highway and turned left.

"Where are we?"

"This here is Eastend. My guess is you've never been here before either."

Leonard said to sit tight until he'd done some explaining. He went into the house and came back out to help with our suitcases. A woman wearing an apron stood under the yellow glow of a porch light.

"That's my mother. She wants to know your name."

Sam hadn't gone back to sleep and he was irritable. He needed to be changed and put down for a spell and it was a formula that always worked, especially if he had a bath first. Tonight it looked like we would both have some realigning to do.

"Hanne. Hanne Lemmons." I waited until we got to the porch to make my declaration. Leonard didn't need to know my name to this point so waiting twenty-five feet was inconsequential.

"Hi, Hanne. Leonard says you've had some car problems. Don't you worry about a thing. You're welcome to stay here until we figure things out. I'm Muriel and Fred, my husband, I'll introduce you to once he gets home. He's at the pool hall. And who might this be?"

"Sam. Sam Lemmons."

"I've always liked the name Sam. It sounds reliable somehow."

Leonard put the two suitcases in the hallway and got back in his truck and drove away. Muriel led me to a bedroom at the back and said she could get some extra blankets and cushions and formulate a makeshift crib for Sam on the floor beside the bed. She said they were keeping the back bedroom ready for her mother but she was too stubborn to come and live with them.

2

MURIEL SAT AT THE KITCHEN table doing a crossword and waiting for her menfolk to return. Fred was later than usual which meant he was losing at pool or winning but more than likely losing and hoping to recoup his losses, and Leonard, because he got to use the truck for the night if he did something with a purpose first, was probably out informing the town that they had guests, a mother and a child, and the mother thought it was a good idea to move to Winnipeg. Muriel preferred to retire early and rise ahead of the sun but she was loath to go to bed now and have Fred come in late making the kinds of commotion she had grown accustomed to over the years: cracking a beer and turning on the TV to catch the late night news. Fred claimed he didn't do much in the way of drinking and Muriel couldn't argue the point; he liked to have one beer after playing pool if he had lost badly or found himself an infrequent winner which meant he had one beer every night when he returned. There wasn't a good deal of variation in a man like Fred, something Muriel found herself thankful for, especially when someone like Hanne Lemmons, a woman travelling on her own but with a child arrives at the door, desperate and scared and owning a car that refused to run. Yes, at times like this Muriel understood the value in an uneventful life.

There was one corner of the crossword that was being ornery and Muriel's rule was to resort to her Del Crossword

Dictionary only after a half hour if her own diligence had proven fruitless. Because Fred was later than usual she turned to it now and found *qat* was a tobacco chewed for mystical experience and that brought her to thinking of how blessed they were that Leonard was no longer immersed in the marijuana fad that was, if the news reported had any credibility, sweeping North America. He had sporadically chummed around with the two Wilson brothers who were Pied Pipers leading the youth of the town down a steep and treacherous ravine until Marty Wilson was carted off by police to a detention centre in Fort Saskatchewan. Muriel always felt compromised and somewhat defeated when she reached out for help from her dictionary, but this was soon replaced with a feeling of great satisfaction and relief. It was always some small detail, some innocuous three letter word that held things up. She was likely the only resident of Eastend who knew what *qat* meant, and she was contemplating how she could maneuver the word into the conversation at her bi-monthly bridge club when she heard Fred stomping the dust off his shoes at the front door.

"You have to be quiet," was how she greeted his entrance.

"What?"

"Keep your voice down. We have guests and they're sleeping."

Muriel summed up the expedition that Leonard had delivered after dark. It occurred to her how little she knew about the why and where of it all.

"She's not very old at all," Muriel explained. "Young by most people's standards and a pretty thing, even after being on the road so long. She has a baby with her. The baby's name is Sam. We considered calling Leonard 'Sam', remember? Her car broke down, which Leonard says he will tend to tomorrow, and she needed a place to stay."

"What in God's name is she doing out in this part of the country by herself?"

"I don't have a clue, dear, but she has the look of someone who needs a hand. It will only be for a day or two until her car is up and running. It will be refreshing to have a young woman in the house."

"She's a runner," Fred said. "She must be running from something and it better not be the law."

"Don't be such a grumbly bear. Wait till you meet her. When you do you'll know she wouldn't harm anyone. Not intentionally."

3

LEONARD WEST WORKED RELIGIOUSLY for Jeremiah Habscheid, the owner of Wilton's Auto, and while circumstances wouldn't normally translate into a deep-seated friendship developing between the two men that was unequivocally what they shared. Jeremiah was the owner, thirty-two years old with a wife, Laura, who was six months pregnant, and Leonard was much younger, had just turned twenty, but Jeremiah and Laura were almost the only people he saw in town. Taking things apart and putting them back together was what Leonard had done since anyone could remember: the family radio, his dad's lawnmower, even the transmission on the Ford truck they owned before they bought the Chevy. There were a few people remaining in town Leonard had grown up with (Leonard hadn't finished high school and wasn't sorry neither) but he liked to be around Jeremiah and his wife because they had ideas that captivated him. Leonard pumped gas and looked after ordering inventory and was officially enrolled as an apprentice mechanic and could already do many of delicate operations his boss was relied upon to do to keep Eastenders mobile. Laura did the books because she could and brought lunch to the garage for the two of them six days a week and she was glad to do it. Jeremiah told Leonard that once the baby was born they would have to start packing their own lunches, but he said so without any real conviction.

They both knew Laura might miss a day or two but she would find a way to help out sooner than later.

The pay Leonard received wasn't much because the business had only been up and running for a few years and Leonard accepted this. He still lived at home and didn't need much. Sunday and Monday were days off for him unless the garage was busy, but some Mondays he would slide by and chat with Jeremiah and pump gas if his boss were pinned underneath a vehicle, and because Leonard was so diligent, Jeremiah told him that one day he could buy into the business and be a junior partner. Leonard liked the sound of that. The two of them would talk nuts and bolts when they had to and talk religion when all the nuts and bolts had been accounted for. Not just any religion; Jeremiah and Leonard were partners in another venture that was completely separate from the garage: they were in the process of creating a brand new religion.

Jeremiah's father had been a firebrand Baptist minister and proselytizing led to his son's inevitable revolt and for years there was no communication between the two. There was now. Jeremiah drove to Medicine Hat four or five times a year to visit and quiz his newly retired father on some of the germane issues of Christianity. Jeremiah (and now Leonard and Laura as well) read anything they could get their hands on regarding religion including texts on Buddhism, Taoism, Hinduism, Confucianism, Judaism and recently, Baha'i. Jeremiah had been metaphorically roasted in hell for so many years that he felt there had to be a nobler path to enlightenment.

Some of the things Leonard had once wanted didn't seem so important now. He viewed his early years with disdain because that was the only way a serious mind could view them. His work and his life felt intertwined now and the purpose of his existence was clear. When Hanne Lemmons had appeared at the side of the road it was an omen of some kind, one he couldn't put into words. He drove to visit Jeremiah and Laura after meeting Hanne, which he planned to do anyway, but he did so with great anticipation because he knew her appearance was about to solidify something in the progression of things. *My people have been lost sheep. Their shepherds have led them astray.*

4

I SLEPT SPORADICALLY and woke up for the last time to the sound of a magpie outside the bedroom window. Earlier, I had changed Sam and we both fell back into a sullen sleep. At first I had some accounting to do to explain where I was and how I had come to be there. The room, I'd been told, was intended for the grandmother and evidence was in the grey floral wallpaper, the dark purple curtains and one large picture of an English country foxhunt, the fox not visible but taking cover in a foxhole and surrounded by dogs. Sam was awake now, swaddled in blankets on the floor beside my bed, looking up at me as if to ask what was next.

"The bathroom's free," Muriel said, standing in the hallway to greet me. "Leonard is at work today but his boss said he could tow your car to the garage. Between the two of them they'll get to the bottom of it. Take your time and I'll have breakfast ready when you're done."

Muriel in the daytime was different from Muriel at night. She was nervous in her own home with a stranger across the table; I could tell she wouldn't be able to calm down until my every need had been served or I was out of the house. She asked a few questions but not in a prying way. She wanted to know where I was from and where I was going, but she didn't ask me anything about Sam's father or where my husband was, though I could tell she was eager to do so. The kitchen window looked out onto Tamarack Avenue and every few minutes a car or truck would drive by and slow down in front of the house. Word had gotten out and people were eager to get a good look at the new girl in town, a girl with a baby in tow.

It was bread baking day, Muriel mentioned, and I offered to help but was told no: after all my travels I deserved a day to myself. I took this as a hint that I should in fact spend the day by myself. I told Muriel that the one thing I regretted not bringing was Sam's stroller because he was an armful to carry and only good for fifteen or twenty assisted steps; she said she had just the solution: a baby carriage in the storage shed that had carted Leonard around town years ago. It was huge with giant wheels and needed a good wipe down from decades of neglect, but soon I was off to explore the town, under a blue and innocent sky, and give its members a chance to get close and personal, and there would be no camouflage because two of the four wheels took turns squealing as I made my way down the road.

Driving into the town at night with its glittering lights gave the appearance of a larger community than it was to walk around. I approached the town surreptitiously, down Pottery Road to Elm before coming out on the business section which was situated on the highway I'd driven in on. I went to Selmon's and bought some throwaway diapers for Sam and a quart of milk. I was accustomed to fussing with cloth diapers but had treated myself for the journey east and I certainly didn't want to be demanding washing time from Muriel, kind as she was. Drivers who passed me on my route waved and storeowners offered hello with an inquisitive edge, as if they knew something but not enough. Muriel had mentioned that Fred worked at Pioneer Elevator so I walked down that way and asked a man coming out of the office if Fred West was around. He said *he* was Fred West and that I must be Hanne.

I told him I didn't want to bother him; I just wanted to say thanks for letting me stay the night. He tipped his hat and I was on my way, and a block later I looked over my shoulder and he was standing in the same spot with two other men watching me squeal my way down the street.

I was about to cross the highway when I saw a tow truck dragging my Plymouth into town, Leonard behind the wheel beaming like he'd just discovered penicillin.

"Well, we got her into town okay. I took a chance you hadn't locked it, which you hadn't, but we're going to need to get the keys from you."

I dug into my purse, which was a mess, and handed them over. I heard someone inside the garage yell in agony about something and Leonard smiled.

"That's Jeremiah, my boss. He wants to meet you some day. Probably won't give your car more than a cursory look today, Jeremiah says, but tomorrow afternoon we'll get on it."

I thanked Leonard and started down the road. He insisted I wait and he ran into the bay of the garage and came out with an oil can and tended to the squeaky wheels.

"That should do you," he said, "but you'll be due for an oil change in another fifteen or twenty miles."

I nodded in agreement, but by the time I realized he was making a joke it was too late to laugh, even politely. Leonard raised his hand in the air as a signal of goodbye.

Sam and I had time to kill and we headed down to the park and along the river which twisted and turned like a snake in a hurry, though the water was low and in about as big a rush as most of the people in the town. The swallows were out in full force and swooped around the carriage as if they were determined to protect the two of us from the mosquitoes that were unmistakably part of the landscape. I sat on a park bench to feed Sam and, despite the diligent swallows, I was bitten three times. Each time I slapped at a mosquito, Sam would stop eating and grin.

It was an enjoyable sojourn so long as we kept moving. I found a play park with a toddler swing that sent Sam into a hysterical giggling fit, and then we walked down to the edge of the small golf course and watched two men who couldn't help laughing at their attempt at playing the game. We headed back to the main drag and found a place called Jack's Café. From outside looking in it wasn't too fancy and I wanted to do something special for Sam. In two days, July 30th, it would have been Samuel's birthday which I wasn't looking forward to, but this was the day Sam was born and he deserved to be recognized. We found a booth as far away from the few customers already seated and the waitress brought a high chair for Sam to sit in. I ordered a coffee and two cupcakes. Candles would have been nice but I didn't want to draw attention to the two of us, but before I allowed Sam to smear his cupcake all over his face I leaned toward his high chair and quietly sang "Happy Birthday". It was one birthday he would never remember but one I would never forget.

I had walked the whole town as far as I knew and when I returned to the house it was filled with the smell of bread soon to come out of the oven and Muriel leaning against the counter with a look on her face that suggested an enemy had been vanquished.

"Take a seat, dear. We'll share this pot of tea, you and me. There's something I need to tell you about Leonard."

5

NEXT TO SUCCESSFULLY OVERHAULING an engine, the favourite thing Leonard got a kick out of was placing his hand on Laura's stomach and feeling her prospective baby kicking like it couldn't wait to get out and join them. That was always the first thing he asked to do when he visited his boss after supper. Then it was down to business.

The truth was they were a bit stumped at their present stage of developing a universal religion. Neither Jeremiah nor Leonard had brought it out in the open, but they were clearly at an impasse. The idea was to create a path leading to spiritual emancipation built in such a way that it would appeal to those dabbling in various sects as well as those wandering aimlessly through life and yearning for direction. The first principle tenant they agreed on was that it made no sense for a religion to include the concept of hell. Hell was negative and Jeremiah in particular had had enough evidence that coercing someone into a particular pattern of behaviour based on such a negative consequence was a foundation for building a fearful society stocked with guilt-ridden citizens. Jeremiah had quizzed his father on this subject many times and it certainly was a main tenant in his father's life. Without hell, he would say, there is no heaven.

So much better, thought the two earnest creators (Laura offered suggestions from time to time but preferred to mostly take notes) to imagine a society where individuals were free to strive for goodness without the anxiety of the possibility of an afterlife of burning flames and eternal suffering. This reaching out that they envisioned had to focus on some higher power. All the religions they had reviewed had a god or two as the focal point (the Hindus had more than 330 million divinities to match every imaginable aspiration) and unlike so many fad religions and cults that had surfaced in recent years, they had no interest in suggesting anyone honour *them* in a deified manner. They were creators, not naturally born leaders. And so, after months of wrangling with the issue, it was the development of the self, they decided, that their members would deem worthy of glorification. Everyone had themselves to contend with and everyone was interested in themselves. All of this was fine and dandy, but the knot in the rope was the structure they needed to provide for followers to make progress. Every religion had a structure of some kind. Rituals deemed worthy of repeating.

What sorts of practices could they put forward that would lay out the journey toward self-fulfillment?

Leonard said, "If the focus is on each individual, wouldn't it make sense that people pray to themselves? If every individual has inside them the power to seek out a better life, rather than praying to a god for guidance, shouldn't they be searching within?"

Jeremiah laced his hands behind his head and leaned back in his chair. It was a thought and he was thinking about it. Laura was thinking too, of course, and besides taking notes (she had already jotted down Leonard's idea) she was also the screen their ideas passed through before gaining acceptance. No one responded for a long time and Laura sat, as she often did when not in the act of taking notes, with her hands cupping her temples and her eyes closed. The kitchen clock was ticking and the old fridge was humming. No one said this would be easy.

"I think the idea is right," she said. "But people need a ladder of some kind to climb or they might only imagine they've arrived somewhere. If you tell some people to sit down and search what they know for a way to make themselves a better person they likely will only come up with what got them to where they are: a person who needs to improve."

"So what do we need to give them?" Jeremiah asked. He thought he already knew but he liked to see Laura involved.

"Well, for example, a minister will direct members of his congregation to the Bible, to texts or parables that sum up the path one needs to consider. These were written so long ago and are so hard to understand for most people, that nothing concrete happens. You need to write a modern Bible of sorts. A series of courses that give people a chance to explore what they need to do."

"For example," Leonard said, "we could write a course on how to control one's temper. I don't know how good it would be but that's one I could do. Also, how to stay patient until you get what you want."

"And how to stay disciplined," Jeremiah said. "I've learned a lot about that in the last three or four years. I could probably do that one."

"That's the sort of thing we need to do," Laura said. "People will only join a religion if they think there's a good reason. Instead of trying to get to heaven or trying to avoid hell, we'll help people to a fulfilled life while they're here."

"Heaven on Earth," Jeremiah said. "That's what we could call the collection of courses. I think this could work but we're going to need some help."

"That's exactly right," Laura said. "The first course you need to work on is 'How to Seek Help When You Need It' and once you understand it you can then turn to others. Even this community has enough people that could help us. Think of all the things the Olenowski's have done for people around here. They would help write a course on 'How to Become a Generous Spirit'. People don't need to know our grand purpose for now. Once we get all of the courses together and polished, then we will invite people to join in. We'll have to start small, of course. This is the beginning of a big project."

"But think about how important this could all be," Jeremiah said.

"We'll probably need to get an editor," Leonard said. "And I could ask Hanne, the young mother who's living with us for now. She might have something to contribute. Anyone who's had a baby has to know something. This will be outstanding. We can get others involved from here, and years from now when people ask where these ideas came from the answer will be Eastend, Saskatchewan."

"Heaven on Earth," Jeremiah said. "I don't think this should just be the name of the book of lessons. Heaven on Earth is the perfect name for our religion."

6

AFTER THREE DAYS at the West residence on Tamarack I could see that it was likely at least three more before my car would be repaired. It wasn't the radiator like he suspected, but a bypass hose. The cylinders had practically seized up and Leonard said without re-doing the engine properly I would own an oil burner that would slowly consume itself. The car was already burning oil, especially on the highway, so I agreed to let him do the work. He said he would try to do most of the repair on Mondays, his normal day off, because if the garage wasn't too busy he could revitalize my old car and he wouldn't charge me much for labour, just parts. I said yes partly because it sounded like a good deal and partly because it was obvious that Leonard was as desperate to offer help as I was to receive it. He had taken a liking to me after three days and was comfortable enough to hang around the house for an hour or so before heading over to visit his boss in the evenings.

Fred didn't interact with me much at all. Three nights a week he was off playing pool and the other two nights he spread paperwork related to the elevator over the surface of the kitchen table and was oblivious to the world around him until it was time for the late night news. Muriel liked me but she loved Sam. She had her routines and was reluctant to accept my help around the house, though folding laundry was apparently something I qualified for. Most days, morning or early afternoon, Sam and I would wheel our way to the park and the river and occasionally the centre of town. People were friendly and waved or said hello and a few called me Hanne though I'd never met them.

Muriel told me raising an only child was more of a challenge than most people could imagine. She explained that Leonard had not had an easy time of it when he first got to high school. He was impatient and short-tempered and frequently resorted to violence with his peers. The school suspended him for a second time and he never went back.

"He's smart, you know. And kind in so many ways. He's getting on with his life now, so we're led to believe, and he's good at what he does and he loves his boss. I ask him what he does over at their house because he goes there every chance he gets and he says the three of them talk about life and how to make it better and that someday Fred and I will get a full explanation. Life around here seems pretty good to me but I guess one could do worse than talk about how to make it better."

Whenever Muriel's half of our conversations veered in this direction I always nodded and agreed with anything she said. I wasn't about to tell her the little I knew about what Leonard was really up to.

Two nights before, a Friday night, Leonard asked if I would like to get out of the house for the evening and go with him to visit Jeremiah and Laura. I mentioned Sam and getting him bathed and into bed and he said his mother had agreed to babysit for two or three hours, no problem. He'd obviously thought things through ahead of time.

Part of me did want to get out of the house because for most of my life there had been compelling reasons not to. They didn't know me and it was unlikely I would ever see them again and Muriel was tickled to have Sam all to herself. She had gone to the library and had a healthy supply of children's books to entertain him.

The Habscheid's house was pedestrian in every way. It was a house they were renting because they were buying the garage property and it was all they could afford. The house cast a small imprint on the vast prairie and the rooms were proportionally diminutive; it reminded me in many ways of the house I had grown up in at Tansor. My visit felt highly anticipated and Laura pulled fresh saskatoon berry tarts out of the oven. We sat around the small kitchen table and I noticed Laura had a notebook staring her in the face.

The flurry of observations that came my way was what I expected: the progress (or lack thereof) on my Plymouth, the warm late summer weather, the local community and how I was or wasn't adapting. How was I finding Eastend? Well, I told them, it was a peaceful place and easy to get around. Try as I might, I couldn't forge a deeper opinion of a place I was only passing through.

Jeremiah explained the project they were working on, recently named Heaven on Earth. He summarized what they had accomplished in their goal to reach out for help in developing ways the commoner might attain personal transcendence. I couldn't believe what I was hearing and it must have shown on my face. I had been through the Pentecostal formula thanks to the Jaggers, and Mr. May's visits over the years had filled me in on communist doctrine, but in this hidden valley in the middle of the prairies I couldn't imagine the two men responsible for resurrecting my car holding down a position of spiritual rejuvenation. When Jeremiah was finished his brief summary, Laura asked if perhaps I might be willing to contribute to the project. The scones were sitting in the middle of the table as yet untouched and it occurred to me, when this question surfaced, if their accessibility depended on my answer.

People accustomed to social banter, I had noticed in my brief time on Earth, had mastered the art of deflecting untenable verbal requests with an expression of neutral and pleasing qualities such that everyone involved felt content even when nothing of substance had been offered. I was still learning. I said nothing straight off because I didn't know how to say that while I recognized their fervour, there was something specious about their vision and I didn't want to hurt their feelings. They *were* earnest and the scones smelled delicious.

Laura relieved the awkward calm by saying, "When I was falling asleep last night I imagined that people asked such a question would say to themselves: what do I know that could possibly be of any use to anyone?"

"You are a wise person," Leonard said, looking right at me. "That was one of the first things I noticed when I first met you. I could tell you were wise beyond your years."

When I heard Leonard's pronouncement I knew it was something he'd heard his mother say. Only someone like Muriel could think up something like that. "Thank you," I said, "for your kind thoughts. I suppose everyone knows something about the world. But my world is so upside down right now. Maybe if I had time to think about it. Then I might be able to help."

"You're right," Jeremiah said. "That's probably the most intelligent thing I've heard for a long time. Of course you can think about it. This project is just beginning and it's going to take some time."

Lemon tea was then served and there were enough scones that allowed each of us to eat two. They were fabulous. Laura asked if I wanted to see the rest of the house which took about sixty seconds but allowed her to have me to herself in the tiny living room.

"I know you have plans to move on eventually," she said, "but I just want you to know that if you stayed I think it would be great. Pretty soon I'll have a baby of my own and he or she could play with your Sam. Leonard has told me all about Sam. Leonard never gets tired of talking about you. Never."

7

FRED WEST WAS A NUMBERS MAN. He had been head operator at Pioneer Elevator for six years and he took great pride in doing the job the way it ought to be done: the right way. Accurate measurements, strict accounting, current market conditions and keeping on top of the machinery were concerns that never left him. People for hundreds of miles around saw him as reliable and trustworthy and a discerning judge of character. Of course, there were some who accessed his facility who were as useful as buffalo chips, but he knew how to handle them. That was part of his job.

Thursday night was Muriel's bridge night out and it was always a relief to Fred when it was hosted at someone else's house. He had no patience for cards or most of the people who played cards. Muriel was an exception, of course. Leonard was out of the house as usual right after supper and before the dishes were done, and Fred was left at home with Hanne and her little boy, Sam. Sam hadn't taken to Fred right away, but it could be said that Sam's early propensity to walk had been aided by living in the same house as Fred. If Sam was teetering at the edge of the coffee table for balance and Fred entered the room, as quick as a lick Sam would take three steps and fasten himself to the couch. After a few episodes of Fred-fear-filled walking, Sam now took five or six steps at a time before his diaper cushioned his fall.

Hanne had helped with the dishes and given Sam a bath and had read him a book before he fell asleep. Walking was taking a lot out of him and he now slept through most nights.

"If you care to watch TV you go ahead," Fred said.

"Are you going to watch anything?" she asked.

"There's nothing on. You might find something though."

"I'm all right."

Hanne made a pot of tea. Fred said he didn't want any so she poured herself a cup and joined him in the living room. It was too early to go to bed. Fred sat in the over-stuffed chair where he always sat, his hands sprawled out on the wide arms of the chair as if an earthquake were imminent.

"No bookwork tonight?" Hanne asked.

"Things are in good order," he said.

Fred was like most of the men living in town. He would talk when he had something to say but didn't shy away from silence. Silence was for thinking, and that was something most people didn't do enough of. He watched Hanne examine the contents of the room. The furniture had come to them through family mostly and had been there for more than twenty years. Muriel had home-stitched lace doilies on the arms of all the chairs and the chesterfield. The lamps were ancient, with frayed tassels hanging down from shades that had yellowed over time. The wood-burning fireplace, brick on the outside, held soot marks from years of use and it wouldn't be long before it would be employed again. He noticed her eyes kept returning to the cuckoo clock that sat inert above a small bookshelf.

"Is the clock broken or does it just need winding?" she asked.

"Both, I guess you could say. It's Muriel's mother's clock and why Muriel took it off her I have no idea. You can wind it up and it will try to run but it doesn't last long. Leonard tried to fix the damn thing once but couldn't do it. Muriel likes the look of it or so she says."

"I might be able to fix it for you."

"*You* could?"

"My dad repaired clocks. I learned a few things."

Fred didn't say anything back for a long time. He was staring at the clock but watching Hanne out of the corner of his eye.

"Well, young lady. I suspect there's got to be a lot of trickery to fixing a clock, but if it's something you could manage you would be a hero around here."

Well, something Fred hadn't considered needed settling was settled. As much as he tried to fight it off, there were a lot of unanswered questions surrounding his house guest and when it was for a day or two they didn't seem important. Leonard didn't appear to be in any hurry to get her car back on the road and daily came up with yet another good reason for the delay, and Hanne had been with them going on two weeks now. Going from a day or two to two weeks changes the flavour of things, was how Fred saw it. If two days can become two weeks then two weeks can become two years. That was how time worked as long as you were alive. How foolish would he look two years down the road if he knew so little about Hanne Lemmons and her son?

"Don't suppose you care to tell some about the place you're from?"

"Well, I could," Hanne said, and she did. She told him about living in Tansor with her father and without her mother or her brother that was to be. She explained how they lived and what their life was like, her father's sudden passing and her living with Old Evans. She spent a disproportionate number of words on Old Evans because he was so interesting and it meant there was less she had to divulge about herself. Through it all, Fred sat there mesmerized by her telling. She told him about some of the neighbours and when she said the name Lodie Stump he asked her to repeat it. Never heard a name like Lodie Stump, he said. She talked for a long time and was thirsty again and this time Fred said he would join her. Once or twice she got him to laughing when she described Mr. May the communist or Ernie Jagger the egg man. She talked and talked like she was responsible for a short summary of her life only it wasn't short at all, and if she kept on talking long enough someone would come home or Fred would grow tired and head to bed and she wouldn't have to address the topic she knew he was most interested in. That's what it felt like to Fred sitting there, fascinated by a young woman who appeared to have lived a thousand lives already. He noticed something he'd taken in the first time he'd seen her at the elevator: she was by most people's standards a beautiful young woman. A girl, really, but with a baby it was natural to lean toward woman. Even with a kid as part of the package he could see she wouldn't last long on the open market.

"Too bad Muriel didn't have any cookies on the go," he said.

"I could make some tomorrow if you like."

"That would be good."

There was a cushion of silence again. Fred knew and Hanne suspected he was contemplating how to ask his next question. How he might cozy up to the wellspring of his curiosity.

"Why Winnipeg?"

This time it was Hanne who wedged stillness into the room. The answer to the question could be long or short, detailed or threadbare, revealing or discreet. She could tend toward subjective and confessional or objectify the sordid facts that made up the trials of her life. The only man who knew all the tainted details of her life was dead now. If the wrong people knew the right things, her intended life would be over. She had been left with one thing worthy of any and all sacrifices that had to be made and she wasn't about to allow any room for compromise.

"Winnipeg is just a place I've wondered about. I've never seen it. It's just my way of getting away from my old life. A chance to start all over again."

The answer was the one Fred had predicted. It was perfect, really. She had outlined her life without restraint and left him with the shadows of conclusions that were not hard to make. Her answer had also told him that this was as far as she was willing to go, that there were parts of her life that only she had the right to own. Fred accepted her position completely.

"Nobody," he said, "would ever track you down in Eastend. Nobody comes here unless they're coming home. Or they've lost their way."

He looked up at her then and they shared a laugh and an understanding.

"Take a look at a map, sometime. They call this the Valley of Hidden Secrets. It's called that for a reason."

8

THE WAY LEONARD STARED you could tell he thought his boss was crazy. Or perhaps he was waiting for Jeremiah to explain what he had told him was just a joke. For the last fourteen months Leonard had worked hard on and constantly thought about the new religion they were working on, and it filled him with an assurance that life was worth living after all. And now this.

"You had to be there," Jeremiah said. "Ask Laura when she gets back from the store. It was fabulous. These people are light years ahead of us and they already have down what we were aiming for, only so much more."

Leonard sat slumped in his chair. He could hear Laura coming in through the back door. "I see Leonard's here," she said. "Perfect timing."

"Laura will confirm everything I'm saying. We saw the notice in the paper and decided to drive to Swift Current and are we ever glad we did. The meeting only lasted about two hours but we spent the day there talking to people involved. They're smart, Leonard. They've thought of everything."

"Who is *they*?" he asked.

"The Church of Scientology. It was founded by a man named Hubbard. All those little courses we were considering? Well, they already have them. It's very deep. Everything they do is to help you become "clear". They say we all are influenced by our past lives and they help you clear that up too. Am I right, Laura?"

"Leonard, don't look so dejected. Just come to a meeting some time and listen to what they have to say. We won't have to spend years working on what we had planned because this man has already done it. They've got literature you can read and study from and you can take these amazing courses in Edmonton."

"Edmonton?"

"Edmonton or Vancouver or Toronto. For now. There will be something opening up in Saskatchewan eventually and who knows, we might be a part of it."

Try as he might, nothing Leonard had to say would dilute their enthusiasm. All they had to say about the organization sounded pretty amazing, he had to admit, but the idea of being the creator of a religion based right here in Eastend was not something he was eager to give up on. He could understand if it was Jeremiah going off on a tangent, but Laura had always been the voice of reason. She had obviously been won over too, and the two of them would not be deterred.

"So that means we won't be meeting like this anymore?"

"Of course we can meet," Jeremiah said. "We can study the course materials together. It's going to make big changes in our lives. You think you feel good about yourself and your role in the world now, wait until you get immersed in Scientology. I'm so excited."

Despite his boss's declaration, Leonard didn't feel particularly good about himself at the moment, and he wasn't even close to feeling excited. He supposed he could go to a meeting at some point. He was doing a job he was good at, better than his boss in fact, and he had been promised a part of the business in the future. But that day he left for home earlier than usual.

When you feel alone sometimes it's best to be alone. He drove down by the river and watched the swallows in their evening feed. Nothing in their world had changed and he envied them.

9

ON THE PRAIRIE, you can feel the weather on your skin. Sam and I looked forward to getting out of the small house every day and we had our favourite haunts. We loved walking along the creek beside the park. It was serpentine and trimmed with wild rose and chokecherry, and one day we saw a shiny black mink cavorting in the water. Fred told me that when you live here for a while you can get up in the morning, stand outside and examine the sky and you know what the weather will be like for the rest of the day. It was all so different from living in Tansor.

Another thing different was the people. Most days Alison Armstrong would come to her front fence to greet us on our walk, then pluck a petunia from her garden and wedge it in the baby carriage for Sam to enjoy. She, like many others in the town, knew I was Hanne and introduced herself to me. On Saturdays I often had the company of five or six kids all vying for a turn to push Sam around town.

I was halfway through my third week in Eastend and Leonard said the car would be up and running in a day or two. I had some decisions to make. Had my car needed only a battery on the way through, I would have been in Winnipeg by now and found something, but the more I thought about it the more I realized that this sleepy little town was as good a place as any to celebrate anonymity. Muriel had been hinting almost from the beginning that I might like to find a home here and one evening when supper was complete, Fred got up from his place at the table and blurted: "I think she should stay." That was all he said before he went off to play pool.

I had left everything behind and because of my circumstances there was no turning back. I still had some money in reserve but I was running low and knew I would have to find a job of some sort. I bought groceries from time to time and I could tell Muriel appreciated that, but realistically I was living in Eastend for virtually nothing and that wasn't going to last forever.

"If I did decide to stay I would have to find my own place," I told Muriel one afternoon.

"I suppose that's true, dear, but there's no rush. Fred is in complete agreement on this. The room you're staying in is yours for now. Otherwise, it won't be used at all."

"And I would need to find some kind of work. I don't imagine that will be easy in a town this small."

"It's always surprising what unfolds," Muriel said. "Everyone here relies on one another in some way and where there's a will there's a way, as they say. I could ask around for you, if you like. The trick to living in a small prairie town is to make some good friends. Everyone needs a good friend. It can get awfully lonely otherwise."

I only had some of the tools my father handed down to me so I found a local jeweller who was willing to let me use what I needed on a Sunday so long as I returned everything early Monday morning. I'd put off working on the clock because if I needed to order any parts it might be months before I could get them in and who knows where I would be by then. I took it apart and found that I would be able to repair it without any new parts. There was a tiny hairball caught up in the gears, some internal rust to remove which can alter the balance of things and, the one serious issue, a cracked bellows, I was able to repair myself. Leonard was off somewhere and Fred was helping a friend move a garden shed, so it was Muriel who volunteered to tend to Sam while I worked away. She was kind enough to stay out of things for the most part, but would swing by with Sam every once and a while and exclaim: "Oh my, isn't that something now." The internal workings of the clock had not been mounted inside the case properly and, when that happens, owners mount their clock on the wall so that it looks balanced but they have no idea the insides are then out of whack. It took me about three hours in total to get it up and running, and when I invited Muriel into the living room to inspect the finished product, tears welled up in her eyes. "Holy moly. I'll have to bring mother over soon. She won't be able to see what you've done but she would love to hear her old clock again."

When Fred got home Muriel started in again. "You should have seen what she did. She oiled the insides using a toothpick. Our Hanne is a genius I would say."

After supper Leonard asked his mom if she would put Sam to bed because he wanted to show me something. She agreed and I was certain he was going to drive me to the garage (only three blocks) to show me that my car had finally been repaired, but instead he took me down a gravel road to the reservoir. The sun was in the early stages of disappearing and the golden light on the burnt out mountains was beautiful.

"This here is where we get our water," Leonard said. "They dam the river and we never run short. Sometimes people drive up here at night and go swimming."

"That's one thing I've never learned to do," I said. "And I don't own a bathing suit."

"The people who swim here at night don't wear bathing suits anyway," he said. "Just if you're interested."

"So how's the car coming along?"

"Tomorrow or the next day. It's almost done. You're battery is barely holding a charge so I got you a rebuild."

Leonard popped in one of his eight track tapes but turned the volume so low I couldn't make out the words being sung. It was his version of atmosphere.

"I like you, Hanne. I need to tell you. I like you a lot."

"And I like you too, Leonard. I like most everyone I've met here."

"You didn't care much about the religion Jeremiah and I am working on. I could tell."

"Well, I don't think it's a bad thing. The two of you are doing what you think is important, at least. It was the way I was raised. I don't feel ready for religion right now."

"I'm going to tell you one thing I would really like to do right now," Leonard said. "I'd really like to kiss you."

I knew I had to be careful. I remembered the stories Muriel told me about how Leonard didn't fit in at school and had turned into a bully to get his way. She said that was all behind him now but who could know for sure.

"You're a fine person, Leonard. Anyone who meets you would say the same thing. But just like I'm not ready for a religion at this stage of my life, I'm not ready to be kissed either. It's just the way it is."

"If I stopped being involved in the religion thing, would you kiss me then?"

"I'm sorry, Leonard. I wouldn't. It has nothing to do with your religion."

He squeezed the steering wheel on his truck and I could see the veins in his arm and neck bulging to the surface. He couldn't contain his emotions any longer and he pressed the flat of his hand against the horn for a long time. When he was finished there was an anemic echo of horn that bounced back to our side of the valley. The sun was lower on the horizon now. The hills not as golden.

"You're going to go away, aren't you?"

"I'm not sure yet. I might go away, I might not."

"If you go away I won't see you again."

"But if I stay you will. Before we head home let's stop at the store. Is the store still open? I'll buy you a pop. I kind of feel like a pop."

Leonard didn't say anything but jammed his hands into his pockets for the car keys and when he did a purple condom rolled onto the bench seat. It embarrassed him, I could tell, but he started the truck and backed up slowly, without any commitment. I had no idea where we were going but relieved that at least it was in the direction of town.

So much of my life had been lived with so little attention paid to expectations of the future, but all that changed after that fateful Halloween. Walking around Eastend not a day passed by that I didn't consider what it would have been like to have both Samuel and Sam with me on my journey. Sam relied on Samuel for many months in a row and Sam now had only me to depend on. Because I was breastfeeding him, no one doubted he was my own child. I was certain that the scenarios fashioned in the minds of the people I had met since coming to this small prairie town were debated in coffee shops and beer parlours and master bedrooms. What they likely thought of me was easy to accept. What they didn't know was a blessing.

316

My father had always enjoyed keeping an eye on the weather, especially the weather that didn't apply to Tansor. He said we were damn lucky to be living where we were because most of Canada suffered from harsh winters and he would often cite the frigid temperatures of places like Edmonton, Saskatoon, and Winnipeg. Fred told me it was warmer in and around Eastend than it was in Winnipeg, but I knew anywhere I took up residence on the prairie would be a shock and in a strange way I was looking forward to the challenge. I could feel the weather changing once September arrived. The kids were back in school and many of the afternoons were bright and sunny but the nights were giving notice of things to come.

I wasn't an accepted member of the community in Eastend, not even close, but I sensed that an invitation had been offered and the decision was clearly up to me. The pace of life I had been living was so relaxed and stress-free, but September proved to test my peace of mind. Leonard finally delivered my car and it ran well, I'll give him that. He even washed and vacuumed it before he handed it over. He was proud of his accomplishment and wore a silly grin on his face as if my revitalized car might offer him another chance to enter my life. Muriel found me a job of sorts. There was an elderly lady living alone down by the river who wanted to continue living in her own house and was willing to pay for her independence. Her name was Emily and her husband had passed away eight years earlier. My job was to show up in the afternoon and do some basic housework, prepare her supper and a lunch for the following day. She wasn't the gentlest of souls and I learned to bite my tongue on many occasions. She did take to Sam, however. I accepted the job on the basis that Sam could come with me and I had a playpen for him to bide his time in when I was busy. Emily was Scottish and had her wits about her, and paid me cash for my services at the end of every day. She felt she had stored up a number of tricks that would come in handy for raising a baby like Sam, and she kept herself busy testing them out every afternoon. Sam was beginning to mimic a lot of what he heard, and Emily had a belief that children learning their colours early was important because the reason boys often grow up colour-blind, according to her theory, was that they weren't exposed to them early on. The way she pronounced "red" I was sure Sam would grow up expecting to spell it with multiple r's.

Muriel and Fred insisted I should continue to live with them and they would only take fifty dollars a month for the privilege, which I knew was ridiculous, but until such time as I got my life into a routine, I didn't argue. Leonard was happy I wasn't moving away and he bought Sam a small winter coat and toque which I had no choice but to accept. Just when everything was falling into place, Muriel's mother, living alone in the country, fell and broke her hip and had to be hospitalized. When the doctor announced that she could only be released either to an extended care home or into someone's private care, my time at the West household came to an end almost as soon as it began. Both Muriel and Fred felt terrible, but it was Fred who suggested I could stay in the farmhouse for free if I looked after the utilities. He said it was way better to have someone living there than to have it ravaged. In the vigorous month of September I was left with my head spinning. I had made a commitment to stay in Eastend, found a job, found a home, lost a home, and found a new one out in the country.

10

LEONARD KNEW HIS WORLD CHANGED the day he found Hanne Lemmons stranded at the side of the road. After sharing only a few words with her he sensed her intelligence and knew she was far more beautiful than he was handsome and she had the sense of self he was striving for. What he would do for her, he realized, was anything. What he needed to do to get her was what he was trying to figure out.

Now that she wasn't going anywhere (who would want to move to Winnipeg anyway?) he knew she was a project he could work towards. The truth was her car could have been completely repaired a week earlier than it had been but his sense was the longer she stayed put the more likely she would stay forever. He wasn't sorry he had taken her down to the reservoir. She said she wasn't ready and, with all he'd imagined she'd been through, he supposed that was reasonable. They were her words that said if she ended up staying she would still be around for him to see. What was that if it wasn't a sign of hope?

He had walked home one lunch hour because he'd changed his pants the night before and gone to work without his wallet. His mother wasn't home and his dad was at work and Hanne was in the bathroom, sharing a bath with Sam by the sounds of it. He stood outside the bathroom door and listened to the splashing of water and the banter between them. He imagined what she looked like frolicking in the warm water, imagined the image of her getting out of the tub and pulling Sam out after her. She dried Sam off first and told him to wait. Then it was her turn to use the towel to remove the tiny drops of water from her skin and she took her time doing so, talking to Sam the whole time. There was a chance she would open the door and step into the hallway to head to her bedroom for clean clothes, and he could be standing there with every right to be home at lunch time in his own house fetching his wallet, but he chose not to let such a thing transpire. He was due back at work by 12:30 and his boss had his own set of expectations.

What Leonard hadn't expected was the way Jeremiah and Laura had turned away from the project he was so passionate about. He still thought it was a good idea, but it was plain neither his boss nor his wife wanted to be involved in any way now. The two of them had gone to Edmonton and taken a course on communications put on by the Church of Scientology. There was no turning back. Despite Laura being only a couple of months away from motherhood, the two of them had decided to move all the way to sunny Los Angeles to work on a special project the church had started. It was called Rehabilitation Project, but Leonard knew nothing about it. Because neither Jeremiah nor Laura could explain it properly, he got the feeling they didn't know much about it either. In any case, they were intent on pulling up stakes immediately and they offered Leonard the opportunity to continue on with the business, pay all the bills required, and help himself to half of any profit margin he could verify on paper. Leonard agreed. If he had his choice, things would have gone back to the way they were, but he knew the economic implications of the new regimen were huge for him. Without the burden of developing the framework for a new religion, he would focus his energy on the business, and his dad was pretty savvy when it came to organizing things and would help him. The first thing his dad suggested was he get a two-year written contract from his boss and that was what he did. Leonard would work hard to build an empire in the town and then he might become the kind of commodity someone like Hanne couldn't resist.

11

IT WAS A LUXURY FOR SAM and I to have a residence to call our own, one without recognizable ghosts from the past lurking in the corners of every room, one without the need to compromise on routines like using the bathroom or making noise if noise needed to be made. The house was close to the same size as the West's house but it felt larger because we had it all to ourselves. Inside, it was like a museum replica of a turn of the century farmhouse, though I believe Fred said it was built in the 1920s. The walls were papered, every one of them, mostly in vertical stripes and ornate floral patterns. The stove had an oven and could be heated with wood or oil; any heat generated there also heated the hot water tank. There was a comfortable claw-footed bathtub, an elaborately carved dining table, a large purple sofa, and a padded rocking chair. The linoleum on the floors had been well-trodden and looked almost rusty in spots but this to me only added to its charm. I retrieved the old Junghans clock from the trunk of the car where it had been stored for months, and just having the reliability of sound in the room made it feel like home. It was a place, finally, where I could catch my breath.

The bedrooms were on the top floor and the stairs leading there were wooden, with a black runner lapping its way up the middle. Sam was walking independently on a regular basis, albeit falteringly, so I made the decision that until the day came when he could traverse the stairs on his own we would confine ourselves to the bottom floor. One of the rooms upstairs had a small bed which I brought down and wedged into a corner of the living room for Sam, and barricaded it with superfluous furniture so he had a makeshift crib to call his own. I slept on the couch and wedged the ironing board at the bottom of the stairs to define the border of our living space.

I was content enough with my surroundings. Sam spent the first few days wandering from downstairs room to downstairs room looking to see where Fred or Muriel or Leonard might be hiding, but soon he was convinced *Fed* and *Mur* weren't to be found; there were only the two of us. There was no TV but there was a radio and an old Symphonic record player. There was also a vast store of records I had never heard of: Count Basie, Louis Prima, the King Sisters, but Sam and I put a different one on every night and danced until bedtime.

When I got Sam to bed I always left the radio on, just barely audible, but loud enough so that my movements around the house wouldn't wake him. Even with the radio on for background noise I was unmistakably alone with my thoughts. When you live in a house with four other people your individual opinions don't surface very often. Now, it was almost as if a dam had broken and the thoughts I hadn't had time to consider all wanted my attention at once.

I thought about what Tansor might be like right now. The house I owned was empty. The oil tank was full but there was no one to turn the heat on and, mild or not, the winter moisture would seep in and have its way with the place, I was sure of it. If circumstances had been different I would have found someone to rent it so it would be looked after in some fashion or other and it would have offered some income. I had no idea what the place would be worth. Eight or ten thousand, maybe more because the land had to be worth something.

There would be taxes coming due and some electricity bills, though to my knowledge only the back porch light was on. What would the government do if someone disappeared and didn't pay their taxes? I guessed that eventually they would put it up for sale and do my paying for me. The house was the one possession I owned that I had to pretend I didn't because the risk I would take to reclaim it was too severe to consider. One thing I could do was write to them and ask about the taxes and offer to pay them so I could keep the place, but even if I went to Maple Creek or Shaunavon and registered a mailbox number they would be able to trace it. The government probably didn't care where I lived so long as I paid the taxes, but someone else might.

What would Lodie be doing now? I assumed she had moved back to her place and had found my welcome note on the table, though it was also possible she never had returned. But she was probably living there by herself and thinking about the last two years like I was. Had she intended to take Sam back when she returned? This I didn't know but it seemed highly likely. She might have gone to the authorities by now and there might be a search warrant out for me: the neighbour lady who had stolen a baby and driven away forever. I didn't trust Lodie or her irrational nature. She gave up on Sam to run off with her estranged husband and Sam deserved better than that. He was my father's son too and I know my father would have done anything in his power to protect him.

I thought often of the people who had been my neighbours and what they would make of my disappearance. The Neilsons knew I was looking after Sam because Lodie had gone off, but what would they think of me now? Were they still staring out their living room window hoping to see their son walking home, older now and wiser? Daisy and Beverly had both been supportive and at times I wished they could drop in and watch Sam walking and telling me he wanted more of what he wanted. It didn't occur to me until several months after Samuel died, but the Neilsons had lost a grandchild in a way. They had lost a son and a grandson in one year and how do you recover from a thing like that?

That's what life is, I realized. A series of events that happen with a not-knowing time in front of them and a knowing time after. Once the event happens there is nothing that can be done to take it back and the same goes for the knowing that follows. We continue to live, waiting for the next series of events and hope that the knowing that follows is something we can live with. Sam was part of the knowing I had with me from my time in Tansor, and he was the one thing that gave me the will to carry on. As long as I had Sam to protect and care for, there was a part of myself that had a purpose.

I enjoyed the twenty-minute drive into town every afternoon to look after Emily. Sam looked forward to it as well, and I would run into people from time to time and they all knew I was Hanne and at least marginally a part of their community. I stopped by to visit Muriel before my shift every Wednesday because I knew Leonard wouldn't be home then and with Muriel there was always some catching up to do. She had her mother living with her of course, and the first visit there Sam toddled his way into the living room to sit on his favourite chair and found a strange lady staring out at a world she couldn't see. Muriel introduced me to her mother, who asked me how her dog was keeping. Muriel signalled thumbs up so I told her mother the dog was doing just fine. Keep the door to the barn open at all times," she said, "and the dog would take care of the rats."

Leonard was so busy with his garage business, Muriel reported, that he started at seven in the morning and worked until five, and had a local high school student there from five to seven every night to pump gas. I was happy to hear that Leonard was getting along, but if I needed gas I always went after five at night before I headed home. The less Leonard saw of me the better for his own sake.

It wasn't long before there was frost on the ground in the morning and it felt like it was cold enough to snow some days. I bought myself a warm winter coat and Muriel knew enough people in town that Sam would be well-equipped against the chilly winds because of the hand-me-downs that came our way. There were enough spaces between the things that had to be done; life felt balanced and easy to cope with. Once a week I stopped in at the library and took out some books for Sam and a few for myself to supplement the small collection of Victorian novels that were housed in the old place. At night and sometimes in the morning I listened to a radio station out of Swift Current and it was there I heard about a farmer near Shaunavon giving away four-month-old border collie pups, so Sam and I made the trip on a Saturday and picked one up. He was the cutest little thing but nervous I guess because he peed on the back seat on our way home. Old Evans had never named the dog he owned and Sam kept calling our little fellow Dog, so that was what we called him. I fed him and we played with him and let him out for long stretches at a time so he would learn to do his business outside. As it got colder and colder, Dog got to spend more and more time inside and it got so he whined to go out when he needed to. It was more work training Sam than Dog because Sam wanted to ride him and pull his tail. Dog seemed to understand his role in the family and when it got to be too much he would bound over the ironing board for some peace of mind upstairs.

❧❧❧

The first snow didn't amount to much but it came before October was over. The hills looked so clean that first morning, it was like Sam and I were living in a completely different place. Dog stayed outside in the afternoons; he slept in the barn and was probably thankful for it on cold days, but despite having a huge doghouse all to himself, he made a fuss every time we drove away and followed the car to the end of the driveway before turning back. By the look on his face he was the most mistreated animal in Saskatchewan.

Emily never went anywhere unless I took her but she still wanted the three inches of snow shovelled from her sidewalk so that was what I did. Sam was content to sit in the middle of her front yard and push the snow around with his mittened hands. When Leonard had handed my car over he said there was antifreeze in the radiator and a pair of snow tires on the back that were slightly used but should do the trick for my first winter. I hadn't seen Leonard at all for several weeks until one afternoon when he knocked on Emily's door.

"Hi," he said. "I came to see if everything was good for you."

"Thanks, Leonard. Things are just fine. The car runs great and I didn't have as much trouble with the snow as I thought. You did a good job."

"I was wondering if maybe you wanted to catch a movie on Saturday? We could go to the Pastime in town. Mom said she would look after Sam if you wanted to go."

"That's a nice offer, really it is, but no. I work here helping Emily six days a week now and we have a dog to look after as well. It just won't work out."

I had been helping Emily Monday through Friday and the day before she had asked if I would consider working Saturdays too. Some ladies from the community always dropped in on Sunday to take her to church and back to one of their houses for supper, which only left Saturday she was on her own. I told her I would consider it before Saturday rolled around, but when Leonard knocked on the door I made the decision to accept. When I told him no as kindly as I could manage it, he stood there looking confounded like he hadn't planned his next move.

"I hear your garage is doing well. Your mom keeps me up to date."

"Busy," he said. "Busy."

"Have you heard from Jeremiah and Laura at all?"

"They phoned once. He sounded kind of weird. So, anyway, I'm really busy too but I'm here if you need anything. Whenever you're ready. Winters can be long around here. Long and lonely."

I thanked Leonard and told him I had to get back to work. He understood getting back to work and he probably had to do the same thing. I knew that eventually something would steer him in another direction. It's just the way life was. It was just a matter of time.

A few days later, Sam and I had just finished supper and someone knocked on the front door. Fred had ventured out to visit a couple to times to make sure everything was working, but his last visit was only a few days earlier so I wasn't expecting anyone. I opened the door to find a man holding a box in his hands; he said he had driven all the way from Maple Creek because he heard I knew how to fix clocks. I told him I knew how to fix most of them but that I hadn't planned on starting up again. He looked at me imploringly and I invited him in. Dog only offered one short woof. He obviously wasn't going to be much of a guard dog.

"If there's any way you could help with this one it would mean a lot. We used to own a clock almost exactly like this one but we lost it years ago when we moved. The movers say they lost it but I sometimes wonder. My wife hasn't wanted a clock since and then I found this one at an estate sale some time back. I need someone to get her running before Christmas."

I told the man I would try but that it could take some time and it would cost forty dollars to fix, maybe more. He was so happy he started dancing on the living room floor. Dog found this odd and woofed one more time. I took his name and phone number and told him I would call when it was ready to go. "If my wife answers tell her you need to talk to Lenny. I need this to be a surprise." He waited until I wrote down "Lenny" and then he left.

And so that fall, without any will of my own, my clock repair business started up; my guess was it was due to Fred West who ran into a lot of people from miles around. By the middle of November I had two more projects to work on. I was reluctant at first because I had made a commitment to put that kind of work behind me, but I knew that as much as I enjoyed looking after Emily, it was a position that had to end eventually. Sam liked to crawl up on a chair beside the arborite kitchen table where I worked and I had to tell him to keep his hands to himself, but despite this he was intrigued with what I was doing and would sit there and watch for half an hour at a time. He would grow up to be his own man and do many wonderful things, I was sure of it, but when he got older it was something I could teach him to do.

12

IN THE MIDDLE OF NOVEMBER we had a significant dump of snow that started in late afternoon and continued on into the evening. I loved the seclusion it brought and Sam and Dog and I were warm enough inside a farmhouse that had offered shelter for more than forty years. I kept checking on the accumulation every hour or so, and then about seven in the evening it stopped. There was no wind and the world felt like it had come to a standstill. The sky cleared and the moon illuminated the pristine landscape. I thought I could see a figure at the end of the driveway, so I put Sam to bed and went upstairs and looked out a bedroom window — there was someone moving up my driveway, no doubt, and he was shovelling away the snow. The figure toiled relentlessly, brushing the dry snow on one half of the driveway to the side and then tackled the second side, working back toward the road. When the figure was close to the house I could see it was Leonard. I hadn't thought much about Leonard for several weeks but apparently he was still thinking of me.

Then the cold weather I had anticipated settled over the landscape. The days were sunny but cold and there was always a wind of some kind. It was cold in the daytime and colder at night and I had to keep the stove on at all times. I kept the doors to all the upstairs rooms closed, trying to keep as much heat as possible on the bottom floor which was our home now. Despite my efforts, because the house was not well-insulated, the cold outside leaked in through windows and doors. The night after the snow I happened to look out toward the road and there was Leonard, standing in the middle of the field, stoically still, his hands in his pockets. He stood directly in front of the house, staring, not rubbing his hands together or shuffling his feet, just stationary like a fence post with nothing to hang on to. There was no sign of his truck anywhere on the main road or in the driveway. It was as if he dropped out the sky, a winter sentinel in waiting.

The same thing happened the next night and the next night too. He had to know I was aware of him because he would have seen the curtains he was staring at moved to the side and my puzzled figure staring back at him. He was hoping I would invite him in. That had to be what was happening. Why else would someone stand there night after night in silent vigil? Every evening he returned; when I went to bed at ten thirty he was in the same spot and when I woke up in the morning he was gone. From the driveway, when I went to town in the morning, it was not apparent where he had stood. Perhaps he walked to the same spot from a different direction each night. Maybe the wind moved the fluffy snow and covered his tracks. It was a mystery, but he was constant, the same time, the same place.

One evening when I got home it was almost dark already. I went inside and quickly prepared pork and beans for supper and fed Sam his favourite, butternut squash. An eerie chill flooded my body when I looked down and saw that Dog's dish was full of dog food. I routinely gave him a half cup in the morning before I let him out and he didn't get any more until after the two of us had finished eating. I was certain Dog had eaten his breakfast installment completely as he always did and that his dish was empty when we left for town. Fred had a key to the house but the two times he came to visit were

Saturdays because he was busy at the elevator weekdays. The bag of dog food was on the counter where it always sat and I always locked up on our way out. I left Sam in his high chair and went upstairs. I turned on the lights to every room and checked the closets. Everything looked the same and there was no one upstairs and no sign there had been. Dog obviously wasn't hungry because he could have eaten his fill if he wanted. I poured all that was sitting in his dish back into the bag and he watched with mild interest before bedding down on his favourite blanket.

I sat by the living room window and waited beside a sliver of curtain-opening for Leonard to appear. I sat there until well after it grew dark and there was no sign of him. When Sam finally needed my attention (and Dog needed me to come to his rescue) I wasn't away from the window more than twenty minutes and when I returned to my post, Leonard was standing in the middle of the field as always.

On the way into town in the morning I decided to stop for gas. It took a while for Leonard to make it to the pumps because he was sprawled out under a car when I pulled up.

"Shall I fill her up?"

"Yes please."

I realized the tank was less than half empty and he would probably wonder why I'd bothered. He filled the car, checked the oil, and put in some washer fluid, the special kind that wouldn't freeze. It came to $9.60 so I handed over a ten.

"Don't bother with the change," I said.

"Great. Thanks a lot. Well, I'd better get back to it. Three jobs on the go today. That was quite the snowfall we had the other day," he said.

"And thanks for clearing my driveway," I said. "You really didn't have to do that."

"Driveway?"

"Last Monday," I said. "You shovelled my driveway from the road to the house."

"Not me," he said. "I would have if I'd thought about it but I would have been late getting out there. Dad slipped and wrecked his back and I had our own place to take care of. You'd think with all his experience with snow he'd know better. Anyway, I gotta go. Let me know if you want to go to a movie sometime."

When I got to Emily's place she said: "Let's forget about housework for today. Why not the three of us go to Jack's for something good. You do such a thorough job around here there's not much to do other than the ironing."

We sat down at a table by the window because Emily adored the mural painted on the wall and she loved to watch people come and go. Two young men came in, stomping their boots at the entrance and I recognized one of them as Fred's co-worker at the elevator.

"I heard Fred hurt his back," I said as they walked by.

"Oh, he's fine. He missed a day of work and then he bought himself a new pair of boots. Always easy to blame it on the boots," he said, and his friend laughed at the joke.

"I heard Fred had taken a fall," Emily said. "You can't be too careful out there. My husband fell about six months before he passed and, you know, I don't think he was ever the same again."

❧❧❧

Wednesday was my longest day because Sam and I got into the routine of heading to town early to visit with Muriel for an hour or so, and then I would shop for enough groceries for the week before heading home. Muriel always gave us lunch when we arrived and now that the weather had turned cold she often had homemade barley soup on the stove. The next time Wednesday arrived we knocked on the door because it was locked. Muriel always left the door unlocked and we knew to just make our way inside, but this time it was locked and knock as I might, Muriel didn't answer. Sam and I walked around to the side windows and rapped on them but there was clearly no one home. I began to worry then because Muriel's mother had so many health issues, and Muriel herself had said many times that she enjoyed her mother's company one day at a time.

We had an hour to kill and we needed something to eat, so we went to Selmons for the week's groceries and had beef jerky and chocolate milk for lunch. Despite the frigid temperatures we ate in the car. It was cold enough that even the ice cream I bought would be fine until my shift was over.

Some days Emily's mind was clearer than others. She asked me if I knew how to knit and I told her I had tried once or twice but had never conquered the skill. Did I want to learn? she asked and I said that I supposed I could try again. Most of Sam's clothes had once belonged to various babies in town and it might be nice to have something to wear that his mother had made. She started in on a series of tales about the knitting she had done over the years and how during the war she knitted sweaters and socks for people she didn't even know. Then she asked me to fetch her knitting and I asked her where it was. She couldn't remember. I looked everywhere in the house, checked every drawer and closet but I couldn't find her knitting anywhere. Then it occurred to me that I'd never seen her knit once since I'd been there. She got herself wound up in a snit about it and said I must have hidden her knitting.

I assured her I hadn't and asked if she was ready for lunch. "I always eat lunch before you arrive," she said, as if it was something I ought to know.

That night on the way home I considered checking in at the West household but decided against it. They would be in the middle of preparing supper and because it was after five, Leonard would be home. The next day I stopped by a few minutes before work began and Muriel was, thankfully, in her kitchen.

"Is everything okay?" I asked.

"I was about to ask you the same question," she said. "I was worried about you. It's silly, I know, but I thought maybe you'd run yourself off the road. I made some delicious chicken and rice soup but I don't imagine you have time to eat it now."

"I came yesterday, as usual, but you weren't here," I said.

"I had to take mother for her six month checkup, remember? I mentioned to you that we would have to do Thursday this week."

I didn't have anything to say to that. Muriel looked tired all of a sudden and she had enough burdens on her lap as it was. We didn't have much time, but Sam made his way into the living room as usual because Muriel's mother always kept an arrowroot biscuit by her chair that she gave him when we left. I've been trying to teach him not to ask people for things. He can ask me, that's different, I'm his mother, but it always seems rude when little kids demand things from adults. Muriel was busy talking about the dress she'd bought in Shaunavon and how now she thought she should take it back, but I was only half-listening to her story. Sam stood in the living room and I thought I heard him say "Cookie?" but there was no cookie to be had today.

13

WILTON'S GARAGE WAS AS BUSY as ever only now it was Leonard who was running the show and Leonard who was taking in half the profit. Jeremiah had arranged some sweetheart deals with a few individuals in town over the years and that was one thing Leonard put a stop to immediately. He didn't have a special relationship with anyone in town (at least not yet) and the labour it took to repair a blown gasket was roughly the same for everyone. At his dad's suggestion, he painted a sign that said LOCAL AND RELIABLE SERVICE and mounted it above the two garage bays where he lived six days a week. His dream was to one day erect an even larger sign that read: LEONARD'S AUTO. The status of his mechanical apprenticeship was up in the air because he didn't have a journeyman supervising his work, but he ignored the dilemma and so did virtually everyone in town. Leonard could do pretty much anything Jeremiah could and there was nothing to complain about.

Leonard became a fastidious keeper of records: again, his dad's influence. At five every day a likeable, gangly teenager named Randy worked for two hours pumping gas and closed up the garage. This gave Leonard a predetermined exit and in the evenings he and his dad would spread the day's accounts out on the kitchen table. For every job completed the customer now got an invoice that was stamped "paid" and listed everything that was done and the cost of the parts. This was revolutionary since, in the past, locals were used to a handshake and receiving the old parts in a plastic bag. Another thing his dad implemented was his phoning of customers into the supper hour a day or two after anything close to major repair had been completed. These were almost always good news calls, but if a tuneup wasn't reacting the way an owner thought it should, Leonard made an appointment to make things right. Within a few weeks he was receiving business from farmers halfway to the next town. Wiltons became the place to go for dependable service and free coffee while you waited.

Three successive Sunday evenings, Leonard received a phone call from Jeremiah who was busy with Laura and their daughter, Ruth, just outside of Los Angeles. It was hard for Leonard to comprehend what they were doing down there, but it appeared to involve building something and it sounded like a lot of hard work. Jeremiah said he had never felt more purposeful in his life and that Leonard should consider coming down to join them. Seek true emancipation from the drudgery of the world. Not once was Leonard asked how the business was going, which he found odd. The weather is heavenly, Jeremiah said. We know you'd love it here.

Some nights, after a cursory scan of the books, he would go to the pool hall with his dad. He wasn't a very skilled player which added to his popularity. There was more peace of mind to be had from losing at pool than wrangling over the foundations of a new religion. Life was good again, despite the winter, and he could only see it getting better.

14

CHASING A BALL, finding a ball, retrieving a ball, and returning a ball so that the process can start all over again was a sport that was a great joy for a dog and a mystery to those who watched dogs. Where would the instinct for such an activity have come from? I imagined dogs roaming in packs before they routinely became domesticated and nothing I could imagine in their life would have offered a genetic rehearsal. An apple or a pine cone could conceivably have fallen from a tree while a dog was nearby; the dog might have enjoyed fetching it, but bringing it back to the tree would have been the end of the game. Dog enjoyed it enormously and it became part of our routine before and after supper. Sam couldn't throw very far but Dog didn't care. When I was cooking supper, Dog had someone to play with.

That was one thing we did to pass the time. There was the radio, of course, and our library books and each other. We are all creatures of habit and our habits leave a beaten trail from somewhere. It was December now and I still had one clock to fix. Some days it was hard to fix a clock. I talked to Sam all the time just like I used to talk to Samuel. Some of what I had to say to him was specific and focused on what he was trying to figure out, but other times I blathered on as if he were interested and I'm sure at times I became like the radio: background noise. I also talked to the dog and sometimes he paid more attention than Sam did. There was the washing to do, the cooking, the cleaning up, but there was a lot of time that wasn't obligated to anything. I watched Sam when he went off by himself and, unless he was hungry or needed his diaper changed, he didn't have any problem filling the time. Thanks to Emily, everything he played with was identified by colour.

Leonard standing in the middle of the field out front was something that was taken for granted. Usually, he was out there close to Sam's bedtime and he never moved until after I went to bed. One Saturday night I turned the lights out and went upstairs, bundled in my winter coat. I crouched by the window and stared at him staring back at the house. It was well past midnight before I went to bed and he was still there, but I couldn't stand waiting any longer. In the morning he was gone again.

The following Monday Sam and I arrived home at our usual time and found Fred parked near our back door, his truck idling against the cold. It had been a long time since he'd driven out to the farmhouse, back when I was settling in, and my first thought was that something in my world was about to be altered. Dog had come and lain on the small porch, waiting for someone to let him in.

"I would have let your pup in but I didn't bring my spare key. How are you two making out?"

I carted Sam and a bag of library books into the house and Fred followed. He sat down at the kitchen table, which is probably what he would have done if he lived there. Then he talked about the weather. Just to get warmed up was my guess.

"On a scale of one to ten, how do you like living out here?"

"An eight, I would say."

The truth was I liked living with just Sam and Dog, but I couldn't rate the place any higher because it was so far from town and there was the Leonard issue.

"Eight is pretty good, I guess. I don't think the prospects for selling the property are very good right now, so we're happy to have you here. Likely, I'll lease the land out to one of two farmers who've expressed interest. That's the way it is these days, they want to use your land but not pay the taxes."

"I'm happy to stay if you're happy to have me."

Something had dried and crusted on the arborite table and Fred set to scratching whatever it was loose with a fingernail. What he'd come for hadn't arrived yet, I was sure of it.

"Remember the Habscheids?"

"Jeremiah and Laura. Yes, I met them both a couple of times."

"Well, they've gone off on some kind of religious rampage as best as I can make out. Down in California somewhere."

"Yes, I heard that from someone."

"I don't give two hoots what the two of them do with their lives, but they've been contacting Leonard and telling him he should do the same thing. He thinks the two of them walk on water. Who knows, maybe that's what they're learning to do down there."

"Leonard wouldn't give up the garage to go down there, would he?"

"Well now, that's what's got the Mrs. and me on the lookout. He's done so well with his mechanical thing it would be a crime to walk away. He likes his work, I know that. We're not sure it's enough."

Sam and Dog were playing fetch and Fred took a minute to observe the action. It was hard to tell between the two of them who enjoyed playing the most.

"Leonard is easy to get along with," Fred said. "It might not be plain to see that because he's so shy. I know he's fond of you a great deal. He doesn't talk to me about it, but he talks to Muriel. He thinks your Sam is pretty special too."

"I'm sure you've got supper waiting for you at home, but can I get you a coffee before you head back?"

"No, Hanne, but thanks. I can't stay. I shouldn't stay. I probably shouldn't even be here. Muriel told me not to come. It's just that . . . we all think the world of you and . . . well . . . maybe down the road — "

"Down the road who knows what might happen. I know I don't. Some things don't happen until you're ready for them. It would be a mistake for Leonard to wait around for the likes of me."

Fred didn't like the sound of that — I could see it on his face. He had run his fingers around the circumference of his plaid hunting hat the whole time and it was likely a size larger from all the rubbing. He didn't say anything for a while and then he got up to go. He took a quarter out of his pocket and balanced it on the top of Sam's head before he wrapped his hand around the doorknob.

"What I'm about to say isn't meant to startle you at all, but last Friday I had to go to a meeting in Moose Jaw about regulations and some confounded legal issues with the elevators in this province. The meeting took up most of the day and before heading home a few of us stopped for a beer and a game of pool. One of the fellas I met was off duty, but an RCMP type. He said they were looking out for a young lady and a baby that may have stopped in Calgary a few months back. He didn't have a picture, just a description, and who knows who it was they're looking for. You don't see the cops around this town much. They drive through once a month and stop for coffee.

The only reason I mentioned it was in case it was information that would come in handy."

☙☙☙

Most nights I stayed up late reading until I was soporific and had no choice but to fall asleep. A few weeks of this and I became outright vertiginous and yet I couldn't make myself go to bed any earlier. It felt like there was someone else in the house but I knew that couldn't be true because I kept the front and back doors locked when we were away. Some nights the wind howled over the rolling hills and the house groaned under the strain and the grey lines on the wallpaper felt like they were getting closer and closer with each passing day. I sometimes wanted desperately to wake Sam up so I would have someone to talk to, but often both he and Dog fell into a deep sleep and they had no interest in what I had to say. What would I say to him anyway? Hi, Sam. I'm your mother. Well, not really your mother. I'm your sister but you can call me Mother because that's who I am to you. I'm your mother because she didn't want you and because your father died and so this is who you ended up with. Be good to me, Sam. Not just now but when you get older. I'll protect you, so don't worry about that. The wallpaper *is* getting closer but it won't harm you. I won't let it. You're safe because you have a dog that doesn't bark but would protect you if he had to and you have your mother who rescued you from a life that would have been worse. Much worse.

In the evenings I couldn't get prairie dogs off my mind. No one in town thought about the welfare of prairie dogs. They had a pretty good life in the summertime so long as they kept close to their burrows. There was coyote and fox and hawk danger out there and you could tell they were wary. But now, with the ground frozen and covered in snow, they were hiding down there and what did they do, I wondered. It had to be lonely for them.

I was tired of thinking but it was hard not to. I thought about what Fred had told me more than I wanted to. I decided most of it wasn't true. I doubted very much anyone had any interest in who I was or where I was living. There was a chance of course, but Fred was trying to stick up for his son. That's what I decided, anyway. The wind was harsh and suddenly the lamp went black and the radio silent. I had a candle but I couldn't remember where I'd put it and I didn't care about it anyway. I slid off the couch and fumbled my way to the front door. I knew what I'd see if I opened it but I opened it anyway. Leonard was standing out there waiting patiently, and the look on his face didn't fall into any category I could name. He just stared. His scarf fluttered to one side because the wind told it to and out there the wind was the boss. I wanted to yell at him. *Go away,* I wanted to scream. *Don't stand out there and think I'll come for you because I won't.* I wanted to do this but I didn't because I had a child and a dog asleep inside. *I want you to stop this nonsense on your own but you won't because people don't stop on their own.* Other people have to stop them.

I closed the door behind me and stood on the hard porch. He didn't move. I stepped into the field and walked in a semicircle around him. He knew I was there, I could tell, but he continued to stare at the house. The snow was dry, like salt crystals that skittered east when disturbed by my footsteps and soon I was standing behind him. He seemed frozen and unable to move. "Go home," I said, and then I yelled at him. "Go home, Leonard. Get away from here!" He must have heard me because he turned around and faced me. He raised his arms from his sides like he was carrying something invisible.

343

"No, Leonard. Leave me alone." He started walking toward me — I stepped back and he kept shuffling his feet, his arms outstretched and yearning. The wind came in gusts and the snow filled the horizon like a frozen fog so I started to run and Leonard came after me. My feet were bare but it didn't matter because I couldn't feel them at all, and I ran across the field and I was getting farther and farther away from the house but I needed to circle back. My feet were slippery in the snow and I fell twice on my way to the back door but nothing deterred Leonard one bit.

I opened the door, locked it immediately, and Dog lifted his head with jaded interest and went back to sleep. My bare feet felt cold, now that I was back inside, and I sat down on the floor and rubbed the circulation back into them. Dog's bowl was filled with food again. Maybe I was feeding him more than he needed. The wind was howling now and I could feel its bitterness slide under the door. If I kept myself safe inside, Leonard would leave me alone. These were the rules, I could see that now, and it was going to be up to me to obey them. Sam would grow up out of harm's way because I would do whatever it damn well took to make it happen. If we stayed inside, we would both be safe from the wind and rain and sleet and snow and the coyotes that stayed up and howled all night long. We would be protected from all the evil that was out there waiting when you least expected it.

Three

1

THE ROADS HAD BEEN BARE FOR ELEVEN DAYS in a
row and, while it didn't feel like spring, it was as good a time as
any. I reported for work as usual on Monday but Emily's door
was locked and no one answered. I was immediately concerned
and pounded on the front and back doors repeatedly. I was
about to give up when the neighbour, Mrs. Foster, came up
the sidewalk and explained apologetically that Emily had
died either late at night on Saturday or Sunday morning. I
could sense something like that was coming, though I hadn't
consciously thought about its natural consequence. Emily had
gradually lost her will to live. The small but sturdy vertebra of
my income in Eastend was gone and so was my desire to stay.

I didn't confront Muriel or Fred with my decision, which
would have been the decent thing to do. I knew they would
try to talk me out of moving and it wasn't just because of my
willingness to take care of the farmhouse. They still held out
hope that Leonard and I would join forces and that was never
going to happen.

I left them a note because when I didn't stop by to visit
Muriel on Wednesday they would know something was up. I
informed them that while I appreciated everything they had
done for me for the last year, my dream of making it all the
way to Winnipeg, as originally planned, was the reason I was
leaving.

I had given some thought to Fred's contention that an off duty police officer had been looking for me and I was convinced it was just a ruse to send me running toward his son. If Leonard, or anyone else for that matter, tried to track me down they could venture east and search for as long as they wanted. I was heading west. I was heading home.

Sam and I left later than I had hoped. We stayed in Medicine Hat the first night, then, to avoid Calgary, we drove toward Lethbridge, through the Crowsnest Pass, and made it as far as Nelson for our second night. It was a lot of driving even though on the map it didn't look like we'd gone very far. The car, thanks to Leonard's repair, ran like it was supposed to and Sam took to the road better than I expected, perhaps because he had Dog in the back seat to occupy him. The closer we got to where we were going the slower our progress. I wanted to return home but I was afraid at the same time. I worried about what might have happened to the house, but mostly I worried about Lodie Stump. I wanted to move back home but I had to figure out a way to make sure it would be possible without there being any issue about who was in charge of Sam. We stayed one night in Osoyoos and another night in Hope before I resigned myself to making the final leg back to Tansor so I could determine exactly where I stood.

From Hope south everything was building toward green. It was raining the day we arrived, but it was warm and it felt joyful and comforting. Even Dog sat up for the last part of our trip, expectant about when he might be let out of the car for more than ten minutes at a time. There wasn't much room in the back seat or the front seat or the trunk because everything I owned, I had with me.

It was almost dark out when I drove up the Lake Road and past my house once, turned back and went up Holiday

Lane as far as the railroad tracks. Sam couldn't manage the ties at anything faster than a snail's pace so I carried him and we walked behind the back acre. The house was in darkness and the one lightbulb left on at the back had burned out as I had expected. Behind Lodie's house a man was working on an old truck in a shed that looked ready to fall over if a wind came up. I watched him for a while and, eventually, a girl that must have been his daughter came out and said something I couldn't hear. The girl looked to be about twelve years old. Lodie may have still owned the house but if she did it was rented out.

It was with mixed emotions that I drove up the driveway to the house. Part of me was happy to be back home, especially since Lodie wasn't living next door, but the house I owned was one I had sworn to never live in again. Sam had just about had it with travel and he wasn't amused when I told him he had to wait in the car. When I told Dog he had to stay he began to whimper.

The outside hadn't changed except that the grass had grown up where it wanted to and one of the small and stunted fir trees had blown over in the wind and narrowly missed the chicken coop. I still had the key to the new lock I'd put on the back door. The door required a solid push to open, perhaps because it had swollen with the winter or the house had settled around it. There was enough light to determine that things inside were exactly as I'd left them. I flipped the light switch but nothing happened. I tried my old bedroom and the living room but nothing. I guess when you don't pay your hydro bill that's what you have to expect, but there couldn't be much owing because there had only been one light left burning. It was late and damp and chilly, and there was a musty smell about the place. Sam was crying like I'd abandoned him for life, so unloading our stuff and getting him to bed wasn't an option. I locked up and returned to the car to find the man from next door peering in the window of the car at Sam and Dog.

"Are you looking for someone?" he asked.

"Not here I'm not. I own this house, I just haven't been around for some time. My name's Hanne. I'm moving back."

"Okay then. Just checking. No one's driven up this driveway before is why I got to wondering."

"You live next door?"

"I do. We bought the house just before Christmas. It needs a little work, but all in due time."

"You bought the house from Lodie Stump?"

"That's the lady who owned it. We wanted to move in earlier but it was messy because she had to get her first husband to agree to the sale. But we've got it now and we like living out here."

"You said Lodie's first husband?"

"I did. She's got a second one now and a baby to boot. They live somewhere in the Glenora area as I recall. Nice couple, those two. Her and the new husband I mean."

The man said once I'd moved in to be sure to drop by and meet his Mrs. The news he imparted was so delicious I didn't mind spending one more night in a motel, and I was so happy I felt like hugging him before I drove away.

I found us a nice clean motel with a bathtub so Sam could get back to his routine. First, we gave Dog a good run and I bought him a can of expensive dog food as a treat. Then Sam and I went to Cecil's Café for supper and they had a booster seat that I propped up in a booth opposite from me and that's where he sat while I told him how life was going to be different now, and I filled him in on all the plans for the house and how in a few years he would get the chance to go to school that I didn't have. The whole time he sat there sucking on a sugar cube, and there was no doubt in my mind he got more than a gist of what I was saying.

❧❧❧

We moved in the next day even though it took two days to get the power hooked up again. I fired up the oil heater in the basement and blasted the dampness out of the house. The first night, I put Sam to bed as it was getting dark, and lit a candle to find my way around. He was close to being old enough for his own bed so he slept with me until such time as I could get him a proper bed. I didn't like the house looking like the house it was and I was determined, no matter how long it took me, to change the furniture and the flooring so that it felt like my new house and not my old house. I had Dog's one and only blanket and, once I laid it on the floor at the foot of the bed, he curled up and went to sleep as if this had been his custom since the day he was born.

On Friday Sam and I walked down our driveway and back up to the house belonging to the man and his Mrs. who turned out to be Edna and Cecil. They had a daughter who was ten, Clare, and another daughter, Sybil, who was a year older than Sam. The three kids busied themselves playing in their bedroom which gave me a chance to get to know my neighbours.

They were curious, of course, and wanted to know where I'd been and how long I'd been gone, so I told them Saskatchewan and said I was staying with relatives. Edna nodded to indicate it was plausible, but I could tell Cecil had his doubts but didn't press the issue.

"There's an old man living not far from here," Cecil said. "Mr. May. I'm sure you know him. Anyway, he poked his head around here a few times once it got cold and I told him no one was living in your house. He came back twice after that and I got the feeling he wanted to slip into your house for the winter so I told him to bugger off. He might be the smallest man I've ever met."

"He is small," I said, "and harmless for the most part. He'll be by in the summer asking for water and trying to start a communist revolution. Just warning you."

"We haven't met most of the neighbours," Edna said. "The fellow across the road, Arty, lives by himself and is raising mink in the large chicken coop on the property. He's about the only one we've met so far."

"People mostly keep to themselves around here," I told them.

In the four days since we had returned, I had been assessing my state of affairs constantly. I owed one year's taxes, due in a couple of months, and I had enough money leftover to make some changes to the house provided I was able to cover my expenses from here on in. I didn't want to do clock repair for the rest of my life, but it was the one skill I had that would stave off starvation for a few years and I planned to advertise in the *Leader* once again. I found out that Cecil was a carpenter by trade and busy at the moment but would soon have some time on his hands. Edna worked as a clerk at the courthouse. She had arranged to split her job with a fellow worker and was looking for someone to tend to Sybil in the afternoons and Clare for another year or so after school and during the summer. They also said they planned to get a cow some day (I thought of warning them about all that would entail, but I kept my mouth shut) and they wanted to raise chickens. The three kids were having a great time playing at something and laughing in the bedroom and eventually I had to be the evil mom and grab Sam and head for home, but it was past eight o'clock when I did so. Before then it was agreed that I would be the one to babysit Sybil starting Monday, Cecil would make some renovations to my property in exchange for towing the chicken coop and the barn from my back acre to his, and in return he would make the changes to the house I had in mind so long as I paid for the materials needed. I was so happy at that moment I wanted to scream or cry, but I tempered my emotion in front of my new neighbours. I understood that everything would stand or fall depending on one person still living in the valley and that person was Lodie Stump.

2

DRIVING BACK FROM TOWN one day I noticed Beverly Neilson getting out of her car and I waved at her in passing. The next evening she came to visit, and because I saw her making her way up my driveway I had a few minutes to decide how much I was going to tell her.

"Well, Hanne Lemmons has made her return. Welcome back."

"Thanks," I said. "Sorry I didn't say goodbye when I left. It was a sudden decision on my part."

"I've been worried about you," Beverly said. "I don't know why, but ever since you left I had a premonition you were in danger somehow. You look fine now. Unless you've been through it no one knows what it's like to lose a child."

Beverly couldn't believe the difference in Sam. He showed her his toys one by one and called her "Beberly". Dogs in general made Beverly nervous, apparently, so despite Dog being the gentlest and least likely candidate as a bite-your-hand-off dog, I put him outside with a bone. I had forgotten how visiting with Beverly was mostly the art of listening.

"There's still no word on our Kurt. I started having weird dreams about him and a friend of mine told me about a fortune teller she knew who is amazing so I decided to give it a try. It meant a trip to Vancouver which Red thought was a complete waste of time and money, but I told him to consider it the equivalent to a month's beer budget. Anyway, I went to visit this lady and it wasn't anything like I expected. There was no crystal ball and she didn't wear loopy earrings, it was just a small room at the back of her house. She asked me to bring a picture of Kurt which I did, and she sat there for a long time before she said anything and finally she said there was a strong impulse coming through and that I could have my money back if I didn't want to hear what she had to say. I told her of course I wanted to hear — that was the reason I came. She told me that, while she couldn't guarantee the message she was getting was correct, it was saying that Kurt was dead and that he was buried somewhere close by. She said some other things after that but I blanked them out. I didn't want to believe in her message then and I still don't. Hope is the only thing I have to hang on to."

Both of us started to cry then. Silently. I felt hot and clammy all of a sudden and even though I knew I should say something encouraging I couldn't open my mouth and I didn't know what to say if I did.

"I'm sorry," she said. "I shouldn't be burdening you with my troubles. You've started a new life for yourself now. I can see that."

I nodded my head and Beverly composed herself. I offered to make her some tea but she declined the offer.

"By the time Lodie came back you'd gone. She asked around about where you were but of course no one knew. Her life has changed completely."

"So I've heard."

"Have you run into her? She seemed desperate to find you at the time. I can imagine she has a few things she wants to talk about."

"I went to Saskatchewan," I said. "I have some family and close friends there. I needed some time away."

"That's what I need," Beverly said. "I would do anything to get away from here and start again. But I can't of course. Despite what the fortune teller said, I need to be here till the day I die in case Kurt decides to come home."

∽∽∽

When Beverly left and walked slowly back down my driveway, there was no one alive I felt sorrier for. She was desperately hoping for some escape from her circumstance and I was the only person who wasn't a fortune teller that knew she would never find one. Sam was close to being weaned and when he wanted more milk he would chase me down with his empty bottle. "More. More." One thing Beverly had said kept coming back to me. *You've started a new life for yourself now.* Everything in the past had to remain there and Sam was my most vital reason for it doing so.

I started babysitting Sybil. It was more like supervising their playtime once Sybil became adjusted to coming to our house. She always brought her favourite doll and Sam had his favourite truck and for the first few days silence was at war with their attempts to negotiate lending rights. It had been my routine to talk to Sam constantly but it wasn't until Sybil was under my care that I realized that Sam was a good listener but wasn't prone to saying much for himself. Sybil was slightly older and more precocious in many ways and her verbal ability was in a constant state of rehearsal. After a few weeks Sam learned to stick up for himself vocally because he came to understand it was the best way to deal with someone like Sybil. Dog felt outnumbered with two kids around and, since the weather was improving every day, he was content to spend the daylight hours roaming around our three acres.

Lodie Stump wasn't in the latest phone book. I assumed her name had changed and I knew I had to talk to her and the sooner the better. Cecil had taken down part of the fence between the two properties and was soon going to drag the two farm buildings over to his place and said he would be willing to start renovating my house the week following. He mentioned running into Lodie downtown, which explained why the following day she showed up at my house just before suppertime. She came alone.

When she drove up I turned on the TV for Sam and stood on the back porch to face her. There were at least a dozen things I had imagined she was going to say and I thought it would be better if Sam wasn't around to be seen or to listen to any of it.

"You went away somewhere," she said.

"Yes, I did. You were gone for a long time and I didn't think you were coming back. You didn't write or anything. I spent a year in Saskatchewan."

Lodie sent the fingers of both hands deep into the roots of her hair as if such a preposterous message needed to be massaged into her consciousness. She looked around her as if to make sure the two of us had no witnesses.

"And you took Sam with you?"

"Of course. He loved it there. He's very adaptable."

Lodie wasn't finished, I could tell. There was a different look about her. Not so much her face or hair, though she was wearing more makeup than usual, but the way she presented herself. She had on a floral dress that looked new, was wearing moderately-heeled shoes and, even with the distance between us, there was a fragrance in the air I couldn't help notice. She bent down and using her index finger removed a spot on one of her shoes in a manner that suggested it had no right to be there. She wanted something, that was apparent, and I was terrified about what that might mean. I noticed the vehicle she had driven up in wasn't her old truck but a new car, red and shiny. She stepped back and leaned against the fender for support.

"I heard you're married now," I said.

"Yes I am. That's what I need to talk to you about."

Something shifted inside of me. I have no idea what it was, and I know our organs are meant to stay put and do what they do, but it felt like my heart had fallen and was now beating rapidly inside my stomach. I was still standing on the back porch and I sat down on the top step, afraid I would fall over if I didn't.

"Bert has gone off on his own," she said. "I'm married again and to a good man and I know how lucky I am to have found him. We have a baby who's three months old. His name is Edward but we call him Eddy. My husband doesn't know most of my past and I might have told him but you were gone and Sam was gone. And anyway, I didn't. It was a mistake, I realize that now, but because so much time has passed I can't take a chance on what might happen. My life is so good right now and I don't want all that's gone on around here to change that."

"So what are you asking?"

"I'm asking that you and I never met. My husband has a job offer in Vancouver and if he takes it we'll be moving in a month or two but there's no guarantee. I'm asking you to carry on with your life and let me get on with mine."

I covered my face with my hands and my whole body started shaking. Lodie walked away from her car and came to the bottom of the steps.

"Is that something you can do?" she asked.

"Yes," I said. "It's exactly the kind of something I can do."

Lodie thanked me and we met halfway down the stairs and exchanged a brief hug. I asked her if she wanted to come in and see Sam. She thanked me but said no — the absence of our history together was something that was better to begin right now. I told her I could see her point and I said goodbye and she drove away; it was the most final goodbye I'd experienced since the day Samuel left me forever.

3

IT TOOK CECIL THREE FULL DAYS to reinforce the chicken coop and the barn and put them on skids and drag them over to his place with his tractor. The small hayloft in the barn had been such a haven growing up I was sad to see it go, but I wasn't sorry to see the end of the chicken coop. I had hated tending to the chickens and now I wouldn't be tempted to try again.

Soon after, Cecil got to work on the house. He changed the flooring in the kitchen and the living room, and once that was complete a small van delivered the furniture I'd purchased at the auction at Whipple Tree Junction the previous week. Gone was my father's dresser, the kitchen table and the sofa chair. I furnished the place with a new bed for Sam, a dresser that matched, and a small but comfy chesterfield for the living room. All of this was accomplished in four days time but that was just the beginning of what I wanted done.

I wanted a workshop for my clock repair business, which felt overly optimistic when the process began. I'd only had one clock to clean since I'd arrived back home. My idea was to have the workshop built attached to the garage. What I described to Cecil was a building that was much like what Old Evans had for his woodworking shop, only smaller, and I asked that a wood heater be installed in one corner so it would be a place I could work separate from the house all year round. What Cecil didn't know was that the structure would extend beyond the garage and completely cover over the location of the dry well that had been filled in.

I could tell when he was working on the flooring that it wasn't the kind of task he enjoyed, but once he got to design my workshop and build something from the ground up it was like I was doing him a favour. In the end the materials cost more than I'd expected but it was worth it. When he was done I had a room for extra storage and plenty of space to have a workstation for my clock repair. He insulated the room, set a small ceramic wood stove in the corner with brick around it, and ran the electricity that was already in the garage into my shop. There were two windows looking out on the grove of fir trees and, maybe because it was new, it felt like a more agreeable place to be than the refurbished house.

Spring rolled into summer and I never did see Lodie again. There was a chance she had moved to Vancouver but I didn't ask. The house was mine. Sam was mine. I enjoyed babysitting Sybil more than I had the whimsical Emily back in Eastend, and eventually my clock repair enterprise began to pick up. Mr. May stopped by for water every Thursday and he now had a small two-wheeled contraption he pulled with his bike that allowed him to transport more water than in the past. I was making more money than I ever had and there was enough to put into a savings account — I knew eventually Sam would start school and he would need more than we'd gotten by with in the past. The world was pretty damn good but not perfect. Perfect for me would have seen the Neilsons move somewhere else but I knew that wasn't going to happen anytime soon.

Early in the summer I felt a tinge of regret about the way I'd left Eastend without saying goodbye to anyone. I sat down and wrote Muriel and Fred and Leonard a letter explaining my decision to move back to where I was raised and I told them all

I had accomplished since arriving. I sent a few pictures of the changes I'd made (not that they knew what to compare it to) and a picture of Sam who was looking more and more like my father with each passing day. I wrote the letter because it felt like the right thing to do. Little did I know at the time that it was the worst thing I could have done.

∾∾∾

It was the last Friday in August and if it wasn't the hottest day of the year it felt like it. I had taken Sam and Sybil to Maple Bay where they had fun splashing around the shallow folds of brinish water under my watchful eye. Unlike my father, I was drawn to the ocean, but I was fully aware of its danger. It was almost five o'clock when we returned and I dropped Sybil off at her house then drove up my own driveway. It wasn't until I was beside the garage that I noticed a truck parked in the backyard, hidden from the Lake Road the way it sat behind the house. I should have recognized it immediately but for some reason I didn't, and as soon as I got Sam out of the car, Leonard got out of the truck and stretched his arms toward the blue sky.

"Leonard," I said.

"Hi, Hanne. This is one big country we live in. It took me four days to get here. How's the car running?"

Dog was in the middle of giving us our welcome-home performance and Sam was cowering behind him, unsure of what to think.

"What are you doing here?"

"I came to visit you. Aren't you happy to see me?"

I invited him in. What else was I supposed to do?

"Where are you staying?"

"I don't know yet. I guess I haven't decided. We got your letter a while back. We thought you'd gone to Winnipeg."

"Well, people's plans change sometimes. You would know all about that, I'm sure."

Leonard said he'd forgotten something in the truck and fetched a toy airplane he'd brought for Sam. "I had one when I was little but it was smaller," he said. "I always thought I'd learn to fly some day."

"Me too," I said.

He offered to take the two of us out for dinner but I told him it wouldn't be necessary, that I could prepare something. I told him it wasn't worth taking someone Sam's age out to eat, but the real reason was I didn't want to be seen in town with him and I didn't want to give him any ideas. I could tell he must have already had some to drive all the way out here uninvited.

"How are your mom and dad doing?"

"Great. Dad just got a raise and Mom volunteers at the senior's home once a week and she's taken up painting prairie landscapes for some reason. They seem pretty happy. You don't have many mosquitoes around here."

"I see one or two a year. We're pretty lucky."

Trying to make conversation with Leonard was awkward. In part I saw him as younger than I was and naïve to boot, but another part of me saw him as a middle-aged man from the prairies. He asked if I had any toothpicks and when I gave him one he sucked on it awhile and manipulated it in his mouth like it was a toothpick-gymnastics routine he'd been working on and was proud of. He was nervous and kept petting Dog to give his hands something to do.

I remembered how I was a desperate and forsaken soul, stranded with no car, and how Leonard's family had taken me in, no questions asked. Anything less than reciprocating was wrong on many levels, but we only had the two bedrooms and two beds and there was nowhere for him to sleep. The couch was a possibility but I didn't want Leonard sleeping on my couch. After we'd finished eating, Leonard jumped up and did the dishes without being asked. I wanted him out of the house and suggested we take a walk down to the creek. Dog and Sam led the way down to my favourite pool and as we made our way across the back acre, Cecil waved from where he was working on revitalizing the old barn. I could tell Leonard was impressed with the lush foliage and serene backdrop of the Cowichan Valley. Fred and Muriel had once driven Sam and me out of Eastend about forty minutes to a small clove of underbrush that had once been a native encampment, and they'd told me they loved going there because it was such a stark contrast to the brown rolling hills that tumbled in every direction from their prairie home. I knew what I was showing Leonard would be reported in detail once he got back. I told Leonard how, growing up, I'd pulled numerous trout out of the creek using worms as bait and he put his hand in the water as if to convince himself it wasn't a mirage.

On the way back to the house, Leonard and Sam took turns giving Dog a chance to fetch a stick and by the time we got back to the house the sun was orange on the western horizon. I was hoping Leonard was about to say thank you for the tour and the visit and that he'd better be on his way, but I knew he wasn't going to do that. He followed me inside and I made some tea. The same kind his mother had introduced me to.

He sat down on the couch, his tea cup cradled in both hands.

"You remember Laura and Jeremiah?"

"I do."

"They want me to move to California and join their Scientology group."

"Is that where you're heading?"

"No, I'm not. I thought about it. It just doesn't feel like something I should be doing."

"So, you're heading back home then?"

"I don't want to go back to Eastend. I want to stay here. An auto mechanic can get a job anywhere. I know we didn't hit if off the first time around, but I want another chance, Hanne. I think we could be good together. "

"It's time for you to leave," I said.

"I haven't finished my tea."

It was time to give Sam his nightly bath and put him to bed. He knew that, and was enjoying the delay.

I sat and waited until Leonard finished his tea. He told me it was good tea and thanked me. I told him he was welcome. He didn't move.

"Just let me sleep on the couch for a week. I'll help out around here. Seven days from today if you tell me it's time to go I'll go. I promise."

"It's time for you to leave now, Leonard."

"I don't want to leave," he said and looked frightened, as if the words that came out of his mouth weren't the right ones.

I picked Sam up and held him in my arms. "I want you out of here now. Sam and I are going outside and we're not coming back until you get in your truck and drive away." I set Sam down at the bottom of the steps and I felt stupid standing there. It was my house and here I was outside and Leonard who should have been outside was inside. It was almost dark out and Sam looked bewildered. He should be getting his bedtime story by now. I waited for a long time but Leonard never came out. The bastard had a lot of nerve sitting in there when he wasn't wanted.

The fence was still down from when Cecil had moved the farm buildings from my place to his and that was where Sam and I walked until we were standing at our neighbour's' back door. Edna answered and I told her I needed to talk to Cecil. She didn't ask why. She could tell I needed help.

I told Cecil that a boy I knew in Saskatchewan was in my house and how he'd come without notice and now he wouldn't leave. I started to get emotional and I was holding on to Sam so tightly he began to whimper. Cecil looked over at our house. "What's the boy's name?" he asked, and I told him "Leonard." He said he would take care of it and grabbed an axe from the woodshed and ducked between the strands of the barbed wire fence.

Edna came back to the porch and asked me to come in. I said no thank you and followed Cecil who was already approaching the back steps. "Don't kill him," I said, and Cecil muttered something I couldn't discern. I took Sam to the doorway leading to my workshop. If I had to I could lock the two us inside.

I heard some yelling followed by a measured conversation that was less than yelling. Then Leonard appeared at the back door and Cecil was behind him, the axe still in his hands. Dog joined them on the porch and wedged himself between the two of them. He barked once and Leonard tripped over him and careened down the cement steps, taking out the railing on his way. It felt like the world had stopped. Dog and Cecil stood on the porch looking down at Leonard, and Sam and I looked horizontally upon the scene that had unravelled before our eyes. The world started up again when Leonard began to moan in agony.

Cecil said we had to get him to the hospital and said he would take him in. I told him I would look after it and he helped me lift Leonard into the back seat of my car.

"You're sure you don't want me to come along?" Cecil asked.

"You got him out of the house for me," I said. "He's in no shape to argue with me now."

Cecil said he and Edna would look after Sam; I had to deliver Sam to his house myself because Sam was confused and didn't know who to trust anymore. Once we got on the road I looked in the rearview mirror — Leonard looked white as a sheet and I thought he might pass out. "I don't feel the least bit sorry for you," I said. "You got what you deserved." Leonard didn't say anything back.

Emergency was busy when we arrived and it took some time before they even examined Leonard. I told them he was visiting from Saskatchewan and had tripped and fallen down the stairs. I waited more than an hour before they informed me he had broken his left ankle and his right arm, and both would be set in casts, and that they would keep him overnight for observation. They asked if I wanted to see him. I told them not at all. I would be back the next day.

It was late in the afternoon of the following day before I ventured back to the hospital. I had Sybil to babysit. I had a life to live. When I got there Leonard was sitting in the waiting room, adorned with an ankle cast and a cast over one elbow. There were two crutches leaning against a chair and he looked demoralized when I approached. He opened his mouth to say something but I cut him off.

"Don't say a word," I said. He struggled to stand up and I fetched his crutches. A nurse in the hallway asked if we wanted the use of a wheelchair and I told her no, we would manage just fine. Once he was sprawled out in the back seat I threw his crutches on the floor.

"I don't know what the hell you were thinking last night. You've got some nerve, Leonard. That was the most ignorant thing you could have done. Cecil keeps asking about you and I told him you deserved to have both legs and both arms broken. Now look at the fix you've got yourself into."

The fix was just as much mine, but I didn't want him to know it. What could I do now but let him stay? His dad would never drive all the way to pick him up and it was obvious he wouldn't be driving for a while.

"You're lucky Sam is in the car or I'd really tell you what I think."

Leonard didn't say anything until we were halfway home. When we got to Berkey's Corner I heard him say "sorry." I turned up the volume on the radio.

Later that night, after Sam was asleep, Cecil knocked on the door and asked if he could have a word with Leonard and, since he didn't have an axe in his hands, I said it would be okay. It was going to be a man-to man-talk, he said, and Edna had just pulled some peanut butter cookies out of the oven if I was interested. Then he winked like my cooperation was implicit.

It was an hour later before Cecil came back. Edna and I had polished off more cookies than a person has a right to consider.

"Well, did you get through to him?"

"I think I explained things to him all right. He told me you were going to let him stay until he could drive back home."

"It's because I know his mom and dad. They're nice enough people."

"I can tell you one thing," Cecil said. "That boy is determined. He said you were the most amazing woman in the world. He wouldn't be the first man to have said such a thing. But . . . "

"But what?"

"It was the way he said it. It was just the way he said it."

4

BEVERLY WOULD HAVE KNOWN Leonard was at my house and must have been busting to pay a return visit to get the lowdown, but she didn't. I fully expected Daisy to drop by but she never did. I saw her from time to time and waved, and she waved back, but she was almost two years older now and had a boyfriend of her own. Not just a boyfriend but a boyfriend with a car. Milo came to the door one time with a gunny sack full of toys which he explained, in his limited fashion, were bequeathed to Sam. I thanked him and gave him a bag of store-bought cookies to take home, but I doubt they made it that far. Cecil told me that the family who was renting the house that once belonged to Old Evans had been reduced to the dad who lived there on his own. His dump truck dwarfed the bungalow-styled house and he kept to himself. Beverly had mentioned that Mrs. Eaton's dog had died and as a result she never made her daily pilgrimage down the railroad tracks, and I told myself I should walk over with Sam and say hello but for some reason I kept putting it off. A few of the pieces that made up the culture of this end of the valley had changed, but for the most part it was much like it had been before I left. Except for the presence of Leonard.

It wasn't easy for him to get around on his crutches because of his broken arm, but the house was so small there wasn't any place for him to go. Rarely did he venture out of the house, though on sunny afternoons he would sit on the top step and absorb the world I was accustomed to. Cecil offered to replace the broken banister and I offered to pay him but he said he had the lumber sitting around looking for a purpose and it was no trouble. He told me this in front of Leonard which I wished he hadn't. As far as I was concerned there was plenty of trouble involved.

Leonard didn't ask for much. Only once did he solicit my services to drive him to town, where he went to the bank and withdrew a wad of bills that plumped his wallet up so that it barely fit into his pocket. He paid me for his keep and helped out with simple things like peeling potatoes or shelling peas and proved useful when I was babysitting Sybil, especially if she and Sam got into a tiff. He slept on the couch and he snored until he fell into a deep sleep and then there was silence. I worried at first because Sam was in his own room and Leonard on the couch was between us. Sam slept well most nights but occasionally woke up in the turmoil of a bad dream. We were into the second week of this arrangement and one morning when I woke up, Sam and Leonard were both sound asleep on the couch.

The days went by and it was as if the ration of words Leonard was willing or able to utter doubled every twenty-four hours. I had made up my mind to take both Sybil and Sam to my workshop to work on clocks as best I could while keeping an eye on the two of them. Eventually, Leonard hobbled out of the house and began to loiter around and Sam wanted him to come in and play. Leonard had the knack of getting the two of them involved in an imaginary game of one sort or another and it wasn't long before they were occupied in a world of their own making. He knew enough not to ask if he could be of assistance with my work, but he asked questions about what I was doing and he was determined to unearth as much of my personal history as he could. He was impressed that I'd completed school by correspondence and he wanted to know more about the books I'd read. I was passionate about my small library of books and he soon found out I was willing to share my obsession endlessly.

"I should read more," he said. "I enjoyed reading when I was working on religion with Jeremiah and Laura. Maybe I could borrow some of your books since I've got some time."

It was obvious Leonard was making what appeared to be a conniving gesture to enter my world, but I decided to play along with it. Reading never hurt anyone. I allowed him entry into my bedroom where I had two large shelves overflowing with books. There had been no evidence of books in the house he was raised in and that likely explained the bewildered look on his face. He ran his fingers along the spines as if he expected the sound of music would result and I noticed he nudged one or two of the slender volumes I owned. I gave him a more substantial hardback, Steinbeck's *Grapes of Wrath,* to start. It was about a journey to the West Coast, different from his but a journey nonetheless, and there were minor references to mechanical issues he might like. I also thought if he managed to get through the entire novel that he might see that the people had been duped into moving west and that what they found when they got there was not what they expected.

I had no explanation for why Dog preferred to hang around Leonard and not with me. Since we got the dog, I was the one who fed him and every night he went to sleep curled up beside my bed. Now his loyalties had changed and he was never more than a few feet from where Leonard stood, sat, or lay down, almost as if he felt guilty for the role he played the night Leonard tumbled off the back porch.

One night he asked to phone home. I was surprised he hadn't asked sooner. I said I could take Sam and Dog for a walk if he wanted some privacy but he said it didn't matter to him. He told his parents he had suffered an accident which was due to his own clumsiness and that he'd broken his leg. He didn't mention his broken arm and he didn't go into detail about how both injuries ended up in a cast, only that he was staying with me for now. I heard him say they would have to take their business elsewhere and I assumed he was talking about his garage patrons. I was only getting one side of the conversation, but Muriel asked how I was making out and I told him to say I was as fine as ever. The last several minutes of the phone call, Leonard went on and on about how beautiful my place was, how there were hardly any bugs, and that the water tasted better than it did at home. When he was finished he phoned the operator and asked about the charges then paid me five dollars for the call.

Sam had a bath every night after supper, a ritual I continued because he was good about going to bed once it was over. Leonard, solicitous to a fault, suggested he read Sam a story in bed and I said that would be okay but I would read to him right after; he had exercised some kind of spell over Dog and I wasn't about to have him usurp my role as a parent. After Sam was in bed for the night, the two of us watched an hour or two of TV if there was anything worth watching. We both liked *Twilight Zone* and *Perry Mason* and I tolerated *Bonanza*. Leonard's favourite was *The Andy Griffith Show*, maybe because Gomer Pyle had his own garage in the show. On Friday and Saturday nights we watched the late night movie and when it was over we discussed our often varying opinions on what we'd viewed over a pot of tea and some cookies. Sometimes we argued vehemently over the premise of a script, but mostly I could see Leonard had sound judgement and I only played the devil's advocate to get him going. Leonard was the perfect gentleman during these weeks of bone-mending and I knew a part of me would miss him when he went back home.

Leonard was going back home. I had made it clear to him on several occasions and he understood that. He would have gone home, I truly believe that, had it not been for three days of torrential downpour that came earlier in the year than usual.

It rained all day Tuesday, and the following day he was due to get his casts removed so I drove him into town. The doctor suggested he take it easy with walking for a few days and I wasn't about to insist he pack up and leave as soon as we got home. When we got back and were heading up the backstairs Leonard noticed through the basement door that had been left open that there was water on the floor. He said it might not be a serious issue and that plenty of basements suffered from dampness in the winter, but it rained hard for the third day in a row and there was water seeping in faster than Leonard, who was supposed to ease his way into walking, could shovel into buckets and dump outside. Thursday and Friday we worked together to keep the water from rising to the level of the oil heater which was what furnished the house with heat in the winter. By Saturday the basement was back to just damp and Leonard said something had to be done because it would be a real mess if the water ever rose as high as the pilot light on the oil furnace.

Leonard knew what to do. He bought a chisel and borrowed Cecil's sledgehammer and created a hole in one corner of the basement on the side that was last to be relieved during the flood. Then he rigged up a sump pump so that if it happened again the water would be pumped outside as soon as the hole filled up. He showed me how the system worked by pouring water in with a hose and it worked like a miracle. "So long as your power doesn't go out," he said, "you'll never need to worry about flooding again."

I can't say exactly what happened after that. Leonard didn't make a move to leave and I didn't insist he be on his way. His ankle was more than mended and we both knew that. With every passing evening the anticipation for our time together on the couch was heightened, and the first time he held me close was during a tense episode of *The Twilight Zone*. Every night after that we snuggled on the couch and whispered our discussions to one another, we were that close. One night we watched *Dr. Zhivago*, a film that I normally would have enjoyed, but on that particular night I felt tired and twice I almost fell asleep. When it was over he kissed me on the forehead and said goodnight and I grabbed his hand and led him away from the couch and into my bedroom.

The next morning we had breakfast as usual, but instead of helping with my babysitting duties he drove his truck into town to look for a job. When he explained his intention I offered nothing to change his mind.

5

THE LAST PART OF THIS DISSERTATION is for you, Sam my man. Some of what you have read on these pages you already knew, but of course much of it you did not and for that matter *could not* know while I was alive. What you do with these pages when you get them is up to you, that goes without saying. You may read them and burn them immediately or you may make the decision to set them aside to revisit from time to time. In my old age and moderate wisdom I have come to realize that one's life is never a complete truth. In my case much of it was lived under a veil of deception, and while I have done my best to prevent any harm coming your way as a result, I apologize for whenever and wherever it has failed.

I was raised without many friends and while I did my best to fight against my impulse for seclusion, I never did develop what most people would refer to as a network of human beings with whom I could share the intimate details of life. A handful, perhaps, but many of them have passed from this world before I have. One of my closest friends, Chris Mann, made an interesting comment when asked to make a speech on the date of his sixty-fifth birthday a few years back, and what he had to say made me envious beyond belief, and I understood then what a fortunate soul he was. He said when he looked back on his life there wasn't one thing he would have changed.

Sadly, there are several key elements to my life I eagerly would have altered given the chance, and I suspect my father, if he were prone to such introspection, would have felt the same. It may have nothing to do with the fact that I have spent a disproportionate part of my life working with clocks, but I feel I have a better understanding about time and the power it bestows upon us. Every tick from every clock I ever worked on has echoed out and into the enigmatic universe and can never be captured again. I can see now that, despite the best efforts people make to repair the past, we have no choice but to accept its indelible script and move on. That is what I have done to the best of my ability, my dearest Sam. Please accept my efforts as genuine, even where they have proven disastrous.

What you have read here began as a diary of sorts. Perhaps more a journal of the significant events that shaped my life. The process began after you had been in school a few years and I began to write down what I remembered. Two things I wanted to accomplish during my time on Earth included learning to fly an airplane and to write something significant enough that it might allow someone to remember me. Well, I am far too old to learn to fly now, but next month, when the weather settles somewhat, I am scheduled to go up in a small plane owned by the son of one of my longest acquaintances. The young man needs to accrue a certain number of hours for some licensing purposes and is more than willing to take me. I'm looking forward to it and I'm hoping I can talk him into flying over the top of the two-humped mountain near what was our home for many years.

I worked away at this journal for a long time which was a good thing because the way the serrated edge of memory wants to work, things emerge from the past with a will of their own. It was after I had completed my journey that I realized that parts of it wouldn't make sense without your knowing the backdrop of characters and lifestyles responsible for instigating the proceedings. This was the hardest thing I could imagine doing and, as is reasonable to expect, most of it is based on conjecture. The people captured here were, I'm sure, invisible to others growing up at this end of the valley, but as a child and even as a young woman, they were monumental characters as large and instrumental as any found in the books I adored.

Because I am as old as I am now and possibly because I have principally led a life of regret, I resent beyond belief the accounting of my life at the beginning of every day. I remember Old Evans saying there was a tedious but necessary auditing of the day's events before the sun went down, but for me the measure of each passing day owns a place within reason; it is the flashbacks I suffer from upon waking.

I was fooling myself when I began this project, as I was convinced it was a valiant but feeble attempt to resolve the issues of my past, but the reality is I wrote this for you, Sam. The details of what happened in the life that encompassed my father and mother were particulars through which I struggled without knowing. This may not be a complete truth you hold in your hands, but it is an Odyssey you deserve to be aware of. However crudely my life has been sculpted, however riddled with despair it has been in the past, the resolve for my life's length and purpose thankfully exists because of you, Sam Lemmons. My only living son. My only brother.

Acknowledgements

Not everything that is considered should be made, but nothing is made without first being considered. As a writer I am grateful for being considered. I am indebted to many who have helped to bring this novel to fruition. Many thanks to everyone at Thistledown Press. The support and encouragement I've received, in the past, from The Gentlemen's Fiction Club (Terence Young, Bill Gaston, Jay Ruzesky, John Gould, and Jay Connolly) has been a blessing. The BC Arts Council was instrumental in offering me resources to complete this project.

Thanks to the biggest small town in Canada, Eastend, Saskatchewan, and all the people I met there, in particular Ethel Willis and Lorraine Armstrong. Fishing tips, gratefully received, were provided by Jeff Diekmeier.

Nothing can deter my editor, John Lent, from seeking the aesthetic truth he believes in. His wisdom is something we all yearn for.

Lastly, thanks to Susan Stenson, my first reader always.